W9-DGJ-939

DEEPER WATER

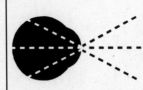

This Large Print Book carries the
Seal of Approval of N.A.V.H.

A TIDES OF TRUTH NOVEL

DEEPER WATER

ROBERT WHITLOW

THORNDIKE PRESS

A part of Gale, Cengage Learning

GALE
CENGAGE Learning·

Detroit • New York • San Francisco • New Haven, Conn • Waterville, Maine • London

GALE
CENGAGE Learning

Copyright © 2008 by Robert Whitlow.
Scripture quotations are from the King James Version of the Holy Bible.
Thorndike Press, a part of Gale, Cengage Learning.

Thorndike Press® Large Print Christian Mystery.
The text of this Large Print edition is unabridged.
Other aspects of the book may vary from the original edition.
Set in 16 pt. Plantin.

LIBRARY OF CONGRESS CATALOGING-IN-PUBLICATION DATA

Whitlow, Robert.
   Deeper water : a tides of truth novel / by Robert Whitlow.
     p. cm. — (Thorndike Press large print Christian mystery)
   ISBN-13: 978-1-4104-2299-6 (alk. paper)
   ISBN-10: 1-4104-2299-2 (alk. paper)
   1. Large type books. I. Title.
PS3573.H49837D44 2010
813'.54—dc22   2009039725

Published in 2010 by arrangement with Thomas Nelson, Inc.

Printed in Mexico
5 6 7 14 13 12 11

To those who live to make the world a
better place:
"Ye are the salt of the earth."
— Matthew 5:13

PROLOGUE

Moses Jones poled his aluminum johnboat through the marshy waters where the Little Ogeechee River mingled with Green Island Sound. The snub-nosed boat rode on top of the water, a slight swirl marking its wake. A set of oars lay in the bow, but Moses preferred a long wooden pole. Quieter than oars, the smooth rod served double duty as a makeshift depth finder.

The old black man slipped the twenty-five-foot-long pole noiselessly into the water until it found the muddy bottom. He glided beneath the outstretched branches of a live oak tree draped in Spanish moss. Around the bend lay one of the best fishing holes on the brackish river. It was night, but the moon shone brightly, and his kerosene lantern sat unlit on the seat.

Moses lifted the pole from the water and balanced it across the front of the boat. He lifted his cap and scratched the top of his gray-fringed head. And listened. The only sounds were familiar night noises: the bullfrogs calling to each other across the channel, the plop of a fish breaking the surface of the water, the cries of crickets in the dark.

Sucking air through his few remaining teeth, Moses let out a long, low moan to let the faces in the water know he was entering their domain. The faces moved from place to place along the inlets and tributaries the old man frequented, from the Tybee River to Wassaw Island. With the water as their grave, they weren't bound to one location. Their cemetery had no tombstones, no iron fences, no flower-edged borders. They could be anywhere.

Moses feared and respected the dead. One day, he knew, he would join them. Whether his face would be young or old, he didn't know.

He rounded the bend and measured the depth of the water. The pole didn't touch bottom. He quietly lowered the concrete block he used as an anchor and let the boat find its place. The slow current took him to the center of the hole. He could bait his hooks by moonlight without having to light the lantern and attract the curiosity of a thousand insects. He lowered his trotlines into the water. A five-gallon plastic bucket set in the bottom of the boat would serve as a makeshift live well. He waited.

Within an hour, he caught five fish that included three keepers. He put the three fish in the bucket. It would be a good night. He felt happy. The hole was teeming with life. He pulled up his lines and rebaited the hooks. The fish bumping against the side of the bucket joined the sounds of the night. When he leaned over to place the lines in the water, she floated up to the surface.

It was the little girl.

Moses squeezed his eyes shut. He wanted to scream, but his lips were clenched. He longed to cry, but his emotions were paralyzed. Memories that couldn't separate fact from fiction raced through his mind. What had he done that she would haunt him so?

He made himself breathe slowly. In and out, in and out. His heart pounded in his ears. Someday, the faces would grow strong arms and pull him into the water to join them. It would be justice. He continued to make himself breathe in rhythm. A bead of sweat escaped his cap and ran down his forehead. There was a jerk on the line he still held in his hand. Every muscle in his body tensed. Maybe tonight was the night of death.

He opened his eyes. All that remained was the dark water.

He wiped his forehead with the back of his hand and pulled in the fish. It was the nicest one yet, fat and lively. His breathing returned to normal. His heart stopped racing.

"Thank you, missy," he said softly.

He wasn't sure if the little girl sent the fish or could hear his voice, but it didn't hurt to be grateful, even to a ghost.

1

"Tammy Lynn!" Mama called out. "You'd think a fancy law firm in Savannah would know how to spell your name."

I left the pantry beneath the staircase and came into the kitchen. With lots of windows, the large kitchen protruded from our wood-frame house like Mama's abdomen a week before the twins were born.

"And is there a new law against calling an unmarried woman *Miss?*" Mama added as she opened a quart jar of yellow squash she'd put up the previous summer.

I deposited two yellow onions on the scratched countertop and picked up the envelope. It was addressed to Ms. Tami L. Taylor, 463 Beaver Ruin Road, Powell Station, Georgia. I'd thought long and hard about changing the spelling of my name to Tami on my résumé. First impressions are important, and I didn't want the hiring partner at a prestigious law firm to think I was a second-rate country singer who went to law school after she bombed out in Nashville.

T-a-m-i had a more sophisticated ring to it. It could even be short for Tamara. As long as I honored my parents in the important things, secretly changing the spelling of my first name for professional reasons wouldn't be a sin. Or so I hoped. I rubbed my finger across the address. I couldn't tell Mama the law firm made a mistake. That would be a violation of the ninth commandment. I kept quiet, trusting silence to keep me righteous in the sight of a holy God. Mama's voice rescued me.

"You're doing well in school, and I'm pleased with you," she continued. "But I'm afraid you wasted a lot of paper and stamps on those letters you sent out. You should have set your sights on working for Mr. Callahan. He might actually give you a job when you get out of school."

"Yes ma'am."

Mama wanted me working close to home, the only secure haven in the midst of a wicked world. Her disapproval that I'd mailed letters seeking a summer clerk position to one hundred law firms across the state wasn't a surprise. It helped a little when I reassured her I'd excluded Atlanta like the hole in the middle of a donut. To live in a place populated by millions of people after growing up surrounded by millions of trees wasn't a step I wanted to take either.

I took the letter into the front room. Our house didn't have a formal living room. The front room served as everything from homeschool classroom to temporary church sanctuary if the preacher stopped by for an impromptu prayer meeting. I plopped down on a sofa covered by a white chenille bedspread and closely examined the return address on the outside of the envelope. I was impressed. Braddock, Appleby, and Carpenter still used engraved envelopes. Most of the rejection letters I'd received arrived at my law school post office box in Athens fresh from a laser printer.

Mama was right. Trying to find a summer clerk job through unsolicited letters to law firms picked at random from a list in the placement office was not the best use of a first-class stamp. I'd already resigned myself to another summer working first shift with Daddy at the chicken plant. I opened the envelope.

Dear Ms. Taylor,
We received your résumé and appreciate

your interest in a summer clerkship with our firm. You have an outstanding record of academic and personal accomplishments. If you have not already obtained employment, please contact Ms. Gerry Patrick, our office administrator, to discuss one of the positions available at Braddock, Appleby, and Carpenter.

If you have taken another job or no longer have an interest in working for our firm, the courtesy of a prompt response notifying us accordingly would be appreciated.

Sincerely,
Joseph P. Carpenter

"Mama," I screamed. "I have a job!" I rushed into the kitchen and tried to hand her the letter. "Read this!"

"Calm down and wait a minute," she said, maintaining her grip on the large knife in her right hand. "I'm in the middle of chopping onions for the squash."

"I'll read it to you!"

I sat at the kitchen table, an oversize picnic table painted white, and in a breathless voice read the letter. Mama scraped the onions into the saucepan.

"Read it again," she said when I finished.

Mama sat across from me and wiped her

hands with a dish towel. I read the letter more slowly.

"And here at the top it says the firm was founded by Mr. Benjamin Braddock in 1888."

"Are you sure it's a job offer? It sounds to me like they just want to talk to you about it."

"They wouldn't contact me this late in the school year if they didn't have a job. Maybe someone backed out and a spot opened for me."

Mama repositioned one of the hairpins that held her dark hair in a tight bun. She hadn't cut her hair in years, and when freed it fell to her waist. Mama and I shared the same hair color, brown eyes, tall, slender frame, and angular features. It always made her smile when someone mentioned how alike we looked. As a single woman, I was allowed to cut my hair, but it still fell past my shoulders. I only wore it in a bun on Sunday mornings.

"Why would they offer you a job?" she asked. "They haven't even met you."

"I laid my hands on the stack of letters and prayed before I mailed them. Then I thanked God for every rejection that came in. He saw my heart and came through at the last moment."

"Maybe, but I'm not comfortable with you claiming his approval so quickly. We need to talk about this. Savannah is on the other end of the state. How far away is it?"

"I don't know." I looked up at the clock on the wall beside the refrigerator. It was 5:10 p.m. "I should call right now and find out if this really is a job offer. That way we can talk it over with Daddy and not guess about anything."

Mama returned to the stove. I waited.

"Go ahead," she sighed. "You're at the edge of the river and need to know what's on the other side."

The only telephone in the house was in my parents' bedroom. When I stopped homeschooling in the ninth grade and went to public high school, Mama never had to worry about me having secret phone conversations late at night. She needn't have worried anyway. Most of my calls were about basketball practice and homework assignments.

I hit the numbers for the unfamiliar area code followed by the seven-digit phone number. The phone rang three times. Maybe the firm didn't answer calls after 5:00 p.m. Then, a silky voice spoke.

"Good afternoon, Braddock, Appleby, and Carpenter."

16

The sound made my mouth suddenly go dry.

"Ms. Gerry Patrick, please."

"May I tell her who is calling?"

"Tami Taylor. That's T-a-m-i."

I couldn't believe I'd spelled my first name. I stifled a giggle while the receptionist put me on hold and let me stew like Mama's squash and onions. I rehearsed my next lines to avoid another long-distance embarrassment. A more mature-sounding female voice came on the line.

"Gerry Patrick."

"Good afternoon, Ms. Patrick. This is Tami Taylor, a second-year law student at the University of Georgia. I received a letter from Mr. Carpenter about a summer clerk position. He told me to contact you."

There was a brief pause. "I have your résumé, but all summer job offers go through my office. I'd know if the firm sent you a letter."

My mouth went dry. "Could you check with Mr. Carpenter?"

"Yes, I want to get to the bottom of this myself."

A much longer pause followed. I counted the red tulips on the top border of the faded wallpaper in my parents' bedroom and prayed that Mr. Carpenter hadn't left for the day. Finally, Ms. Patrick spoke.

"It's fortunate for you that you called. I'd signed a stack of rejections this afternoon without knowing Mr. Carpenter made a copy of your résumé. Your turndown letter was in the mail room."

"Thank you." I swallowed. "Do you know why he offered me a job?"

"Not a clue. Mr. Carpenter isn't here, but his assistant confirmed the letter. Are you interested in the position?"

"Yes ma'am."

"I'll e-mail the details."

"Uh, I'm home on spring break, and we don't have a computer with an Internet connection."

I felt my face flush. The only computer in the house was an outdated one used for educational programs with the twins. Powell Station didn't boast a coffee shop with Wi-Fi.

"Do you have access to a fax machine?" Ms. Patrick asked.

I frantically racked my brain for a solution. "No ma'am. Would it be all right if I called you in the morning? By then I'll be able to track down a way for you to send the information."

"I'm usually here by nine o'clock. These jobs don't stay open for long."

"Yes ma'am."

I hung up the phone. Challenges raised by my family's lifestyle weren't new. Daddy always said obstacles were opportunities for personal character growth. However, that didn't keep routine problems from causing pain. I returned to the kitchen.

"I talked to Ms. Patrick, the office manager. It's a real job," I announced with reduced enthusiasm.

"What details did she give you?"

"She's going to send me information as soon as I figure out a way she can transmit it." I didn't mention the disdain I sensed in Ms. Patrick's voice.

"And that won't tell you anything about these people or their values, morals, beliefs, lifestyles."

I tried to sound casually optimistic. "No ma'am, but it's just a summer job at a law firm in Savannah. What could be wrong with that? I'll only be there for a few months, and it will give me an idea what to expect in a real law —"

"We'll talk it over with your father when he gets home," Mama interrupted.

I shut my mouth. When Mama invoked the title "father," it meant nothing could be discussed until he arrived.

We would be eating chicken and dumplings for supper. Thick noodles, chicken broth, and a few chunks of chicken went a long way toward feeding our large family. The slightly sweet smell of the dumplings competed with the pungent onions in the squash.

"Do you need help with supper?" I asked, leaning on the counter and sniffing.

"No, thanks. Everything is cooking. Why don't you check on the twins? I left them working on an essay."

I was eleven years old when Ellie and Emma were born, and we'd shared a bedroom since the first day they came home from the hospital. With preteen excitement about everything related to babies, I welcomed them into my world with open arms and a room decorated with balloons and a white poster board proudly announcing the girls' names in fancy script surrounded by flowers. My enthusiasm was instantly tested by a double dose of demands.

My first job was to change the girls' diapers and take them to Mama for the middle-of-the-night feeding. For months, I slept in fits and starts as I listened to the tiny infants sniffle and snort while I wondered whether they were hungry or feeling an uncomfortable gas bubble. If one cried, the sound immediately became stereo. But I didn't complain. Every child was a blessing from God.

Daddy put an old rocking chair in my bedroom, and my arms grew accustomed to holding the babies close to my heart. I kissed their heads enough to wear off the newborn fuzz. Later, when they were toddlers, they often ended up in my bed, especially on cold winter nights when the best warmth is found in closeness to a loved one.

Now, they welcomed me home with hand-drawn pictures and silly poems. The three of us couldn't fit in my bed, but we still enjoyed sitting in our pajamas on the circular rug on our bedroom floor and talking in the moonlight until the little girls' eyelids drooped.

I walked up the creaky stairs to the second floor of the house. No sounds came from the bedroom, a hopeful sign of serious educational activity. I peeked in the door. The twins were sitting across from each other at the small table beneath the room's wide, single window. My bed was to the right of the window. The twins slept in homemade bunk beds on the opposite wall. Both dark-haired heads were bent over sheets of paper.

"How's it going?" I asked.

Ellie looked up with blue eyes that could have made me jealous. "We're almost finished."

"Yeah," Emma echoed. "We wrote about different things so Mama wouldn't think we copied."

"Do you want me to check your papers when you finish?"

"Yes," both girls responded.

My side of the room was immaculate. The same couldn't be said for the twins'. Emma was the neater child, but without Ellie's cooperation, they both received blame for messiness. I straightened up their side of the room while they continued writing.

"Done!" Emma announced.

"I'm on my last paragraph," Ellie said.

"Keep working. I'll read Emma's paper."

Across the top, the older of the twins had written: "Deism and the Founders of Our Country."

For a woman who never went to college, Mama was an amazing teacher. Not many twelve-year-olds could spell *deism,* much less give a credible definition of the belief and explain in clear, simple terms how several signers of the Declaration of Independence viewed God as a cosmic clock-winder passively watching events unfold on

the earth below. The twins would be prepared for public high school. Except for
calculus and AP physics, I never made less
than an A in high school.

"Show me your research," I said to Emma.

She handed me a stack of index cards,
each one labeled with the reference. I
checked the quotes in the paper against the
information on the cards and corrected a
handful of grammatical errors. While I
worked, Ellie finished her paper and looked
over my shoulder at her sister's work.

"You should have put a comma before the
conjunction separating two independent
clauses," Ellie said, pointing to one of my
corrections. "Everybody knows that."

Emma pushed her away. "Wait until she
reads your paper. It's full of mistakes."

"Stop it!" I commanded.

Emma and I sat on the bed and went over
her paper. It was a very good first draft.

"How long have you been working on
this?"

"About two weeks. Mama wants it finished
by Friday."

Ellie's essay was titled "Thomas Jefferson's Bible." She focused on the rationalist
beliefs of the primary author of the Declaration of Independence. There was overlap-
ping research with her sister's paper, but

also information unique to Jefferson, including a discussion of the founder's personal New Testament with all the references to miracles carefully cut out. Ellie was a better writer than her sister, but I was careful to make an equal number of corrections and suggestions.

"That's all for today," I said when we finished. "I'll tell Mama how well you're doing. Supper will be ready in a few minutes."

"I'll pray," Emma volunteered.

Our homeschool experience was saturated with prayer. Deism had no place in Mama's theology. God was omnipresent; a truth that both scared and comforted me.

We held hands while Emma prayed. I smiled when she included a heartfelt request for God's blessing upon Ellie.

"And thank you that Tammy Lynn will be home with us in a few weeks for the whole summer. In Jesus' name, amen."

I squeezed both small hands. To spend a summer in Savannah would require convincing more than my parents.

2

The twins and I went downstairs to help
Mama set the table. From the kitchen I
could see the dirt basketball court where
I'd spent many hours practicing my three-
point shot. While putting the forks in place,
I glanced out one of the windows in time to
see my eighteen-year-old brother, Kyle,
leading a Hereford steer by a rope halter
toward the feedlot on the opposite side of
the family garden. A senior in high school,
Kyle worked part-time for a local livestock
broker. He'd already made enough money
buying and selling beef cattle to buy an old
pickup truck and a secondhand hauler.
Trailing behind Kyle and the steer were our
two dogs, Flip and Ginger. The dogs spent
their lives outside and never entered the
house. I would have loved a little indoor
dog, but Mama and Daddy said our home
wasn't Noah's ark.

Daddy always took a shower before he left

the chicken plant, but I knew he carried the smell of fifty thousand chickens in his nostrils. As a line boss, he supervised a score of women who processed the naked, headless birds that a few weeks before had been tiny yellow chicks. For five summers I'd worked on Daddy's crew as an eviscerator, a fancy word for the person who cuts open the chicken and scoops out its internal organs. No part of a chicken was foreign to me.

My sixteen-year-old brother, Bobby, had finished his work in the garden and was sitting on the back steps quietly strumming his guitar. Bobby had been singing in church since he was a little boy; the guitar was a recent addition.

"He's writing his own songs," Ellie said as she took out a pack of paper napkins. "Bobby," she called through the screen door. "Make up a song for Tammy Lynn."

Bobby increased the tempo and volume. "Tammy Lynn! Tammy Lynn!" he called out. "Where have you gone? Why did you leave me here alone? I waited till dawn, but you never came home. Now, all I can do is moan."

I looked at Mama and rolled my eyes. "Are you going to let him do that?"

Mama smiled. "As long as he sings about

his older sister, I'm not going to worry too much about it."

The dogs started barking and ran around the corner of the house to the front yard.

"Daddy's coming," Ellie said. "I'll set Tammy Lynn's place. I want her next to me."

"No, she's next to me," Emma protested.

"Put her in the middle," Mama said.

I heard the front door open, and the familiar sound of my father's uneven footsteps as he walked across the wooden floor. When Daddy was in the army, a drunken soldier shot him in the right foot. Two surgeries later, Daddy was left with a misshapen foot and a VA disability check that made the monthly payments on our house. He claimed the injury was a blessing in disguise, which sounded reasonable except for the pain on his face during cold weather. Daddy wore insulated rubber boots and two pairs of socks at work, but I think the foot still hurt because of the cool temperatures in the plant. When he came into the kitchen and saw me, he smiled.

A smile from Daddy after I'd been away from home for a few weeks at school could make me cry, so I lowered my gaze. I crossed the floor and gave him a quick hug.

"It was cloudy today until I saw you," he

said, kissing the top of my head. "Did the girl from Dalton give you a ride home?"

"Yes sir. She didn't mind coming through the mountains."

"Did you give her gas money?"

"Yes sir."

Kyle and Bobby came inside and began discussing the status of the garden with Daddy. It was early spring, but our family used the entire growing season. In north Georgia, that meant early harvests of cabbage, leaf lettuce, and broccoli.

Unless company came for supper, Mama served meals from the stove. As soon as she called out, "Supper's ready," there would be a few minutes of chaos until all seven people were seated at the table. No one dared nibble a piece of corn bread until Daddy bowed his head and prayed a blessing. Then, conversation broke out on every side. Our family might be quiet around outsiders, but with one another we didn't hesitate to talk. Tonight, Daddy's focus was on me.

"Tell me about your classes," he said after his first bite of dumplings.

"This semester I'm taking secured transactions, introduction to labor law, municipal corporations, and civil procedure."

"Which class do you like best?"

"Municipal corporations. It's the study of

city government law. The professor is a woman who worked for a firm in Seattle, Washington."

"How did she get to Georgia?" Mama asked in surprise.

"Lawyers move all over the place," I said, planting a tiny seed.

I ate a bite of squash and onions. Compared to Seattle, Savannah was next door. As supper continued, I brought Daddy up-to-date on my strictly regulated life — going to class, eating, studying, sleeping, reading the Bible, and praying.

"And I've been playing basketball. Several girls at the law school invited me to join a team that plays in a graduate school intramural league. We're undefeated in our first five games."

"Have you scored a basket?" Kyle asked mischievously.

"Of course," I replied.

In high school, I'd averaged fifteen points a game during my senior year.

"Ellie and I have been practicing every day since the weather warmed up," Emma said. "Will you play with us later?"

"Maybe tomorrow."

Mama had put extra effort into the meal because it was my first evening home. I complimented every dish individually and the entire meal collectively.

"Have you lost weight?" Daddy asked.

"Maybe a little. I do miss home cooking." Mama smiled in appreciation.

"We'll have you home in a few weeks so we can take care of you," Daddy said. "When is your last exam?"

"I'm not sure about the exact date," I replied with a glance at Mama, who shook her head.

"The plant is running overtime," Daddy continued. "The company has taken on quite a few new growers, and production is way up. An experienced hand like you can really pile up the cash if you take all the available overtime."

"Is there a place for me?" Bobby asked.

"Next year when you're older would be a better time for you to get on as a temporary worker," Daddy replied.

"Could you ask?" Bobby persisted. "I'll still take care of my share of work in the garden. I want to save enough money to buy another guitar."

"What kind of guitar?" Mama asked sharply.

Bobby smiled. When he did, he looked like Daddy. "Don't worry, Mama. I want a better acoustic, not electric. Some of the best are made by a company called Taylor, so it would already look like it had my name engraved on it."

I wanted to yield my place on the eviscerating crew to Bobby right then. It didn't take long to master the art of cutting open a chicken with razor-sharp scissors and removing its entrails.

"I'll check with Mr. Waldrup," Daddy replied.

Mama surprised me with a lemon meringue pie for dessert. The peaks and valleys of white and light brown meringue were as pretty as a photograph of the Alps. I held the knife in my hand, almost hating to cut the pie.

"What are you waiting for?" Ellie asked impatiently.

I lowered the knife and destroyed perfection. Seven pieces later, the pie pan was empty.

"The twins and I will clean up," I said to Mama when we finished eating. "Sit on the porch with Daddy."

In spring and fall, Daddy liked to sit in the swing on the front porch after supper. It was his way of unwinding after the hectic activity at the chicken plant with its loud noises and fast pace. It was quiet at our house. Except for an occasional logging truck, we rarely heard vehicles passing by on Beaver Ruin Road. That left only the evening sounds of nature — in early spring a few katydids, in summer a more varied chorus. I especially enjoyed it when a great horned owl would issue a call. Daddy liked to hoot in return, drawing the bird into conversation. When I was a little girl, he would interpret the owl's hoots and make up stories about the owl's life. I loved owl stories.

After the twins and I finished cleaning the kitchen, I took my Savannah letter to the front porch. Daddy and Mama were sitting on the swing. The sun was down, but the sky still displayed a broad band of orange. Daddy had his arm draped over the back of the swing behind Mama's shoulders.

"Is now a good time to talk?" I asked Mama.

"Yes," she said.

Emma opened the front door and came outside.

"It's not a good time for you," Mama said to her. "Stay inside with Ellie."

Emma frowned but shut the door. I sat on the edge of the porch with my feet propped on the steps.

"Your mama says you got a job offer with a law firm in Savannah," Daddy said. "Tell me about it."

"Do you want to read the letter?"

"Yes."

I handed it to him.

"They misspelled your name."

"The spelling of my name isn't the important part," I replied with a twinge of guilt. "It's hard to get a summer clerkship like this one. The lady in the job placement office told me less than twenty-five percent of the second-year class is able to find a legal job with a law firm, fewer still with a law firm like this."

"What do you know about Braddock, Appleby, and Carpenter?" Daddy asked, reading the names slowly.

I told him about my conversation with Gerry Patrick, leaving out the intrafirm miscommunication concerning the offer.

"There's no harm in getting information about the job, is there?" I asked, trying not to sound whiny.

Daddy handed the letter back to me. "Not if you keep your heart right."

The condition of my heart was somewhat shaky, so I stuck to practical arguments.

"Bobby could take my place on the chicken line. And Savannah isn't as far away as Seattle."

"Did you apply for a job in Seattle?" Mama asked in alarm.

33

"No ma'am. I was just making a point about the relative closeness of Savannah."

Daddy pushed the swing back and forth a couple of times.

"I guess you could tell the lady in Savannah to send the information to Oscar Callahan's office. Didn't you list him as a reference on your résumé?"

"Yes sir, and if the Savannah job doesn't work out, I'll definitely talk to Mr. Callahan about working a few hours a week for him."

"Which is a much better idea than running off to a strange place to be with people you don't know anything about." Mama spoke rapidly. "Where would you live? How will you be able to afford the rent? What kind of cases does this law firm handle? You don't want to be representing criminals. Divorces would be just as bad. And the attorneys who manage a large law firm won't share your moral convictions."

These topics and many others had been discussed in great detail before I started law school, and I didn't want to revisit the debate. I remained silent. The band of orange had lost its hue. The sky was totally gray.

"I only have one question," Daddy said after a minute passed. "Will you honor your parents?"

I knew what he meant.

"Yes sir."

Later that night I tiptoed into the darkened bedroom. Emma's voice from the top bunk startled me.

"Tammy Lynn."

"Quiet! You're supposed to be asleep."

"Exactly how old were you when we were born?"

I did a quick calculation. "Almost seven months younger than you are now."

"And you didn't mind sharing your room?"

"No, I was excited. But just like now, you were noisy when I wanted you to be quiet."

"I don't mind sharing the room with you when you come home."

"Thank you. I like being with you too."

I sat on the bed and slipped off my shoes and socks.

"When are you going to get married so I can have a baby to play with?"

"Don't be silly," I answered. "I've never even been kissed. Good night."

Emma sighed. Then sighed again.

"What is it?" I asked.

"Isn't Savannah the city founded by General James Oglethorpe for people in

England who couldn't pay their bills?" she asked.

"Yes. Were you eavesdropping on my conversation with Mama and Daddy?"

"What's Savannah like now? We only studied about the 1700s."

"I've never been there, but it's very pretty with a lot of little parks and squares."

"How do you know that?"

"I read about it in a book that had pictures and information about historic places."

"If you take the job, does that mean we won't see you this summer?"

"I'll try to come home or maybe you can visit me."

"Would Ellie come too?"

"Of course, but it would be up to Mama and Daddy."

There was a moment of silence.

"I want you to be here with us. This is like you're moving away forever and never coming home."

I could hear a tremor in Emma's voice. I came over and stroked her hair. My eyes had adjusted to the dark, and I could see a forlorn expression on her face. I kissed her on the forehead.

"I love you wherever I am."

"But it's not the same if you're not where I can see and touch you."

I felt a pang of remorse. My focus had been totally selfish. There was great benefit in spending a summer at home. The love of family wasn't a daydream — it was the most enduring reality in my world.

I always slept better in my own bed. I woke up when Chester, the family rooster, began to crow but managed to tune him out and sleep for another thirty minutes until a finger tapped me on the cheek. Through bleary eyes I couldn't tell if it was Emma or Ellie.

"Who is it?" I asked.

"Guess."

"Ellie?"

"That's right. Are you going to get the eggs?"

I pulled the sheet next to my chin. Not having to get up for class made the bed feel extra nice.

"Who's been doing it?" I mumbled.

"This is my week, but I wanted to help with the biscuits."

Too many thoughts were now in my head to allow another snooze. "Okay. I'll get the eggs."

I got up and pulled on a loose-fitting cotton dress. The women and girls in our family never wore pants, and we made most of our day-to-day clothes. Learning how to sew was part of our training. When I went to high school, Mama was nice enough to buy me some inexpensive skirts, dresses, and blouses at Wal-Mart. Store-bought clothes blunted the stigma of our private dress code, but I still stood out as a feminine island in an ocean of unisex apparel. Snide questions and critical stares were inevitable, but it helped that a few girls in the school came from families with similar rules. Those girls were my closest friends.

The high school basketball uniforms could have been an impossible fashion obstacle to overcome. Mama played basketball in high school and was willing to bend on the rules, so long as the coach ordered a uniform with extra-long shorts that reached to my knees and a shirt with sleeves that came close to my elbows. At first glance, it looked a couple of sizes too big, but no one paid attention to the length of my shorts or my baggy shirt after I hit a nice shot or made a crisp pass for an assist. People in the church criticized my parents for making an exception. Daddy told me not to worry about it.

I maintained the dresses-only rule through college and law school. I could always look Mama in the eye and answer truthfully when she asked me if I'd worn pants or blue jeans.

I splashed water on my face, slipped my hair into a ponytail, and went downstairs. I grabbed the blue metal pail used to collect the eggs. The twins and I had decorated the pail with a chicken motif that included primitive portraits of some of our hens against a chicken coop landscape. I stepped outside into the cool morning air.

The wire enclosure where the chickens stayed was to the left of the basketball court. The birds stayed inside at night but were released to forage in the yard during the day. Flip and Ginger would bark at them, but our chickens' greatest enemies were possums.

Mama preferred white-shelled eggs, so we owned leghorns. We kept one rooster and four to six hens. Compact and muscular, our chickens bore little resemblance to the flaccid birds delivered to the processing plant in town. Daddy raised pullets to replace hens whose egg production declined. We never ate our hens. When they clucked their last cluck, the chickens received appropriate burial in the large pet cemetery at the edge of our property.

I went inside the pen. Chester charged in full-attack mode, but I ignored him. Top law students who could handle intense questioning by a tough professor would probably flee from Chester. The rooster came right up to my feet before giving a loud, self-satisfied squawk and strutting away.

I slowly entered the coop. Our hens were named after female characters in Shakespearean plays. Mama used an edited version of Shakespeare's works, with the bawdy jokes deleted, as part of her homeschool curriculum. Each bird's nesting box was marked with a carefully printed card: Juliet, Olivia, Viola, Cressida, Cleopatra, and Lady Macbeth. It was a noble company with Chester as their lord.

The hens knew what I intended to do and began protesting and pecking my hand as I slipped it into each box to pull out a warm egg. However, once the egg was gone, they abandoned the boxes and fluttered to the ground. Collecting eggs was the easy part of raising chickens. Cleaning the coop was the hard job. The coop needed cleaning. I hoped Mama had told one of the boys to do it. I carried the pail into the kitchen.

"Five for five," I announced.

"They're producing nicely," Mama replied. "There are more eggs in the refrigerator. Wash what you gathered this morning in vinegar and scramble up as many as you think we'll need."

Mama varied the breakfast menu. We often ate oatmeal or cereal with fruit, but once again she wanted to do something special in honor of my return. She knew I loved fluffy scrambled eggs with crisp bacon. The bacon was already beginning to sizzle in the skillet, and the biscuits were in the oven. I cracked open the eggs in a metal bowl and added salt and milk to make them lighter.

Kyle and Bobby didn't start spring vacation until the following week. They came into the kitchen dressed for school in slacks and short-sleeved collared shirts. My brothers blended in much easier than I did at their ages. Not only did women have to suffer the pain of childbirth, they also bore the reproach of nineteenth-century fashion in a twenty-first-century world. I beat the eggs harder to drive out my thoughts. Resentment led to the sin of bitterness.

The first bite of eggs after Daddy prayed was worth the early morning effort. Mama gave me two extra slices of bacon. Breakfast was a quiet meal. Everyone was thinking about the day ahead.

"I'll call Mr. Callahan's office," I said to Mama and Daddy. "I think his secretary gets there at eight thirty. I'd like to see him too, if he's available."

"Do you want me to go with you?" Mama asked.

"No ma'am," I answered a bit too quickly. "I mean, there's no need."

Daddy left for work, followed a few minutes later by my brothers, who rode to school in Kyle's truck. I cleaned up the kitchen while Mama and the twins began the school day. When I turned off the water, I could hear the sound of Mama's voice in the front room. She loved teaching. It would leave a big hole in her life when the twins reached high school age.

My homeschool years were pleasant memories. The yard, sky, woods, and the pond down the road were our science laboratory. I could identify many trees by leaf and bark. Math was incorporated into the practical functions of the household. Mama put a premium on being able to perform math mentally. Calculators weren't allowed; paper and pencil discouraged.

By age seven, I was reading the text in picture books and finished the entire Chronicles of Narnia a year later. Much of the day was spent reading. The county librarian, Mrs. Davis, would order anything Mama wanted through the state lending program. Twice a month, the old books went to town, and Mama returned with new ones. I'd read many of the classic works of literature required by my college English courses by the time I was in the ninth grade. Only the more controversial books didn't make Mama's list. When I finally read them, I usually understood why.

The twins were old enough that much of their study was self-directed. Mama guided them from the sidelines. She used a questioning format similar to my law school professors. After I started the dishwasher, I went into the front room. The twins were studying the Bible.

"Why do you think the apostle Paul thought he was serving God by persecuting the early Christians?" Mama asked.

"He was sinning," Ellie answered.

"But he didn't know it at the time. How is it possible for a person to believe he is obeying God when in fact he is doing the opposite?"

Emma knew what to say. "Where do we look for the answer?"

Mama gave references from three Pauline letters. "It's somewhere in those chapters. When you find the answer, write down the verses that apply. Then, I want you to think of at least one modern example of the same kind of mistake made by the apostle Paul."

The girls immediately opened their Bibles. Mama's question made me uncomfortable. I looked at the clock on the wall.

"I'm going to call Mr. Callahan's office."

3

Mrs. Betty Murphy answered the phone at Oscar Callahan's office. When I asked if I could talk to the lawyer, she put me on hold for a few seconds, then told me to come in anytime before noon.

"And can I have a fax sent to the office?" I asked. "It has to do with a job offer from a law firm in Savannah."

"Sure, honey. I'll be on the lookout for it."

I left a message on Ms. Patrick's voice mail and hoped she'd retrieve it in time to forward the information. Then I ran upstairs, showered, and dressed in a blue skirt and white blouse. I had a matching jacket that turned the outfit into a business suit but left it in the closet. I put on low black heels and slipped the letter from Savannah into a small black purse.

"May I borrow the car keys?" I asked Mama when I returned downstairs.

"You look fancy," Emma said.

"Like a woman preacher," Ellie added.

Our church allowed women to exhort the congregation. Mama rarely exercised the privilege, but when she did, her eyes blazed with the fire of God so that chills ran up and down my back.

"I'll tell Mr. Callahan to repent," I said, turning around in the center of the room. "I wore this outfit several times when I gave a presentation at school."

Mama reached over and touched the fabric of the skirt. "That's a nice blend."

"Is it modest enough?" I asked a bit anxiously.

"Yes. You look very professional."

"I'd hire you," Emma said. "And get you to sue Ellie for breaking the porcelain figurine that Aunt Jane brought back from her trip —"

"Emma," Mama interrupted. "Open to 1 Corinthians 6 and read what Paul wrote about Christians suing each another."

"I was joking," Emma protested. "I forgave her the next day."

"I know, but it's a good time to learn a lesson about lawsuits between Christians." She turned to me. "Take the van. Don't worry about putting any gas in it."

■ ■ ■ ■

With a family of seven, a large passenger van was a necessity, not a luxury. Daddy selected the model, and Mama chose the color. She loved blue, and our vans were always somewhere between navy and azure. We didn't take long trips. Common destinations were town, church, and the homes of relatives. One of the boys washed the van on Saturday, but it couldn't stay spotless to the bottom of the dirt driveway. A light coat of red Georgia clay immediately coated the back bumper and created a film across the rear window.

I turned left onto Beaver Ruin Road and followed it a mile to a freshly paved two-lane highway. The highway zigzagged across the hills of north Georgia, making sure no crossroad was left out. I knew every curve and dip of the route well enough to navigate it in a driving thunderstorm. I reached the edge of town. Powell Station had a single main street with two red lights, a business district three blocks long, and a U.S. post office. For travelers, it was a forgotten slow spot in the road. To me, it was the hub of our lives.

Oscar Callahan was the only lawyer in

town and jokingly claimed a monopoly on a business that didn't pay well. However, he'd made enough money to build a large home surrounded by a fifty-acre pasture where Angus cattle grazed in idyllic contentment. Kyle thought the lawyer's stock was the best of the breed in the area.

The basis for Mr. Callahan's success was his representation of workers injured in the small manufacturing plants, textile mills, and chicken processing facilities scattered across the region. If a worker sprained a knee, hurt a hand, or ruptured a lumbar disc, Mr. Callahan got the case. Insurance defense lawyers from Atlanta came north to litigate against him at their peril.

I first met Mr. Callahan when I was ten years old and Mama took me to his office for a field trip. He took an immediate interest in me, and that first field trip led to other visits during which we talked about everything from the U.S. Constitution to what it was like inside the county jail. When I graduated from high school, he sent me a check for a hundred dollars along with a note telling me I could become a lawyer if I wanted to.

Mr. Callahan's roots in Powell Station ran deep. His grandfather was one of the most famous preachers in the early days of our church. The lawyer and his wife attended a more traditional congregation, but he understood people like my parents and me.

I parked the van in front of a corner building at one of the two traffic lights. Mr. Callahan had remodeled the plain brick structure years before and installed nice wooden double doors with his name, "Oscar Callahan — Attorney at Law," in large brass letters across the top. The building was painted white. Even after the paint began to chip, it was a classy place. Everybody in town considered his office a landmark.

The inside of the building was cool on even the hottest days. It was the coolness of the interior that impressed me as a little girl. Our house didn't have air-conditioning, and we survived summer with fans that did little more than circulate the heat. The church sanctuary was air-conditioned, but people supplemented the anemic system with funeral home fans. Mr. Callahan didn't concern himself with what he had to pay the electric co-op. The oversized cooling unit behind the building never stopped humming.

Thick, deep carpet covered the floor beneath my feet. A leather sofa and eight chairs lined the wall. Neat rows of sporting, hunting, and women's interest magazines were displayed on a coffee table. Mrs. Murphy, a gray-haired woman, sat in the corner of the room behind a dark wooden desk. A man in overalls was talking to her. I stepped toward her desk but kept a respectful distance.

"Either Harriet or I will call you as soon as your settlement check comes in and set up a time for Mr. Callahan to meet with you," Mrs. Murphy said to the man.

"When do you think it will get here?" the man asked. "My wife's got her eye on a new double-wide, and we don't want it to get away."

"Within a couple of weeks."

"That might be too late."

"Who's selling the trailer to you?"

"Foothills Homes."

"I know Mr. Kilgo. Would you like me to call and let him know what's going on with your case?"

"Yes'm."

The client turned away, and Mrs. Murphy smiled at me.

"Here's your fax," she said, handing me a few sheets of paper. "He just got off the phone, and I'm sure he would like to see you. You look great, very professional."

"Thanks."

Beyond the reception area was a library

that also served as a conference room. Opposite the library was Harriet Smith's office. In her early forties, the secretary had worked for Mr. Callahan over twenty years. Beyond the secretary's office were a file room and two smaller, unfinished offices, one of which Mama wanted me to occupy upon graduation from law school. Mr. Callahan had never brought up the subject during the short stints I'd worked at his office organizing files. However, he'd agreed to serve as a reference on my résumé.

The door to the lawyer's office was open, and I could see his feet propped up on the corner of his desk. A tall man, Oscar Callahan was sixty years old with a full head of white hair and intense, dark eyes. It was easy to imagine his grandfather as a fiery preacher. Mr. Callahan looked over his gold-rimmed reading glasses and rose to his feet.

"Welcome, Tammy Lynn," he boomed out. "It appears the transformation into sophisticated lawyer is well on its way."

Mr. Callahan motioned for me to take a seat. The lawyer had large hands that he used to emphasize points in conversation. He laid his glasses on his desk and pointed at the papers in my hand.

"Did you get your fax?"

"Yes sir."

"Is it from Savannah?"

"Yes sir," I answered in surprise.

Mr. Callahan nodded. "Joe Carpenter called me about you the other day. We were in law school together. He's a tight-lipped blue blood from the coast, and I'm the wild-eyed son of the red clay hills, but we've always gotten along fine. I've seen him at bar association meetings over the years. Did he offer you a summer job?"

I held up the papers. "Yes sir, I think so, but I haven't read the terms."

"Well, an offer is like bait on a hook. It doesn't count for anything unless a fish bites it. Look it over while I finish reviewing this medical report."

Mr. Callahan put on his glasses and resumed reading. I looked down at the three sheets of paper in my hand. Even the fax cover sheet had a classy look. I turned to the next page, titled "Summer Clerk — Offer Memorandum." My eyes opened wide at the amount of money I would be paid. The weekly salary would be greater than what I would make in two grueling weeks, including overtime, at the chicken plant.

The impact of a legal education on my economic future struck me like never before. If the law firm paid this much to a summer clerk, the compensation for first-year associates would be even more. I quickly calculated a likely annual salary in my head.

The rest of the memo was related to dates of employment, a prohibition against working anywhere else while employed by Braddock, Appleby, and Carpenter, an agreement that all my work product would belong to the firm as well as receipts from billings, and a confidentiality clause as to both terms of the offer and any proprietary information obtained during my employment. I wondered what in the world I might learn that would be valuable enough to sell. When I glanced up, Mr. Callahan was peering over his glasses at me.

"How does it look?" he asked.

I started to hand the fax to him, then stopped.

"I'd like your opinion, but I can't show it to you," I said. "It has a confidentiality clause."

The older lawyer laughed. "Consider me your personal attorney for a few minutes. A confidentiality clause doesn't prohibit consultation with a lawyer. I'll review it pro bono."

I sheepishly handed the offer sheet to him. He read it in a few seconds.

"The price of raw legal talent is going up,"

he said. "That beats hugging dead chickens, doesn't it?"

"Yes sir."

"And they're going to toss in a name change for free."

I didn't answer.

"Oh, don't worry about it," the lawyer said with a chuckle. "Everybody knows your mother as Lu; no one calls her Luella."

"Except my grandmother and Aunt Jane." I paused. "Mama and Daddy think the different spelling of my name was a mistake by the law firm."

"Do you want to confess your sins to me?"

I remembered my comment about telling Mr. Callahan to repent.

"I can use it for the summer, then go back to the correct spelling."

"Don't worry about it. T-a-m-i has a nice look to it. I've never been fond of Oscar but couldn't come up with an alternative."

"You'll always be Mr. Callahan to me."

The lawyer laughed. "I'm sure I will."

"What else do you know about the firm?" I asked.

Mr. Callahan handed the fax back to me. "As you can see from the letterhead, the Braddock firm has been around for a hundred years. Samuel Braddock is a descendant of the founder. I don't know Nelson

Appleby and told you about Joe Carpenter. How many lawyers are there? Sixteen or seventeen?"

I glanced down at the letterhead and counted. "Fifteen."

"I did a little research for you," Mr. Callahan said. "According to the firm website, less than half are partners. The rest are associates hoping they get invited to join. The firm's representative clients include a couple of shipping companies, several banks, blue-chip corporations, large foundations — the cream of the crop." Mr. Callahan smiled. "I doubt any of their lawyers would be interested in representing a man who rips the rotator cuff in his right shoulder while unloading a trailer in one-hundred-degree heat."

My face fell. "Do you think it would be a bad place to work?"

The lawyer held up his hand. "No, no. Don't let my bias on behalf of working folks taint you. I shouldn't have said that. There are many honorable places to land in the law. One of the best pieces of advice I ever received was to dabble in a number of areas, find what brings the most personal satisfaction, and become an expert in it."

Listening to Mr. Callahan's practical wisdom made me wish he would offer me a summer job. Even if he paid me chicken-plant wages it would be plenty of money for me, especially since I could live at home.

"It's a long way from Powell Station," I said, hoping my wistful comment might lead the conversation in that direction.

"You've gone a long way from here already. And I bet you've taken the best your family has to offer along with you. If you take the job in Savannah, folks are going to meet the kind of person who made this country great in the first place."

"What do you mean?"

Mr. Callahan looked past my right shoulder. He stared so long that I turned and followed his gaze to an old photograph of his grandfather on the wall. Preacher Callahan didn't look like he knew how to smile.

"You know exactly what I mean," the lawyer continued, his eyes returning to mine. "You're different, and it won't take long for anyone to find it out. Most people focus on the externals: the way you dress, the fact that you don't go to movies, the obedience to parents, the way you honor the Lord's Day by not doing anything on Sunday except go to church meetings. They don't realize that what makes you special is on the inside — your integrity and strength of character. That's rare, especially when

56

joined with your intelligence."

Mr. Callahan's words made me uneasy. It sounded like an invitation to pride. I kept silent.

"Is it all right for me to share my opinion?" he asked.

"Yes sir. That's why I'm here."

The lawyer tapped his fingers on his desk. "Just the answer I expected, and although my ideas don't always line up with your beliefs, hear me out. When I look at you, I appreciate what my grandfather and those like him stood for. The strict ways don't work for everyone, but in your case they do. And I'm open-minded enough to acknowledge the good done by God's grace when I see it."

"Yes sir."

"So, what are you going to do about the job?" the lawyer continued.

"Could I work for you?" I blurted out.

Mr. Callahan smiled. "That's not the bait in the water. But to be honest, I thought about it after Joe Carpenter called me. I even prayed about it."

My eyes opened wider.

"Does that surprise you?" he asked.

"No sir. I mean, I guess it does a little bit."

"I believe in prayer," the lawyer said.

"What does the Bible say? God blesses the children of the righteous to how many generations?"

"A thousand generations."

"Did they teach you that in law school along with the rule against perpetuities?"

"No sir. It's in Deuteronomy."

Mr. Callahan nodded and spoke thoughtfully. "Well, I'm only two generations removed from a very righteous man, and all my life I've felt the stirring of his influence in my soul. When I prayed about offering you a job, the Lord told me to 'ask for a continuance.' When does a lawyer request a continuance?"

"When he's not ready to try a case."

"Or when the case isn't ready for the lawyer to try."

I mulled over his words for a moment before responding. "Do you think I have to learn more before I'm ready to make a decision about coming back to Powell Station?"

"Maybe, but don't treat my opinion like someone standing up at the church and saying, 'Thus saith the Lord.' I don't claim infallibility or divine imprimatur. And it's not just about you. I need time to decide what I'm going to do over the next few years. Someday, I want to spend more time feeding my cattle than fighting with insurance companies. Unless I simply close the doors when I retire, I need to bring in a younger lawyer or two who can develop rapport with my clientele in preparation for taking over my practice."

I knew the meaning of patience. Instant gratification wasn't part of my upbringing.

"Yes sir. Can I share what you've told me with my parents?"

He leaned forward and clasped his hands together. "I'd expect you to. And if you need Internet access or use of the fax machine while you're home, come here."

"Thank you."

I stood up. Mr. Callahan spoke. "Don't let go of the good planted in you."

"Yes sir."

As I drove home, I couldn't shake a deep longing that, in spite of his comments, Mr. Callahan might offer me a job. It would be a gracious next step along the path to independence. As I rounded a familiar curve, I appealed the lawyer's decision to a higher judge.

"Lord, could you tell him a continuance isn't necessary?"

After supper that night, Daddy, Mama, and I returned to the front porch. After making sure neither of the twins was eavesdropping,

I told them about my meeting in town. I left out the part about praying that Mr. Callahan might change his mind. Mama started to interrupt a few times, but Daddy put his hand on her arm.

"That's it," I said when I finished.

"So, the Spirit still moves on his heart," Daddy said. "Why would he wander from the fold?"

"His mother didn't like our ways," Mama replied. "And a family that isn't of one mind is a house divided. It will fall."

"But he's aware of his heritage," Daddy answered. "Do you think Pastor Vick and some of the elders should visit him?"

Mama was silent for a moment as they rocked back and forth. "It would be a glorious homecoming."

I stared across the darkening yard, not sure what my parents' interest in Oscar Callahan's spiritual pilgrimage meant to me. I needed them to make a decision. The Braddock, Appleby, and Carpenter job offer wouldn't remain outstanding indefinitely. If I didn't accept it, and Mr. Callahan didn't change his mind, my summer would be spent with thousands of dead chickens. I cleared my throat.

"What about Savannah?" I asked.

"We'll seek the Lord about it tonight,"

Daddy said. "And tell you in the morning."

Daddy's comment wasn't a religious put-off. He and Mama believed in praying until they received a definite answer. I'd seen the light shining beneath their bedroom door in the middle of the night when an issue of importance to the family required guidance from the Lord. People at our church would tarry at the altar as long as it took to find peace.

"I'll pray too," I answered.

"It's right that you should," Mama replied. "A cord of three strands isn't easily broken."

4

Moses Jones lived in a waterfront shack on
an unnamed tributary of the Little Ogeechee River. Years before he'd selected a
place so marshy and uninhabitable that no
one would have an interest in disturbing his
privacy. No mobs of angry white men looking for a scapegoat threatened him.

It took several months to build his single-
room dwelling with scrap lumber and ply-
wood. When he finished, it rested on stilts
four feet above the ground. Twice hur-
ricanes damaged the house, but each time
Moses scavenged enough lumber to rebuild.

It was a ten-minute walk through the
woods to the lean-to where he kept his
bicycle beside a narrow road. Every Monday
morning, he pedaled into Savannah where
he spent the day collecting aluminum cans
to sell at the recycling center. He didn't pick
up cans alongside the road. Moses had an
arrangement with several bars and pubs that

allowed him to haul away their beer and soft drink cans in return for cleaning around the back of their buildings. Included in his wages at one of the pubs was a free meal. The high point of Moses' week was sitting on a delivery dock savoring a plate piled high with spicy chicken wings.

After he sold the cans, Moses would buy a few fishhooks and fill up a plastic bag with free food from the community food pantry. Clothes and shoes were castoffs that couldn't be sold at a local thrift store. He washed his clothes once a month at a Laundromat. People mistakenly considered him homeless. They didn't know about his shack in the woods. He never begged or panhandled.

The old man's most expensive regular purchase was the kerosene that powered his stove, heater, and lantern. He'd strap a five-gallon plastic container onto his bike rack and fill it with fuel at a hardware store. Five gallons of kerosene would last a long time in the warm summer months when he only used it for cooking, but in the winter he had to buy more. Winter was hard on animals and hard on Moses.

Fish and an occasional squirrel he caught in a metal trap were his sources of fresh protein. Moses liked fish coated in cornmeal and quick-fried; a gray squirrel grown fat on acorns from live oaks provided a different taste in meat. He drank water boiled in a large pot and poured into milk jugs. Alcohol hadn't passed his lips since he'd worked years before as a bolita runner for Tommy Lee Barnes.

Moses slept on eight pillows wrapped in an old sheet and laid on the floor. It was a lumpy mattress, but it was a lot easier hauling pillows through the woods than trying to carry a mattress. He had a folding table and two aluminum chairs, but he never had guests. It had been five years since his last visitor, a duck hunter who surprised him one morning. The hunter stopped for a brief chat then moved on. There weren't any ducks in the area, and the hunter didn't come back.

In good weather Moses cooked outside, which kept his shack from getting smoky or burning down. He kept the kerosene lantern for emergency use and rarely lit it. Except when he went night fishing, he lay down to sleep at dark and woke at dawn.

The old man kept his most prized possession, his johnboat, locked and chained to a tree. The key to the rusty lock hung on a leather strap around his neck. In winter Moses slept in the shack, but the rest of the year he liked to spend several nights a week on his boat. When he finished fishing, he'd tie up at a dock of one of the many houses that lined the waterway in every direction. He preferred the docks as moorings. Too many times, he'd tied up to a tree only to have a snake, spider, or an army of ants invade the boat in the middle of the night.

After he found a spot for the night, he'd remove one of the seats in the johnboat and roll out two rubber mats that he placed on top of each other in the bottom of the boat. He'd stretch out on the mats, drape mosquito netting over the edge of the boat, and watch the stars overhead while the boat gently rocked in the river. The faces in the water couldn't see over the edge of the boat, and after so many years, the memory of innocent blood running off his hands into the river rarely played across his mind. He felt at peace.

However, like a hidden log just beneath the surface of the water, Moses' habit of tying up at the river docks concealed an unknown danger.

After putting on my pajamas, I took my Bible and journal downstairs to the front room. I turned on a small lamp and knelt in front of the sofa. God could speak quickly, or he might make me wait. To set a timetable for an answer would be disrespectful to his sovereignty. God was merciful, but prayer wasn't always meant to be a desperation plea by someone wanting a quick fix to a thorny problem.

Divine guidance about a summer legal clerkship with Braddock, Appleby, and Carpenter would have to come indirectly. Savannah, Georgia, didn't appear in the sixty-six books within the black leather cover, and the references to rabbinical lawyers, especially in the New Testament, weren't very complimentary. Any impression I received would be closely scrutinized by my parents.

I started by spending time thanking God for his past love and faithfulness. Although completely sufficient in himself, the Lord, like any parent, appreciated the thanks of a grateful child.

As I thought about God's goodness, I remembered a time in high school when I didn't have the money needed for a week-long trip to Washington, D.C., and the deposit for the trip was due on a Monday. Without telling anyone except my parents, I prayed for the funds, and after church on Sunday morning a man in our church gave me a check for the exact amount I needed.

Remembering how I felt at the time, a wave of emotion touched me, and I wiped a tear from the corner of my eye. More instances of God's goodness came to mind. I momentarily pushed aside the reason for my private prayer meeting.

I loved the Psalms and decided to quote Psalm 100 from memory, placing special emphasis on the verse about entering his gates with thanksgiving and his courts with praise. A civil courthouse was light-years from the place where David worshipped the Lord with all his might, but while meditating on the vast differences, a prayer welled up within me. I knew the next words from my mouth would be important.

"Lord, wherever I go, may I make the court of law a place of praise."

It was a beautiful thought. To find a place of holiness in the midst of a secular courtroom was something I'd never considered, and I marveled at a new facet of God's greatness. I might not shout "Hallelujah" in a judge's face, but my soul, like Mary's, could magnify the Lord, and my spirit could rejoice in God, my Savior. And the truth was even greater than that. Wherever I set my foot, not just a courtroom, could be a place of worship.

My mind raced ahead. The practice of law

itself could be a place where I praised the Lord. I repeated, "Lord, wherever I go, may I make the court of law a place of praise," several times, pausing at different points for emphasis until each word was a brick laid on the solid foundation of faith. My tears returned. The prayer fit my life's journey. Since I was a little girl, I'd been called to live a holy life — every thought, word, and deed sanctified to the Lord. Now I could glimpse how this might be fulfilled in a new way in the future.

Lifting my hands in the air, I began to walk back and forth across the room. This was the time to tarry in secret. Not to rush. Praise offered in the night bears fruit in the day. I sat on the couch and made notes in my journal. When I finished, I peeked around the corner and saw the light shining underneath my parents' door. I didn't have an answer to my summer job question, but I was content. I'd received a greater good.

Before getting into bed, I stepped quietly over to the bunk bed, gently laid my hands on the twins, and asked that the grace poured out on me this night might also be theirs. Giving was always a part of receiving.

"Good morning," Mama said when I came into the kitchen with a half dozen fresh eggs.

She stared at me. "What happened to you, Tammy Lynn? You're radiant with the joy of the Lord!"

"Yes ma'am. Last night —"

The twins came bursting into the room in the heat of an argument. Emma accused Ellie of switching a pair of good socks for a pair with holes in the toes.

"I know the good ones are mine!" Emma said. "I put them in the top drawer when I folded my clothes."

"We both have a good pair and a bad pair," Ellie responded. "She's gotten them mixed up."

Mama pointed upstairs. "Go back to your room and come back when you have this worked out."

The twins stomped out. Mama turned to me. "Wait till your daddy is here to tell me. He's going to stay a few minutes after breakfast so we can talk."

It was an oatmeal morning. Mama had fixed a huge pot that we dished out and garnished with fresh fruit, raisins, brown sugar, and nuts. Emma and Ellie returned after sorting out the sock controversy. Daddy and the boys joined us. I sat quietly and ate my breakfast.

Several times Mama glanced at me. Nothing excited her more than the move of the

Spirit in a person's life, especially for one of her children. After breakfast, she shooed the twins from the room. Mama scooted close to Daddy and spoke.

"Walter, let her go first."

Daddy looked surprised. "Why?"

"Just listen."

I quietly told them what happened the previous night. At first Mama gave a slight nod or two, but by the time I finished, she'd gotten up from the bench and began walking back and forth across the kitchen, much as I'd done the previous night. When I finished, Daddy pointed at her and grinned.

"The twins are going to get some good preaching during Bible study this morning," he said.

"I can't sit still when the Spirit is moving like this," Mama said.

"So, you think it was the Lord?" I asked.

Mama looked to heaven and raised her hands in the air.

"That's a 'yes,' " Daddy answered, rising from the bench. "I'll get my Bible."

He returned with the tattered Bible he used at home.

"You know most of this by heart, but I want to read it," he said, turning the pages.

He began in Matthew 6, just before Jesus' reference to the lilies of the field. I loved listening to Daddy's voice. He read the Bible as if it was a letter from a loved one. He finished and looked at me.

"The most important thing is to seek first the kingdom. That's what you did last night. I told your mama that if your heart was fixed on the Lord, it would be the sign we needed." He paused and looked at her. She nodded. "You have our permission to take the job in Savannah if that's what you believe you're supposed to do."

It was a serious moment. I felt a shift in responsibility for my life to my own shoulders. A touch of fear gripped me.

"But what do *you* think I should do?"

"Exactly what you did last night," Mama answered. "Hear his voice and obey it."

"He didn't say anything about the job."

"What is in your heart to do?"

"My heart is desperately wicked," I began.

"Stop it!" Mama commanded. "Don't abandon your faith."

Daddy spoke more gently. "Have confidence in God's goodness. Isn't that what you felt last night?"

"Yes sir."

I looked at their faces. I knew they loved me. I knew Jesus loved me. I shut my eyes for a few seconds. No visions appeared behind my eyelids. I opened my eyes and looked at Mama.

"What does your heart tell you?" she insisted.

I tried to look past the darkness at the core of my being and spoke slowly. "I think God has opened a door for me to go to Savannah, even though I don't know what's on the other side."

"Then finish out the semester and go to Savannah with our blessing," Daddy said.

Mama hugged me. "You'll be back. I know it."

After Daddy left for work, I called Braddock, Appleby, and Carpenter. As the phone rang, I imagined what the firm's office might look like. With fifteen lawyers and support staff, it would be too large for a grand old house converted into a law office. Most likely, the firm was in a modern office building. The receptionist transferred me to Ms. Patrick.

"This is Tami Taylor in Powell Station," I began. "Thanks for faxing the information about the job."

"I hope you've made a decision. There are other deserving candidates."

I took a deep breath. Even with Daddy's permission, I felt tentative. "Yes ma'am."

There was an awkward moment of silence.

"And?" Ms. Patrick asked.

"I'd like to accept," I responded quickly before fear jumped on my back.

"I'll notify Mr. Carpenter. Any questions about the terms of the offer?"

"No ma'am."

"Then sign it and mail it to my attention. Will you need help finding a place to stay?"

"Yes ma'am."

"Would you like to live alone or with a roommate?"

I hesitated. Alone would be expensive, and I needed to save as much money as possible. But a roommate could be risky. In college, I shared a dorm room with a teammate from my high school basketball team. We were different, but she respected my beliefs. She wore headphones while listening to her music and never brought a boy into the room while I was there. I kept the room immaculate and helped her pass freshman English and chemistry for nonscience majors.

"A roommate would be fine if we have a chance to talk before making a decision," I replied.

"One of the summer clerks is a girl from Atlanta. Do you want her name and number?"

"Yes ma'am." I grabbed a pen and a piece

of paper from Mama's nightstand.

"Here it is," Ms. Patrick said in a few moments. "Julie Feldman. She's finishing her second year at Emory."

I swallowed. Feldman sounded Jewish. Our church believed the Jews were God's chosen people, but I'd never had to choose one myself. Ms. Patrick rattled off a phone number and e-mail address that I scribbled on the sheet of paper.

"Give Julie a call or send her an e-mail. She's already been down to look for a place to stay."

"Are there any other summer clerks?"

"Yes, a young man who grew up in Charleston. He's attending Yale."

My eyes opened wider. The thought that my neophyte legal work would be compared to that of an Ivy League law student was instantly intimidating.

"Okay. I'll get in touch with Julie."

Ms. Patrick spoke in a more pleasant tone of voice. "Call if you need help or have other questions. You'll have a great time in our program. Summer associates get to sample everything Savannah has to offer."

"Yes ma'am."

I hung up the phone. Ms. Patrick might be upbeat about everything Savannah had to offer, but it sounded ominous to me.

Social pressures to conform were constant, but never welcome. I didn't relish the prospect of a future laden with the smorgasbord of sin. Not that I feared temptation. Doing the right thing was easy compared to defending my conduct to skeptics. I glanced at the slip of paper in my hand and decided not to contact Julie Feldman until I returned to school where I had constant Internet access. I'd made enough quick decisions about my future in the past twenty-four hours.

Mama and the twins were in the front room. I quietly watched them for a minute from the doorway. Emma and Ellie had their heads close together as they shared a science book. The sock dispute had vanished like the morning mist above the ground outside. Mama was sitting in a rocking chair reading a devotional book.

I'd loved my homeschool years with Mama. I wasn't naive about turning back the clock, but the refuge of home always seemed more precious when thinking about the hostile world at the end of the dirt driveway.

I spent the rest of the morning with Mama and the twins. The routine of the day restored my equilibrium. After helping fix bacon, lettuce, and tomato sandwiches for lunch, I mailed the summer clerkship agreement to Savannah. Turning toward the house, I absorbed every detail of the scene. I hoped my anchor in the hills of Powell Station was strong enough to hold me fast in the murky waters of Savannah.

Late that afternoon, I took two pillows to the front porch and positioned them on the swing so I could lie down comfortably.

The swing creaked as I shifted my weight. Flip and Ginger, hearing the sound of the swing, ambled around the corner of the house and took up their customary positions in the dirt beneath the porch.

I studied the massive poplar tree in our front yard. The new leaves showed no sign of the stress that would come with the onslaught of summer's heat. I wiggled my toes, which appeared as large as the trees on a distant hill. Before I realized it, Emma was tapping me on the shoulder.

"Wake up!"

I blinked. "Was I asleep?"

"Don't pretend you were praying," Emma said. "Is Mama going to let you live in Savannah this summer?"

Out of the corner of my eye I could see Ellie standing just inside the house.

"Ask her," I responded.

The twins ran toward the kitchen. I got

out of the swing and followed.

Emma and Ellie were firing questions at Mama when I entered the kitchen. They knew that if they could persuade Mama to change her mind, it would negate my plans. Arguing with me would be a waste of time.

"Fix the spaghetti sauce for supper while I talk to your sisters," Mama said to me.

She took the girls onto the back steps. In a few seconds it was quiet. I opened two jars of canned tomatoes, added other ingredients from the spice pantry, and placed the pot of chunky sauce on the stove to simmer. Mama and the twins returned. She looked at me.

"Did you promise Ellie that she and Emma could visit you in Savannah this summer?"

"No ma'am," I said, and then continued quickly when I saw Ellie about to explode. "I told her a trip might be arranged if you and Daddy gave permission. I don't even know where I'm going to stay."

Mama turned to Ellie. "Is that what she said?"

"I'm not sure. I was sleepy."

"A trip to Savannah isn't like a drive for a picnic at the park. And I don't want to be like Jacob and have all my children leave and go down to Egypt. Unlike Canaan during the time of Joseph, there isn't a famine in Powell Station."

"But it meant the whole family got to be together," Emma said.

"Go upstairs and straighten up your room," Mama told the girls.

"I'm sorry if I caused a problem with my mention of a visit," I said when they left the room.

"It was a helpful diversion," she replied. "They love you so much the thought of your absence hurts. A trip to see you gives them something else to think about."

I stirred the sauce. "Do you think the whole family could visit? It would be a chance for the twins to see the ocean for the first time."

Mama lifted a huge pot of water for the noodles onto the stove. "Goodness. That would be a big undertaking. You know how busy summer is around here."

The job in Savannah was the major topic of conversation at the supper table. My role in the decision didn't come out, but I saw Kyle and Bobby give each other a knowing look. It made me wonder what secret dreams they held about the future. A wave of fear washed over me that they might not be seeking God's will. It would crush me if a member of our family became a prodigal.

"I've sought the mind of the Lord about this," I said as a quick lesson to my siblings. "It's not an act of selfish independence or rebellion. Daddy and Mama are going to give me their blessing."

"And I'll be blessed if I can take your spot at the plant," Bobby added with a hopeful glance at Daddy.

"I'll mention it to Mr. Waldrup," Daddy said. "But are you sure you want to work inside on the line? I could try to find a place for you as a catcher."

The catchers went into the chicken houses, grabbed the birds, and crammed them into cages for transport to the processing plant. It was hot, nasty, physical labor.

"Did working on the line bother you?" Bobby asked me.

The days standing in the chill of the plant with razor-sharp scissors in one hand and chicken guts in the other were a numbing blur.

"The language of some of the women is bad," I replied. "But the chickens don't have much to say, and the smell is better than what you'd face as a catcher."

"What do the women say?" Emma asked.

Mama shook her head, and Emma plunged her fork into her spaghetti.

5

Sunday morning, of course, we went to church. I put my hair in a tight bun and helped the twins get ready in their long dresses that reached to their ankles. Everyone in our van had assigned seats. I occupied the referee position between Ellie and Emma. It was about three miles to the church. The sanctuary was a large redbrick building with opaque white windows. Families similar to our own streamed into the parking lot. It was the one day during the week when normal looked like us. We took our usual seats about a third of the way from the front on the left side of the sanctuary.

Pastor Vick, a large man with a bald head and a booming voice, spoke with an eloquence that made my advocacy professor at the law school look like an oratorical amateur. This morning, he preached from Ezekiel 47. Daddy read the Bible with tender love; Pastor Vick could make the meekest verse echo with the thunder of Sinai. His text came from Ezekiel's vision of the river flowing from the temple in Jerusalem.

He measured a thousand cubits, and he brought me through the waters; the waters were to the ankles. Again he measured a thousand, and brought me through the waters; the waters were to the knees. Again he measured a thousand; and brought me through; the waters were to the loins. Afterward he measured a thousand; and it was a river that I could not pass over: for the waters were risen, water to swim in, a river that could not be passed over.

Pastor Vick then described the apostate condition of the Israelites in a way that left no doubt as to the parallel for the present. That part of his sermon was always easy to hear. But then he turned his attention to the people sitting in the pews. Rhetorical questions were his most deadly bullets.

"That was their abominable condition, but what about you? Are you satisfied with dipping your toe into the river of God's glory and pretending you've sold out to Jesus? Is knee-deep water enough for you to play in and call yourself committed to the gospel? Do you believe you're righteous because the water laps around your waist?" Pastor Vick let his eyes scan the entire congregation. "Are any of you willing to cast yourself into the river of God where only Jesus can hold you up? Who will go into deeper water?"

My stomach quivered; a familiar feeling that meant an arrow shot from the pulpit had found its mark. I glanced sideways at Mama. Her attention was riveted on the front of the church. As Pastor Vick continued, my uneasiness increased. The river of God was both fearful and wonderful.

"The river is wide, the river is deep," Pastor Vick continued. "And only those whose eyes are fixed on Jesus can enter its waters. If that describes you this morning, the altar of God beckons you."

At the invitation, I was one of the first people to walk down the aisle and kneel in prayer. Being away at school for most of the year, I didn't have the option to hold back until another Sunday. I had to respond when the Spirit moved. One of the elders laid his hands on my head and prayed a long blessing. I rose to my feet encouraged. Outside the church, Mama gave me a hug.

"Watching you blesses me," she said simply.

It was the highest compliment I could imagine.

Mid-afternoon, the female law student giving me a ride back to school picked me up. Everyone stood in a line in the front room for a hug. My suitcase waited beside the door.

"Let us know your exam schedule," Mama said. "So we can pray."

"We love you," Daddy added, his eyes sparkling with a mixture of happiness and sorrow. I could see him swallow after he spoke.

Kyle and Bobby gave me obligatory brother hugs. The twins grabbed me so tightly that I had trouble breathing.

I carried my suitcase to the car and put it in the trunk. I didn't look back until the last instant. Mama, Daddy, and the twins were standing on the front porch watching the car drive away, taking me back to the outside world.

I lived alone about a mile from the law school in Athens. My one-room apartment was a converted motel, but I'd joked to Daddy that it wasn't fully saved. It contained a stove, a compact refrigerator, a couple of cabinets, and a three-foot countertop with a sink. I brought in a twin bed, a small wooden table picked up at a garage sale, and a webbed lounge chair where I sat to read. My computer was on a desk in front of the single window that provided a view of the parking lot.

After the sun went down and the Sabbath was over, I turned on the computer and sent an e-mail to Julie Feldman, introducing myself and asking about her living arrangements for the summer. I closed my eyes and prayed before clicking the Send icon. I didn't want to be selfish or wasteful with money, but I liked the peace and quiet of living alone. It made life so much simpler.

None of my classmates at the law school knew the depth of my religious convictions, and their ignorance was my bliss. In Pastor Vick's terminology, I lived among the Babylonians without defiling myself with their idols or offending them with my differences. I didn't belong to either the Young Democrats or the Young Republicans; both groups were far from the truth. I was simply the girl with long hair who wore skirts and dresses to class and baggy sweatpants when playing basketball or going out for a run.

When I unpacked my suitcase, I found letters from Emma, Ellie, and Mama. I'd left them notes hidden in places where they might not be found for a couple of days. Emma had drawn a picture of me with red hearts around the border. Ellie drew me as a scarecrow running away from a giant Chester the chicken. I saved Mama's letter for last. She expressed her thankfulness for my sensitivity to the Lord, passed on a few words of encouragement, and concluded by reassuring me that every thought of me brought her joy. Even though I'd just been home, the letters made me homesick.

I studied for a couple of hours and checked my computer. I had an e-mail from Julie Feldman. My heart went to my throat as I moved the cursor to open it. I immediately noticed there was an attachment with pictures.

Hi, Tami,

Got your e-mail. Look forward to a fun time with you this summer at B, A & C. Wish you'd called sooner. I just signed a lease for an apartment in an older home near Greene Square. I'd gone back and forth about taking a beautiful (but pricey) place overlooking the river that would have been great for two. The woman who owns it is going to be in Spain for the summer.

Can you imagine that!

I'm sending pics and details of two other places I found and a photo of me taken a couple of months ago. Lynn Bynum is the leasing agent who helped me. Gerry Patrick at the firm knows her. The apartment on Price Street is not far from me. Call quick if you want to take one of these. There's a lot more about me on MySpace-.com. See you in a few weeks.

Julie

I read the e-mail four times. I'd heard that some of the students at Emory could be snobby. Julie sounded nice enough, although her definition of fun was likely the same as Ms. Patrick's invitation to sample all Savannah had to offer. It was a relief not having to decide whether to room with someone for the summer.

I clicked on Julie's picture and watched it load from the top of the screen to the bottom. She had black hair that fell to her shoulders, a full figure, and wore glasses that made her look very smart. Her Jewish ethnicity was apparent in her face. Dressed casually in a blue sweater and jeans, she was sitting on a bench in front of a huge tree on the Emory campus. There was an open book in her hands that was the same civil procedure casebook we used at Georgia; however, Julie was holding the book upside down and staring at an unknown object in the distance. It was a posed shot, but the purpose of the photo with an upside-down book and faraway look in her eyes wasn't clear. I didn't try to access Julie's myspace.com page. I avoided the personal side of the Web because it was so full of lies and perversion.

I opened the photos of the places mentioned in the e-mail. There were multiple photos of the two apartments and a PDF file giving the specifications of each. The apartment near Julie's place was the second story of a detached garage, and the second location was an end unit of a block of townhomes. I was shocked to discover that one month's rent for the townhome equaled three months at my apartment. The garage apartment was even more expensive. I quickly closed the files. I would need to phone Ms. Patrick and find out about a cheaper place to live.

The following morning at 5:30 a.m. I rolled over and opened my eyes. There were no chickens to tend, but I enjoyed getting up for an early morning run and loved breathing the fresh air of a new day. On even the coldest days of winter, I bundled up for a forty-five-minute jog that included a mile-long section alongside the Oconee River. While I ran, I rejoiced. It wasn't a time for intercession, and I didn't try to make it serious. I simply enjoyed the world God created and the physical strength he'd given me.

I covered the last half mile in a sprint that made my heart pound. When I finished, I walked across the parking lot, breathing heavily, with my hands on my hips. I drank two large glasses of water while I cooled off, showered, and dressed for the day. The runner's rush and the glasses of water curbed my morning appetite, and I didn't cook a complicated breakfast. Fruit, yogurt, and a hard-boiled egg were typical. While eating, I prepared for the day's classes. Information learned in the morning stayed with me better than what I studied at night. Most law students didn't crack a casebook in the morning and dragged themselves to class on a skid of strong coffee. I'd never finished a cup of coffee in my life.

After my first class, I went to the placement office and told the job placement director about the Savannah offer. She congratulated me and wrote down the information for her statistics. The placement office had rooms with phones and computers for students to use in job search activities. I closed the door and phoned Ms. Patrick.

"Your acceptance of the job arrived in the mail this morning," she said.

"Really?" It was amazing that an envelope could travel from Powell Station to Savannah in less than two days.

"Did you contact Julie Feldman?"

"Yes ma'am." I told her about my e-mail from the Emory student. "The places Julie sent me are not in my budget. I need to save as much money as possible."

"I'm looking at your résumé and see that you've worked with the elderly."

"Yes ma'am. I enjoyed it."

Starting in college, I'd found part-time work as a sitter for older women in nursing homes. Some were demanding; others docile. It was easy work that allowed time for study when my clients slept. One reference on my résumé was a woman whose mother I'd cared for.

"Would you be interested in staying with an elderly woman in Savannah?" Ms. Patrick asked. "Her daughter is a client of the firm and told me recently that her mother needs a live-in caregiver to spend the night. The mother is self-sufficient, but she's reached the age where it's better to have someone around the house on a regular basis. She lives in a beautiful old home a few blocks from our office. I don't know what the family would be willing to pay, but the daughter mentioned room and board if I could think of a woman to help."

A free place to stay within walking distance of the office sounded like a sign from heaven.

"Yes ma'am, but I don't want to violate my contract with the law firm. I promised to devote all my efforts to firm business."

Ms. Patrick laughed so loudly that I felt embarrassed. "I appreciate your integrity, but you're a summer clerk, not a first-year associate. Seventy-hour workweeks aren't part of the plan. This is your last opportunity to enjoy a law office without any responsibilities. When I talk to Christine Bartlett, I'll tell her what you'll be doing at the firm so she can take that into consideration."

"What's her mother's name?"

"I don't know her first name. I've always called her Mrs. Fairmont. She's an interesting woman."

Interesting could mean a lot of things, and staying with a woman in her own home would be a lot different from the controlled environment of a nursing facility. I immediately thought about the use of alcohol. I had no intention of becoming a dying alcoholic's barmaid.

"And I'm sure they would have a lot of questions for me." I paused. "I'd have a few too."

"Do you want me to pursue it?"

"Yes ma'am," I said quickly. "But I know from experience that compatibility is important. You can pass along Mrs. Frady as a reference. She's listed on my résumé."

I'd stayed several hours a week with Mrs. Frady's mother for over a year until the eighty-six-year-old woman died. I'd fought off bedsores, spooned chipped ice into her toothless mouth, brushed the old woman's hair, given simple manicures, decorated her room, and tried to make her last days on earth as pleasant as possible for a person trapped in a body that deteriorated before my eyes. So many people thanked me at the funeral that I was embarrassed. Any Christian should have done the same thing.

"She's kind. Her mother and I hit it off from the start."

"I'll call Christine and get back to you."

Late that afternoon I checked my e-mail at my apartment and immediately noticed a message from an unknown sender with the subject line "My Mother in Savannah."

It was from Christine Bartlett. She wanted to talk to me as soon as possible and left both an office and a home phone number. I didn't have a cell phone and made my phone calls through my computer connection. I looked at the clock. It was almost suppertime, the telemarketer time of day. I would eat and call later.

I ate in silence. The TV in the room wasn't plugged in; however, it was impossible to escape invading noise from the people living on either side of me. I used earplugs at night, but during the day, I sometimes tuned out distractions by daydreaming. Tonight I imagined that I was eating at home, sitting between the twins with Mama at one end of the table and Daddy at the other. Emma and Ellie were talking about our laying hens, and Bobby asked Daddy if he'd talked to Mr. Waldrup about a summer job. Mama had a slightly sad look on her face that I took to mean she was missing me. I missed her too.

I washed the dishes in the tiny sink. Compared to cleanup following a meal at home, kitchen duty in my apartment couldn't be called work. After a few minutes, I returned to the computer and placed the call. Mrs. Bartlett answered on the third ring. She had the smooth accent of the coast.

"Is this a good time to talk?" I asked.

"Oh, yes, Ken and I are relaxing with a glass of wine on the veranda at our place on the marsh. Let me put you on the speakerphone so he can hear as well."

I heard a click and some background noise.

"We're both here," Mrs. Bartlett said. "Gerry tells me you'll be moving to Savannah in a few weeks to work for Braddock, Appleby, and Carpenter."

"Yes ma'am."

"You'll love Samuel Braddock. He's one of the sweetest men in Savannah. He was Daddy's lawyer. He could have retired years ago but still works like a junior associate."

A male voice spoke. "He lets Joe Carpenter run the firm. Joe is a good lawyer, but I can't say he's one of the sweetest men in Savannah."

Mrs. Bartlett spoke. "Nonsense, I'm sure you'll love working there. Gerry told me all about you, and I took the liberty of calling Betty Lou Frady. We had the best talk."

"I enjoyed caring for her mother; however, she was in a nursing —"

"And she went on and on about you. Says you're tall and carry yourself like a New

York model. So many young women these days slouch around and don't stand up straight enough to carry off a decent debut. Do you have a boyfriend?"

"No ma'am."

"I've got several young men I want to introduce you to while you're here this summer. My boys are grown and married, and we have two grandchildren, although I try not to look too much like an old granny. Stay out of the sun. I used to think a tan was a sign of good health. Now, I'm fighting the wrinkles."

"How is your mother's health?" I asked, trying to redirect the conversation.

"She was doing great until the first of the year. Living alone and walking to her volunteer job every day. Then they diagnosed her with, what is it, Ken? It's not Alzheimer's."

"Multi-infarct dementia."

"It sounds horrible, but she just has moments when things don't click right. My brother and I think it would be nice if someone stayed with her at night. The cleaning lady is at the house three or four times a week, and her gardener checks on her every time he comes by to water the flowers and take care of the bushes, but that doesn't cover the evening hours. She keeps one of those things around her neck at night in case she falls and can't get to the phone, but her problems are mental, not physical."

"Does she remember to check in with the monitoring service in the morning?"

"Half the time, I don't think she calls them. She's so fixated on getting that first cup of coffee that nothing and no one can stand in her way. We both drink it black and strong and love Jamaican blue. That's probably one reason her heart is acting up."

"What's wrong with her heart?"

"It races away every so often, but she's never had a heart attack. The biggest problem is her high blood pressure. That's the cause of the multiproblem thing."

"What medications is she taking?"

"Goodness, I don't know what they're all for. Of course, she takes something for high blood pressure, a pill to regulate her heart rate, and a blood thinner, but the doctors are always switching things around so much that I can't keep up with them. All that information is written on the door of the medicine cabinet in the kitchen. Gracie, the woman who cleans the house, fills up Mother's pillbox on Monday."

"How often do you see her?"

"I pick her up for lunch every week or so. For years she was so wrapped up in her own social circle that she didn't have time for mine. Recently, her friends have been dying off left and right. I've taken her to two funerals in the last six weeks. It's sad when the fabric of life begins to unravel. I never want to get to the place where I embarrass myself in public. Better to go with dignity."

"Christine," Mr. Bartlett interrupted. "Don't you think it would be a good idea to invite Ms. Taylor to meet your mother?"

"Absolutely," Mrs. Bartlett responded. "I've enjoyed this chat on the phone, but there's nothing like meeting in person. I realize you'll only be here for a short time this summer, but we still need to convince Mother that it's a good idea to have a live-in caregiver."

"You haven't asked her?"

"Not yet. I'm still planning my strategy. The last time she had a houseguest was when Nicholas Harrington moved in and tried to convince her to marry him. My brother had to fly in from Majorca to settle that problem and send him on his way. I can tell her she's doing you a favor by letting you spend the summer. That will keep her from suspecting the truth."

"I think it would be better —"

"Could you come this weekend?" Mrs. Bartlett continued. "Friday evening would be perfect. Ken and I will put you up at a bed-and-breakfast around the corner from Mother's house. We'll have a light snack at her place on Saturday morning, and after we all meet, you and I will slip away for a private chat in the kitchen. If everything is a go, you can ask Mother to let you spend the summer with her."

"I wouldn't feel comfortable inviting myself —"

"Don't worry. I'll set everything up. I know how to get her to do what I want." Mrs. Bartlett laughed. "She taught me how to get my way, so I learned from the mistress of manipulation. She doesn't even recognize her own tricks when I use them on her. Did Gerry give you the address for the house?"

"No ma'am. And I don't feel comfortable deceiving your mother about the reason for my interest in staying in her home."

"How sweet," Mrs. Bartlett responded. "Mrs. Frady told me you were a deeply religious girl. I think that's admirable. Mother has a lot of antiques and valuable artworks. Everything's insured, of course, but irreplaceable. Before we found Gracie there was a bit of petty thievery going on at the house."

"My concern —"

"And we're not deceiving Mother," Mrs. Bartlett continued. "Just creating a scenario that will work for her good. A circuitous route is often the best way to get from A to Z, and half an explanation cuts down on needless anxiety. Haven't you found that to be true when working with the elderly?"

"Yes. I guess so," I said, remembering my conversation with my parents.

"Don't worry. We'll do everything with integrity."

"Okay, but I'll need to arrange transportation."

"You're not flying, are you?"

"No ma'am. I don't have a car. I can try to find a ride to Savannah, but we're just back from spring break, and most students at the law school will be staying on campus this weekend."

I heard muffled voices; then Mr. Bartlett spoke. "Don't worry about it. I'll arrange for a rental car. What time are you finished with classes on Friday?"

"Two o'clock."

"And your address?"

I gave him the information.

"I'll have a car delivered to your place at three on Friday and e-mail you the information about the bed-and-breakfast," he said.

"And I'll be by to pick you up Saturday morning so we can go to Mother's house together," Mrs. Bartlett chimed in. "What's your cell phone number?"

"I don't have a cell phone."

"How in the world do you survive without a cell phone?" Mrs. Bartlett didn't try to conceal her shock.

"I'm sure Mrs. Frady told you I was punctual and reliable in my care for her mother. We worked out a satisfactory arrangement for communication."

"But no cell phone? Why would a young —"

"I look forward to meeting you," Mr. Bartlett cut in. "We'll get in touch with you at the bed-and-breakfast."

Mr. Bartlett ended the call.

I spent a few moments imagining the ongoing conversation between the couple before Mrs. Bartlett calmed down and took another sip of wine. If she thought the absence of a cell phone was an indicator of a radical lifestyle, she was in for a few more lessons once she got to know me better.

6

Not many people in Savannah remembered Moses' face or knew his name. Those who did were dying without anyone to take their places. Only a handful of longtime residents remembered the wiry young black man who always wore a gold Georgia Tech cap. That cap had been Moses' trademark when he was younger and earned him the nickname Buzz. Moses kept the pieces of that hat in a plastic bag at his shack on the river. It reminded him of happier days.

Unlike several of his cousins who spent hours and hours on the pedestrian walkways near the river, Moses never tried to pick up extra money playing sloppy jazz on a pawn-shop saxophone or drumming the bottom of five-gallon plastic buckets. Around other people, he contented himself with the once-a-week rattle of a plastic bag full of empty aluminum cans.

Not that he wasn't musical.

Moses sang in church when his great-auntie took him as a boy. She had a fine voice, and Moses didn't hesitate to sing as loud as his ten-year-old vocal cords would let him. He could memorize most songs after hearing them once or twice. His rambunctious singing and outgoing personality attracted the attention of one of the deacons, who recruited him to work for Tommy Lee Barnes. Brother Kelso bragged that he gave ten percent of the money he earned from his take as a ward captain in the bolita racket to the church. It was enough money to earn him a seat of honor on the deacon board until a new pastor came to the church and kicked him out. Moses never tried to be a hypocrite; it took too much energy. His great-auntie died, and the church folks looked the other way when they saw Moses coming.

But a gift given is forever.

Sitting at the edge of a flickering fire on a spring evening, Moses could feel the blues rise up within him like the tidal surge in the nearby river. The first sounds came through his cracked lips with a soulful sigh and hum. Another sigh and longer hum would follow. And then emerged words in rhythm that gave substance to sorrow and turned it into a thing of bittersweet beauty. Moses used

101

the blues to keep despair at bay. And they helped vanquish the sick feeling that came whenever he remembered the blood that once stained his hands.

However, melancholy songs in the night weren't an antidote for fear. Most people would have been afraid to live alone on a marshy, deserted stretch of a black-water river. Moses wasn't afraid of solitude. Fear kept Moses alone. It was a fickle companion that wore two faces. The panic he felt when the faces rose to the surface of the water caused adrenaline to course through his veins. Afterward he experienced the exhilaration of survival. And the satisfaction that once again, he'd cheated death.

But on those nights he didn't sing.

The following afternoon, I called Gerry Patrick to thank her for putting me in touch with Mrs. Bartlett and then told her about my upcoming visit.

"Did Christine talk your ear off?"

"Both of them. She had very nice things to say about Mr. Braddock."

"He's a true Southern gentleman. Will you arrive in time on Friday to visit the office?"

"I'm not sure. What time do you close?"

"Five thirty."

"No, it will be later than that when I get

into town. Is the office open on Saturdays?"

"Most of the associates show up, but the doors are locked. I'd rather you come when I can give you a proper tour and introduction to the attorneys and staff."

"That makes sense." I paused before continuing. "If staying with Mrs. Fairmont doesn't work out, I'd like to look for another place to live while I'm in town."

"Of course. I'll send you contact information for Lynn Bynum, the location agent the firm uses. She knows what's available in any price range. Don't be bashful about asking for help. We send Lynn plenty of paying business."

Ms. Patrick seemed to have resolved her reservations about my receiving the job offer without her input. Perhaps she was a churchgoer.

"Julie Feldman mentioned Ms. Bynum in her e-mail." I said.

"Yes. We're in synagogue and Hadassah together."

My eyes opened wide.

"That's nice," I managed.

"Let me know if I can help in any way."

That evening I called home and unleashed a torrent of information upon Mama about all that had happened with Mr. and Mrs.

103

Bartlett.

"What do you think?" I asked when I finished and took a deep breath.

"You're bumping up against the world in a new way," Mama said calmly. "The daughter sounds like a person who's looking for someone to do for her mother what she ought to be doing herself."

"Yes ma'am."

Mama rarely missed a chance to point out an example of American self-centeredness. When we studied other cultures in homeschool, I was amazed by the differences in attitudes toward relatives that existed between civilized countries and those considered more backward. Mama said *sacrifice* was in the Bible and the dictionary but not in most people's hearts.

"A free place to stay would be a blessing," she continued, "but you've got to ask the Lord if he is sending you to help this woman. His will is all that matters. If he's in it, you'll find the grace to withstand the pressure."

"Yes ma'am."

"Daddy and I will pray about it and let you know if the Lord shows us anything."

"Thanks. Any other news from home?"

"Not much. Ellie was the last one to find her note from you. She thought you might have forgotten about her, which made it that much sweeter when she found it under the stuff piled on her nightstand."

"Maybe that will convince her to clean more often."

We talked about the routine things of life for several more minutes before saying good night. Talking to Mama always gave me strength. My mind had been racing too much about the uncertainties in Savannah. With the sound of her voice in my thoughts and earplugs lodged firmly in my ears, I slept peacefully through the night.

I hurried home from class on Friday and opened the curtain all the way so I had a clear view of the parking lot. I packed my suitcase and put everything nice I owned into a garment bag. I didn't want to make the final decision about what to wear until I was in Savannah. Each time a car entered the parking lot, I went to the window to see if I recognized it. Most of my neighbors were either students without much money or young people working marginal jobs. A white van with a magnetic car rental company sign on its side pulled into the parking lot. It was an unusual choice, but I was used to driving a van. I grabbed my wallet and went outside.

"I'm Tami Taylor."

"We're here with your car," the rental company employee said.

A silver convertible with the top down came around the corner of the building and pulled into a spot beside the van.

"Is that the car?" I asked, my mouth dropping open.

"Yeah. I need to see your driver's license, and we have some paperwork for you to sign."

The car had a white leather interior. I had trouble focusing on the forms. I skimmed the fine print prepared by a lawyer in a faraway office and signed at the bottom.

"What kind of car is it?" I asked.

"A new Jaguar. We got it in this week. You're the first person to lease it."

I glanced over my shoulder and saw that one of my neighbors was standing in his doorway watching.

"It's a rental car," I said.

"Sweet," he responded with a nod of his head. "Let me know if you need company. It'll drive better with someone in each seat."

I finished signing the paperwork. The man driving the van handed me a card.

"Call this number when you want us to pick up the car on Monday. It's got a tank of gas, but there's no need to return it full.

That's included in the rental."

"Sweet," the neighbor in the doorway echoed. "You can take the whole complex out for a joyride."

I smiled awkwardly. The men from the rental company got in the van and left.

"My name is Greg Overton," my neighbor said, stepping forward. "I don't think we've met."

"I've talked with your girlfriend a few times. Where is she?"

Greg opened his arms. "Working at the pizza parlor. She doesn't get off until ten o'clock tonight. We've got plenty of time to take that beauty out for a spin. We could even go by and see her if you want to."

I brushed past him and continued toward my door. "I'm leaving town in a few minutes."

"Don't be in such a —," I heard before I shut my door.

I leaned against the door for a few seconds to compose myself. I thought about the silver car and imagined myself behind the wheel. I put my hand to my mouth and began to giggle. In a few seconds, I was doubled over with laughter. The idea that I would be driving such an expensive automobile was so outlandish that I didn't know what to do but laugh.

I wished the twins were with me. They would scream with delight at the thought of riding in a convertible. The closest thing to a convertible they'd experienced was a quick trip around the yard in the back of Kyle's pickup truck.

I finished packing my suitcase. When I came outside with my suitcase and garment bag, there was a small crowd of people standing around the car.

"Are you the lawyer who lives here?" a teenage girl asked.

"I'm a law student."

"It looks like you've already won a big case," said an older man wearing a dirty T-shirt.

I pushed the button on the key that popped open the trunk. The trunk was large enough to swallow my luggage. I got in the car and started the engine.

"Buckle your seat belt," the girl called out.

I smiled at her. "Always."

I found the switch that raised the top and pressed it.

"No!" the girl yelled. "Drive with the top down."

The top closed over my head. After the expanse of the sky as my roof, the inside of the car seemed claustrophobic. I flipped the switch that returned the top to its boot. The boy waved when he saw me. I put the car in reverse.

When I stepped on the gas, the car rocketed out of the parking space. The crowd jumped back. I slammed on the brakes and jerked to a stop. Greg Overton laughed and pointed at me. I felt my face flush. I put the car in drive and drove gingerly across the parking lot.

As I crept along, the responsibility of operating such an expensive piece of machinery hit me. Even the slightest dent or ding would stand out like a broken leg. I stopped at the exit for the parking lot and waited until there wasn't a car in sight in either direction before pulling into the street.

The route out of town took me near the law school. I stopped at a light and heard someone call my name.

"Tammy Taylor! Is that you?"

It was one of the law students on my basketball team. She was standing on the sidewalk, waiting to cross the street. I waved nonchalantly.

"Hey, Donna."

"What a beautiful ride! When did you get it?"

"It's not mine. A man in Savannah rented it for me. I'm going down there for a weekend visit."

The girl's green eyes grew even bigger. "I didn't know you had a boyfriend."

"He's not a boyfriend. He's married."

The light turned green, and I had to pull away before providing a more complete answer. In the rearview mirror I could see Donna staring after me. Our next game wasn't until Tuesday, and she would have plenty of time to broadcast erroneous information to others before I could provide the facts. I debated turning around, but when I looked again in my mirror, she was gone.

As I drove along the city streets, people on the sidewalk and other drivers turned to stare. I was used to stares for dressing differently, but this was a new kind of stare. Two college-age boys yelled at me, and a balding man in a Corvette nodded my way when I pulled up next to him at a traffic light. It was a relief to leave the city behind.

The route south from Athens led me through the heart of middle Georgia. I'd tied my hair in a ponytail that swirled in the breeze. I passed through several small communities. The most picturesque was Madison, a town spared the torch by Gen. William Tecumseh Sherman during his march to the sea after the destruction of Atlanta.

The restored antebellum homes lining the main street of town seemed grander from my seat in the convertible. And I looked at the houses in a new way. My car would fit in perfectly parked in front of one of the fine old homes.

I reached the outskirts of Milledgeville, the early capital of Georgia, and pulled into a convenience store to buy a bottle of drinking water. When I got out of the car, I could see my reflection in the plate-glass window of the store. With my collared, short-sleeved blouse, knee-length skirt, and plain sandals, I looked totally out of place beside the stylish sports car. I took my hair out of the ponytail and shook it. Through the strands in front of my face, I saw a man walk out of the store and glare at me with a hostile look that scared me. I sat back down in the car, flipped the switch to raise the top, and locked the vehicle before entering the store.

When I came outside, the man was putting gas in a blue van that looked a lot like the one parked in our front yard in Powell Station. In the front passenger seat I saw a middle-aged woman with her hair in a bun and behind her several children hanging out the windows. It could have been my own family a few years earlier. The man saw me and clearly broadcast a message of judgment against a frivolous, sinful girl who shouldn't be driving a fancy convertible and shaking out her hair in front of a convenience store. Daddy would never have looked at someone the same way, but there were men in our church who would.

In a more subdued mood, I drove away from the store and merged onto the interstate. The next fifteen miles I spent my time praying that the lure of wealth and the things it offered wouldn't ensnare me in sinful pride and compromise.

The interstate deposited me directly into the downtown area of Savannah. I stopped and lowered the top of the car. No one paid attention to me as I drove slowly into the historic district. I'd read about Savannah's twenty-one squares and the restored homes and buildings surrounding them. But as I drove along, the information and images were jumbled in my memory. There would be plenty of time later for leisurely exploring on foot.

My destination was a massive postbellum residence near the home of Juliette Gordon Low, the founder of the Girl Scouts. The bed-and-breakfast was built by a confederate blockade-runner who served as inspiration for Rhett Butler in *Gone with the Wind*. I slowed to a stop in front of the opulent three-story residence with iron railings in front of ornate windows. Carrying my own luggage, I entered the house where I was greeted by a stylishly dressed hostess.

"I'm Tami Taylor," I began. "I have a reservation."

"I'll have someone show you to your room. Mr. Bartlett made all the necessary arrangements" — the woman leaned forward — "including gratuities for the staff."

A porter who looked about the same age as my brother Kyle took my suitcase and garment bag. I followed him to the third floor where he opened the door to a very feminine room with high ceilings and a collection of antiques that surrounded a four-poster bed.

"The Mary Telfair room," he announced as he placed my suitcase on a stand. "It's decorated in Eastlake and named for the daughter of an early governor and plantation owner. The house is mostly vacant tonight, and I'll be glad to show you rooms appointed in Renaissance/Revival and French Empire, the architecture of the house itself. We also have a great wine selection."

Mama had taught me about art and classical music, and I could instantly recognize a Rembrandt and identify Beethoven within a few notes, but my knowledge about antiques and wine could be summarized on a 3 × 5 index card. Jesus made simple furniture and drank wine, but I'd never been around antiques, and no wine had ever touched my lips.

"You know a lot about antiques?" I asked.

He grinned. "I'm a senior at the Savannah School of Art and Design."

I reached for my purse. The young man held up his hand.

"No, it's taken care of. I'll be downstairs until eleven o'clock tonight if I can give you a tour or help in any way. What time would you like turndown service?"

"What?"

"Someone from housekeeping will prepare your bed."

"I'm a country girl from the mountains," I answered with a smile. "I've never been in a place like this in my life."

The boy leaned forward. He had nice eyes. "Most people who pretend to be experts about antiques and fine wine make fools of themselves. I've studied a lot to learn a little."

"Thanks. I guess I'd like turndown service about ten o'clock."

I peeked into the bathroom. It had a claw-foot tub. The twins would have so much fun in a room like this. I eyed the queen-size bed. The three of us could spend the night together, so long as I slept in the middle to prevent pushing and arguing.

After all the excitement of the day, I felt tired. I pulled back the covers, lay down, and stared at the ceiling. Every detail of the room was a work of craftsmanship.

I dozed off and woke with a start. It was almost 9:00 p.m. I hurriedly made the bed so it would be ready for turndown service.

The bathroom was stocked with four kinds of bubble bath and salts. None of them had been opened. I read the labels, debating whether to indulge. I turned on the water in the tub. The sight of water splashing against the bottom of the tub ended any debate. I'd taken bubble baths as a child, but the sensation of bath salts would be something new.

I lay exulting in the warm water until time to put on my pajamas in anticipation of the turndown service. For extra modesty, I slipped on the complimentary robe I found in the armoire and sat in a chair beside the bed. I didn't want to wrinkle the bedspread. Precisely at 10:00 p.m. there was a knock at my door. When I opened it, the young porter and a woman from housekeeping were there.

"Would you like a nightcap?" the porter asked as the woman brushed past me and walked to the bed.

I touched the top of my head. The robe was a nice extra, but I'd not slept with a cap on my head since I was a little girl on cold nights in the middle of winter. Some of the women in our church would wear a scarf as a head covering when they exhorted, but it wasn't mandatory. I could tell the porter was still trying not to laugh.

"I meant a hot drink, glass of milk, something like that," he managed.

"Oh, no thanks."

My face went red, and I turned away. The woman had finished folding down the comforter on the bed and placed a chocolate in a gold wrapper on one of the pillows. I didn't look back at the porter as the woman passed me on her way out of the room.

"Thank you," I mumbled.

The door closed, and I quickly locked it against a further faux pas. At least I knew the French words for a "social blunder."

7

I woke up early and snuggled deeper into the covers for a few seconds before slipping out of bed to open the drapes. From the window, I could see the fountain in the middle of Lafayette Square and a white church with multiple spires pointing toward the morning sky. I wanted to jog around the borders of the historic district without worrying about traffic, and very early on Saturday morning seemed the perfect time. After dressing, I noticed an envelope slid underneath the door of my room.

My heart jumped. It was probably from the nice young porter telling me not to be embarrassed and offering to take me on a tour of the city. Turning down his invitation would only increase the awkwardness I felt. I bent over and picked up the envelope. It had the name of the inn on the outside. I opened the envelope and took out a sheet of paper.

I'd misjudged the porter. Mrs. Bartlett had left a phone message at the front desk asking me to meet her in the parlor at 10:00 a.m. I put the note on the nightstand beside the bed and went downstairs. The staff was setting up the dining room for breakfast. There was no sign of the porter.

It was a slightly muggy morning. After stretching, I ran south along Broughton Street to Forsyth Park, the largest patch of green in the downtown area. I explored the park and ran around a fountain with a statue of a Confederate soldier facing north on top. I left the park and ran south all the way to the Savannah River. Large container vessels slowly moved upriver to the port area. I ran along River Street, past Factor's Row and the Cotton Exchange. The streets were deserted. I felt the gates of the city had been opened just for me. As I jogged, I prayed that everywhere I set my feet would be a court of praise.

I crossed West Bay Street and reentered the historic district. After several wrong turns I finally stumbled upon Lafayette Square. There wasn't a place for a long, wide-open sprint, but I ran twice around the square at top speed before coasting to a stop.

When I returned to the B and B, preparations for breakfast were complete, a lavish spread of food that included everything from grits to quiche.

After taking a shower, I selected a bright dress that shared colors with the fruit platter downstairs. The dress reached to the midcalf of my leg. While I brushed my hair, I practiced standing up straight. Mrs. Bartlett was right about one thing. Good posture was always in style.

Downstairs, I sampled most of the items on the breakfast buffet. At home I ate a big breakfast because there was work to do that would burn up plenty of calories. Breakfast at the buffet was decadent — food for the sake of food. I bowed my head for a blessing before starting and kept a thankful attitude all the way to the final pastry.

After I finished, I returned to my room, brushed my teeth, and applied a very faint hint of lipstick not much darker than my natural color. Sunday mornings at home were makeup-free, but Mama said God ordained beauty to females in the human family and subtle enhancements were acceptable — as long as there was no intention to allure. The only times I saw Mama wearing makeup were rare occasions when Daddy took her out to dinner. She claimed her attractiveness to him was based on inner qualities, not her outward appearance. Daddy whispered to me and the twins that he thought Mama was the most beautiful woman, inside and out, in the whole world.

I was blessed with naturally long eyelashes, and in college I'd experimented with a light touch of eye shadow. I liked the change, but I'd always quickly rubbed it off. Each time I put it on I thought it looked nice, but I'd never left the bathroom with it in place. This morning I gave it another try. Perhaps it was the fancy room or being in a new town, but this time I didn't remove it. Also, there was no chance of causing a man to sin since I would only be meeting with Mrs. Bartlett and her mother.

I sat in a comfortable chair in the corner of the narrow foyer that served as the lobby. The people coming and going seemed at ease with the sumptuous surroundings. Or perhaps they were pretending. A well-dressed woman in her fifties came in, and I nervously swallowed, but she wasn't Mrs. Bartlett. A grandfather clock chimed the hour. I thought about reading a magazine, but nothing on the coffee table looked interesting. At 10:15 a.m. a short, slightly overweight woman with reddish-blonde hair burst through the front door and scanned the room. I stood up.

"Mrs. Bartlett?"

"Yes, yes," she said. "You must be Tami."

I tried not to stare at Mrs. Bartlett's obviously dyed hair as she approached. It was accentuated with highlights that would require a lot of maintenance. She was wearing a blue silk blouse, black slacks, and sandals that revealed a pedicure as flawless as her hair color. I held out my hand, but Mrs. Bartlett ignored it and gave me a hug that included a European greeting. She had to rise up on her toes to deliver the peck on both my cheeks.

"You certainly are statuesque," Mrs. Bartlett continued.

"Yes ma'am. I played basketball in high school."

"An athlete? You'd never know it now, but I had a five handicap in golf until about ten years ago. I beat Ken all the time, although I never mention it in public. My putter can still work magic, but I have no distance off the tee."

"Please tell Mr. Bartlett I appreciate the car and thanks for providing such a beautiful place to stay," I said.

"You can tell him later. He's going to meet us this afternoon. Come on, the valet is holding my car at the curb."

Mrs. Bartlett took off.

121

"Do you ride in a cart or carry your bag when you play golf?" I asked as we rapidly descended the front steps.

"Carry my bag? That would be a plebeian thing to do. I get my exercise walking on the beach early in the morning."

"I ran down to the river and through the historic district this morning," I said. "I enjoyed looking at the houses."

"A runner? I thought you were old-fashioned. There are plenty of registered houses. And every one has a story with many chapters."

Mrs. Bartlett was driving a white Mercedes. She handed a twenty-dollar bill to the valet who opened the door for each of us.

"Mother's house is just a few blocks away on West Hull near Chippewa Square."

"Did you grow up there?"

"No, no. My father would never live in this part of town. She bought the house after he died about fifteen years ago. I grew up at Beaulieu on the Vernon River."

Mrs. Bartlett drove like she walked. Fast. Fortunately, the short streets didn't provide enough space between stop signs to give her the chance to do more than stomp the gas pedal then slam on the brakes. I couldn't imagine what it would be like to ride with her on the interstate. After several quick

122

turns she came to a stop alongside the curb.

"Here we are. Built in 1860, just in time for the original owner to ride off to the war and get killed at Cold Harbor."

It was a square two-story brick structure with tall narrow windows on the first level and broad front steps. On the side of the house was an attached screened porch. Two large live oaks were planted between the house and the sidewalk. An iron railing extended from the steps down the street on either side, then turned toward the rear of the house.

"It's beautiful," I said.

"She wanted it and got it," Mrs. Bartlett responded crisply. "I thought it was a mistake at the time, but it's worth four times what she paid for it. Mother knows how to manage her money. Her father made a mint in real estate, and it rubbed off on her."

We walked up ten steps to the front door. I could see there was a basement with windows partly below street level. Mrs. Bartlett rang the door chime.

"I have a key, but she hates it when I walk in unannounced. It will make her happy to pretend we're here for a formal visit."

After a long wait, a white-haired woman shorter than Mrs. Bartlett but with a similar figure opened the door. She had bright blue eyes that narrowed slightly when she looked at me and made me feel like she was sizing me up in a split second. Mrs. Fairmont was wearing a carefully tailored yellow dress and white shoes with low heels. A string of pearls encircled her neck. Mrs. Bartlett kissed both her mother's cheeks.

"This is Miss Tami Taylor," Mrs. Bartlett said, "the young woman I told you about who is going to work for Samuel Braddock's firm this summer." She turned to me. "Samuel and Eloise Braddock have been here for cocktails many times before going to the opera."

Mrs. Fairmont took my hand in hers. She was wearing a large diamond ring accented with emeralds on her right hand.

"Good morning, child," she said in a slightly raspy voice steeped in a coastal accent.

"Pleased to meet you," I answered.

Mrs. Bartlett patted her mother on the shoulder and entered the house. Mrs. Fairmont still held on to my hand.

"The house has double parlors," Mrs. Bartlett called back from the interior. "It's not an uncommon design. Mother, was Gracie here yesterday? Everything looks so nice. I like the way she arranged these flowers. Where did she get them?"

Mrs. Fairmont stayed by the door, holding my hand. Her skin was wrinkled with age, and her knuckles revealed a touch of arthritis. She put her other hand on top of mine.

"You have nice hands," she said.

"Thank you."

"Enjoy them while you can."

"Yes ma'am."

"Don't block the door, Mother," Mrs. Bartlett called out. "Where do you want us to sit?"

Mrs. Fairmont looked up at me. "Do you prefer green or blue?"

"Blue is my favorite."

The house had two parlors separated by a foyer that faced the main stairway to the second floor. On the right was a pale green room; to the left one painted an ephemeral blue.

"That is the green room," Mrs. Fairmont said, gesturing with her bejeweled hand. "And this is the blue room."

Both rooms contained beautiful furniture, original paintings, and mirrors in gilt frames. I wondered how grandchildren and great-grandchildren fared in the house. A wrestling match between Kyle and Bobby could have caused thousands of dollars of damage. Mrs. Fairmont went into the blue room and sat in a side chair. Mrs. Bartlett motioned for me to join her on a cream sofa.

"You have a beautiful home," I said. "Mrs. Bartlett told me a little of its history."

"The couple who sold it to me did most of the restoration," Mrs. Fairmont said. "Before that, it was a rooming house. Can you believe it? Workmen and laborers renting rooms by the week." She leaned forward. "If I could understand the creaks in the night, I'm sure there are many stories to tell. Did you know our voices will echo in the universe until the end of time?"

"That's a silly notion," Mrs. Bartlett cut in. "A sound doesn't really exist if it can't be heard, like a tree falling in the forest when no one is around."

"What do you think?" Mrs. Fairmont turned her blue eyes toward me.

"Well, the Bible says God keeps a record of every word that's spoken and will judge us by what we've said."

Mrs. Fairmont nodded in satisfaction toward her daughter. "See, Christine, it's the same thing, only I didn't know God agreed with me."

"Let's not get into anything controversial," Mrs. Bartlett said. "I'd like to know more about Miss Taylor's background."

Controversial could be a synonym for my

background, but I knew how to exercise discretion. As I talked, I emphasized my commitment to God and family without going into detail about the rules that guided my conduct. Mama said a question was an open doorway to proclamation of the truth, but I didn't want to come on too strong. Mrs. Fairmont seemed especially interested in our life in the country and asked questions about the garden and the chickens. Mrs. Bartlett interrupted when I described my homeschool experience.

"Your mother taught you Shakespeare?"

"Yes ma'am. I memorized long passages from several plays and quite a few sonnets."

Mrs. Bartlett shook her head. "Of course, I've heard about the homeschool movement, but I thought it an inferior model. Mother and I both attended private schools."

"It can be the best and the worst," I said. "The fact that I did well in high school, college, and now law school is proof it can provide the foundation for a successful academic career."

"Do you embroider?" Mrs. Fairmont asked, her eyes getting brighter.

"Please, Mother, Miss Taylor is obviously a traditional girl, but it's not fair to expect her to embroider."

"No ma'am. I can cross-stitch with a pattern, but I've never tried to create my own designs. I'd love to see some of your embroidery."

"It's in the bedrooms and upstairs along the hall," Mrs. Bartlett replied. "Mother doesn't allow anything in these rooms that isn't museum quality."

Mama proudly displayed my crude cross-stitch in the front room.

"I can't embroider anymore," Mrs. Fairmont sighed.

I saw a tear run down the older woman's cheek. I glanced at Mrs. Bartlett, who had picked up a ceramic figurine.

"Are you all right?" I asked the older woman.

Mrs. Fairmont wiped away the tear with a lace handkerchief she pulled from the side pocket of her dress.

"Please excuse me. It's not about the needlepoint. I've been crying for no apparent reason recently. It's one of the symptoms of a condition I have called multi-infarct dementia."

I couldn't hide my surprise.

"You're still smarter than I am," Mrs. Bartlett added with a nervous laugh. "And I'm not sure it's a good idea to study too much about medical things. That's why we have doctors. Talking about health problems can make anyone depressed. Did you tell me where Gracie bought the flowers?"

Mrs. Fairmont looked directly at me and spoke. "What do you think? Should I educate myself during lucid moments or try to ignore the fact that the blood vessels in my brain are slowing dying?"

"Please, Mother," Mrs. Bartlett spoke with agitation. "That's not a fair question to ask Miss Taylor. Do you have the coffee brewing?"

Mrs. Fairmont stared at me for a few seconds. Her face softened.

"Yes, of course," she said. "Let me serve you. I have decaf for me and regular for you and Miss Jackson."

Mrs. Fairmont used her arms to push herself from the chair. Mrs. Bartlett waited a few seconds then also rose from her seat.

"I'll help. Miss Taylor can relax here."

Standing very erect, Mrs. Fairmont slowly walked from the room. Mrs. Bartlett held back. When her mother was out of sight, she leaned over and whispered to me.

"I'm sorry she brought up her condition so abruptly. She's always been quick to offer her opinion about anything from politics to religion, but recently it's gotten worse. Did you see how quickly she forgot your name? A year ago she would never have made a social blunder like that. Most of the time, she can take care of herself. Still, I'd feel better if there was a watchful eye in the house every now and then. Any loving child would want the same thing. How do you want your coffee?"

"Uh, I'm not a coffee drinker. Does she have any tea?"

"Yes, but it might upset her if you don't drink coffee. I'll fix you a cup with cream and sugar, and you can pretend to sip it."

Mrs. Bartlett left, and I gave the parlor a closer inspection. Unlike my grandmother's home, the house didn't smell musty. The plantation shutters on the tall front windows were open and let in plenty of light. A compact but ornate glass chandelier hung overhead. The fresh flowers in a glass vase on a small round side table were an explosion of color. There was a fireplace in the parlor, and I peeked into the other room to see if it also contained one. Neither grate had been used in a long time. A well-preserved rug with ornate flower designs covered the floor.

My inspection was interrupted by the quick patter of tiny feet on the wooden floor and a sharp bark. Around the corner came a light brown Chihuahua. The dog stopped when it saw me and blinked its oversize eyes. I lowered the back of my hand to the floor as a sniff offering. The dog moved forward cautiously, stopped, and looked over its shoulder.

"Hello, little boy or girl," I said. "I bet you've never met anyone who worked in a chicken plant. I've washed my hands since then so you probably can't smell the chickens."

The dog inched forward and stretched out its head toward the back of my hand. I could hear a low growl in its throat. I kept still, aware that smaller breeds can be quicker to bite than larger ones. The Chihuahua took another step forward and sniffed my hand and fingers. The growl receded. I reached around and scratched the back of the dog's neck. The dog's eyes closed in satisfaction. I could see it was a male.

"What's your name, boy? I bet it's fancy. Sir Galahad would be nice. We have chickens at my house with unusual names."

The dog was wearing a narrow red collar decorated with rhinestones. Still scratching his neck, I repositioned the collar so I could see the dog's name tag. When I saw the engraving, I smiled.

"Flip. I have a dog named Flip, but he

lives outside and sleeps in the dirt under the front porch in the summer. Have you ever slept in the dirt? Do you know what dirt looks like?"

I picked up Flip and held him in my lap as I continued to stroke him. I was careful not to let his tiny feet touch the sofa. Mrs. Bartlett and Mrs. Fairmont returned to the parlor. Mrs. Bartlett was carrying a silver coffee service. Her mother followed with a plate of miniature pastries.

"Careful!" Mrs. Bartlett cried out.

The dog launched himself from my lap. Barking ferociously, he skidded across the floor toward Mrs. Bartlett, who stuck out her left foot to keep him away. The tray tipped to the side. I jumped up and rushed toward her as the tray moved the other way and the coffeepot slid to the edge. Flip, his teeth bared, continued to bark and dance around her feet. Mrs. Fairmont stood motionless with her mouth slightly open.

"Stop it!" Mrs. Bartlett said. "Get away!"

Like a basketball player scrambling for a loose ball, I lunged to the floor and grabbed the wiggling animal with my right hand. But it was too late. Mrs. Bartlett lost control of the tray. The pot flew off, followed by three cups, saucers, the sugar container, and a cream pitcher. The sound of clattering metal and breaking china in the quiet house was deafening.

Mrs. Bartlett swore. The black coffee was pooling across the wooden floor toward the rug. Instinct took over. I grabbed the coffeepot, knelt on the floor, and positioned my dress between the coffee and the rug. I pressed down with my hands in an effort to block the progress of the coffee. The long length of my dress came in handy.

"Someone get a washrag or paper towels," I said.

Mrs. Bartlett hurried out of the room. Mrs. Fairmont stared at me and seemed stuck in the moment. I could feel the coffee against my free hand. In spite of my efforts, it was continuing to creep toward the rug. There was nothing else to do. I sat down on the floor between the coffee and the rug. I could feel the hot coffee on my thigh, but it wasn't warm enough to burn me. I looked up at Mrs. Fairmont. Flip calmed down, and I held him in my lap. The old woman put the pastry tray on a chair.

"Get up, child. It's not worth ruining your dress to clean up a spill."

"I couldn't let it ruin the rug. I can wash the dress, but I don't know how you would clean a rug like that."

Mrs. Bartlett returned from the kitchen

with washcloths. Flip started barking again. Mrs. Bartlett handed the washcloths to me and quickly backed away. I slipped to my knees and tossed the cloths on the rest of the coffee. The rug was saved.

"I thought you were going to keep that dog in his room," Mrs. Bartlett said, turning toward her mother. "I called and reminded you this morning."

"He must have been in my bedroom," Mrs. Fairmont said apologetically. She looked down at me. "I'm so sorry about your dress."

Mrs. Bartlett turned to me as if just realizing what I'd done. "How courageous of you," she said. "To sacrifice your outfit."

"I'm not sure how courageous it was, Mrs. Bartlett. It was coffee, not a hand grenade."

I stood and moved one of the washcloths across the floor with my foot.

"It's that dog's fault," Mrs. Bartlett said, refocusing on Flip. "This isn't a house for a dog, no matter what you think. Especially a vicious one!"

Mrs. Fairmont, a dazed look in her eyes, stared at Mrs. Bartlett without saying a word. I picked up Flip and could feel a growl in his throat. I rubbed his back.

"Take him away!" Mrs. Bartlett said. "And lock him up in that dog palace you created for him."

Mrs. Fairmont seemed to reconnect with her surroundings.

"If Miss Taylor will carry him, we'll put him in his room."

"Yes ma'am."

I followed Mrs. Fairmont through the foyer.

"I'll call Gracie and have her come right over and clean up this mess," Mrs. Bartlett called after us. "She doesn't have a regular house to clean on Saturday, does she?"

"I can take care of it," I said over my shoulder. "Find the broom and a dustpan."

I patted Flip on the head and whispered in his ear. "I understand. You're just protecting your territory like your wolf ancestors."

8

"I have a place for Flip in the basement," Mrs. Fairmont said.

We walked down a short hallway past a paneled room that looked like a den or study. Bookshelves lined the walls on either side of a large television. Mrs. Fairmont turned and faced me.

"I keep Flip with me all the time," she said in a soft voice. "He even sleeps on my bed, although Christine doesn't know it. We'll take him downstairs, but it would be cruel to leave him there all the time. Does your family have a dog? Living on a farm like that, I'd expect you to have a dog."

"Yes ma'am. We have two dogs; one is named Flip."

"Really! What breed?"

"Mixed. Our Flip probably weighs about fifty pounds."

"My baby weighs six pounds, four ounces."

We went down to the basement. Light streamed in from the windows I'd seen from the front of the house. Mrs. Fairmont's home was three stories in the rear and opened onto a courtyard/garden. Windows lined the wall and let in light and the view. A wall ran down the center of the room. To the left was an open space used for storage. Mrs. Fairmont opened a door to the right, and we entered a suite with a kitchenette. A dog bed surrounded by chew toys lay in the middle of the floor. There wasn't any other furniture.

"Was this was one of the rooms for rent?"

"Yes. It's really a little apartment. No one has lived here since I bought the house. It's what they call a garden apartment."

"May I take a look?"

"Sure."

Still carrying Flip, I stepped across the living area into a bedroom with French double doors that opened onto a brick patio with a wrought-iron table. There was an old brass bed that looked like it hadn't been used in years.

"It has a nice view of the garden, but it sure doesn't look like a palace," I said without thinking.

"Christine is prone to exaggeration, as I'm sure you've noticed if you've been around her more than five minutes." Mrs. Fairmont sniffed. "She claims this house is worth three times what I paid for it."

I recalled Mrs. Bartlett's statement as "four times" but kept my mouth shut.

Mrs. Fairmont took Flip from my arms. The little dog licked her chin.

"Nice kisses," she said. "Now show us how you got your name."

She put the dog on the floor and made a circle with her right index finger. The Chihuahua stepped forward and did a backward somersault. It happened so fast that I didn't get a good look.

"Will he do it again?" I asked.

Mrs. Fairmont swirled her finger and Flip obliged. She leaned over and patted him on the head.

"I've never seen a dog do that," I said.

"He's a smart boy."

"What else can he do?"

"Love me," Mrs. Fairmont said, looking at me with her blue eyes. "When no one else does."

She gave Flip a treat and closed the door to the room. I listened for a moment but didn't hear any scratching or whining. We returned upstairs. The coffee on my dress now felt clammy against my legs. Mrs. Bartlett was in the hallway near the kitchen. She had a cordless phone in her hand.

"I can't get Gracie," she said, clicking off the phone.

"I said that I'd be glad to finish cleaning up," I said, trying not to sound disrespectful. "All I'll need are paper towels, a broom, and a dustpan."

"Gracie moved all the cleaning supplies to the closet near the porch," Mrs. Fairmont said.

I followed Mrs. Bartlett through a small formal dining room. Before reaching the porch, we came to a space designed as a coat closet. I grabbed what I needed, returned to the parlor, and began cleaning up the mess. Mrs. Fairmont sat down and rested her head against the back of the chair.

"All this commotion has taken away all my energy," she said. "I need to lie down for a few minutes."

"Not yet. We're not finished with our visit," Mrs. Bartlett replied. She pointed across the room. "Tami, I see a splatter of coffee all the way over there."

I went to the kitchen, moistened some of the paper towels, and while the two women watched, cleaned the floor, pushing the bits of glass into a single pile.

"You missed some glass beneath Mother's chair," Mrs. Bartlett said.

I turned on my knees so that my rear end was facing Mrs. Bartlett to hide the laughter threatening to explode. I didn't mind cleaning up the mess, but Mrs. Bartlett's bossiness was a comedy of the absurd.

"I need to moisten some more towels," I said as I stood and left the room.

I reached the kitchen, a compact room at the rear of the house, and let myself giggle for a few seconds.

From the kitchen sink I could see more of the small formal garden with its carefully manicured shrubbery and an array of spring flowers. A brick walkway wound through the garden that featured a fountain in the middle — a great place to read the Bible and pray. I turned off the water along with my daydream. I had no idea whether I should live in the house or not.

At the entrance to the parlor, I heard Mrs. Fairmont say, "What on earth gave her that idea? To presume after one visit that I would want her to live —"

"Oh, Tami," Mrs. Bartlett interrupted. "Thanks so much for helping us clean up this mess. You're a dear to do it and come to the aid of two helpless old women."

"You're welcome."

I resumed my work without any desire to laugh. I didn't mind being a servant, but

Mrs. Bartlett's deception and supercilious statements about helplessness after she'd bragged about her golf game and long walks on the beach made me mad. I used the broom and dustpan to scoop up the broken pieces. Mrs. Fairmont didn't speak a word. A few more wipes of wet paper towel across the floor, and no sign of the morning's disaster remained. I looked up and saw Mrs. Bartlett mouthing words to her mother. I wanted to stuff a washcloth into Mrs. Bartlett's mouth.

"What should I do with the dirty cloths?" I asked icily.

"There's a clothes drop at the end of the hall," Mrs. Bartlett said. "Follow me."

As soon as we left the room, Mrs. Bartlett turned to me. "Give me a few minutes alone with Mother. She's ecstatic about the idea of you staying with her, but we need to work out the details in private."

"That's not what . . . ," I began, but Mrs. Bartlett was gone.

I found the dirty-clothes drop. Mrs. Bartlett's subterfuge was an out-and-out lie, and I had to set the record straight. If honesty destroyed the chance to stay rent-free in a beautiful house, then there had to be a low-rent apartment on a bus line somewhere in Savannah. I returned to the parlor. The two women were sitting in silence. I could feel the tension. I moved to the edge of a cream sofa and started to sit down.

"Stop it!" Mrs. Bartlett cried out. "Don't sit down."

I jumped to my feet and looked around.

"Your dress is drenched in coffee," Mrs. Bartlett said. "It might bleed onto the sofa."

"Get a towel for her to sit on," Mrs. Fairmont said.

Mrs. Bartlett looked at her mother. "But I thought —"

"Get a towel from the upstairs linen closet," her mother insisted.

Mrs. Bartlett turned to me. "We won't be staying long. I'm sure you'd like to change out of that dress and into something clean."

Mrs. Bartlett left the room. As soon as her footsteps could be heard going up the stairs, I spoke rapidly.

"Mrs. Fairmont, I didn't come here to invite myself to live in your house. That's not the way I was raised. The office manager at the law firm gave my name to your daughter because I've helped take care of people with health problems in the past. I talked on the phone with Mrs. Bartlett, and she was kind enough to arrange my trip to Savannah. She even rented a car and put me up at the bed-and-breakfast on Abercorn Street last night. I completely understand if you don't want a houseguest for the ___"

"Ken arranged for the car and lodging," Mrs. Fairmont interrupted. "If you ask me, he's a saint for putting up with Christine. Fortunately, the boys take after their father."

"Yes ma'am. But I want to be completely honest with you. This meeting was a setup."

Mrs. Fairmont eyed me as she had at the door upon my arrival.

"Do you like Flip?" she asked.

"Yes ma'am."

"More important," she said with emphasis, "he likes you. I've never seen him take to a stranger like he has to you."

"I'm used to being around animals. They know a lot more than we give them credit for."

"Yes, they do. How long will you be in Savannah this summer?"

I gave her the dates of my employment with the law firm.

"Would you be willing to stay in the downstairs apartment?"

"Yes ma'am," I said, startled.

Mrs. Fairmont leaned forward. "If you stay downstairs, it means Flip will have to sleep with me."

"Yes ma'am," I replied, smiling. "It would

143

be a sacrifice on your part, but you would have no other reasonable option."

"And you're not wanting to be paid anything?"

"No ma'am. Although I'll be willing to help around the house."

"You've proven that this morning when you didn't have to."

Mrs. Bartlett returned with a peach-colored bath towel in her hand. "Will this one do? It was underneath the nice ones."

Mrs. Fairmont nodded. "Yes, and Miss Taylor and I have agreed that she will spend the summer with me."

Mrs. Bartlett's mouth dropped open. "But you were adamant —"

"Oh, that was the multi-infarct dementia speaking," Mrs. Fairmont replied lightly. "I'm in my right mind now. Miss Taylor, didn't you say your first name was Tami?"

"Yes ma'am."

"I can see how it will be positive for Tami and me if she spends evenings and nights here. I suggested the downstairs apartment, and she agreed."

"What about the dog?" Mrs. Bartlett asked.

"I'll find a comfortable place for him." Mrs. Fairmont winked at me.

I spread the towel on the sofa and sat down.

"Tell me more about your family, especially your twin sisters," Mrs. Fairmont said. "I went to school with twins, and we've been friends ever since."

Forty-five minutes later Mrs. Bartlett patted me on the arm as we left.

"Well, you're going to be a successful lawyer if you can manipulate people like you did my mother."

"I didn't manipulate her. I told her the truth."

"I'm sure. And nothing but the truth." Mrs. Bartlett sniffed. "Somehow, you got Mother to do what we wanted and made her think it was her idea. That's hard to do."

I didn't try to argue. We made a jerky trip back to the bed-and-breakfast. Mrs. Bartlett stopped the car in front of the inn and called her husband.

"Ken can't meet us," Mrs. Bartlett said after a brief conversation. "He's had something come up. But Mother already called him and told him that you were going to be her guest for the summer. Can you imagine her being that excited about it?"

"I'm looking forward to staying with her too."

"I'll be running on my way," Mrs. Bartlett said. "I wouldn't want to bore you with my activities of the day."

"From now on should I contact you or your mother?"

"Try Mother first; here's her number." Mrs. Bartlett took a card from her purse and wrote it down.

"Mother's first name is Margaret, but her close friends call her Maggie."

"I'm sure I'll be more comfortable with Mrs. Fairmont."

"Of course. She can be contrary at times, but after your performance this morning, I doubt you'll have any problems with her. The fact that you could handle that vicious dog of hers was very impressive."

I opened the door of the car and got out. "Please tell Mr. Bartlett how much I appreciate the arrangements you made for my trip."

With a wave of her hand, Mrs. Bartlett sped away from the curb. I went to my room, cleaned up, and changed into a long blue skirt, yellow short-sleeved blouse, and white tennis shoes. I packed my suitcase and garment bag and carried them downstairs.

"Do you know where the law offices of Braddock, Appleby, and Carpenter are located?" I asked the hostess on duty.

"It's on Montgomery Street." She drew a map. A different porter than the young man who'd helped me the previous evening carried my luggage to the car.

It took about five minutes to reach the law firm. A prominent, brick-framed white sign in front announced "Braddock, Appleby, and Carpenter — Attorneys at Law." I pulled into a parking lot covered with ornamental pavers. Several nice cars were in the lot, but none as fancy as my convertible.

The office was a two-story structure built of old brick with a slate roof and lots of windows framed by dark shutters. Two balconies were inset at either end of the second floor. The entrance was guarded by a set of small stone lions in front of large wooden double doors. Everything about the place spoke of prosperity and attention to detail. Mr. Callahan's chipped white office in Powell Station couldn't have served as a storage shed for this building. I wanted to peek inside, but I wasn't dressed for success and didn't want to give a wrong first impression.

The reality of what lay ahead hit me.

I wasn't admiring just another nice building. I was parked at the place where I would be working in a few weeks and, if God granted me favor and success, be employed for many years to come. I imagined myself walking into the office wearing the blue suit I'd worn to Mr. Callahan's office. But a blue suit wouldn't banish fear. Inside the beautiful office would be people smarter than me, more sophisticated than me, and better able to excel in the legal community than me. My mouth suddenly went dry.

I'd made a terrible mistake. I needed one more summer at the chicken plant before venturing into the world on my own.

I heard the sound of a motorcycle turning into the parking area. It was bright red with a fat rear tire. The rider crouched over the handlebars, circled in front of my car, then drove directly toward me. I reached over to start the engine, but the rider held up his hand. He was wearing a red helmet with white Mercury wings on either side. He turned off the motorcycle. I didn't want to get into a conversation with a member of a local motorcycle gang. The rider took off his helmet and approached. To my surprise, he was a nice-looking young man in his twenties with blue eyes and light brown hair bound in a very short ponytail. He was wearing blue jeans and black boots.

"I'm visiting and about to leave," I said.

"Who were you visiting?" he asked.

"No one. This is where I'm going to be working in a few weeks. I've got to go."

"Then I'll see you soon. I'm one of the lawyers."

"You're a lawyer?"

The man released the band that held his hair and ran his fingers through it.

"And a motorcycle rider," he replied. "Nice car."

"It's a rental."

"It's still a nice car." He stuck a tanned hand over the side of the car. "I'm Zach Mays, an associate with the firm."

I remembered his name on the letterhead. Zachary L. Mays. He was near the bottom of the list of attorneys. There was an asterisk beside his name and a reference indicating that he was also licensed to practice law in California.

"Tami Taylor, one of the summer clerks."

"I heard the firm was bringing in a clerk or two. What did you think of the offices?"

"I didn't go inside. I just wanted to know how to find it."

"I can give you a tour. One of my jobs as an associate is to make sure summer clerks have a positive experience with the firm."

"No, thanks. I'm sure you have a lot of work to do."

"There's always work to do. Come on."

He pointed to the other cars. "None of the named partners are here. And there isn't anything on my desk that can't wait a few minutes."

I still wanted to drive off, but he reached out and opened the car door.

"No, Mr. Mays," I said. "I'd rather not."

He laughed. "Call me Zach. Save that title for the real bosses."

The young man didn't let go of the car door. I had no options. Self-conscious about my clothes and hoping my face wasn't red, I got out of the car.

"Okay, but I won't take much of your time. I don't want to impose."

"It's not an imposition. I know how tough it is to come from law school into an environment like this. It hasn't been that long since I was a summer clerk."

We walked across the parking lot. Beautiful flowers, bushes, and ornamental trees surrounded the building.

"Did you clerk here?" I asked.

"No, Los Angeles. I went to law school at Pepperdine and worked for a firm in the city with a big admiralty practice."

I'd heard of the law school but didn't know anything about it.

"I've been in Savannah for two years," he continued.

"How do you like it?"

"It's different from Los Angeles."

We passed the guardian lions. Zach swiped a card through a security device, and I heard the door click. He held it open for me.

We entered a high lobby open to the top of the building. The floors were covered in dark wood, and a curving staircase led to the second floor. Oriental rugs and ornate furniture were arranged throughout the area.

"This is amazing!" I exclaimed.

"And from what the partners tell me, it's paid for. Follow me. Downstairs is where the elite hang out."

Zach led me through the lower level that contained the partners' offices and two conference rooms. After seeing the lobby, I wasn't surprised at the opulence at every turn.

"Where is your office?" I asked.

"Upstairs. Do you want to take the elevator or the stairs?"

"I think the stairs are more elegant."

"Tell me about yourself," Zach said as we made our way back to the lobby.

"I'm a second-year student at Georgia and grew up in a rural area in the northern part of the state."

Zach glanced at me. "When you're asked that kind of question this summer you need to open up a lot more. People want to learn about you so they can decide whether you'll be a fit for the firm after you graduate."

"That makes sense."

The staircase was designed for a woman wearing a regal gown. However, the upstairs was a different world. In both directions there were open areas divided into small cubicles. It was like a beehive.

"This is where a lot of work takes place," Zach said. "Except for the partners' executive assistants, all the clerical, word processing, and bookkeeping is performed here." He pointed to an enclosed office. "That's where the office manager works."

"Ms. Patrick?"

"Right."

We came to a row of small, separate offices, each with its own window. Several of the doors were closed.

"These are for the associates and top paralegals. The closed doors mean someone is pretending to work on a Saturday."

"Why do you say pretending?"

Zach stopped, knocked on a closed door, and opened it before anyone inside could respond. A young woman dressed in casual clothes was sitting behind her desk with papers spread out in front of her and a dictation unit in her hand.

"This is Myra Dean, a paralegal in the litigation department," Zach said. "She is working, not pretending."

He introduced me.

"Sorry to interrupt," I said.

"No problem," she replied in a voice with a Midwestern accent. "Zach should have known I wouldn't be sitting here reading the sports page."

"Except in the fall when Ohio State is playing football."

The woman smiled. "On my own time."

Zach closed the door and continued down the hall.

"Myra was a bad choice to catch goofing off. She's in Joe Carpenter's group. If she wasn't a hard worker, she wouldn't have lasted a week."

He stopped at another closed door. "This is a sure bet."

He knocked and opened. A balding man was sitting with his feet propped up on his desk and holding a book about golf.

"Zach, knock and wait for an answer before barging in here!" he snapped before he saw me. "Oh, who's your lady friend?"

"Tami Taylor, one of our summer clerks. Just giving her a tour. This is Barry Conrad.

He works in the transactions area."

Conrad held up the book. "And on my slice. Are you a golfer, Ms. Taylor? It's a great way to develop client relations."

"No, I play basketball."

Conrad looked at Zach. "Do we have any clients who play basketball?"

"I don't know. Who's paying for your golf study?"

"The firm. I'm billing it to professional development. Mr. Braddock wants me on the course at four o'clock this afternoon with the management team for Forester Shipping Lines. If I don't do something about my driver and hold up my end of our foursome, it could cost us thousands."

"Keep your shoulders square to the ball and don't rotate your hips too soon," Zach said, adopting a pretend golf stance.

"Get out of here."

We left the office, and Zach shut the door.

"Is Mr. Conrad a partner?"

"No, he's a permanent associate. He swallowed his pride when he wasn't asked to join the firm. It's not a bad life. The pay is good by Savannah standards, and there's no management responsibility."

"How long has he been here?"

"Maybe fifteen years." Zach added, "That's fifteen years averaging fifty to sixty hours a week working plus time spent in his office reading a golf manual or following his fantasy football team."

We stopped before an open door.

"This is my space," he said. "Come in and have a seat."

I hesitated. "I really need to be on my way."

Zach held up his right index finger and shook it. "What is lesson number one?"

"Open up and tell about myself when asked a question by one of the lawyers."

"Good. Rule number two. Don't miss an opportunity to talk to one of the lawyers when given the chance to do so. We're all busy and won't ask you to spend a few minutes with us unless we intend to use it efficiently."

"Yes sir."

"Don't call me sir or mister. My name is Zach."

"Okay."

"Come in."

He led the way into a small office. Directly in front of me was a window that overlooked the parking lot. I could see my car with Zach's motorcycle beside it. Two miniature motorcycles rested on the front of the lawyer's desk. In neat rows on the wall were framed diplomas and other certificates.

On the corner of his desk facing me was a picture of a very attractive young woman with a white flower in her blonde hair. Next to that picture was a photograph of an older couple I guessed to be his parents. The man in the picture had long hair that was gray around the edges, and the woman was wearing a dress that would have looked in style in the late 1970s. Zach picked up a legal pad and took a pen from the top drawer of his desk.

"Tell me about your spiritual journey," he said.

"My spiritual journey?" I asked in surprise.

"Yes, it's an allowable question under the antidiscrimination guidelines."

"Why do you think I have a spiritual journey?"

Zach held up three fingers. "Rule three about being a successful summer clerk. Never answer a question in a way that makes you seem evasive. It's easy to spot a phony. Better to be forthright and honest than beat around the bush and give what you think is a politically correct answer that will help you land a job upon graduation."

"I'd never do that."

"Good. Start by giving me a straight answer."

I sat up in my chair. A head-on challenge required fearlessness in the face of attack. Zach Mays probably didn't have the power to revoke the summer job offer, but even if he did, I wouldn't compromise.

"I've been a Christian since I prayed with my mother at the altar of our church when I was a little girl."

"Did your spiritual journey stop there?"

"No, it's a lifetime relationship with Jesus Christ that affects every aspect of life. I'm always trying to learn and grow."

"Do you believe there are other ways for sincere people to find God?"

"No, there is only one way."

"It's your way or the highway?"

I didn't like to be mocked, but it was part of the persecution of the righteous. At least I knew where I stood when an assault came.

"My beliefs aren't based on my opinions. The Bible says that Jesus is the way, the truth, and the life. No one can come to the Father except through him."

"Doesn't that sound narrow-minded?"

"It is narrow-minded. But truth doesn't depend on popular consensus or opinion polls. The Bible also says the road that leads to eternal life is narrow, and only a few find it. Pretending that someone who tries to live a good life or believes in the god of another religion will make it into heaven is a cruel deception."

"And you're convinced about your religious perspective?"

"Enough to tell you what I believe without beating around the bush." I looked directly into his eyes and took a deep breath. "If you had a wreck on your motorcycle later today and died on the side of the road, would you go to heaven?"

The corner of the lawyer's lips curled up. Whether in a smile or a sneer, I couldn't tell. He pointed to the picture of the beautiful woman on his desk.

"Who do you think that is?"

"I don't know."

"That's my older sister. She's a nurse at a clinic in Zambia."

I wasn't going to be easily deterred. "My question deserves an answer."

Zach ignored me. "She's a missionary in Africa."

"A Christian missionary?"

"Yes."

"Has she talked to you the same way I am?"

The lawyer shook his head. "No, actually, I'm the one who led her to faith in Jesus Christ. It happened at a summer camp for homeschoolers we attended in Oregon. One year she realized the faith of our parents had to become real for her."

I sat back in the chair. "You were home-schooled?"

"Since kindergarten. The first time I entered a public school classroom was to take a course at a local community college when I was sixteen. My high school graduation was sponsored by a homeschool association in Southern California."

I couldn't believe what I was hearing. I pointed to the picture of the older couple. "Your parents?"

"Yes. They were part of the Jesus movement and lived in a Christian commune for a number of years."

"A Christian commune?"

"Yep. Remember how the early believers in the book of Acts didn't claim any private property but held everything in common for the good of all?"

"Yes."

"That's what my parents and some of their friends did. Does your church believe that part of the Bible?"

"We believe every word of the Bible."

"Do you follow the part about sharing everything with other Christians?"

"Not exactly the same way, but we give to people in need. Members of the church have helped me financially even though they didn't have to."

"That's good, but it's not having all things in common. My parents held on to the ideal for years but gave up on group Christianity when I was about ten years old. After that, we lived in the same area as people in our fellowship, but every family had its own checkbook. It takes a zealous group of believers to be biblical in every aspect of their lifestyle."

I'd always considered myself and those like me the epitome of zeal, not in a prideful way, but in humble recognition of our responsibility to walk in the light given us. Suddenly, new biblical revelation I'd not considered loomed before me like a fog bank.

"What are you thinking?" the lawyer asked, interrupting my thoughts.

"Do I have to reveal my secret thoughts as part of the interview process?"

"No."

"And you haven't been taking notes."

The lawyer laughed. It was a pleasant sound.

"I won't be preparing a memo to Mr. Carpenter about the details of this conversation. It would require too much background information that he wouldn't understand."

"So why did you ask your spiritual journey question?"

Zach smiled. "I could tell that your beliefs dictated the way you dress. But your preferences could have been caused by a lot of things."

"It's not a preference; it's a conviction," I responded firmly. "We believe in modesty for women and that there should be a difference between the sexes in clothing. Women should wear skirts or dresses."

"You've never worn blue jeans?"

"Not one day in my life."

The lawyer started to speak, then closed his mouth. "I'll have time this summer to learn more about you," he said.

His comment made me feel like an insect under a microscope. I looked for an air of judgment or condemnation on his face but didn't detect it. As we walked out of the building, I told him we shared the common bond of a homeschool education.

"Until I attended the local high school," I said.

"And played basketball?"

"Yes. I'm on an intramural team now."

Outside, it was a pleasant day with a breeze blowing. The humidity of the previous afternoon had been swept away. Zach opened the car door for me. I hesitated.

"What brought you to Savannah?" I asked.
"It's a long way from Southern California."
"We'll save that for later."
"But that violates rule number one."
Zach smiled. "Rules don't apply to me."

9

Moses Jones awoke to the sound of footsteps on the dock. He opened his eyes and peered through the mosquito netting. It was early morning with a heavy fog rising from the surface of the river. The fog covered the dock and kept him from seeing in the dim light. A different fear crawled over the gunwale of the boat.

"Who be there?" he called out, his voice trembling slightly. "That you, Mr. Floyd? I done told you, she ain't here!"

"Chatham County Sheriff's Department. What's your name?"

Moses sat up in the boat and pulled back the netting. Two sets of dark brown pants, khaki shirts, and shiny black shoes came into view. When he could make out faces, he saw two young deputies — one white, the other black. He took a deep breath and relaxed. These were flesh-and-blood men.

"Moses Jones, boss man."

The black deputy spoke. "Who gave you permission to tie up at this dock?"

Moses looked at the rope looped over the wooden piling. He couldn't deny his boat was connected to the dock. He quickly appealed to a broader reality.

"The river. It don't belong to nobody," he said.

"The river belongs to the State of Georgia," the same deputy responded. "And this dock belongs to the folks who live in that house over there."

Moses peered through the mist but couldn't see a house.

"Don't strain your eyes," the white deputy said. "There is a house there, and the people who live there built this dock, which is private property. You're trespassing."

"No sir. I didn't set one foot on this here dock. I've just been a-sleeping in my boat, not bothering nobody but myself."

"Do you have any identification?" the black deputy asked.

"I ain't got no driver's license. I don't own a car."

The deputy pointed to the white bucket in the front of the boat. "What's in that bucket?"

"Two little ol' fish that I'll cook for my dinner," Moses replied, then had an idea.

"Would you gents like 'em? They're nice-size croakers, plenty of meat and plenty of bones."

"Are you trying to bribe us?" the white deputy asked.

"Uh, no sir, boss man. I'm just sharing my catch."

"We don't want your fish," the black deputy said. "Do you have a fishing license?"

"Yes sir. I sure do. I be totally legal."

Moses kept his fishing license in the bottom of his tackle box. He opened the box and rummaged around until he found it. He handed it up to the deputy, who inspected it.

"This expired two months ago."

Moses' face fell. "I guess the date slipped right past me. What are y'all going to do to me?"

The two deputies glanced at each other. The black one spoke.

"Mr. Jones, there are surveillance cameras on several docks up and down this stretch of the river. A man fitting your description has been illegally tying up his boat for months, and a lot of people have complained. We're going to have to take you to the jail."

"What about my boat?"

"It will be confiscated as evidence," the white deputy replied.

"What do that mean?"

The black deputy spoke. "It will go to the jail compound too. We'll keep it in the lot where we put stolen cars."

"But this boat ain't stole! It was give me by Jabo Nettles, the bartender who used to work at the Bayside Tavern. He got to where he couldn't use it 'cause of his sugar."

"Do you have a registration for it?"

"What's that?" Moses asked, bewildered.

"Mr. Jones, get out of the boat and come with us."

Sunday mornings, I usually stayed at my apartment. There wasn't a church in the area similar to my church in Powell Station, and I preferred solitude with God to apostate religion. I had a drawer full of cassette tapes of sermons by Pastor Vick and guest preachers at our church. I'd listened to some of them so many times that I'd almost memorized the messages.

Two men from the rental car company came to pick up the convertible. I'd carefully checked the car to make sure it hadn't been scratched or dinged by another vehicle. It was a good lesson in the burden imposed by the objects of wealth. Watching after them was a hassle.

"How fast did you get it up to?" one of the men asked as he checked the mileage.

"Not above the speed limit."

The man looked at his coworker and rolled his eyes. "And I only had two beers last night. High-performance cars like this have to be pushed every so often to keep them running right. Use or lose it."

The other man eyed me. "Isn't that right, sweetheart?"

I set my jaw. "Do you want me to contact the district manager of your company and ask him why one of his employees called me 'sweetheart'?"

The man held out his hand. "I was only trying to be friendly."

"Professional would be a better goal." I put the car keys in his palm. "Thanks for picking up the car."

I peeked out the window of my apartment and could see the two men shaking their heads as they talked about me. Modest apparel helped keep males at bay, but it wasn't armor that prevented all attacks. The closest I'd come to physical harm happened in high school. One of the boys on the basketball team surprised me with a crude grab around the waist and attempted to kiss me on the lips while we walked in the dark from the gym to the bus. He received a stinging right hand to the cheek that knocked him back a couple of steps and left a mark I could see the following day at school.

After the men from the car rental company left, I spent the remainder of the afternoon reading a devotional book written by a sixteenth-century Puritan writer. The old saints had a better grasp of the demands of the gospel than contemporary Christians. In Oliver Cromwell's era, believers like my family would have found a welcome seat around the cultural campfire. Sometimes, I felt like I'd been born 350 years too late.

As soon as the sun set I called home. Mama held the phone so Daddy could listen. I told them about the rental car without the detail that it was a convertible and described the bed-and-breakfast simply as a clean place to stay. I provided a lot more information about my meeting with Mrs. Fairmont. Mama interrupted when I told about Flip and the use of my dress to save the rug.

"I never made you clean up a spill with your dress," she said.

"But you made me willing to do it. There's no telling what the rug on the floor was worth. I'm presoaking the dress in the sink right now. I think the stain will come out."

"And don't get any ideas about bringing a Chihuahua into our house," Daddy added. "I can tell you liked the little fellow, but if a dog can't scare possums away from the chicken coop or chase squirrels out of the cornfield, it won't find a place around our table."

"When was the last time Flip and Ginger ate in the kitchen?" I asked.

"You know what I mean," he replied.

I could picture the twinkle in his eyes.

"I won't bring home a pet without permission," I reassured him. "But a house dog might be just what you and Mama need after we're all grown and on our own."

"That's a ways off," Mama said. "Emma and Ellie seem slow to mature. Yesterday they got in an argument that would have shamed a pair of five-year-olds."

"The relationship between Mrs. Bartlett and her mother lacked maturity too," I said.

Mama and Daddy listened as I told them about my honesty with Mrs. Fairmont and her response.

"That cleared the way for her to ask me to live with her," I said. "What do you think?"

As soon as the question escaped my lips, I realized I'd made a terrible mistake. I'd accepted the invitation to live with Mrs. Fairmont without obtaining my parents' permission. It was an amazing lapse of protocol for an unmarried woman. Letting me make the decision to work in Savannah for the summer did not give me unfettered authority over my life. I could hear Daddy and Mama talking softly to each other on the other end of the line but couldn't make out what they were saying. If they rejected the arrangement, I would have no option but to call Mrs. Fairmont and Mrs. Bartlett and ask their forgiveness for prematurely acting without permission. Daddy spoke.

"Go ahead and stay with Mrs. Fairmont if you have peace about it. But don't be surprised if her daughter gives you trouble at some point."

"Yes sir," I said with relief. "I'll try to be a blessing to both of them, and it will help me save more money for the school year."

After my near miss on the Mrs. Fairmont issue, I decided not to mention my visit to the law firm. Mama would cross-examine me closely, and I wasn't prepared to discuss Zach Mays' comment concerning the communal lifestyle of Christians in the book of Acts or in Southern California in the 1970s and 1980s. It was a lot easier telling Mama and Daddy how much I loved them and ending the call.

■ ■ ■ ■

Relieved that I'd found a place to live during the summer, I spent the final weeks of the school year in a sleep-deprived blur of academic activity. Second-year scores were very important because they would be part of a student's academic record during the fall hiring season. Post–law school job offers at firms like Braddock, Appleby, and Carpenter were often contingent on maintaining a certain level of academic achievement. I wanted to do well for several reasons, but especially because God's children, like the prophet Daniel in pagan Babylon, should excel.

Our basketball team finished the season undefeated. The other girls accepted my explanation about the convertible but gave me a nickname — Jaguar. I talked twice with Mrs. Fairmont, who agreed that the Friday before I started work on Monday would be a good time to arrive in Savannah. Daddy would help me move.

The night before Daddy was going to come help me, I began separating my belongings into two piles, one for Savannah, the other to be stored in Powell Station. Before unplugging my computer, I checked

my e-mail. I had a message from Mrs. Bartlett.

Hi, Tami,
Change of plans. Another one of Mother's friends died today. Can you believe it!
The poor woman dropped dead in the dining room at The Cloister. Her funeral is
going to be in Brunswick late Saturday
afternoon. Mother is going down there
tomorrow to stay with the family and won't
be back until Sunday. We'll be at the
house by 2:00 p.m. See you then.
                          Christine Bartlett

I read the e-mail three times, trying to
twist an alternate meaning from it. Mrs.
Bartlett expected Daddy and me to haul my
belongings to Savannah on the Sabbath. I
didn't like putting my suitcase in a car on
Sunday. I quickly wrote her back.

Dear Mrs. Bartlett,
My father is taking off work to help me
move on Friday. Could arrangements be
made to allow us into the house tomorrow? After unloading my things, I could
stay in a motel until Sunday if you prefer.
Please allow me to do this. It would be

greatly appreciated.

Sincerely,
Tami Taylor

I prayed hard for fifteen seconds and sent the e-mail. I began packing my things in marked boxes but left my computer running. My anxiety level rose higher and higher. I checked the computer five times before a response came from Mrs. Bartlett. My heart pounded as I opened it.

Tami,
  Got your message but it won't work. See you Sunday.

Christine Bartlett

I sat down on my bed too frustrated to cry. I couldn't handle something as simple as arranging the date of arrival for my summer job. I kicked myself for sending an e-mail instead of calling. I would have had a better chance of appeal on the phone. I had no option but to ask Mama and Daddy what to do. Daddy answered the phone.

"I'm looking forward to seeing you," he began as soon as he heard my voice. "I worked overtime earlier this week so I wouldn't have to take but two hours of vacation. I'll be on the road as soon as the sun rises."

"There's a problem," I said. "We can't go tomorrow. One of Mrs. Fairmont's friends died, and she'll be out of town. The house won't be open until Sunday afternoon."

"Sunday afternoon?"

"Yes sir."

There was silence on the other end of the line.

"What am I going to do?" I asked as tears now threatened to break to the surface.

"Have you talked to the law firm about starting work on Tuesday? I could try to change my schedule at the plant and ask off on Monday."

"I just found out tonight. I could call the law firm tomorrow. But what if they're not willing to be flexible?"

"Call anyway." Daddy paused. "I know you want to honor the Lord's Day and keep it holy."

"With all my heart. It's just hard when there are other people involved."

"Every test is an opportunity," he replied.

It was one of Daddy's sayings, a call to be optimistic about any problem. It always sounded more convincing in theory than in practice.

We agreed to talk in the morning. Daddy would delay going to work until I talked to someone at the law firm. After the call ended I didn't have the heart to continue packing but did so by faith. The Lord commanded the Israelites to prepare to leave Egypt even though the way to the Promised Land would be fraught with perils.

I spent most of my prayer time early the following morning asking for God's favor upon my call to the law firm. I debated whether to appeal directly to Joe Carpenter, but since I'd never talked to him I asked for Gerry Patrick instead. It was barely 8:01 a.m. Fortunately, Ms. Patrick was in.

"Good morning, Tami," she began in a chipper voice. "Christine Bartlett is thrilled that you're going to be staying with her mother. It sounds like you really impressed both of them."

"Yes ma'am, but there is a problem with my move from Athens to Savannah."

"What sort of problem?"

I explained the delay due to the death of Mrs. Fairmont's friend. "Would it be possible for me to start work on Tuesday?"

"When did you say Mrs. Fairmont will be home?"

I hadn't mentioned the day. I swallowed. "Sunday afternoon."

"Can't you move in on Sunday?"

"I'd rather do it on Monday."

"The firm has arranged a special catered

luncheon for the summer clerks on Monday. All the partners and associates will be there, and with vacation schedules, it may be the only time this summer when everyone will be together," she continued with emphasis. "The one day you need to be here is Monday. A key part of the summer clerk program is the opportunity for the partners to get to know you."

I remembered Zach Mays' rules. "Yes ma'am. I'm aware of that. I want to meet people."

"Good. Then you'll be here?"

In desperation, an idea was born. "Ms. Patrick, are you Jewish?" I asked.

"Yes."

"Do you keep the Sabbath?"

"Not as strictly as my rabbi uncle in Fort Lauderdale would like me to," she said after a brief silence.

I took a deep breath. "I'm a Christian, and my family keeps Sunday as our Sabbath. We don't do any work on Sunday and spend the time after church services in rest and spiritual reflection. It would violate my religious convictions to move my furniture on Sunday."

"I'm not familiar with the New Testament teaching on the Sabbath."

It wasn't a question, and the inflection in

Ms. Patrick's voice didn't sound like a request for a biblical explanation.

"Are you asking for a religious accommodation under the federal antidiscrimination laws?" she continued coldly.

"No ma'am," I answered hurriedly. "I'm not raising a legal issue or trying to put the firm in an awkward position. I'm appealing to you as a person. I've agonized over this ever since I received the news from Mrs. Bartlett last night."

"And I don't question your sincerity. But I'm not sure I can give you an answer. I'll need to check with Mr. Carpenter and let you know what he says."

My heart sank. No matter how well Ms. Patrick tried to explain my position, the reaction of one of the senior partners to my predicament was easy to imagine.

"Could you talk to Zach Mays instead?" I asked. "I realize he's an associate, but he understands something about my background."

"Zach Mays? How do you know him?"

I had no choice but to mention my brief visit to the office.

"Can you stay on the line while I see if he's in the office?" she asked.

"Yes ma'am."

While I waited on hold, I listened to classical music. It was a Bach organ concerto, composed to the glory of the God, whose laws the world now tried to ignore. It was a moment of musical irony. Ms. Patrick returned.

"I mentioned your dilemma to Zach. He thinks you should definitely be at the luncheon on Monday and offered to solve your religious objection by meeting you at Mrs. Fairmont's house on Sunday to unload the furniture for you. He also suggested that you read a verse from the New Testament about an ox falling in a ditch on the Sabbath and the owner pulling it out. I wrote down the reference — Luke 14:5."

"Is he also willing to load the truck in Athens?" I asked, chafing at the young lawyer's advice. "My ox is in two ditches at once."

"He didn't mention it. Do you want me to connect you to him?"

"No ma'am. I'm sorry. It's nice of him to offer to help."

"Zach is a fine young man and an excellent lawyer. There's no pretense with him."

"I'll call my father and get his advice. He's the one who will be helping me move. Oh, and please don't mention this to Mr. Carpenter. I wouldn't want to trouble him."

"I can't promise confidentiality," Ms.

Patrick responded stiffly. "Everything related to personnel issues is an open topic for the partners. That's a part of my job."

"Yes ma'am. I understand. I'll call back later today."

I ended the call. People who didn't want to honor the Sabbath used Luke 14:5 as an excuse for just about any activity. I phoned home. Mama answered.

"Is Daddy still there?" I asked.

"Yes, I'll get him."

"We're both here," Mama said after a few moments.

I told them about my conversation with Ms. Patrick, leaving out Zach Mays. Daddy spoke.

"We prayed about the situation last night and this morning," he said. "Your mother and I both agree that this is a Luke 14:5 situation. The ox represents your livelihood, and now that you tell us about the Monday luncheon, it's clear you need to be there. If the only way to make sure that happens is for us to move your things on Sunday, then that's what we'll do. I'll be at your apartment by ten in the morning. Try to have all your boxes ready by sundown on Saturday."

"Yes sir," I mumbled.

"What?" Mama asked.

"Thank you," I said. "See you then."

10

When Daddy arrived, I threw open the door of the apartment and ran out to greet him before he turned off the motor. I threw my arms around his neck as soon as his feet touched the asphalt.

"Well, that's a nice welcome," he said.

"It's good to see you, Daddy," I said. "Sorry about what I'm putting you through."

He kissed the top of my head in the usual spot.

"Don't mention it again. Let's get your ox out of the ditch and load him on the truck."

All the stuff going to Powell Station was loaded in the front of the truck. To the rear was the furniture I would use in Mrs. Fairmont's basement apartment, my summer clothes, pots, pans, and dishes, toiletries, and books to occupy my free time in the evenings. Daddy's foot was bothering him, so I jumped in and out of the truck to arrange the load. When we finished, Daddy tied a blue tarp over the top of the pile and lashed it down.

"There's a chance of rain this afternoon as we get near the coast," he said.

We left town and followed the same route I'd taken to Savannah. Being with Daddy, my spirits lifted. I liked riding with him in Kyle's truck ten times better than driving an expensive convertible with the top down. As we rolled along, I asked question after question about the family.

"Bobby starts at the chicken plant tomorrow," Daddy said.

"Is he going to be an eviscerator?"

"No, it wouldn't be good to throw him in with all those ladies. He's going to work on the loading dock."

"Coming in or going out?"

Dealing with frozen dead birds in cardboard cartons was much easier than the noise and stench of the live ones in wire-mesh crates.

"Coming in," Daddy replied.

Kyle's truck didn't have air-conditioning, and the late spring air blowing through the window was warm. I brushed a strand of hair from my face and returned it to the ponytail behind my head. I looked at Daddy.

He was a relaxed driver, not stressed by the responsibilities of being on the road. Before he met Mama, he worked for a couple of years as a long-distance truck driver.

"What was it like driving across the country?" I asked.

"I liked it. But once I got married, I didn't want to be away from your mama for weeks at a time. Then when you came along, I had to come home every night and plant a new kiss on top of your head."

"What did you do about driving on Sunday?"

"My partner did it. He was a Seventh-Day Adventist. I drove on Saturday; he drove on Sunday. It worked out good for both of us."

"Did you ever go to California?"

"Los Angeles."

"What was it like?"

"Oh, the land out there is dry but green where they irrigate. It made me think about the verses in the Bible where the desert blooms like a rose. It's a fragile place. Unless people pipe in water, not much can live there. There are trees up in the mountains, but no forests on the flats."

"What about the city?"

He shrugged. "Every truck terminal is the same whether it's in Omaha or L.A. I couldn't tell you much about Los Angeles except that once it started it never seemed to stop. I never made it all the way to the Pacific. We'd drop a load, eat a steak at a truck stop, and head back."

I stared out the window. Trees had always been part of the landscape of my world. I wondered if there were trees where Zach Mays' family lived.

"One of the attorneys at the firm in Savannah is from Los Angeles," I said.

"How did he get to Georgia?"

"I'm not sure."

We stopped for gas.

"Do you want me to drive?" I asked.

Daddy stretched and rubbed the back of his neck. "That would be nice. I talk about being a long-distance truck driver, but those days are long gone."

The gears on Kyle's truck grated when I started off. Once I reached highway speed, Daddy leaned against the door frame and went to sleep. His ability to catch a nap at a moment's notice amazed me. He could stretch out on a blanket beneath the poplar tree in front of the house and doze off within seconds. Flip and Ginger would see him and curl up at his feet.

A small convoy of large trucks passed us, and I thought about Daddy driving across the country. I wondered what other dreams he'd sacrificed to be home at night to kiss me on the top of the head. Like Daddy's truck-driving career, my summer job at the law firm in Savannah might be no more than a detour through Los Angeles on the way to a greater good.

Daddy didn't wake up until we were close to the coast. He sat up and blinked his eyes as we passed a mileage marker.

"Did that say twenty miles to Savannah?" he asked.

"Yes sir. You must have been really tired."

"It's been a long week. Your mama got her money's worth out of me yesterday. I spent several hours in the crawl space underneath the house spreading tar paper on the ground and treating for termites. Do you want me to take over?"

"Yes sir, I'll pull off at the next exit. I don't trust myself shifting gears on the short streets of Savannah."

We entered the historic section of the city, and I gave directions.

"You already know your way around pretty good," he said as we made the third turn in four blocks.

"Yes sir. It's not far to her house."

The spring flowers I'd enjoyed during my first visit were giving way to summer's less-vibrant colors. Daddy had never been to Savannah.

"It doesn't remind me at all of Los Angeles," he said as we passed the James Oglethorpe statue in Chippewa Square.

"It's not Powell Station either," I said, wiping perspiration from my forehead. "There aren't any mountain breezes."

We made a final turn, and I pointed to the house.

"That's it, the one with the two large live oaks in front and ironwork up the steps. You can park at the curb."

"How is living in a fancy place like this going to affect you?" he asked as the truck rolled to a stop.

"Don't worry. I'll be living in the basement like a scullery maid."

Daddy didn't smile. "Don't underestimate the power of the world to pull you into its grip."

I pointed to my heart. "The truth you and Mama put in here is as alive as you are."

I led the way up the steps and pushed the doorbell. Mrs. Fairmont answered wearing an expensive blue dress with pearls around her neck and the same diamond rings on her fingers. I introduced her to Daddy. He shook her hand and bowed slightly.

"Hello, dear," she said to me. "Did you

185

have car problems? I was expecting you yesterday."

My eyes opened wider. "No ma'am. I thought you were out of town at a friend's funeral. Mrs. Bartlett sent me an e-mail the other night telling me you wouldn't be home until this afternoon."

Mrs. Fairmont waved her hand in dismissal. "I told Christine about the change in plans. Didn't she get in touch with you? And it was a cousin who died, not a friend. The funeral was yesterday morning, and I came directly home. Sometimes Christine is worse about remembering than I am." The older woman's eyes brightened. "Today is a good day. I woke up feeling chipper this morning. How do you like my dress?"

"It's beautiful," I managed, still processing the information that Daddy and I could have driven to Savannah on Saturday.

"You have your father's eyes," Mrs. Fairmont said. "Come inside."

"But thankfully she mostly looks like her mother," Daddy said as we entered the foyer.

I turned to Daddy and mouthed an apology. He smiled and shook his head.

"Would you like to see Flip? I told him you were coming."

"Yes ma'am."

"Have a seat in the blue parlor while I get him. He's in the courtyard."

We went into the blue parlor. It was exactly the same except for a new arrangement of flowers. I heard the patter of little feet. Flip dashed into the room and began barking furiously. Daddy and I both lowered our hands in greeting. The little dog sniffed me briefly then spent more time examining the back of Daddy's hand. Daddy scratched the dog's neck.

"Another friend." Mrs. Fairmont beamed as she came into the room. "Your whole family must have a way with animals."

Mrs. Fairmont sat down, and Flip jumped into her lap.

"I never let him do that when Christine is here," she said. "Now, Mr. Taylor, I want to thank you for letting Tami stay with me this summer. Are there any instructions about her conduct you want to share with me? I've raised two children, imperfectly I must admit, but I'm willing to do what I can to help mold her character."

To my surprise, Daddy launched into a laundry list of guidelines, most of which would have been suitable for the twins. He included everything from cleaning my living area and helping with household chores to not staying out late at night and notifying

187

Mrs. Fairmont when I wouldn't be home for supper. She nodded her head in agreement.

"That's very helpful," she replied when he finished. "I'll try, but you know how young people can be."

"Tammy is a fine young woman," Daddy replied. "All her mother and I ask is that you do the best you can. Now, we'd better unload her things from the truck."

Daddy got up from the chair and left the room. Slightly numb, I followed him outside.

"What was that all about?" I asked as soon as we reached the front steps. "Why mention all the rules to her? It sounded so juvenile."

Daddy put his hand on the side of the truck and faced me. "You'll do all those things and more, but it satisfied Mrs. Fairmont, didn't it?"

"Yes sir."

"It was for her benefit, not yours. She needs to see herself giving you more than a bed to sleep in at night."

We each carried a box into the house. Mrs. Fairmont was standing in the hallway with the door to the basement open.

"I'd better stay here," she said. "I don't want to chance my luck on the stairs."

Daddy followed me into the basement.

"It's a plain room," I whispered. "Mrs. Bartlett thinks the dog lives down here. It was rented out years ago when this was a boardinghouse."

I pushed open the door and stopped in shock. The efficiency apartment had been completely redecorated with new carpeting and furniture. I peeked into the bedroom. Light streamed in onto a pretty twin bed. There was a white chest of drawers with matching nightstand. I opened the door to a bathroom that was sparkling clean.

"It's been totally redone," I marveled.

I bounded upstairs.

"Mrs. Fairmont, it's beautiful! You shouldn't have gone to so much trouble."

"Gracie and her nephews did all the work. It was fine as a hide-out for Flip when Christine came for a visit, but not fit for a young lady like you."

I leaned over and hugged her.

"Thank you," I said.

None of my secondhand furniture would look right in the garden apartment, so it only took thirty minutes to unload the truck. Everything else would spend the summer in Powell Station. It was work, but not as much as I'd expected. Mrs. Fairmont went into the den. Every time we passed the room on the way to the basement door, I could see her sitting in a chair, staring out the windows.

"I'll unpack the other things after the sun goes down," I said to Daddy after I hung my dresses up in a long, narrow closet in the bedroom.

We went upstairs. I knocked on the door frame of the den. "We're finished," I announced.

Mrs. Fairmont didn't respond. I couldn't see her face. I turned to Daddy, who gave me a questioning look. I walked softly across the room.

"Mrs. Fairmont? My father is leaving now. He'd like to say good-bye."

I reached the chair. Flip was curled up on the floor at Mrs. Fairmont's feet. The old woman continued staring. I reached down and gently touched her on the arm. She jerked so violently that I stepped back.

"I'm sorry," I said. "I didn't mean to startle you."

Mrs. Fairmont rubbed her temples. "I have a headache. Did you hear the bird flying around inside the house? We need to open all the doors and let it out. It came in through the veranda."

She pointed to a screened-in porch that overlooked the garden. I opened the door.

190

All I saw was a set of beautiful wicker furniture and some green potted plants.

"Mrs. Fairmont," I said calmly, "there's not a bird in the house. The doors are all closed."

Mrs. Fairmont frowned and shook her head. "I heard it as plain as you talking right now. Be quiet and listen."

We were all silent. Mrs. Fairmont waited a few moments then sighed.

"It's gone." She looked up at me with sad eyes. "Or I had a hallucination. That can be part of my illness. What have I been doing?"

"Sitting in this chair and staring out the window while we brought in my things and put them in the basement."

"Gracie says I sit and stare at nothing. It's like my brain freezes up, and I don't know it. I'm so scared that I'll put something on the stove and won't watch it."

"Maybe I can cook for you," I said.

Mrs. Fairmont stared out the window in silence so long that I thought she'd had another brain freeze. She turned in her chair and saw Daddy. He stepped forward and gently took her hand in his.

"It was nice meeting you," he said. "I have to leave now. It's a long drive home."

"Yes, it is," she responded then continued staring.

Daddy and I quietly left the room.

"Her condition may be more serious than her daughter realizes," Daddy said as we walked down the front steps. "Keep a record of what happens for her family and the doctors. And pray there will be a chance to tell her about Jesus."

"Yes sir."

We reached the truck.

"Are you going to be okay on the drive?" I asked.

"Remember, I've hauled freight to California. The nap refilled my tank. I'll be in Powell Station by bedtime."

I longed to go with him. He hugged me and deposited a last kiss on the top of my head.

"Call us."

I nodded, not wanting to speak as emotion welled up in my heart. Daddy got in the truck and pulled away from the curb. I watched him leave, turned, and went inside the house.

Mrs. Fairmont was sitting in the den. She'd turned on the TV to an afternoon show. She muted the volume and motioned for me to come into the room.

"I'm better now," she said. "I drank a sip of water, and it washed away the cobwebs of my mind."

"That's good."

"But I know that water isn't the cure for what's wrong with me. Did I say anything stupid? I hate embarrassing myself."

"You were staring out the window," I answered slowly as I debated whether to mention the imaginary bird.

Mrs. Fairmont continued. "Your father is a good man. I can tell by the way he looks at you that he loves you very much."

"Yes ma'am. I'm blessed to have my family."

Mrs. Fairmont pointed at the TV. "This show is about children abandoned by fathers who turn up years later looking for a handout after the child becomes a financial success. What do you think about that?"

I watched the silent images of people pointing fingers and arguing with each other. The camera flashed to the studio audience, some of whom were on their feet yelling. It gave me a queasy feeling.

"That the producer of the TV show is more interested in entertainment than solutions. I wouldn't watch something like this."

Mrs. Fairmont glanced at me with a frown on her face. "You're probably right, but I want to hear what the host tells them to do. Why don't you go downstairs and finish unpacking your things."

I went downstairs but didn't unpack. My first action was to pray that God would spiritually cleanse the beautifully decorated apartment. I went into the bedroom and knelt beside the bed. I prayed for about thirty minutes, then turned my focus to Mrs. Fairmont.

The spiritual warfare to be fought for the elderly woman's eternal destiny was real, and I would need all the help heaven could muster. I asked God for grace and the ability to discern his voice directing my steps. A few seconds later, a deep male voice faintly called my name.

"Tami!"

I'd never heard the audible voice of God. My guidance had been less distinct, but nonetheless effective. I'd learned to trust the impressions that came to my spirit as divine communication, a birthright I enjoyed as one of God's children. Passages of Scripture about the experiences of Moses, Samuel, and Isaiah raced through my mind. I shut my eyes tighter and clenched my hands together. I quickly settled on the response of the boy Samuel when the Lord spoke to him in the middle of the night.

"Speak, Lord," I said under my breath. "Your servant is listening."

I waited. In a few seconds the voice spoke again, only louder.

"Tami Taylor!"

I kept my head bowed.

"Speak, Lord, for your servant is listening," I repeated.

I waited, but the voice didn't continue. The hair on the back of my neck stood up. I opened my eyes, but the narrow bedroom was empty. I heard a loud knock that made me jump.

"Are you in there?" the voice repeated. "It's Zach Mays from the law firm."

I looked toward heaven and saw nothing except the white ceiling. At least I now knew that God didn't talk like the young lawyer from California.

"Just a minute. I'll be right there," I called out.

I checked my appearance in the bathroom mirror. I certainly didn't look like I'd been to glory. After loading and unloading the truck, I resembled a chicken plant worker more than an aspiring lawyer. I quickly brushed my hair and splashed water on my face.

When I opened the door, Zach Mays was standing there wearing blue jeans and a white T-shirt with a big tomato on it. He had his hair pulled back in a short, tight ponytail. His motorcycle helmet was under his arm.

"I'm here to help you get your ox out of the ditch," he said with a smile. "Am I too late?"

"My ox turned out to be a kitten," I answered. "Since I visited a few weeks ago, Mrs. Fairmont has totally redone this place. I didn't need the furniture I brought from my apartment at school." I paused. "Does Mrs. Fairmont know you're here?"

"I sneaked in through the garden," he joked.

"I mean, she's not doing well mentally. She's confused and disoriented."

"No, I didn't notice anything unusual when she let me in."

At the mention of confusion, the absurdity of what I'd thought moments before hit me. Mrs. Fairmont imagined a bird flying around inside the house; I opted for the audible voice of God from the top of the stairs. Both of us were out of touch with reality. I started to chuckle, tried to stifle it, then burst out laughing. Zach stared at me in bewilderment.

"Mrs. Fairmont seems like a nice lady," he said. "I'm sorry she's having mental —"

I held up my hand. "No, no. It's what you said."

"What did I say?"

"My name," I managed. "Twice."

"And why is that so funny?"

I laughed again. Zach Mays probably thought I was certifiably crazy, but I couldn't stop. I motioned for him to come into the apartment. He eased onto the sofa and placed his helmet beside him. I plopped down in a chair and wiped away the tears streaming down my cheeks.

"I'm sorry," I said, taking a couple of deep breaths. "I was in the bedroom praying when you called my name from the top of the stairs. I thought it was the voice of God."

"You think I sound like God?"

I shook my head and stifled another wave of laughter. "I've never heard the voice of God, but under the circumstances, my imagination played a trick on me. I didn't know there was a man in the house, and when a male voice calling my name came out of nowhere, I assumed it must be a messenger from heaven. I guess I'm not making a very good second impression, but at least I'm not trying to hide anything."

"Good application of rule number three."

I remembered an older rule of hospitality. "Would you like a warm bottle of water?"

I asked. "I haven't been to the grocery store and don't have anything in the refrigerator."

"No, thanks."

"I need one."

I took a bottle from one of my boxes. It was tepid from the ride in the truck.

"I didn't see your convertible out front," Zach said.

"It was a rental. My daddy brought me and my belongings in a pickup truck this morning. We finished unloading a few minutes ago, and he's headed home." I pointed to the boxes on the floor. "All I have to do is unpack. There isn't much to do. I'll save most of the work until tomorrow."

Zach looked around. "The apartment is nice."

"Yes, and please understand I wasn't making fun of Mrs. Fairmont's mental condition. The reason I'm living here is to help take care of her."

"That's what Gerry Patrick told me."

I stared at Zach Mays. I'd never invited a man into my apartment at school. In my confusion about his voice, I'd allowed him across an invisible line without realizing it.

"We should go upstairs," I said quickly. "Mrs. Fairmont may be wondering what's going on."

I inwardly kicked myself at the wording of

198

my last comment and stood up.

"Do you laugh a lot?" Zach asked.

"Only when something funny happens, usually to me."

"Are you going to let that side of you come out at the law firm?"

"I doubt it. And I can promise you one thing — I won't make the mistake of thinking Mr. Braddock paging me on the office intercom is the voice of God." I stepped toward the door. "We really should be joining Mrs. Fairmont. It's rude not to."

Zach's motorcycle riding boots clunked on the stairs. I peeked into the den. The elderly woman was sleeping in her chair with a black-and-white movie blaring from the TV. I touched my lips with my index finger and quietly entered the room. The remote control was on a stand beside Mrs. Fairmont's chair. Flip was curled up at her feet. When he saw me, he jumped up and growled, but I leaned over and scratched the back of his neck. With my other hand, I picked up the remote and turned off the television. Mrs. Fairmont stirred slightly then relaxed. I gently lifted her feet and placed them on an ottoman and positioned two pillows around her so that she wouldn't slip to the side. I gave Flip a final pat on the head and backed out of the room. I motioned for Zach to follow me into the foyer.

After we were safely out of earshot of the den, I said, "Thanks for stopping by. I'm sorry I acted like such a silly girl."

"No, it's okay. I'll see you tomorrow morning."

"Is that when all the other summer clerks begin?"

"The girl from Emory starts then. Vince Colbert has been here for a week."

"Is he the clerk from Yale?"

"Yes, and he seems like a nice guy. Very smart. He's a Christian too."

11

Moses Jones lay on his back on the bottom bunk and stared at the cheap mattress overhead. The man who'd slept above him since Moses was arrested had gone to trial and not come back. Moses didn't know if that meant his bunkmate had been released to go home or convicted and sent directly to the state penitentiary. He'd heard both stories from his cellmates. Rumors in the cell block were as plentiful as mosquitoes on the marshes of the Ogeechee in July.

Jail had changed a lot since Moses spent six months behind bars for hauling moonshine when he was in his early twenties. The old Chatham County jail had been torn down, replaced by a new one with air-conditioning, an indoor exercise facility, and completely integrated cell blocks. The deputies who arrested Moses drove him past the spot where blood once stained the curb. Moses turned his head and stared for a few seconds at the place that still refused to give up its secret.

In the new jail, prisoners with white, black, or brown skin lived close together. English and Spanish profanity shared equal airtime. There was tension between the three groups, but nothing as bad as the racial hatred Moses experienced in his younger years.

Moses' boss, Tommy Lee Barnes, couldn't have run his bolita racket without black runners, but they had to dodge beer bottles, curse words, and racist remarks to collect their fees. Eventually, Barnes was arrested for aggravated assault and spent two years at the Reidsville penitentiary in a ten-by-ten cell filled with men of different races. Moses heard that confinement with a black man caused the heart attack that ultimately killed the gambling kingpin.

Now, men of all races in the cell block shared one common physical characteristic — body art. The quality of images varied. A prisoner might have a flower worthy of Monet on his forearm and a tiger that resembled an anemic house cat on his shoulder. One man in the next bunk had a grim Reaper on his back that he'd asked a local tattoo artist to transform into a motorcycle rider. The result was a wreck that left no survivors. Moses was the only one in his cell block without adornment. The only marks on his wrinkled black skin were from long-forgotten fights and scrapes in the woods. Because of Moses' age, no one bothered him.

Soon after he arrived, Moses was given the task of emptying all the trash cans in the building. It took two hours, twice a day, to complete his rounds pushing a gray plastic buggy through the cell blocks, bathrooms, offices, and food service areas. He often hummed softly to himself while he worked. All the wasted food bothered him. When he cooked at his shack by the river, he never had any leftovers except skin and bones.

Moses dumped the trash into a large container behind the dining hall. When he went outside, he always peeked through the fence at his boat. It was in exactly the same place, chained to a light pole. The chain comforted him. It was a shiny new one, much stronger than the one he owned, and it would be hard for anyone to steal the boat. Some of the cars in the lot only stayed a night. Others had been there since the first time Moses peered through the fence.

Two days after his arrest, Moses talked to a young black detective for a long time. He

told him about the faces in the water. The
detective listened and wrote things down on
a sheet of paper. He refused to tell Moses
when he might be released to go home.
Weeks passed. The old man felt as if he'd
been dropped into a hole in the bank of the
river and forgotten. His soul needed to sing,
but there wasn't a solitary place to do it.

At least he had plenty to eat. The meat
dishes weren't as tasty as fresh fish dipped
in cornmeal and fried in a skillet over a
kerosene fire, but institutional food kept
away hunger. Dessert was the best part of
the meals. Moses only had a few teeth left
in his mouth, but he joked that all of them
were sweet.

I woke up early and quietly left the house
for a morning run. Included in my loop was
a jog past Braddock, Appleby, and Carpenter. I slowed my pace as I passed the office.
It was barely light outside, and there weren't
any cars in the parking lot. I remembered
my prayer a few weeks earlier in Powell Station.

"Make this a place of praise," I said.

I enjoyed a burst of energy as I ran around
Forsyth Park and back to Mrs. Fairmont's
house. There was no sign of Mrs. Fairmont.
I drank two glasses of water and took a

banana downstairs. I sat at the wrought-iron table outside my bedroom, ate the banana, and prayed.

After I showered, I put on my blue suit. The first day of work was a time to look my best. With my hair spilling past my shoulders, the only thing out of ordinary about my appearance was the absence of makeup. I applied just enough lipstick to slightly enhance the color of my lips.

When I went upstairs Mrs. Fairmont wasn't in the den or the kitchen. I approached the bottom of the stairs and looked up. It didn't feel right leaving the house for the day without telling her good-bye. I put my foot on the first step and debated whether to go upstairs. I didn't want to invade Mrs. Fairmont's privacy. Flip appeared at the top of the stairs and looked down at me.

"Is she awake?" I whispered.

I heard a door close.

"Mrs. Fairmont," I called out. "Good morning. It's Tami."

The elderly woman appeared, wearing an elegant green robe and slippers. Her hair looked like it hadn't been brushed. She blinked her eyes and peered down the stairs.

"Where's Gracie?" she asked. "Are you her helper?"

"No ma'am. I'm Tami Taylor. You're letting me live in the basement apartment this summer while I work for Mr. Braddock's law firm."

Mrs. Fairmont rubbed the side of her face. "My mind is foggy this morning."

"I'm leaving for work in a few minutes. Is there anything I can do for you?"

"Did you make the coffee?"

"No ma'am. Would you like some?"

"That would be nice. Cream and sugar."

Mrs. Fairmont shuffled away from the top of the stairs. Flip followed her. I went into the kitchen and started the coffeemaker. I checked the clock. I wanted to get to the office promptly at 8:00 a.m. and wasn't sure exactly how long it would take to get there on foot. I didn't want to be late, but I was living in the house to serve Mrs. Fairmont's needs. I watched the coffee begin to drip into the bottom of the pot. While I waited, I wrote a note that I left on the kitchen counter, thanking Gracie for renovating the downstairs apartment and telling her how much I looked forward to meeting her.

As soon as enough coffee dripped down, I poured a cup and added cream and sugar. I held the cup carefully while climbing the stairs. Halfway up, I thought about the spilled coffee incident in the blue parlor and had to fight off a giggle that threatened to cause the brown drink to slosh over the edge of the cup. I made it to the top of the stairs and knocked on the door frame of a room with the door cracked open. A bark from Flip confirmed that I'd found Mrs. Fairmont's bedroom. I slowly entered.

"It's Tami. I've brought your coffee," I announced. "With cream and sugar."

Mrs. Fairmont was sitting up in bed with pillows behind her. Like the rest of the house, the bedroom was filled with beautiful furniture. The bed had four massive posters and an ornate headboard. A tall bookcase filled with books stood against one wall. Against another wall was a long dresser with a large mirror above it. The top of the dresser was covered with family pictures. On the corner of the dresser was an old black-and-white photograph of a bride in a long elaborate gown and a groom wearing a tuxedo.

"Sorry, child. I was confused a minute ago," Mrs. Fairmont said. "I wasn't really awake. You're the young woman with twin sisters who have blue eyes."

"Yes ma'am," I replied, surprised at her recall of such a small detail. "Where should I put the coffee?"

"On the nightstand."

I set the cup in front of a picture of two girls in old-fashioned dresses.

"Who is that?" I asked.

Mrs. Fairmont turned her head. "That's Ellen Prescott and I at Forsyth Park. She came from a poor family but received a scholarship to my school. It was Ellen's little daughter who was murdered. She had blue eyes, just like your sisters. They never found the body."

I involuntarily shuddered. "How old was she when she died?"

"About ten or eleven. Ellen married late in life to a man with a lot of money and never had another child. She and her husband died in a car wreck a few years later."

Mrs. Fairmont reached over and raised the cup to her lips. Her right hand shook slightly, but she didn't spill a drop.

"That's good coffee for decaf," she sighed. "Thank you."

I moved away from the bed. "I'm leaving for my first day of work at Mr. Braddock's law firm. I'll see you this afternoon."

"Run along. With Flip's help, I'll try to hold on to my sanity."

I stopped for a last glance at myself in the mirror in the green parlor. I looked appropriately professional and resolute. I practiced a quick smile that left me unsatisfied. People complimented me on my smile, even though the right corner of my lip curled up slightly higher than the left. I turned away from the mirror before a vain thought lodged in my brain.

The early morning sun served notice that it would be warm by the end of the day. I walked briskly down the steps and turned in the direction of the law office. My shoes didn't have high heels, but it was different from navigating the uneven sidewalks in running shoes. My feet crushed acorns left from the previous year's crop. I noticed details that had escaped me during my morning run. All of the houses were old, but there was remarkable variety in the use of brick or wood, the shape and placement of windows, the design of the front doors, and countless other nuances. I didn't try to take it all in at once. I knew that by the end of the summer, the walk to work would be as familiar to me as the woods on the west side of our house in Powell Station.

I passed a man walking his dog and two joggers running in the opposite direction. I crossed several intersections and reached Montgomery Street. The law office was several blocks from the Chatham County Courthouse, a modern structure uninfluenced by the beautiful area nearby. Traffic was busier on Montgomery Street, and when I reached Braddock, Appleby, and Carpenter, my heart began to pound in my chest. A few cars were in the parking lot.

"Make this a place of praise," I began to repeat under my breath.

I knew the prayer was right, but it didn't send peace to my heart. I'd felt less nervous trying to make a crucial free throw at the end of a conference tournament basketball game. I took a deep breath when I reached the front door and opened it.

The receptionist sat to the right of the sweeping staircase. My low heels clicked on the wooden floor.

"May I help you?" she asked.

"I'm Tami Taylor, one of the summer clerks," I said, hoping my voice didn't shake. "I'm here to see Ms. Patrick."

The receptionist spoke to someone on the phone.

"Have a seat," she said to me. "She'll be down in a few minutes."

I sat in a wooden chair with curved arms and legs. The front door of the office opened, and a young woman entered. It was Julie Feldman, also dressed in a dark suit and white blouse. Without noticing me, she approached the receptionist. Julie was shorter than I'd imagined from the pictures sent via the Internet and a lot cuter. Her black hair was cut short. The receptionist pointed in my direction. Julie's eyes met mine, and she smiled. She sat down on a leather couch beside my chair and introduced herself.

"Are you nervous?" she asked.

"Yes."

"Me too. I've talked to two of my friends who have been working for a week at big law firms in Atlanta. They told me not to treat it like summer camp. Their firms don't want them to get bored, and the partner in charge of summer clerks has a bunch of activities planned to keep them entertained. I told them Atlanta may be different from Savannah."

Julie spoke rapidly, her dark eyes alert.

"All I know is that we're going to a luncheon today with the lawyers," I replied. "Ms. Patrick says it may be the only time all the partners are with us."

Julie nodded. "I've talked to her a bunch. Mr. Carpenter told me to meet with her this morning."

I wondered why I'd not received personal contact from the senior partner. Perhaps it was because I was a fill-in.

"What's he like?"

"Okay, I guess. He came to the law school for an interview day. I didn't think he liked me, but then I got the job offer. Did you find a place to live?"

I told her about Mrs. Fairmont's house.

"You're not far from my place near Greene Square. We'll have to go out together some at night."

My defenses flew up. "It depends on Mrs. Fairmont's condition. Staying at her house is actually a second job."

"What do you mean?"

"She has health issues," I replied, not wanting to give details that Mrs. Bartlett might want to remain private.

Julie lowered her voice. "Maybe you can sneak out after hours. I've already been to River Street twice. It's a lot of fun."

A middle-aged woman with dark hair and reading glasses on a chain around her neck came down the stairs and introduced herself. It was Gerry Patrick. Ms. Patrick was the same height as Julie. She gave Julie a quick hug and shook my hand.

"Did you move in yesterday?" she asked me crisply.

"Yes ma'am. Mrs. Fairmont completely renovated the downstairs apartment."

"That's good to hear. Let's go to a conference room. Vince Colbert is already here this morning. He's working on a project for Mr. Braddock."

When Ms. Patrick turned away, Julie leaned over and whispered, "Vince must be a gunner."

We went into one of the plush downstairs conference rooms Zach had shown me during my first visit. Ms. Patrick sat at the end of the table and offered us coffee or water. She then pushed the intercom button on the phone.

"Deborah, send Vince into conference room two."

I crossed my ankles under the shiny table. Opposite me was a massive oil painting of a harbor scene from the early nineteenth century. I could see bales of cotton piled on a wharf in front of a row of sailing ships. Scores of people filled the scene. The detail in the painting would have taken a long time to create.

"Is that Savannah?" I asked.

"Yes," Ms. Patrick said. "Mr. Braddock lets the art museum keep it for a year then brings it back to the office for twelve months."

The door to the conference room opened and a tall, lanky young man with wavy brown hair and dark eyes came into the room. He was wearing a dark blue sport coat, gray slacks, white shirt, and burgundy tie. He was carrying a very thin laptop computer in his right hand.

"Vince, meet Julie Feldman and Tami Taylor," Ms. Patrick said.

When I shook the male clerk's hand, I noticed a large, rectangular-shaped scar on it. The skin was oddly wrinkled and lacked pigment. I quickly glanced up. His eyes were on my face. He released his grip and sat on the opposite side of the table with his right hand out of sight.

"Vince already knows what I'm going to tell you," Ms. Patrick began. "But Mr. Carpenter wanted the three of you to have a sense of starting together."

She distributed cards that would give us access to the building twenty-four hours a day and rapidly outlined a lot of details about office procedures: names of support staff and their job duties, locations of copy machines and the codes to input when using them, Internet research policies, areas of specialty for each of the lawyers, and office schedules. Vince's fingers flew across the keyboard. Neither Julie nor I had anything to write on. Ms. Patrick didn't seem to notice.

"Will all this be included in an information packet or should I take notes?" I asked when she paused.

"You can copy my notes," Vince replied.

He slid the computer across the table. Julie and I leaned in and looked at the screen. He'd typed in almost every word on a template that made it look like a corporate flow chart.

"That works for me," Julie said.

"I don't own a laptop computer," I said, trying not to sound whiny. "Does the firm supply one?"

"Not for summer clerks," Ms. Patrick replied. "The younger lawyers bring one to meetings, but most partners don't. It's a generational difference."

I concentrated hard through the rest of the meeting. At least my memory, forged in the front room of the house in Powell Station, went with me everywhere. And it never needed rebooting.

"That's it," Ms. Patrick said in conclusion. "Any questions?"

I didn't know what to ask and kept my mouth shut. Julie spoke. "How will we circulate through the different sections of the firm?"

It was a good question, and I wished I'd thought to ask it.

"You'll find out at the luncheon. There isn't time during the summer for you to spend a lot of time with each partner. Anything else?"

"Is there a dress code?" I asked.

"This is a traditional firm with clients who expect a professional appearance at all times. We don't wear blue jeans on Friday."

"That's fine. I don't own a pair of jeans."

The other three people stared at me. I'd needlessly blurted out controversial information. I wanted to crawl under the table.

"Any other questions?" Ms. Patrick asked after an awkward pause.

I pressed my lips tightly together. The progress I'd made with Ms. Patrick after meeting with Christine Bartlett had been nullified by the events of the past few days.

"Very well," the office manager said. "Vince, you can return to your project with Mr. Braddock. Julie, Mr. Carpenter wants to meet with you in his office. Tami, wait here."

Left alone in the conference room, I had nothing to do but stare at the painting. Many of the figures on the wharf were slaves, toiling without pay in the burning heat as they loaded the heavy cotton bales onto the ships. I suspected the painter intended to portray normal life. However, normal in one era can be barbarian to the next. The slaves, a people oppressed for no reason except the color of their skin, illustrated that truth with a massive exclamation point. The painting was an indefensible snapshot of injustice. I sighed. Oppression took many forms, and often, the society of the day didn't recognize it.

Ms. Patrick returned to the conference room. I started to offer an apology but before I could start, she spoke.

"Come with me," she said from the doorway. "You're going to assist one of the paralegals this morning."

There was no denying my relegation to the bottom rank of the summer clerks. I recognized the large open work areas that were filling with people. We walked down a hall to an open door.

"Myra," Ms. Patrick began, "this is Tami Taylor."

The paralegal glanced up from a stack of papers on her desk. "Welcome, nice to see you again."

Ms. Patrick looked at me with raised eyebrows.

"Zach Mays introduced us when I came by the office on a Saturday a few weeks ago," I said.

Ms. Patrick waved her hand to the paralegal. "She's all yours until 11:30."

"Thank you," I said to Ms. Patrick's

217

departing back.

Myra reached forward and picked up a thick envelope. "I'm in the middle of a project that has to be finished before the end of the day. Do you know where the county courthouse is located?"

"Yes ma'am."

The paralegal pulled back the envelope. "Unless you think I'm old, call me Myra."

"Okay."

She handed me the heavy envelope. "This is a response to a motion for preliminary injunction that needs to be filed this morning. Mr. Carpenter has a hearing in this case tomorrow, and the other side needs twenty-four hours' notice. We have electronic filing in federal court but not in the state courts. There are two copies. Have both of them stamped at the clerk's office, then take one to Judge Cannon's office. Bring the other back here, and I'll have a courier take it to the opposing counsel's office."

"I could take it," I offered.

"It's in Brunswick. It would be cutting it close for you to drive down and back before lunch."

"Oh, I don't have a car."

Myra stopped and stared at me. Stares had always been part of my life, but a new environment inevitably provoked a rash of them. Without further comment the paralegal turned her attention to the documents on her desk, and I backed out of the room.

My earlier confidence was gone. As I walked down Montgomery Street, the hopelessness of my situation washed over me. I had no business working in Savannah. My success was as unlikely as one of the slaves in the painting making the transition from dock laborer to cotton merchant.

I reached the courthouse and climbed the steps. After passing through security, I found the clerk's office where a helpful middle-aged woman date-stamped the response to the motion. But when I tried to pick up both copies, she held on to one of them

"One of these needs to go in the file. You can serve the other," she said.

"No, I need to take it to Judge Cannon's office. There's a hearing tomorrow afternoon."

The clerk pointed to a copy machine. "Then make another copy."

I panicked. "I didn't bring my purse and don't have any money."

An image of myself hot and sweaty, running back to the office, flashed through my mind.

"Which law firm do you work for?" the

woman asked.

"Braddock, Appleby, and Carpenter."

"Use their copy code."

"I'm a summer clerk. It's my first day, and I don't have it with me."

The woman made a face that showed me I'd reached the end of her patience.

"Call and get it," she said.

"I don't have a cell phone."

The woman rubbed her hand across her forehead and through her hair. Without saying anything else, she reached under the counter and retrieved a black notebook. She flipped open the book and turned it so I could see the firm name with a number beside it.

"Thank you," I replied gratefully.

I made two copies in case I hit another unforeseen roadblock. I left the clerk's office and found Judge Cannon's chambers on the directory beside the elevator. It must have been a day for criminal court, because several of the people who joined me on the elevator looked like criminals. No one spoke, but two of the men stole sideways glances at me. I quickly stepped out when the door opened.

The judge's office had an anteroom where an older woman sat behind a scarred wooden desk. Public administration of justice didn't pay as well as the private practice of law. I identified myself and handed the envelope to the woman.

"The judge has something for you to deliver to Mr. Carpenter," the woman said in a raspy voice. "I was going to mail it, but you can deliver it in person."

"Yes ma'am. I'll be glad to."

She gave me a sealed envelope. Holding it tightly in my hand along with the service copies of the response to the motion, I retraced my steps to the law firm. It was hot, and I was doubly glad I'd not had to make an extra trip. By the time I reached the foyer of the law office, the cool air felt good on my hot face. I climbed the stairs to Myra's office. Her door was closed. I knocked.

"Come in," she said.

"Here it is," I announced. I laid the stamped copies on her desk. I held up the other envelope. "The judge's secretary gave me this to deliver to Mr. Carpenter."

"Take it downstairs to his office," she said without thanking me and resumed her work.

I didn't know where to go so I wandered the hallway looking for clues. I opened one door. An older man with a bald head and wearing glasses glanced up in obvious irritation.

"Sorry," I mumbled and quickly closed the door.

At that moment, Julie Feldman entered the hall.

"Where's Mr. Carpenter's office?" I asked in relief. "I have something to give him from a judge."

"He's on a conference call with a client, but his secretary is in there," she replied, pointing to a door next to the one I'd opened.

"What does he look like?" I asked in an anxious voice.

"Uh, he's tall with gray hair and a goatee. He reminds me of an actor whose name I can't remember. Some guy who used to be in old movies."

"Good," I said with relief. "What are you doing for him?"

Julie held up a thick file in her hand. "He gave me a research project, something about competing security interests in forklifts and other equipment at a big factory that's about to go into bankruptcy. There are claims by two banks and three companies that sold the equipment. I'm supposed to read all the documents and prepare a chart telling him which companies are secured as to each piece of property and for how much."

"That sounds interesting," I replied.

Julie gave me a strange look. "Are you kidding?" she asked.

"No."

Julie shook her head. "I'll see you at lunch. Until then, I'll have my head stuck in article nine of the uniform commercial code."

I entered the office, which was as fancy as the office at the courthouse had been plain. I introduced myself to a woman in her thirties and gave her the envelope from Judge Cannon.

"Have a seat," she said, motioning to one of two chairs in front of her desk. "Mr. Carpenter will want to meet you as soon as he finishes his conference call."

I sat down and waited. Fifteen minutes passed. The secretary ignored me. Both Julie and Vince Colbert were already busy on projects. I knew it was only the first day, but I already felt behind. Another fifteen minutes passed. In between phone calls, which she seemed to be able to handle without consulting Mr. Carpenter, the secretary's fingers flew across the keyboard. I wanted to be productive. But there was nothing to do except become intimately familiar with every detail of the room. More time passed. Finally, the secretary seemed to notice my existence again. She picked up the phone and told Mr. Carpenter that I was waiting to see him. The office door behind her opened, and a man matching Julie's description entered the room.

Mr. Carpenter had a slender build and extended his hand in a way that struck me as slightly effeminate. However, when I shook his hand, the grip was firm.

"Ms. Saylor," he said in a smooth voice.

"It's Taylor," I corrected, perhaps too abruptly.

"Sorry," he said. "Tami, right?"

"Yes sir."

We entered his office. It was about the same size as Mr. Callahan's office. Apparently, Mr. Carpenter liked boats, because the walls were covered with pictures of yachts.

"I've been on the phone with so many people this morning the names are running together."

He sat behind a large desk with a leather inlaid top and stared at me for several seconds without speaking. I shifted in my seat.

"You have a lovely office," I said.

His phone buzzed and he picked it up. "Put him through," he said after listening for a moment.

I started to get up, but he motioned for

me to remain. The call involved a domestic relations case. Mr. Carpenter represented the husband who had filed for the divorce. I picked up that the man on the other end of the line was the lawyer for the wife. The main issue had to do with division of property.

"Our answers to your discovery set valuation of the marital estate at twenty-two million and change," Mr. Carpenter said. "I think we should be able to arrive at an amicable resolution. My letter of the fifteenth is a starting point, but there is room for discussion on several items."

Mr. Carpenter listened for a long time. I watched his jaw tighten and his lips turn downward.

"Bob, I don't think you want to go there," he said. "We can divide the pie, but if you try to throw it in my face, this will get messy."

It seemed like a silly comment, but the way Mr. Carpenter said it sounded ominous. He listened again, then spoke in a steely voice.

"If that's the way you want it, we'll litigate into the next decade. Have your paralegal call Myra Dean to set up the depositions." He paused. "And tell Mrs. Folsom my previous proposal is off the table. Our next

225

offer will be less — a lot less."

He hung up the phone and looked at me.

"Welcome to Savannah," he said cheerily.

I gave him a startled look at his easy transition from threatening to friendly. "Thank you, sir. I appreciate the opportunity."

"Gerry tells me you're living with Margaret Fairmont. She's a gracious lady. Her husband was a great friend of Sam Braddock."

"Yes sir."

"And I have your résumé somewhere in here."

The lawyer leafed through a short stack of papers on the corner of his desk.

"Have you met Vince and Julie?" he asked as he continued to search.

"Yes sir."

"And you already know Zach Mays?"

"Not really. I met him a few weeks ago when I stopped by the office on a Saturday. He's been very helpful in helping me acclimate to the firm."

"Good, good. Zach is an earnest young man who isn't afraid to ask hard questions. Here it is," Mr. Carpenter announced, holding up a sheet of paper.

I watched while he skimmed the one-page summary of my life.

"That's right. You worked for Oscar Callahan. It's the reason I pulled your résumé out in the first place. Oscar gave you a glowing recommendation. If he'd stopped representing mill workers for petty injuries and crawled out of the mountains, he could have been one of the best litigators in the state."

"Yes sir," I said, not sure if agreeing with Mr. Carpenter would dishonor Mr. Callahan.

"His grandfather was a preacher, wasn't he?"

"Yes sir."

"If I recall, he was the leader of some kind of obscure religious sect that wanted to turn back the clock to the Dark Ages."

I swallowed, not sure if this was a time to defend the faith or accumulate more information.

"Is that what Mr. Callahan told you?"

"How else would I have picked up that bit of trivia?" Mr. Carpenter slapped his hands together. "Enough of that. Let's get down to business. Your summer at the firm will be a good mix of work and pleasure. I hope your experience will be intellectually stimulating. Law school prepares you to take tests, not practice law. We'll have plenty of projects that will involve research within your comfort zone, but there will also be practical opportunities to broaden your experience."

"Yes sir."

"I'm glad you had a chance to hear my side of the opening salvo in the Folsom divorce case. I don't handle many divorce cases, but our firm is deeply involved in J.K. Folsom's corporate dealings, and he doesn't want another law firm to know his business. J.K. pays our top hourly rate for representation. Using you to assist with research and deposition preparation, I can keep his bills lower."

My stomach went into a knot. I'd wanted to avoid domestic practice. Mr. Carpenter continued. "Have you taken a domestic relations course in law school?"

"No sir."

"That's not a problem. We'll see how fast you can get up to speed in an unfamiliar area. We have a couple of treatises in the law library. Read them to get a foundation and dive into the fray. Divorce work is exciting because the emotions of the parties run wild. It's key for the lawyer to keep her cool when others around her are losing theirs."

Even when talking to a summer associate, I could tell Mr. Carpenter utilized dramatic pauses.

"Sounds like Kipling," I managed, remembering a poem I'd memorized in home-school.

Mr. Carpenter nodded approvingly. "Yes, it does."

He buzzed his secretary and gave her instructions about giving me access to the file. He stood up, signaling an end to our meeting.

"I'll see you at the luncheon. Until then, the library is your home."

The secretary spoke as I passed her desk. "I'll have a packet on the Folsom case ready for you by early afternoon," she said. "In the meantime, the case number is 207642."

"Thank you," I replied without much feeling. "Where is the firm library?"

"On this floor at the west end of the building."

Not being able to see the sun in the hallway, I wasn't sure which way to turn, but I guessed the opposite end from Mr. Braddock's office. I didn't want to walk unannounced into another lawyer's office. When I cracked open a wooden door and peeked inside I saw bookshelves. Sitting at a table with papers spread out before her was Julie Feldman.

"Are you alone?" I whispered.

"Not now."

I sat down on the opposite side of the

table. Even with the advent of computer research, the firm still maintained an extensive library of books. Several computer terminals for online use were in a row along one wall.

"How's it going?"

"I'm shuffling papers and trying to understand what they say." She looked up. "I haven't taken a course in secured transactions. I know a few terms but none of the principles. I'm completely lost."

"I loved my secured transactions course. It was taught by one of the best professors at the law school, and I enjoyed figuring out the different rules. But Mr. Carpenter has assigned me to a big divorce case. I've not taken a domestic relations course, and the only thing I know about divorce is that God doesn't like it."

Julie's eyes opened wide. "That's unreal. I spent last semester doing research for one of the best divorce lawyers in Atlanta. She handles a lot of high-profile breakups and knows all the tricks of the trade. Reading her files was more interesting than most of the novels my mother keeps on the nightstand in her bedroom."

The irony of our predicament made me smile.

"Are you thinking what I'm thinking?" Julie asked.

"What? That we're both being pushed out of our comfort zones?"

"No. We should switch projects."

I shook my head. "Mr. Carpenter knows I haven't studied domestic relations. He wants to see how quickly I can learn a new area. It's part of the summer experience."

"But we could help each other."

Julie's suggestion surprised me. Law school was competitive, and a summer clerk opportunity raised the competition to a higher level because a job, not just a grade, was at stake. Even if we didn't talk about it, I'd expected jockeying for a permanent job to affect all my interaction with Julie Feldman and Vince Colbert.

"How would we do that?"

"Talk about stuff. You can help me with these documents, and I can give you pointers about the divorce case. Where is your file?"

"I won't have it until this afternoon. I'm supposed to be reading a treatise on divorce law in Georgia, but I'm not sure how many there are or which one is the best."

Julie looked at her watch. "Here's what we'll do. It will be just like my study group at school. Help me figure out what I'm supposed to do for an hour and a half. Then,

I'll take you through a domestic relations treatise for an hour. I know which one to use. After lunch, we'll spend time identifying your specific issues. And we'll end the day in the guts of article nine of the uniform commercial code."

I felt a weight lift from my shoulders.

"Okay."

I took my chair around to Julie's side of the table. The next hour and a half flew by as I organized the documents, located the key language in each one, and showed Julie the important dates.

"Which company are we representing?" I asked when we took a break. "I've been treating this like an exam question to unravel, not a case to win."

"This one." Julie pointed to a stack of documents. "I didn't want to influence your opinion by letting you know in advance. Later, we can try to figure out how to make our case stronger."

"You're going to be a great lawyer. You have something law school can't teach."

"What's that?"

"Wisdom."

Julie rolled her eyes. "Whatever. I'll get the divorce book. Do we represent the husband or the wife?"

"Does it matter?"

"Not as much as it used to. Unless there are little kids, it's all about the money."

Julie went to the shelves and returned with a dark green volume. "You remind me of a rabbi," she said as she sat down.

"Why?"

"You think about stuff that rabbis care about. Clothes, what God thinks about divorce, wisdom, ethics."

"What do you care about?"

Julie looked at me and laughed. "See what I mean? That's a rabbi question if I ever heard one. You can't turn it off, can you?"

"No," I admitted with a small smile.

"That's okay. You're not going to offend me. My cousins in New York are ultraorthodox. They're always telling me what to do and think." Julie opened the treatise. "Do you know the divorce rate among Christians?"

"A few years ago, it was about thirty percent, the same as everyone else. But that doesn't mean all —"

"I think it's higher, now," Julie interrupted. "Closer to forty percent. Guess what the divorce rate is for ultraorthodox Jews?"

"I don't know."

"About three percent. Tell me, whose belief system is working? Of course, I'm not orthodox and don't want to be, so I won't have the benefit of those statistics." She opened the book and flipped over a few pages. "Let's see. Here's where we should start."

Julie launched into an efficient explanation of the divorce laws in Georgia. I didn't like the subject matter, but it was much easier receiving it spoon-fed by a friendly face than groping along under the sharp questioning of a polemic professor. An hour later, the door opened. It was Vince Colbert, his laptop in his hand.

"Mr. Braddock sent me. It's time for the luncheon."

12

Julie chatted with Vince while we walked down the hall. I lagged behind. Her lack of antagonism to my beliefs was nice, but her casual attitude threw me off balance, as if she could trivialize the truth by rejecting it in a friendly way.

"Vince is our designated driver," she called over her shoulder. "He knows where to go."

Several lawyers were leaving the building at the same time. Introductions were made as we passed through the reception area and out to the parking lot. The bald lawyer I'd disturbed when I opened his door grunted when I offered an apology and returned to a conversation with one of his colleagues. Joe Carpenter wasn't in the initial group. Zach Mays was also missing. We reached Vince's car, a new BMW.

"Sit up front," Julie told me. "Your legs are longer than mine."

Vince looked at me as if evaluating the length of my legs. I blushed before opening the door and sliding into the passenger seat.

"Did you play sports in high school or college?" Julie asked me as soon as we were settled.

"Basketball in high school. Intramurals since."

"I played soccer in high school," she replied. "My father claims I'd have gone to Harvard or Yale if I'd not headed so many balls. What's Yale like?"

Vince backed out of the parking lot. "It's a law school. There are a lot of smart people."

Vince rested his hand on top of the steering wheel. The scar on the back of his hand was very visible. It made me wonder what would happen if it was unprotected against the sun.

"Did you play sports in high school?" I asked him.

"No."

"Are you going to take notes during lunch?" Julie asked.

"Yes."

"I wish you would transfer to Emory and join my study group," Julie said. "We need someone like you. But that would be a big comedown from Yale."

If I hadn't spent the morning with Julie, I would have considered it a sarcastic comment.

"She's serious," I added. "Julie would love having you in her study group. We accomplished a lot more this morning by working together."

"I'm not in a study group," Vince replied. He glanced at me. "Are you in a study group?"

"No, I'm a loner."

"Me too," he said.

I turned and saw Julie roll her eyes. The look caught me off guard and made me giggle. I put my hand over my mouth to suppress an outburst. Vince glanced sideways at me. The car swerved slightly.

"Are you okay?"

"Yes. Julie is trying to make me laugh."

"There are rabbis who laugh," she responded. "It's kosher."

Vince didn't say anything and stared straight ahead. I suspected he wanted to get out of the car and away from two crazy, immature women as soon as possible.

We turned into the parking lot of a plain-looking building on the outskirts of the historic district. A small sign beside the door identified it as "The Smith House — Private Parties Only." Gerry Patrick was standing beside the door.

"Have you been here before?" Julie asked Vince.

"For the rehearsal dinner before my sister's wedding," he said. "She was married in Savannah."

We got out of the car. One of the lawyers came over to Vince, and the two left us. Julie put her hand on my arm and stopped me.

"You'd better keep that laugh under control and out of sight," she said in a soft voice. "It may be kosher, but it's also unprofessional. I thought Vince might drive onto the curb and mess up the alignment on his car."

"It's your fault. Making fun of me because I'm a loner."

"Don't you think I know what it's like to be alone? I went to a college that didn't have enough Jewish students to fill a table for eight. I almost assimilated."

"What's that?"

Julie started walking toward the door. "Lost my distinctiveness in an effort to blend in."

"That's one type of pressure I understand."

Ms. Patrick greeted us. "How was your morning?"

Julie briefly told about our working together. I could tell Ms. Patrick was surprised.

"That's good," she said, looking at me. "Being part of a team is a good idea, especially on big projects. Go inside. Your places at the table are marked."

The inside of the building was dark, and it took my eyes a second to adjust to the change in light. The interior had the look and smell of tradition. The walls were paneled in dark wood and decorated with old English hunting scenes. There was a coat and hat room to the right of the front door and a bar area to the left. An older lawyer with an ample waistline, wispy white hair, and blue eyes was talking to Vince, but when we entered, he came up to us.

"Sam Braddock," he said, extending his hand.

Mr. Braddock began asking questions that made it clear he'd never seen our résumés. While Julie was summarizing her educational background, the door opened and Zach Mays came in, accompanied by a tall man who looked about the same age as Mr. Braddock but with ramrod-straight posture and assertive eyes. It was Nelson Appleby, the admiralty lawyer. When he shook my hand, I was surprised to notice that the veins on his stood out like those of a patient in a nursing home. His voice, however, was steady.

"Ms. Taylor, I think we're sitting next to each other at lunch," he said.

We moved into a large room with a table set up in the shape of a T. At the end of each table was a place for one of the named partners. Everyone stood around and talked for a few minutes until Mr. Carpenter arrived. A younger associate who looked frazzled came in with him.

My seat was to the left of Mr. Appleby with Zach Mays across the table from me. To my left was Barry Conrad, the lawyer I'd met when I first visited the firm. I started to ask him about his golf game, but he immediately began talking to the lawyer on his left. I heard the sound of a glass being tapped with a spoon and turned in my chair. It was Mr. Carpenter.

"Welcome to the firm luncheon in honor of our summer law clerks, Vince Colbert, Julie Feldman, and Tami Taylor. Before we begin the meal, I'd like each of them to tell us why they decided to spend the summer at our firm and an interesting or unusual fact about themselves. Tami, please go first."

I'd not known an introductory speech was part of the program. Going first made it worse. My stomach suddenly felt queasy and my mouth went dry. I took a quick sip of water and stood up. Everyone was looking at me. I licked my lips. Julie, who was sitting beside Mr. Carpenter, gave the same eye roll she'd delivered in the car.

"It's an honor working here this summer," I began. "I'm here because Mr. Carpenter sent me a letter offering me a job."

There was a smattering of laughter.

"And after praying about it and discussing the job with my parents, I decided to accept it."

The smiles were replaced by a few puzzled expressions.

"I look forward to working with as many of you as possible. I want to learn, and I'm willing to work hard." I paused and glanced at Zach. "There are many unusual facts about my life, but one that I share with Zach Mays is a homeschool education. Thank you."

I sat down. No one clapped or said anything. Vince was next. He was from Charleston and mentioned his family's longtime personal connection to Mr. Appleby as the reason for his interest in working for the firm. As an interesting fact, he described his Eagle Scout service project, in which he created a training program to teach and implement household safety in lower-income areas and a database of needy families to receive help. The program was adopted in Charleston County as part of a United Way initiative. There was polite applause when he finished.

Julie stood up. "I'm here because Savannah has always been my favorite city on the coast." She hesitated and then spoke with feeling. "I wouldn't trade two Charlestons and three Wilmingtons for one Savannah."

Several lawyers pounded the table in agreement.

"I'm as excited about being here as I was spending two months last summer sailing across the Caribbean with my father. We visited over a dozen ports including the Caymans and the Virgin Islands. I didn't think about law for eight weeks and spent most of my time working on my tan."

"You can come on my boat!" one of the younger lawyers called out.

"Mine's newer and bigger!" another lawyer countered.

"And you're married," Mr. Carpenter said, pointing to the second lawyer. "Thank you, clerks. Enjoy lunch."

I looked across the table at Zach. He avoided my eyes.

"What's this about a homeschool?" Mr.

Appleby asked the young associate. "You never mentioned that before."

"Who taught it? Your mother?" Conrad added.

Zach looked at Conrad with a steely expression. "Yes. All the way through high school. She was an excellent teacher."

Having caused this problem, I wasn't going to abandon Zach and sit on the sidelines.

"The tutorial system was the preferred method for educating European royalty for hundreds of years," I said. "And several modern studies have proven it works well today, even if the parents aren't college educated."

Mr. Appleby spoke. "My brother and I had a private tutor when our family lived in Nigeria. My mother taught grammar and literature; the tutor handled math and science. I've always thought those were the best years of my education. I was way ahead of my peers when we moved back to Baltimore."

I saw Conrad turn in his chair and begin talking to the person next to him.

"Tell me more about your educational background," Mr. Appleby said to me.

I started to give a two-sentence answer, then remembered Zach's advice about taking the opportunity to talk when asked a

243

question by one of the partners.

"I'd be glad to."

It was an easy subject. I'd defended home-schooling against all comers for years. Mr. Appleby asked several insightful questions, and I talked steadily through the salad course up to arrival of our entrée, a seafood dish as rich as anything I'd ever eaten. Once, I looked at Zach and silently offered to pass the ball to him, but he gave a slight shake of his head. This was my chance to impress Mr. Appleby. So, I continued talking.

"And do you believe this type of education makes you a better law student?" Mr. Appleby asked.

"Yes sir. I didn't wait until law school to learn how to analyze an issue and evaluate possible solutions."

Mr. Appleby turned his attention to Zach, and they began to discuss a case involving a Norwegian shipping company. I couldn't follow the unfamiliar admiralty terms. Learning the law of Georgia was challenging enough; the prospect of applying U.S., Norwegian, and international law to a legal problem was overwhelming. As a waiter took away our plates, Mr. Appleby looked at his watch.

"It will be too late to call Oslo when we

get back to the office," he said. "Send Bergen an e-mail outlining our position so he can read it in the morning. If he wants to continue to do business with our client in the port of Savannah, there will have to be concessions on the container surcharge and agreement on the arbitration language."

Dessert was a custard dish that dissolved on my tongue and sent shivers down my spine. I wanted to ask for the recipe so I could make it for my family, but I didn't want to draw attention to myself. Julie didn't seem to have that problem. I could hear her laughing loudly at the other end of the table.

Mr. Carpenter stood and tapped his glass again. The room became quiet.

"I hope you've enjoyed this luncheon. Every time we do this, it makes me wish we spent more time together as a firm."

I heard Conrad clear his throat. Mr. Carpenter continued.

"We don't have any prizes to give away, but there is a drawing of sorts for our summer clerks."

I sat up straighter.

"Judge Cannon has agreed to allow our summer clerks to handle minor misdemeanor cases under appropriate supervision. These are pro bono matters. The clerks won't be providing as important a contribution to the community as Vince did with his Eagle Scout project, but every citizen of the land deserves legal representation. Ms. Taylor picked up an order authorizing this work at the courthouse this morning. The judge is authorizing the firm to delegate the cases; however, I think it would be appropriate for the clerks to have a hand in the selection process."

He paused. I suspected his last comment was meant to be a play on words, but no one laughed. He held up three folders.

"Each of these folders contains a brief description of a case and an order from Judge Cannon specially authorizing you to make an appearance on behalf of the defendant."

One of the younger lawyers called out, "When I was a summer clerk I had to represent a man caught playing video poker!"

Mr. Carpenter spoke. "And as I recall you gambled with his future, and he spent ninety days in jail."

"Bob lost a hundred dollars playing the machines while investigating that case," another lawyer said.

"If our clerks will step forward," Mr.

Carpenter said, "I'll let them choose their fate."

Julie stood beside Mr. Carpenter. Vince and I joined her. Mr. Carpenter held out the three folders.

"Ms. Feldman," he said.

Julie chose the one in the middle and opened it.

"State v. Ferguson," she said. "I think he's charged with impersonating a public official — a water-meter reader."

"Say that fast three times in front of the judge," one of the lawyers said.

"Why would someone do that?" Julie asked Mr. Carpenter.

"Allegedly," Mr. Carpenter corrected. "Meet with your client and investigate the facts; then we'll talk about a theory of the case." The senior partner pointed to the lawyer named Ned. "Mr. Danforth, I want you to supervise Ms. Feldman's efforts on behalf of the defendant."

"Can we do it on my boat?" the lawyer asked.

"Not without appropriate adult supervision," another lawyer responded.

The flirting banter in the room made me uncomfortable. I glanced at Julie, who didn't seem upset by the innuendos. Mr. Carpenter turned to Vince.

"Your turn."

Vince selected the file on the left and opened it.

"State v. Brown," he said. "Operation of a motor vehicle at excessive speed while racing and improper muffler."

"A racer!" one of the lawyers called out. "Where was he arrested?"

"At 10746 Abercorn Street."

"That's near the new mall," the lawyer replied. "He and his buddies were probably dragging between stoplights."

Mr. Carpenter spoke. "Russell, since you're such an expert on street racing in Chatham County, I want you to work with Vince."

"Do I get to drive his BMW?" the lawyer asked.

"Only with proper adult supervision," Mr. Carpenter replied.

Several people laughed. Mr. Carpenter looked at me.

"That leaves you, Ms. Taylor."

"Without a choice or a chance!" one lawyer called out.

I took the file from the managing partner and opened it. There were multiple sheets of paper filled with charges. The number of counts was overwhelming. At first, I suspected that I'd gotten some kind of serial criminal by mistake. But as I read the charges, I realized each count was identical except as to location of the offense.

"*State v. Jones,*" I said, quickly turning the pages until I reached the final one. "Twenty-four counts of trespassing. Mr. Jones illegally tied up his boat for the night at twenty-four private docks."

"Allegedly," Mr. Carpenter said. "Not necessarily illegally."

"Yes sir," I replied, although it seemed hard to imagine twenty-four instances of honest mistake or sudden emergency.

"Who would be a suitable mentor?" Mr. Carpenter asked as he looked around the room. No one raised his hand. I glanced at Zach, whose eyes were lowered like a schoolboy trying to avoid the teacher's gaze.

"Sounds like a first cousin to an admiralty case," Mr. Carpenter said. "A lower-level type of piracy on the high seas. Mr. Mays, I want you to help Ms. Taylor."

Zach raised his head, and I studied his reaction. He had a fixed expression that appeared to be a cross between a forced smile and a grimace. I returned to my seat. General conversation resumed in the room.

"Thanks for helping," I said to Zach.

"I'm a man under authority," he replied.

Mr. Appleby left the table. I leaned forward. "Are you upset with me for mentioning your homeschool background?" I asked in a whisper. "I didn't mean to embarrass you."

Zach shook his head. "No, there's just a lot of pressure with my workload. I didn't need another project on my desk."

"I'm sorry. I won't ask for much help."

I left the table and went to the restroom. No one else was there. I stood in front of the mirror. Challenges surfaced by the minute at the law firm. I wasn't convinced that I hadn't embarrassed Zach Mays. I washed my hands and lightly touched a wet paper towel to my cheeks and forehead.

When I returned to the dining room, everyone was getting ready to leave. Zach and Mr. Appleby were near the door. I started to go to them, but heard Julie call my name.

"Tami!"

I turned around as she came up to me.

"Your case sounds like a lot of work," she said. "Do you think you'll have to interview the owners of every dock where your client tied up his boat?"

"I haven't thought about it," I replied.

"I'd subpoena every one of them," Julie said. "Rich folks don't want to show up in court, and if they don't testify it will knock out a count."

I held up the folder in my hand. "I suspect at least a few of these people would make an appearance, and the punishment for two counts probably wouldn't be much different than for twenty-four."

"But you may be able to wear down the prosecutor and get your client a good deal."

I wasn't interested in a strategy session, but when I looked back to the door Mr. Appleby and Zach were gone.

"Ned says we may raise a Halloween defense for my client," Julie continued. "We could claim he was delusional and believed every day is Halloween. The water-meter outfit was his costume of the day."

"You haven't talked to the client yet."

Julie laughed. "I'm kidding. I wouldn't ask him to lie, but Ned has a great sense of humor. This firm isn't nearly as stuffy as I thought it would be."

Several more lawyers came over and introduced themselves. Julie received most of the attention.

"Is there a firm directory?" Julie asked as the crowd thinned. "I won't be able to remember everyone's name."

Vince patted his laptop. "I have that information in a file."

Julie put her arm in his. "We've only been

251

here half a day, and already I don't know what I'd do without you."

Ms. Patrick joined us. "That went nicely," she said. "I'm glad you were all able to be here."

"Yes ma'am," I replied.

On the return trip to the office, Julie talked nonstop from the backseat while Vince and I sat in silence. She repeated several stories told by the lawyers at her table.

"Did you hear anything interesting?" she asked as we pulled into the firm parking lot.

"Just a few comments from Mr. Braddock about the project I'm working on," Vince said. "Nothing that would interest you."

"Tami?" Julie asked.

"Mr. Appleby wanted to talk about home-school education," I said as Vince parked the car.

"Yeah, it took courage to mention that," Julie said. "It was way outside the box. What was his reaction?"

"Positive. His family had a private tutor when he lived in Africa as a boy."

"Cool."

Julie got out of the car and walked rapidly toward the office. Vince lagged behind, and out of courtesy I stayed with him.

"Did you have offers from other law

firms?" he asked as we walked across the parking lot.

"No, I was surprised when I got the letter from Mr. Carpenter."

"What were you going to do?"

"Work as an eviscerator in a chicken plant."

"Cutting open the chickens?"

"Yes. How did you know?"

"The Latin root of the word."

I laughed. "Do you type in Latin?"

Vince smiled slightly. "No, but I'd like to learn more about homeschooling from someone who went through it and became academically successful."

"Why?"

We reached the front of the office. He opened the door for me.

"I like to learn, especially from a person with strong convictions. Maybe we could go to lunch?"

"I'm sure they will have other events on the schedule."

We reached the hallway. Vince turned toward Mr. Braddock's office suite.

"Thanks for the ride," I said.

"You're welcome."

I stopped by Mr. Carpenter's office. His secretary had made copies of the documents in the Folsom divorce file. Even at this early stage of the proceedings, it was thick enough to require a large, expandable folder. Carrying it with both hands, I returned to the library. Julie glanced up when I entered.

"Did Vince ask you out?" she asked.

13

I gave her a startled look.

"Don't act so innocent," she responded. "Anyone with half a brain could tell he was interested in you."

"How?"

"Did he ask you out?" she repeated.

"He mentioned lunch, but I didn't commit."

"Yeah." Julie nodded with satisfaction. "He's nerdy but nice, and tall enough for you. The chemistry is explosive when two loners get together. I wondered about the scar on his hand. Do you think his whole body is scarred? Usually something like that is the result of a childhood burn. It may explain why he didn't play any sports."

"I'll let you ask him personal questions."

"Oh, he'll tell you when he's ready. Guys like him are waiting for a sympathetic ear to pour out their innermost thoughts and feelings."

"How can you be so sure?"

Julie sniffed. "My family spends a lot of time psychoanalyzing our relatives and friends. All the best psychiatrists are Jewish. It's part of our cultural DNA. Some study Freud and get a fancy diploma and charge hundreds of dollars an hour for what the rest of us do for free."

"Then why aren't you in medical school?"

"Organic chemistry, and I'm more of a talker than a listener. At least once a week, I want you to tell me to shut up."

"I don't tell people to shut up."

"You will if you want to help me become a better person. Plus, I'm bound to get on your nerves. We'll both need to regularly vent and clear the air." Julie pointed at the folder in my hand. "That looks heavy. Drop it on the table and let's see what's going on in the dirty corners of the Folsom household."

We spent the rest of the afternoon dividing our time between Julie's project and mine. The selfishness and sin that had brought the Folsom family to the place of breakup was depressing. I focused on the financial data. Julie read the file like it was a cheap romance novel.

"I can't believe what he did to her ownership in this company," I said as I reviewed the minutes from a corporate meeting. "He bought back her shares at a fraction of their fair market value."

"Shares that he gave her in the first place," Julie responded. "Folsom transferred the stock to his wife so she could put it up for collateral against a construction loan for the North Carolina mountain house titled in her name. Then, he let his mother-in-law stay in the house every summer for five years. Mr. Folsom is a prince who should be protected from his gold-digging wife."

A few minutes later I handed Julie a memo attached to a financial statement. "A wicked prince with a harem. He's paying five thousand dollars a month in child support for a little boy his wife doesn't know about."

Julie read the memo. "What a jerk! I guess it's better than dodging his responsibilities, but I'm not sure how Mr. Carpenter intends to camouflage those payments. The accountant labeled it 'Miscellaneous Benevolence,' but that won't get Folsom through a deposition."

Mid-afternoon we switched to Julie's project. After an hour of online research, I helped her draft a memo about the competing parties' interests in the collateral. I located a Georgia Court of Appeals decision that really helped our position. No one else came into the library. Late in the day, Julie stood up and stretched.

"This is a good place to take a nap."

"Shut up and get back to work," I said from my place at the worktable.

Julie looked surprised.

"I wanted to get it out of the way," I said with a smile. "It's been hanging over me all afternoon."

Julie shook her finger at me. "That's not the way it works. It has to be said with feeling in the right context. I won't cater to your Protestant guilt trip."

"I've never told anyone to shut up in my life."

"There's a lot you've probably never done. This summer is going to be a space trip into the unknown."

I sat back in my chair. "Can I ask you something serious?"

"Yes, but only because you found the Paxton case."

I waited. Julie sat down across from me.

"Okay," she said. "I'm listening."

I put my hands against the edge of the table. "People are always trying to pressure me to do things that violate my Christian beliefs. When that happens it creates stress and awkwardness. Problems build my character, but I'd like to be able to relax around you and not have to defend myself all the time. Would you let me be who I am without trying to change me?"

Julie was silent for a moment. "Would you let me be who I am without trying to change me?"

I was caught. It was my privilege and duty to tell Julie about Jesus. My inner conflict couldn't be hidden from my face. Julie continued.

"Several Christians have tried to prove to me that Jesus is the Messiah and get me to pray to him. But it never made much sense to me. Jews don't try to convince everyone to agree with them. We rarely agree ourselves. It's the way life is lived, not the words spoken, that is important."

"That last part is the truth," I said.

"Okay. Do we have a deal? Neither of us tries to change the other."

I thought about my parents and what they would say. "No. I can't do that."

Julie stared at me for a second, then reached across the table and patted my hand. "Good. We'll have more fun if nothing is off-limits. I'll try to corrupt you, and you can try to convert me."

Ms. Patrick came into the library. "Mr. Carpenter left the office for a meeting earlier this afternoon and asked me to check on you at the end of the day."

Julie told her what we'd done, giving me extensive credit for helping her.

"That's good," Ms. Patrick replied. "I told Mr. Carpenter you were working together, and he gave his permission. However, the lawyers will also want to see how you handle assignments on your own." She looked at her watch. "You can leave anytime after five o'clock. It's five thirty now, so be on your way."

"Can we leave our work in here?" I asked.

"Yes. We're in the process of creating a cubicle space for both of you on the second floor if you want it, but this is a better research environment."

Ms. Patrick left. Julie and I put everything back in our files. It seemed like I'd been at the firm a week, not a day.

"Do you want to grab a beer?" Julie asked when we finished. "There are several nice pubs along the river. I'll buy the first round."

"No, thanks," I replied nonchalantly.

"That would have been a good place to say shut up," Julie responded. "You'll catch on."

We reached the reception area. Julie headed toward the door. I hesitated at the base of the stairs. Julie turned around.

"Aren't you leaving?"

"In a minute. I need to talk to Zach Mays about my criminal case."

"It can wait."

I glanced up the stairs, then followed Julie out the door. It was sticky hot.

"Can I give you a ride?" Julie asked. "Not to get you drunk along the river, but to the house where you're staying."

I didn't relish a hot walk in my business clothes. "Thanks."

Julie drove a new compact car. She had a yellow plastic flower taped to her dashboard. A scent wafted from it.

"It's an air freshener," Julie said when I reached out and touched it.

"Reminds me of the mountains."

"Your new boyfriend is still working," Julie said as we passed Vince's car. "If the firm is only going to hire one new associate, you and I should probably consider this a summer vacation. Vince is a lock."

"That's a lot more likely than the boyfriend part."

"How many serious boyfriends have you had?" Julie asked as she turned onto Montgomery Street.

"Less than you."

That's all it took. During the short ride to Mrs. Fairmont's house, Julie told me more than I'd wanted to hear about her love life. She'd even been engaged for two months when she was a senior in college.

"But I caught him with one of my sorority sisters when he thought I was out of town for the weekend. That's when I decided to go to law school."

"Here it is," I said, pointing to the curb.

"Cool," Julie said, peering through the windshield. "I'm in a garage apartment. You're in the mansion."

"My apartment is in the basement," I said. "But it's very nice."

Julie stopped the car. "Call me if you change your mind about grabbing a beer."

I got out without responding and walked up the brick steps. I could hear Flip barking inside. Unlocking the door, I stepped into the foyer.

"Mrs. Fairmont. It's Tami! I'm home."

Saying the word *home* touched me in a soft place. This place wasn't home, but the English language didn't provide an alternative that fit. There was no response from Mrs. Fairmont. I checked both parlors then walked down the hall, past the kitchen, and to the den. The elderly woman was sitting in her chair, her eyes closed.

"Mrs. Fairmont," I repeated.

She stirred in her chair and slowly opened

her eyes. She appeared disoriented.

"I'm Tami Taylor," I said. "I'm living in the basement apartment."

"I know that," Mrs. Fairmont replied, touching a tissue to her nose. "And you just finished your first day as a summer law clerk working for Sam Braddock's firm. Gracie has fixed a nice supper for us, and while we eat, I want you to tell me all about it."

There was a small pot roast with carrots and potatoes in the oven. It was still warm. A simple tossed salad was in a metal bowl in the refrigerator. I took out the food and fixed two plates while Mrs. Fairmont set the table in the dining room.

"What kind of dressing do you want on your salad?" I called out.

"French," she responded.

I carried the food into the dining room. Mrs. Fairmont was already sitting in her seat with Flip on the floor beside her.

"What would you like to drink?" I asked reluctantly.

"Water with lemon would be nice."

I brought two waters and joined her at the table.

"This has been a good day," she said. "After Gracie finished straightening up the house, we spent the afternoon organizing some of my papers and memorabilia. Christine may throw everything away when I die, but at least she'll know what she has. But all the work made me so tired that I fell asleep and didn't hear you come in."

"I didn't want to startle you."

"Don't worry about it. Let's eat."

"Could we pray first?" I asked.

Mrs. Fairmont returned her fork to its place. "Go ahead."

I prayed a simple prayer of thanks for what we'd been able to accomplish and a blessing on Gracie for fixing our supper. The pot roast was fork tender and very juicy.

"Gracie was in a singing mood," Mrs. Fairmont said as she nibbled a piece of carrot.

"What kind of songs?"

"Anything you want to hear. She knows show tunes from way before you were born, songs from her church, the blues. I accuse her of making up her own songs, but she won't admit it. Flip follows her around the house when she's singing. He doesn't want to miss a note."

The normalcy of Mrs. Fairmont's thoughts and speech made me want to squeeze in as much conversation as possible. She had other ideas.

"But my life is dull and almost over. I want to hear about your day."

She listened attentively. When I mentioned the luncheon at the Smith House, she interrupted me.

"My husband owned that building years ago and rented it to a printing company. The printing company moved to a bigger location, and Harry sold it to the people who redid the interior. The last time I was there was for a wedding reception."

"Was it for the Colbert family? Vince Colbert is one of the other summer clerks. He's from Charleston, but his sister had a reception at the place where we ate lunch."

"Do you know who married his sister?"

"No ma'am."

While I talked, Mrs. Fairmont ate a good supper. I nibbled in between sentences and ate faster when she left the table for a few minutes. We carried our plates into the kitchen.

"You'll have to invite Julie over for supper," she said. "Let me know, and I'll ask Gracie to do something special. She cooks a very nice pork loin topped with a cranberry sauce."

"That might not be the best choice. Julie is Jewish, but I'm not sure she follows any dietary laws."

Mrs. Fairmont raised her eyebrows. "Gracie doesn't know much about kosher cooking."

I fixed Mrs. Fairmont a cup of decaf coffee.

"Let's sit in the blue parlor," she said. "I promise not to spill a drop."

It was pleasant in the peace of the parlor. More than any other time since my arrival in Savannah, it reminded me of Powell Station. Mrs. Fairmont sat in a chair contentedly looking at interior decorating and antique magazines. From time to time, she would mark a page with a Post-It note. I curled up in a corner of the sofa and read my book about the Puritans. Flip hopped onto the sofa and let me scratch his neck.

"I'd like to call my parents before it gets late," I said after time had passed.

"Go ahead."

I used the phone in the kitchen. Mama answered then let me talk to the twins before they got ready for bed. After I finished with them, Mama held the phone so she and Daddy could both listen while I told them about my day. They were very interested in the conversation with Mr. Appleby about the merits of a tutorial education and Zach Mays' homeschool background. I felt a twinge of guilt in revealing Zach's history as new information. I didn't give details about my work projects, focusing on the people instead. As I talked, I realized the anxiety I'd felt in the morning when I arrived at the office had subsided. It was a new world, but at least I'd established a beachhead.

"It sounds like you're off to a good start," Daddy said. "Take it each day at a time."

"Yes sir."

"Can you tell us more about the cases you're working on?" Mama asked.

"No ma'am. The confidentiality rules are strict. But as a clerk I won't have much contact with clients. I think most of the day will be spent doing research and getting to know the lawyers in the firm."

"Don't compromise your convictions," Daddy said.

"Yes sir."

"And we'll be praying for the Jewish girl," Mama added. "They're the vine; we're the branch."

"Yes ma'am. I'm going to read Romans 9–11 before I go to sleep."

I hung up the phone and returned to the parlor. Mrs. Fairmont was still sitting in her chair, but her head was tilted forward, her eyes half-closed. She yawned when I entered.

"I'm not much of a hostess," she said. "Especially for a young woman like you."

"No, this has been a great evening, just what I needed after all the pressure of my first day at work. I'm ready to go downstairs and read. But we should test the intercom connection between the basement and your room."

"I don't think I'll ever use it."

Mrs. Fairmont stood up and told Flip to go outside.

"Can we check it anyway?" I asked.

"Suit yourself."

I followed Mrs. Fairmont as she slowly climbed the stairs. Flip rejoined us and scampered past.

"He seems happy that it's bedtime," I said.

"He's always happy. That's one reason I'm glad he's with me."

We entered the bedroom. A sudden urge to hug the older woman came over me. I leaned over and gave her a quick embrace. She remained stiff.

The intercom was on a bureau covered with personal items expected of an elderly woman like Mrs. Fairmont, who was meticulous about her appearance. On the corner of the bureau was the intercom unit. I found an outlet, plugged it in, and set it to "A."

"I'll run downstairs and call you," I said.

I went to the basement and checked the

white box beside my bed. I set it on the same channel and pressed the Call button. I heard it beep, but there wasn't any answer. I pressed the Talk button and spoke.

"Mrs. Fairmont, press the Talk button and say something if you can hear me."

I heard Flip barking.

"I'm here," she said.

"Now press the Call button," I said.

I waited a second, then heard the double beep signaling a call. I pressed the Talk button. "Hello."

"Hello," Mrs. Fairmont responded.

"We're connected." I hesitated a moment. "Could I say a good-night prayer? My family does it every night when I'm at home."

There was a scratchy silence, and I wondered if I'd gone too far too fast.

"Are you praying?" Mrs. Fairmont said. "I can't hear you."

"No ma'am. If it's okay, I'll start now."

I said a simple prayer of thanksgiving and blessing.

"Good night," I said when I finished.

There was no response. The static of the intercom continued for a few seconds, then stopped.

I put on my pajamas, read Romans, and prayed. It had been a long time since my prayer list had grown so much in a single day. When I laid my head on the pillow the creaks and pops of the old house didn't disturb my sleep.

14

I loved routine, and my early morning run provided a comfortable beginning point for the day. Savannah's historic district offered many interesting places to see, and I didn't want to settle into the same route. So, I included a longer loop along the river before climbing a set of ancient uneven steps to the plateau on which the city was built. I ran down Bay Street to Bull Street and turned into the heart of the town's old section. I went around some unfamiliar squares before winding my way back to Mrs. Fairmont's house.

Flip greeted me inside the door, but Mrs. Fairmont didn't make an appearance before I left for the office. I brewed coffee and left her a good morning note. My route to the office wouldn't vary. Shortest was best. I wore a casual khaki skirt, a blue blouse, and white sandals. The sandals were much more comfortable than the low heels I'd worn the previous day. I passed the same people walking their dogs and arrived at the office a few minutes before 8:00 a.m. The door was locked, and I slid my card to open it.

I went to the library, but Julie wasn't there. I picked up the folder for *State v. Jones*. The door opened. I glanced up, expecting Julie, but it was Vince Colbert.

"Good morning," he said. "Ready for another day?"

"Yes."

He handed me several sheets of paper. "My notes from the meeting with Gerry Patrick and a pictorial directory of the firm I put together from the website."

He'd cut and pasted every partner and associate's picture along with a brief personal summary and description of practice areas.

"Thanks, this is great. Do you have a copy for Julie?"

"I only did it for you, but I'll run another for Julie. Where is she?"

"Not here yet."

Vince glanced down at the floor. "Do you have lunch plans?"

It wasn't even 8:15 a.m.

"No, but don't you think we should be flexible in case one of the lawyers asks us out?"

"I'm flexible," he said, looking up. "Just

let me know if you can't make it. I'll be working on a project for Mr. Appleby in the main conference room."

"Okay."

Vince left, and I went upstairs. The clerical staff was milling around, and I saw more coffee mugs than computer screens switched on. The door to Zach's office was closed. I knocked.

"Come in," a voice answered.

Zach, his tie loosened around his neck, was facing his computer. He was wearing the same clothes from the previous day.

"Have you been here all night?" I asked in surprise.

He stretched and rubbed his eyes. Strands of light brown hair had escaped from his ponytail. His eyes looked tired.

"Yeah. Sit down. I had to catch the Norwegians first thing Oslo time. One of their ships was scheduled to leave Gdansk in a few hours bound for New York or here. We just wrapped up a deal memo a few minutes ago to keep the business."

"Did Mr. Appleby stay up too?"

Zach smiled. "No, he talked to our client yesterday afternoon and gave me the guidelines I had to work within. The rest was left up to me."

It was a lot of responsibility. I looked at

the young associate with new respect.

"Are you going home now?" I asked.

"For a few hours. Then I'll come back and draft the long form agreement. The deal memo is solid, but I'll feel better when everything is tied up."

"Did they agree to the right kind of arbitration clause?"

"You remembered. Yeah, any disagreements will be resolved through a dispute resolution firm of maritime experts based in London."

I started to leave.

"No, wait," he said. "Why did you come to see me?"

"I won't bother you. I wanted to talk to you about the case assigned to me yesterday at the luncheon, but it can wait."

"Let me see the file," he said.

I handed it to him. He read the charges.

"Moses Jones," he said. "Drawn out of the water by the local police and thrown in the pharaoh's prison. How many counts of trespassing?"

"Twenty-four."

Zach handed the file back to me.

"Should I file a motion for bond?" I asked.

"No, go to the jail and talk to Mr. Jones. They usually set bond in cases like this when the person is arrested. Advise him not to give a statement to the police." Zach yawned. "I could give more help if he'd been abducted from a Portuguese freighter in the Malaysian Straits. We have a firm that knows the exact amount of ransom to offer. I just don't have time to do much with you until I catch a break in my caseload. Until then, you're on your own."

I left Zach's office hurt and confused. When I returned to the library, Vince was giving Julie her copy of the materials he'd prepared for me. Julie was wearing black slacks and a tight-fitting top. She smiled when I entered.

"You should have gone with me last night," she said. "There was a great blues band at one of the clubs along the river."

She turned to Vince. "Vinny, does blues music make you happy or sad? I think it can go either way. For me, hearing about someone else's problems puts my own in perspective. But it makes one of my friends sadder."

Vince glanced down at his laptop and didn't answer.

"Isn't it the same with Southern gospel music?" Julie asked me. "You know, lyrics describing life as a peach pit until Jesus spits it out so that it can grow into a tree that reaches to heaven."

I wanted to tell Julie to shut up, but before I spoke, I saw a spark in her eyes that let me know she was baiting me.

"That's the worst idea for a song I've ever heard," I responded. "And you're confusing the Gospel of Matthew with 'Jack and the Beanstalk.' I'm not a big fan of Southern gospel music, but it's nothing like the blues. In Southern gospel, hardships are real, but sorrow is not the final destination."

"That's poetic," Vince said.

"I need to get to work," Julie said, rolling her eyes. "You can continue the music theory discussion without me."

"I'll check with you about eleven thirty," Vince said, moving toward the door.

After he left, Julie turned to me. "Sounds like a lunch date. Did he call you last night and ask you to go out with him today?"

"No, first thing this morning."

"I may be wrong about gospel music, but I know men. All the world's greatest match-makers are Jewish."

"That's why I'm praying to Jesus and asking him to find the right husband for me. You know Jesus is Jewish, don't you?"

"Yeah, a lot of Jews have a touch of the messiah complex in them," she replied. "Let's work on *Folsom v. Folsom*. A dose of divorce will keep you balanced as you go forward with Vinny."

We spent most of the morning sorting through financial documents and memos to and from Mr. Carpenter and J. K. Folsom. The business dealings were as confusing as a shell game at the county fair, but one thing became clear — Mr. Folsom didn't want his estranged wife looking in every place he'd hidden money. Julie contacted the law firm she'd worked for in Atlanta, and a paralegal e-mailed research and pleadings Julie had prepared in two other cases.

"Are you sure this is okay?" I asked. "The agreement I signed with the firm said it owned my work product."

"I didn't sign anything in Atlanta." Julie shrugged. "Beth is a friend who wouldn't do anything wrong. It's mainly research and sample questions, not facts about an identified client."

I had to admit that the information was very helpful. Julie had done a good job.

"Did you make up all these interrogatory and deposition questions?" I asked.

"No. Most of them were pulled from other files and transcripts. I organized them and made them fit our case, just like you'll do for Folsom."

"I wish I had something like this for my

criminal case," I said. "I talked to Zach Mays for a few minutes early this morning, but he stayed up all night working for Mr. Appleby and doesn't have time to help."

Julie looked at her watch. "Uh-oh, that reminds me. I'm late for a meeting with Ned about our bogus water-meter reader."

She grabbed her file, a legal pad, and rushed to the door. "Have a good lunch with Vinny," she said. "Maybe you can hold hands under the table."

After she left, I worked steadily on a long list of questions for Mr. Carpenter to ask Marie Folsom during her deposition and didn't check my watch until the library door opened. It was Vince.

"Sorry," he said with a sad face. "Mr. Appleby asked me to have lunch with him. I'm in the middle of a big project, and the general counsel for our client is coming into town from Birmingham. It may be the only face-to-face contact I have with the client all summer, so I can't miss it."

"Sure," I replied. "We'll do it some other time."

"How about tomorrow?"

"Maybe," I replied noncommittally.

Vince left. I stood and stretched. I'd reached a good stopping place in my work and wasn't sure what to do next. I picked

up the thin folder labeled *State v. Jones.*
There was no use delaying. One lesson I'd
learned from Mama was that if I didn't
begin a project, it wouldn't get done. I went
to the reception area.

"Where is the jail?" I asked an older
woman on duty after I introduced myself.
"Is it near the courthouse?"

"Used to be, but they moved it to the new
complex with the sheriff's department." She
gave me an address and told me it was
several miles away.

"Does the bus line run there?" I asked.

She gave me an odd look. "Why would
you want to take a bus?"

"I don't own a car."

"Is your visit to the jail personal or business?"

"Business."

"Then ask Gerry to let you use the firm
car."

"The law firm has a car?"

"Of course. The runners use it, and it's
available to the lawyers if one of them needs
a vehicle." She smiled. "I understand the air
conditioner works. That and a motor is all
you'll need in Savannah."

I went upstairs to Ms. Patrick's office. She
was eating a salad at her desk.

"May I use the firm car so I can visit a

client at the jail?" I asked somewhat breathlessly.

"Probably, unless it's checked out."

"Who keeps that record?"

"The receptionist on duty."

I returned downstairs. The woman saw me coming and spoke before I asked a question.

"Yes, it's here, and no one has reserved it until later this afternoon. I should have told you."

I turned around and climbed the stairs. Ms. Patrick made a photocopy of my driver's license, and I signed several sheets of paper without reading them.

"The receptionist can give you directions and the keys."

"Thanks," I said, then stopped. "Oh, and I had a wonderful evening with Mrs. Fairmont last night. She's a very gracious lady. We talked a long time at dinner and spent a time together in the parlor. She was completely lucid. I appreciate you putting me in touch with her daughter."

"I hope things continue to go well," Ms. Patrick said, returning to her salad.

I stepped outside into the heat, which made me doubly thankful I wouldn't have to stand on a street corner, waiting for a bus or ride in a smelly cab. I found the car.

It had just been returned, and the air conditioner began to cool the interior by the time I left the parking lot. Several minutes later I parked in front of the Chatham County Correctional Center. The size of the sheriff's department complex surprised me. It was larger than I suspected.

I didn't feel very confident. I'd gritted my teeth all the way through criminal law and procedure, and the law school course trained us to argue a case before the Supreme Court, not figure out the best way to dispose of a petty criminal offense. I wasn't even sure how to conduct an effective interview.

I presented the order from Judge Cannon to a female deputy in the lobby area of the jail. She left with the order. Beyond the lobby was a large open room with chairs and phones on either side of clear glass. It wasn't visiting hours, and the room was empty. To my surprise, the jail smelled as clean as a hospital. The woman returned and handed the order to me.

"Wait here until someone brings the prisoner from lockup," she said. "Jones is a trusty so they may have to track him down."

I didn't know what "trusty" meant, but it made me feel better about meeting a man who lived behind bars. A door behind the woman opened and a male deputy appeared.

"Tami Taylor?" he asked.

"Yes sir," I answered before realizing it probably wasn't necessary to be so formal.

The deputy grinned. "Follow me."

The door clicked shut with a thud behind me. We walked down a short hallway to another door that opened when the deputy pushed a series of buttons. I could see surveillance cameras mounted on the wall. If the twins had been with me they would probably have waved to the cameras.

We entered another room with several numbered doors around an open space. None of the doors had windows in them. A deputy sat behind a desk at one end of the room.

"He's in room 5," the deputy said.

"Do I go in alone?" I asked.

"I don't think Jones is a security risk," the deputy answered. "If you have a concern, you can leave the door open. Deputy Jenkins and I will be on the other side of the room."

"All right." I nodded grimly.

I approached the door and pushed it open. It contained a small table and four plastic chairs. Standing by the table was an old black man with graying hair.

"I'm Tami Taylor," I said. "Are you Mr. Jones?"

"Yes, missy. But you can call me Moses."

The man extended his hand. It felt like old leather. His fingernails were cracked and yellowed with age. I let the door close. The deputy was right. Moses didn't look like a serious threat to my personal safety.

"You be my lawyer?"

"Sort of," I said, then quickly added, "I'm a law student working for a law firm in Savannah this summer. One of the firm's lawyers will be supervising what I do for you."

I put a blank legal pad on the table. We both sat down. I clicked open my pen. I wanted to be professional and efficient.

"First, I need some background information. Your full name, Social Security number, and date of birth."

Moses turned his head to the side and made a sucking noise as he drew air into his mouth. I couldn't see more than a couple of teeth.

"Moses Jones is all I go by. My mama, she give me another name, Tobias, but I don't never use it. I lost my Social Security card. The boss man, he pays me cash under the table. What else you want to know?"

"Date of birth."

"I was born on June 5."

"What year?"

"I'm seventy-one years old," he said, "if that helps you figure it."

I wrote down the date and other information on the legal pad.

"And your address?"

"I ain't got none."

"You're homeless?"

"No!" he said with more force than I expected. "I got me a place down on the river, but it ain't on no road or nothing."

"Are you married?"

"No, missy. I ain't had a woman in my life for a long time."

"Any children?"

"I had one, a boy, but he be dead."

"I'm sorry."

Moses leaned forward and his eyes became more animated. "I never seen his face in the water. If'n I did, I don't think I could stand it."

"What water?" I asked.

"The black water. In the night. That's when the faces come up to look around. They don't say nothing, but I can read their thoughts. They know that I know. They be calling out to me."

I wrote down his words. When I saw them on the legal pad, it made me feel creepy. I

284

looked up. The old man was staring past my shoulder. I quickly turned around. All I saw was the blank concrete wall.

"Do you see something in this room?" I asked hesitantly.

"No, missy. But the faces ain't never far from me. You from Savannah?"

"No."

Moses Jones was obviously delusional and had mental problems much more serious than twenty-four counts of misdemeanor trespassing in his boat. He needed professional help. No one in our church ever admitted going to a psychologist or psychiatrist, but it made sense to me, at least until God came in to straighten out a person's life.

"Well, you may need to talk to someone about that later," I said.

"I told the detective all about it. He asked me a lot more questions than you."

"Which detective?"

"I don't know his name. He be young and black."

"Did he question you about tying your boat up to docks where you didn't have permission?"

Moses nodded his head. "Yeah, but I told him the river, it belong to God who made it. How can anyone own a river? It always be moving and changing. You can't hold on to water like you can a piece of dirty ground."

I was startled by his logic. In a way, it made sense.

"But when a person builds a dock on the river, that's private property," I answered. "That's why you were arrested, because you tied up your boat where you didn't have permission."

"Who'm I going to ask? Will a man be happy and hug my neck if'n I come up on his house in the dark, beat on his door, and say, 'I want to tie up for the rest of the night. I won't hurt a thing. My rope, it don't leave a mark. And I'll be slipping away at dawn light?'"

"The law says you have to get permission."

"You be the lawyer. Make the law right so I can leave this jailhouse with my boat."

"Where is your boat?"

"In amongst the cars behind that tall fence. I can see it, but I can't touch it. I don't know if it be leaky or not."

"It's here at the jail?"

Moses nodded.

"I'll check into that for you. Have they set your bond?"

"I reckon, but I ain't got money for no

bondsman. My boat ain't worth nothing to nobody but me."

"Have you had a court hearing of any kind?"

"I ain't been before no judge, if'n that's what you mean."

"So they'll leave you in here indefinitely for trespassing?" I asked, expressing my private thoughts.

"That be your job, missy. Most of the time, the lawyer be the one to get a man out of this jail."

"Okay."

I opened the folder and looked again at the twenty-four counts. The scenario seemed clear. I spoke slowly.

"You would fish at night and tie up at a private dock for a few hours of sleep until the sun came up."

"Yes, missy. That part be true. I never took nothing that weren't mine." He looked away. "Except for some other stuff."

"What other stuff?"

"At the taverns where I cleaned up. I'd grab cooked food, a knife, a fork. Not every week, only when I was extra hungry or needed it."

All theft is wrong, but these newly admitted offenses weren't part of the case I had to resolve, and I wasn't a prosecutor. I sat back in my chair.

"So what is our defense to the charges against you? They've listed twenty-four counts of trespassing when you tied up without permission at private docks. I agree with you that the river belongs to God, but the docks are private property."

Moses looked at me and blinked his dark eyes. "I want my boat back and to get out of this jailhouse so I can go to the river and catch fish. I won't bother nobody else. Never again."

"Will you stop tying up at private docks?"

He rubbed his hand across the top of his head. "I been on that river before there be docks. I reckon I can say to myself they ain't there no more."

"Does that mean you won't tie up there?"

"Yes, missy. That be exactly what that mean."

15

I watched Deputy Jenkins escort Moses out of the interview area. I wasn't sure I'd conducted an adequate first interview or not. I glanced down at my single page of notes. There didn't seem to be any benefit in asking the old man about each count. I'm sure the story was the same. I considered my options.

I could remind the judge that God, as the Creator of all things, owned all the rivers of the world and looked favorably on baby Moses when his basket trespassed onto waters reserved for Pharaoh's daughter. Such an argument, while creative, wouldn't make me look like a competent lawyer-in-training. I could follow Julie's advice to subpoena the twenty-four dock owners to trial and hope none of them showed up. While trying the case would give me courtroom experience, it would also drag Zach Mays away from his more important work at the firm.

The best course of action was obvious. Moses Jones ought to plead guilty to the charges with a promise not to trespass in the future. After receiving a stern lecture from the judge, he could be placed on a short period of probation. I reached the lobby.

"Could I find out the name of the detective who interviewed my client, Moses Jones?" I asked the woman deputy on duty.

"Give me the case number."

I handed her the file. She opened it and returned my notes.

"You might want to keep this."

"Thanks."

"Wait here."

She left for several minutes. While I waited a deputy brought in a woman in handcuffs accompanied by two small girls. She stood forlornly with the little girls holding on to her legs while the officer spoke on a walkie-talkie to someone in another section of the jail. I stared, unable to pull my gaze away from the tragedy. The woman looked at me with eyes that pleaded for help. I took a step forward, then stopped. I had no right to intrude. The deputy took the woman by the arm and led her into the lockup area with the children trailing along behind.

The woman officer returned.

"It's Detective Branson. He's on his way up to see you."

"He's willing to talk to me?"

"I showed him the order from the judge."

A different door than the one I'd taken to the interview area opened, and a black man in his thirties wearing a casual shirt and dark pants entered.

"I'm Sylvester Branson," he said.

"Tami Taylor."

"Come with me."

I followed him through the door into a suite of small offices.

"Have a seat," the detective said.

On the detective's desk was a picture of a woman and two girls about the same ages as the ones I'd seen a few minutes before.

"You're working for Braddock, Appleby, and Carpenter?"

"Yes sir."

"Mr. Carpenter represented my father and his brothers in a civil case several years ago. He's a great trial lawyer, one of the best cross-examiners in this part of the state."

"That's what I've been told. I hope to see him in the courtroom while I'm here."

"Did he send you down here to represent Moses Jones?"

"In a way. He asked Judge Cannon to ap-point summer clerks to work on misdemeanor cases so long as another lawyer in the firm supervised our work."

The detective didn't say anything. I shifted in my chair, not sure about the proper way to proceed.

"When I met with Mr. Jones, he mentioned that he had been interviewed by a detective," I said.

"That's right. I talked to him."

"Could you tell me what he told you?"

Branson tapped a folder on his desk. It was much thicker than mine.

"After waiving his Miranda rights, he talked freely about the charges."

"Did he sign a statement?"

"Yes, but I won't give it to you now. You can obtain a copy once you file the proper request with the court."

"I'm going to have to research how to do that." I bit my lower lip and tried to think of something else to ask. I decided to broach the ultimate issue. "If Mr. Jones wants to enter a plea, could I talk to you about that?"

"No, the district attorney's office will have the case assigned to a prosecutor. All plea negotiations are handled by the prosecutor."

"Who has the case?"

"I'm not sure. No one has contacted me."

I ran down my mental checklist. "Is there a bond set in Mr. Jones' case?"

"Yes, it's five thousand dollars."

"I don't think he has much money."

"That's why he's still in jail and represented by an appointed lawyer."

"I'm sorry. That was a stupid question."

The detective smiled. "No need to apologize. There are a lot of lawyers in Savannah who ask stupid questions. They could use a dose of your honesty."

"Have you talked to any of the people who claim he tied up his boat at their dock?"

"One of my assistants and a deputy verified the information contained in every count listed in the accusation. The complainants are from the same homeowners association."

"Can you give me the name of the association?"

The detective opened the file and read a name.

"Was there any physical damage to the docks?" I asked.

"Is there any mention of criminal damage to property in the charges?"

"No."

"Then it's not part of the case at this time."

"Good. Do you think the complainants

would oppose probation for Mr. Jones if he promised to stay away from their docks?"

"That wasn't discussed. Their primary goal is to put a stop to your client's trespassing. This area is only partially developed, and there is still a lot of marshy wilderness. It's disturbing when a stranger comes around a private residence. Break-ins have occurred."

"But nothing linked to Mr. Jones?"

"Not at this time."

I looked at a certificate on the wall of the detective's office. It had something to do with proficiency in the use of a weapon I'd never heard of.

"Is there anything else?" the detective asked.

"Yes, I think Mr. Jones may need treatment from a mental health professional."

"That's already started. He's meeting with a counselor who, I believe, placed him on medication."

"Thanks."

I got up to leave but then sat back down. "I appreciate your patience, but there is one other thing I don't understand. Did Mr. Jones talk to you about seeing faces in the water?"

"That's the reason for the referral to mental health."

"He said he talked to you about the faces in the water for a long time."

The detective didn't respond.

"Is that right?" I asked.

The detective closed his file. "Any conversation with Mr. Jones is difficult. Your client has a tendency to talk about what he wants to."

"Thanks for taking time to meet with me. I'm just learning what to do and really appreciate it."

"I'll walk you out. Give my regards to Mr. Carpenter."

When we reached the entrance area, I remembered the woman with the two children.

"Oh, a woman in handcuffs was brought in a few minutes ago," I said to the detective. "She had two little girls with her. Can you tell me what she did wrong?"

"Running a meth lab in her kitchen. One of the other detectives is talking to her now."

"What will happen to the children?"

"Probably stay with a family member if someone is suitable. Otherwise, they'll be placed in foster care."

"It's a sad situation."

"Would you like to represent her too?"

"No," I said quickly. "I don't think I'm going to be a criminal defense lawyer."

■ ■ ■ ■

During the return trip to the office, my mind went back and forth between Moses Jones and the woman with the little girls. My first encounters with people in jail had left me thinking more about their tragic circumstances than the punishment they deserved.

Back at the office I returned the keys to the receptionist.

"Did you fill it up with gas?" she asked.

"I didn't think about it. Should I —"

"I'm kidding," she interrupted. "Did you have trouble finding the jail?"

"No ma'am."

I went to the library. It was empty, and everything looked the same as when I'd left for the jail. I worked alone on the Folsom case for over an hour before taking a break. It was quiet in the library, which helped me concentrate, but I had to admit that I missed Julie. The door opened, and I looked up, expecting to see her. Instead, it was Zach Mays. He'd changed clothes and shaved.

"Gerry told me you were working in here," he said. "Can I interrupt?"

"Sure."

He sat across the table from me. "I feel better after sleeping for a few hours. Do you ever stay up all night studying?"

"Never, I always plan ahead. Not that I'm saying you don't organize your time," I added quickly. "In law school there aren't negotiations with businessmen in Norway. All our classes are on eastern standard time."

Zach's long hair still looked slightly damp. "I shouldn't have told you that I was too busy to help you," he said. "I was tired."

"That's okay. I understand."

"And I want to apologize."

My attitude toward the young lawyer rotated 180 degrees. Confession was one of the most trustworthy signs of genuine faith.

"Thank you," I said as sincerely as I could.

Zach smiled. "And to prove my repentance, I'll take you to the jail so we can talk to our mutual client. What's his name? Mr. James?"

"Moses Jones, and it's too late. I've already interviewed him, along with the detective who questioned him about the charges."

Zach sat up straighter in his chair. "What did you find out?"

I gave him a detailed account of my initial investigation. He listened without comment until I finished.

"I'll do a conflict of interest check on the homeowners association," he said. "We may represent it. Ned Danforth does a lot of that type of work for Mr. Braddock's clients."

"Would that disqualify us from the case?"

"No, but it might give us an advantage in talking to the homeowners. What about Jones' prior criminal record? If he's had multiple convictions, it would impact a plea agreement."

"I didn't ask."

"And the detective didn't mention it?"

"No."

"Search the state and county websites."

"Do you know the links?"

"No, you track them down. Also, contact the administrator at the district attorney's office and find out the prosecutor assigned to the case. We can meet with that person together." Zach pointed to my folder. "Make a copy of everything in the file for me."

"Okay."

"Jones sounds like an alcoholic who's pickled his brain and sees dead people floating around in the jar with him. Did you ask him if he recognized the faces in the water?"

"No, it was weird, something that should be explored by a mental health worker, not me."

Zach rubbed his chin. "You're probably

right, but I'm curious. Next time, I'll ask him."

After Zach left, I went to the downstairs copy room, and after one false start, navigated my way through the codes and buttons to make the copies. I organized Zach's folder exactly the same as my own and took it to his office. He wasn't there so I left it on his desk. On the corner near the photograph of his parents was a light blue envelope with Zach's first name written in a woman's hand across the front.

I used one of the computer terminals in the library to research Moses' background. There were countless defendants named Jones, but only one with the first name Moses. I found a felony conviction for illegal transport of moonshine whiskey that corroborated Zach's suspicion that Moses' brain had been damaged by alcohol. I didn't know much about bootleg liquor, but I'd read that a bad batch could cause blindness, brain damage, or death. The county database didn't reveal any other convictions or subsequent arrests.

It was close to 5:00 p.m. when I called the district attorney's office. After waiting on hold for several minutes, the woman who answered the phone told me the case had been assigned to an assistant DA named

Margaret Smith.

"May I speak to her?" I asked.

After another long wait a female voice came on the line. "This is Maggie Smith."

I identified myself and the purpose for my call.

"My first taste of the criminal justice system came when I was a summer clerk for the Braddock firm," she said. "I'll never forget it. My client was charged with simple battery of his fifteen-year-old stepson. I wanted to see my client behind bars, not set free. That case, and the fact that Braddock, Appleby, and Carpenter has never hired a female attorney, are two big reasons why I decided to be a prosecutor."

"How many other female summer clerks have worked at the firm?"

"Several, but no women have ever made it onto the letterhead. Don't get me wrong, it's a nice place to spend the summer and looks decent on your résumé, but unless things have changed, there won't be an opportunity for employment after law school. The history of male bias at the firm is conclusive, and everyone in town knows it." Smith paused. "Hold on while I pull the Jones file. I don't recall seeing it come across my desk."

While I waited, I wondered why God

would miraculously open a door of opportunity with a brick wall behind it.

"I have it," the assistant district attorney said.

"When did you work here?" I asked, still thinking about her comments.

"Five years ago. Try to forget what I said. I guess I'm still bitter at the double standard. You might be the one to break the gender barrier."

"There's another girl at the firm this summer."

"Really? I was the only female clerk my year."

"Did they hire an associate?"

"Yeah, Ned Danforth, but he never clerked. Let's see now, twenty-four counts of simple trespass. Can't your client read a No Trespassing sign?"

"Actually, I'm not sure he can read. Were there signs posted on the docks?"

"I don't know. It's not a legal requirement to post private property. Look, I know Joe Carpenter wants you to gain experience by making my life miserable with motions and frivolous hearings, but I don't have time to play games. There are a lot of serious cases on my docket. Do your investigation; talk to everyone who lives on the Little Ogeechee River if you like; then make me a plea offer.

If it's reasonable, I'll recommend it. On a case like this, I doubt Judge Cannon will give us a problem, and your client can get on with his life."

"Okay."

I wondered if I would sound as confident and forceful as Maggie Smith after I'd been practicing law for five years.

"And best of luck to you and the other girl working at the firm. There's always a first time for everything. If you get a job offer, I'll buy you a double of your drink of preference."

"That would be sweet tea for me."

"Whatever. Get back to me with your proposal."

A few minutes after I hung up the phone, Julie returned, looking frazzled.

"Do you like dogs?" she asked.

"Yes."

"Then I wish Mr. Carpenter had given you my case. Ned and I got a list of the State's witnesses to interview. We drove through several run-down neighborhoods trying to track down people and ask them what they'd seen. I've never run into so many dogs in my life. Ned is allergic to dogs so he sent me to knock on doors." Julie pointed to her right leg. "Can you see the dog slobber on my pants?"

I leaned forward. There was a distinct shiny streak from mid-thigh to below her knee.

"I got that from the biggest, hairiest dog I've ever seen. A dog like that has no business living in Savannah. He should be in the northern tip of Maine."

"At least he didn't bite."

"I was afraid it was a preliminary lick before he chomped down. I ran out of there as fast as I could go."

"Were these nice neighborhoods?"

"No, the owners spend all their money on dog food. There was one house with two pit bulls. I refused to go inside the gate. A man heard the dogs snarling and came to the door. I yelled questions to him across the yard."

"What did you find out?"

"We didn't talk to everyone, but a few people remembered Ferguson because he wandered around after pretending to look at the water meter. I think I've figured out what he was doing."

"You've given up on the Halloween costume defense?"

"Yeah," Julie answered. "I'm serious. I think Mr. Ferguson was scoping out houses to rob."

"But you said the neighborhoods weren't

upper class."

"Exactly. Poor people prey on other poor people. There were houses with burglar bars on the windows that I wouldn't want to go inside if the door was left wide open."

"And dogs in the yards."

"Yeah, the people bought those brutes as an alternative to a sophisticated security system."

"Is your client linked to any of the robberies?"

"I hope not, but if he's charged with burglary, it would be a felony and take the case out of my basket."

"When are you going to the jail to talk to him?"

"He's not in jail. He's out on bond working his real job."

"What does he do for a living?"

"Get this. He works for the city's animal control department. That's probably how he got access to a meter reader's uniform."

"And explains why he isn't afraid of dogs."

Julie rubbed her arm across her forehead. "Are you ready to leave? I haven't needed a shower so badly since I played soccer on a muddy field in middle school."

"I'm not trying to make you stay."

"Let's go together. I'm giving you a ride home. I want every detail about your lunch date with Vinny. Did he ask you out to dinner? Did he talk about his last girlfriend and why they broke up?"

"I didn't go to lunch with Vince. He had to meet with Mr. Appleby and a client."

"What did you do?"

"I went to the jail and interviewed my client."

"Then tell me about that. At least you didn't have to worry about getting mauled by a pack of dogs."

After meeting with Tami, Moses finished his first trash run of the day. Then the deputy in charge of the dining hall ordered him to clean the tables. Each stainless-steel table was surrounded by four metal stools bolted onto strips of metal that extended like spokes from a central post. Fights during mealtime were rare at the jail, but if an inmate did lose his temper, a chair couldn't be used as a large blunt object.

Moses carried a plastic bucket of water in each hand. One bucket contained warm, soapy water; the other, clean rinse water. After wiping off each table and chair, he dipped a rag in the rinse water and removed the soapy residue. Moses didn't just clean the surface of the tables; he also scrubbed under the rims. The deputy gave him a screwdriver to dislodge fossilized pieces of chewing gum. Moses worked slowly. Getting done in a hurry wouldn't earn him any reward except an earlier return to his cell where he had nothing to do but lie on his bed.

The tall girl who talked to him said she wasn't a lawyer but then acted like one. It didn't make sense. She reminded Moses of the young woman with blonde hair who'd met with him a few days earlier. She said she wasn't a doctor but then acted like one. The blonde-haired woman asked questions about his health, wrote notes on paper, listened to everything he told her, and told the jail nurse to give him a green pill every morning. Moses dutifully swallowed the pill, but he knew getting back to his life along the river was the only medicine he really needed.

As he cleaned the tables he thought about the tall, dark-haired girl who wasn't a real lawyer. She looked familiar. That's why he asked if she lived in Savannah. Moses knew a lot of people by face if not by name. He'd met hundreds of people when he worked for Tommy Lee Barnes as a bolita runner and could remember faces for years and years.

A bolita runner collected money from the

players of the simple betting game and handed out slips of paper that served as proof of the numbers chosen. Beginning early in the morning, Moses went all over the city calling on regular players and trying to attract new ones. At precisely 6:00 p.m., five winning numbers between 1 and 100 were announced by randomly selecting five numbered Ping-Pong balls from a large bag. Prior to the drawing, Moses and one of the other runners tabulated the most popular numbers of the day, and Tommy Lee would remove those numbers from the sack to avoid a big loss.

Tommy Lee made the daily drawing exciting. He had a preacher's voice and always asked a pretty girl to stick her hand in the bag and draw out the Ping-Pong balls. Runners notified winners the following day and delivered their winnings. Moses liked counting out the greasy dollar bills to a winner. Even with payouts, Tommy Lee would make a couple of hundred dollars a day. Each Friday, Moses would take envelopes of cash to the police officers who let the game operate. Mr. Floyd, Tommy Lee's boss, paid the mayor's office directly.

The tall girl who wasn't a real lawyer reminded Moses of a girl he'd known during the time he worked for Tommy Lee

Barnes. She didn't play bolita, but the old woman who owned the big house where the girl lived guessed ten numbers every Wednesday. When the girl saw Moses on the sidewalk outside the house, she would tell him to go away. Moses would nod respectfully and sneak around the corner where he would wait for the old woman to come out to meet him. If she had a winning number, Moses would pick up the ticket and redeem it for her.

Moses wasn't sure what had happened to the girl. She would be an old woman herself by now. Once or twice, he thought he'd seen her face in the water, but it didn't make sense that she would be there.

16

By the end of the first week, I had begun to doubt Ms. Patrick's promise that a summer clerk job at Braddock, Appleby, and Carpenter would be more fun than toil. Mr. Carpenter added two more projects to my workload and three more to Julie's stack. She and I worked together on the Folsom case, and I revised her memo on the secured transaction issue, but we had to go our separate ways on the new projects. She worked directly with Mr. Carpenter. I found myself reporting more and more to Robert Kettleson, a senior associate who confidently informed me that he was next in line for partner.

Kettleson, a tall, skinny man, communicated with me via e-mails that he typed at all hours of the day and night. He wanted my responses in writing so there would be no doubt about my opinion. The process bothered me, but I had to admit it forced me to be very careful in my research.

I had no time to work on the Jones case. When I asked Zach about it, he pointed to the files on the corner of his desk and told me justice for indigent defendants like Moses Jones would have to wait another week. At least the old man had food to eat and a roof over his head.

Late Friday afternoon, Julie returned to the library and plopped down on the other side of the table.

"Are you coming to work tomorrow?" she asked. "Please say no because I don't want to be the only clerk who abandons the office to spend a few hours at Tybee Island beach. Why don't you come with me? We're both pale as white bread, but we could lather up with sunscreen and pretend we're from Nova Scotia."

"Nova Scotia?"

"If that's not exotic enough, you can be Norwegian and I'll be Lebanese."

"I don't own a swimsuit."

"You're kidding."

Apparently my face told her the truth.

"Don't worry about it," she continued. "I'll buy one for you and put it on my credit card. You can pay me back when we get our paychecks next week."

"Do your orthodox cousins in New York

310

go to the beach?" I asked.

"Yeah, there are places where they can go and be among the faithful on certain days of the week, but they don't wear —" Julie stopped. "Rabbi, are you that conservative?"

"Yes."

"Wow. You are hard-core."

Her words stung, but I stayed calm. "I have strong convictions about modesty," I replied quietly.

"Okay. Suit yourself, or rather don't if it offends your morals. My parents want me to walk on eggshells around my cousins, which is one reason I don't like to visit them. But I still want to know if you're going to spend the day at the office. If you do, it will make me and Vinny look bad."

"You already talked to Vince?"

"He agreed to take the day off. I didn't say anything to him about the beach, but if it was okay with you, I wanted to invite him to join us. Two girls and one guy would be irresistible odds."

"The two of you can go."

"And steal him from you? He's not my type."

"I'm not sure he's my type."

"What is your type?"

"I'm not sure. I haven't met him."

"Don't be so dense," Julie snapped. "You

have to meet men to find out who you're compatible with. I'm trying to help you, but you're not making it easy. You'll never find out the truth about other people or yourself with your nose stuck in a Bible or a prayer book."

"I don't use a prayer book, and I didn't ask for help."

"But you need help. Lots of it. I'm sure glad we're not sharing an apartment. I don't think I could stand your self-righteous attitude 24/7. You're so uptight I'm surprised your eyes open in the morning!"

My uptight eyes suddenly stung with tears I vainly tried to blink away. Most people didn't keep attacking after I made my convictions clear. Julie saw that I was upset and swore.

"I'm sorry," she said.

I quickly wiped my eyes. "Everything you say makes sense except that I believe God controls my future. I can't abandon my confidence in him. To do that would be to deny who I am as a person." I pulled a tissue from my purse and blew my nose. "Does that make any sense to you?"

Julie shrugged. "You fanatic religious types are all alike."

"People judge me because of the things I do and don't do. But I'm not a mixed-up mess of legalistic rules and regulations. I'm a child of God who wants to live in the freedom from sin Jesus provides through his death on the cross."

"Okay, okay," Julie said. "You can step down from your pulpit. My efforts to corrupt you are over for the week."

This time I didn't cry. I pressed my lips tightly together before I spoke. "I guess I'll walk home."

"No need to get hot and sweaty. I'll give you a ride. I said I was sorry."

Partway home, Julie broke the silence. "You've never had a boyfriend?"

"No."

"My Jewish intuition tells me that's about to change."

We reached Mrs. Fairmont's house. Julie stopped the car.

"So, are you going to the office tomorrow?" she asked.

"No. I wouldn't do anything to try to gain an advantage."

"Good. I'll call Vinny. This summer is our last chance to have fun before we have to enter the real world of work."

I opened the door. "If you go to the beach, use plenty of sunblock."

"You won't recognize me on Monday. I may not look Lebanese, but in a couple of days I'll be able to pass for an Israeli."

I could hear the TV blaring when I entered the house. I peeked into the den. The TV might be on, but that didn't mean she was watching it. Mrs. Fairmont's eyes were closed. She tried to maintain a schedule, but I'd learned that even though she went to bed early, her sleep patterns were irregular. Twice when I'd come upstairs to the kitchen in the night, she had been awake watching TV. Flip didn't seem to mind. He matched his sleep schedule to hers. The little dog barked and came over to me for a welcoming scratch behind the ears.

"Mrs. Fairmont," I announced.

She stirred. Her eyes fluttered open and glanced in my direction.

"Who is it?" she asked with alarm in her voice.

"Tami Taylor. I'm staying with you this summer."

The older woman's lapses of short-term memory made my heart ache. I picked up Flip, who licked my chin.

"Flip knows me," I said as I let the tiny dog lick my chin. "I'm staying in the basement apartment and working for Mr. Braddock's law firm."

Mrs. Fairmont stared at me. Generally, it

only took a few comments to tether her mind in reality.

"Where's Gracie?" she asked.

"Gone for the day."

"Did she let you in the house?"

"No ma'am." I held up a key. "Your daughter, Mrs. Bartlett, gave me a key."

Mrs. Fairmont pushed herself up from the chair. "I'm going to call Christine this minute. She has no right giving out keys to strangers!"

I deposited Flip on the floor. This was the most serious spell of confusion I'd witnessed.

"What do you want me to do while you call her?"

"Wait on the front steps would be the polite thing to do," she answered curtly as she walked unsteadily toward the kitchen. "Proper young women don't barge into a house uninvited."

"Yes ma'am."

Keeping the key in my hand in case she locked the door behind me, I retreated toward the front of the house, but I positioned myself by the hallway door in the green parlor so I could hear the conversation in the kitchen. I wasn't sure whether Mrs. Fairmont would remember Mrs. Bartlett's phone number. There was silence for several seconds, then I heard Mrs. Fairmont begin talking to someone about her house key. After a couple of sentences she stopped talking.

"Yes, I took my medicine," she said. "Gracie always gives it to me."

A longer period of silence followed.

"Are you sure?" she asked. "Samuel Braddock?"

After a shorter silence, she said, "No, I can take care of myself."

I heard her hang up the phone. I quickly moved through the foyer and outside to the front steps. I waited, praying that Mrs. Fairmont had regained connection with reality. The front door opened. She stared at me again.

"Christine says you're staying here so you might as well come inside, but I don't want you telling me what to do."

"I'm here to help."

Mrs. Fairmont turned and walked away. I stood in the foyer and watched her climb the stairs to the second floor without looking back. Flip followed her. I went into the kitchen and hit the Redial button on the phone. Mrs. Bartlett answered.

"What is it now?" she asked.

"It's Tami Taylor. I overheard your mother's phone call. She thought I'd gone outside, but I was listening from the parlor. I came in from work a few minutes ago, and she didn't recognize me. Usually, her confusion goes away after we talk for a minute or so, but this time it didn't. It's the worst spell she's had since I've been here."

"Where is she now?"

"Upstairs."

"No, I'm not!" a voice screamed behind me.

The sound startled me so violently that I dropped the phone. It hit the floor with a sharp crack. Flip barked and ran around the kitchen.

"Who are you talking to?" Mrs. Fairmont demanded with fire in her eyes.

"Your daughter, Christine," I managed.

I picked up the phone and handed it to her. "Here. Talk to her yourself."

Watching me with suspicious eyes, she put the phone to her ear. "Who is this?" she demanded.

I couldn't hear the other side of the conversation, but the expression on Mrs. Fairmont's face slowly changed. I stepped backward to the far side of the kitchen and waited. Mrs. Fairmont closed her eyes several times as she listened. I inched closer, fearing she might faint.

"Yes, yes," she said, followed by, "No, no."

She handed the phone to me. "Talk to her."

"Hello," I said.

"Has she calmed down?" Mrs. Bartlett asked.

"I think so."

"I can't drive into town tonight. Ken and I have a dinner engagement that has been on the books for months. She'll be all right in a few minutes. These things pass. It's even happened with Gracie."

"But what do I —"

"Call my cell phone or 911 if there is a true emergency, although if you're patient she'll be fine. You can take care of this. That's why I hired you. Good night."

The phone clicked off. Mrs. Fairmont was leaning against the counter with her eyes closed and her hand resting against the right side of her face. It was such a sad sight that the remaining tears I'd bottled up at the office when Julie attacked me gushed out in compassion. Mrs. Fairmont opened her eyes. The fire was gone. She looked tired.

"Why are you crying?" she asked.

"Because I care about you. I'm here to help you. The last thing I want to do is upset you."

"I don't feel well," she said.

"May I help you upstairs?"

She started shuffling toward the door. I followed behind her. Flip stayed out of the way but close to her feet. When she reached the steps, Mrs. Fairmont grasped the railing tightly as she climbed. Halfway up, she wavered, and I reached out my hand to steady her. She reached the landing at the top of the stairs, then walked slowly to her room. I followed.

"Here's the intercom, if you need me," I said, making sure it was still turned on. "I have one in the basement. Press the Call or Talk button, and I'll be here as soon as I can."

She sat on the edge of the bed. "What's happening to me?" she asked.

"You were confused."

She rubbed her temples. I noticed she was wearing shoes that didn't match.

"Why don't you lie down and rest?" I suggested.

She leaned back on the bed and closed her eyes. I gently removed her shoes and positioned a pillow under her head. The air-conditioning was on so I put a lightweight cotton throw over her legs and feet. I picked up Flip and put him on the bed. He curled up near her feet.

"I'll be back in a little while to check on you," I said, turning toward the door.

"You can sing a song now," she said softly.

I came closer to the bed. "What kind of song?"

"You know, the kind you sing every night before I go to sleep."

I thought back to some of the songs Mama sang to me when I was small. All of them had biblical themes.

"All right," I answered softly.

My brother Bobby was the best singer in our family, but I could carry a tune. I decided humming might be a good way to start. I leaned close to Mrs. Fairmont's head and began to hum a melody whose roots lay in the spirits of early Christian pioneers. Mrs. Fairmont's facial muscles relaxed. When I switched to words, she took a deep breath. In a few seconds, she was asleep.

I didn't stop.

I finished that song and started another. Mrs. Fairmont was unconscious, but I wasn't singing to her mind — the lyrics were intended for her spirit. I knelt on the floor beside her bed, continued through three songs, then tapered off to another hum. I finished by praying in a soft voice for healing, salvation, and blessing. When I lifted my head, Flip was watching me through a single, drooping eye. I slipped quietly from the room.

320

Several hours later, I came upstairs in my pajamas for a drink of cold water before going to bed. Mrs. Fairmont was sitting in the den watching the late-night news. I peeked in at her. An empty dinner plate was on a table beside her chair.

"Hello, Tami," she said when she heard me. "Did you have a good day at work?"

"It was challenging," I answered.

"You must have worked late. I had a long nap and feel much better. Gracie left supper, but your plate is still in the refrigerator."

I'd been so upset by the events earlier in the evening that my appetite had disappeared. "I may eat it tomorrow."

"That's fine. I'm going to bed after the news is over. Good night."

"Good night."

Saturday morning, Mrs. Fairmont was back to normal. I brewed her coffee and fixed a light breakfast that we ate at a table on the veranda that opened into the den. She didn't mention the chaos of the previous night, and I didn't see any benefit in bringing it up. While I watched her carefully spread orange marmalade to the edges of an English muffin, I thought about her irrational anxiety and felt a lump in my throat. Aging was part of life, but I wished people could leave earth in a blaze of glory like Elijah, not spiral down into pathetic incompetence.

"Are you all right?" Mrs. Fairmont interrupted my thoughts.

"Yes ma'am. Would you like another cup of coffee?"

"That would be nice."

I went to the kitchen. The doorbell chimed. Flip charged in from the veranda to warn the possible intruder of the dog's fierce presence. I followed him into the foyer and opened the door. It was Zach Mays with his motorcycle helmet under his right arm.

"I hope I'm not too early," he said.

"What are you doing here?"

"It's a nice neighborhood. May I come in? Did you just wake up?"

"No, I've already run four miles that included a quick trip by the office. The parking lot was empty at six thirty."

The young lawyer stepped into the foyer. "I'll be there later today but wanted to go for a ride before it gets too hot."

"Mrs. Fairmont is on the veranda. I'm getting her a fresh cup of coffee."

Flip, continuing to growl, circled Zach's feet.

"Will he bite?" Zach asked.

"I'm not sure. It's probably a good thing you're wearing boots."

Zach followed me into the kitchen. Together, we went to the veranda.

"Mrs. Fairmont, do you remember Zach Mays?"

The old woman extended her hand. "No, but it's good to see you again. Please sit down."

For the next thirty minutes, we enjoyed a pleasant conversation. Mrs. Fairmont asked Zach questions. She was mostly interested in people he'd met whom she knew. I didn't try to sort out the cast of characters. The intricacies of Savannah society seemed as complicated as Chinese history. At a pause in the discussion, Zach looked at me.

"Are you ready to go?" he asked.

"I'm not working today."

"I'm not talking about the office. I meant for a ride."

"On your motorcycle?"

"Make sure you wear a good helmet," Mrs. Fairmont said.

"I have an extra with me," Zach replied. "It's strapped to the bike."

"But I've never ridden a motorcycle." I paused. "And I don't have any jeans. I wouldn't feel comfortable behind you on the seat."

"You don't have to put your arms around my waist, and you can wear anything you like," Zach replied. "I have a sidecar. It's not much different than the fancy convertible you were driving, just a little bit closer to the ground."

"It sounds like fun," Mrs. Fairmont said. "Ferguson Caldwell used to own a motorcycle. He took me for a ride."

"I'm not sure," I said.

Zach held up his hand as if taking an oath. "I promise not to go any faster than you like. If you feel uncomfortable, we'll just go around the block, and I'll drop you off by the front door."

I was wearing a loose-fitting blue skirt and a white short-sleeved blouse. "I need to do the breakfast dishes," I said.

"I'll help," Zach volunteered.

"Go ahead, I'll be fine," Mrs. Fairmont added. "It's so pleasant out here this morning."

In the kitchen I studied Zach's face. "Why are you asking me to go for a ride?" I asked.

"I'll tell you later," he replied. "I promise."

There wasn't time to call my parents and get their counsel. I had to decide myself. My mind leaned toward no, but my mouth must have been connected to another part of me.

"Okay, but not long."

It only took a few minutes to clean up the kitchen. Zach loaded the dishwasher exactly the same way I did. I went downstairs, brushed my teeth, and tied my hair in a ponytail. I threw some things in a casual handbag. Zach and Mrs. Fairmont were on the veranda, continuing their conversation about Savannah.

"I'm ready," I announced.

"Have fun," Mrs. Fairmont said.

I followed Zach outside. Parked alongside the curb was a big black motorcycle with a sidecar attached to it.

"I thought you had a red motorcycle," I said.

"I do. This one belonged to my parents. It's twenty years old. I used to ride in the sidecar when I was a kid. That's when I fell in love with motorcycles. My father was going to sell it last year, so I bought it from him. I couldn't stand the thought of it leaving the family."

The passenger carrier had orange flames flickering along the side.

"You make it sound like a family heirloom."

"In a way, it is." He handed me a black

helmet also decorated with the orange flame motif. "This is my mother's helmet. It should fit."

I pulled the helmet over my head. It rested snugly against my ears. A plastic shield covered my face.

"It feels claustrophobic," I said, speaking extra loud so I could be heard.

"You'll be glad the first time a june bug crashes into your face at fifty miles an hour." Zach slipped on his helmet. "And you don't have to yell," he said in a voice that echoed inside the chamber. "There is a microphone connection embedded near the right corner of your mouth. It helps with the guided-tour portion of our ride."

"Testing, one, two, three," I said.

He tapped the side of his helmet and nodded. "I'll help you get settled in the sidecar."

He held out his hand, but I ignored it and stepped in. As I sat down, I quickly slid my legs forward, making sure my knees remained covered. My feet barely reached the nose of the narrow car.

"It has plenty of legroom, doesn't it?" Zach asked.

"Like a limo." I reached down with my hands. "Where's the seat belt?"

Zach threw his right leg over the motorcycle seat. "There isn't one. If a motorcycle wrecks, staying attached to it isn't always the safest thing."

He started the motor and revved the engine. It caused the sidecar to vibrate. I couldn't believe I'd left the peace and safety of Mrs. Fairmont's veranda to sit a few inches off the ground beside a motorcycle operated by a man I barely knew.

"Ready?" Zach spoke in stereo into my ears.

I nodded grimly.

He looked over his shoulder at the street and pulled away from the curb. The first thing I noticed was the immediate sensation of speed. The street seemed to fly past.

"How fast are we going?" I shouted.

"About thirty. You don't have to yell. It might make me wreck."

Some of the streets in the historic district were in need of repair, and we bumped along for several blocks. The helmet limited my view so I turned my head from side to side. Everyone we passed stopped to stare. If the twins had been on the sidewalk and saw me ride past attached to a motorcycle and wearing a black helmet with orange flames on the side, they would have fainted.

"Where are we going?" I asked.

"To a smoother road."

We left the historic district and turned

onto President Street Extension, a broader, four-lane highway. The motorcycle picked up speed, and I could feel the wind rushing past my arms and neck. Even though it felt fast, I noticed that Zach stayed in the slow lane, letting most of the cars pass us.

"How do you like it?" Zach asked.

"Better than the back of a pickup truck," I admitted.

We left the city behind, but both sides of the road were still marked by commercial development. We stopped at a light, and I looked at the street sign.

"Are we going to Tybee Island?"

"Yes. Have you been there?"

"No."

"Is that okay?"

"Sure."

I doubted Julie and the rest of the bikini crowd would be out this early. Without the presence of girls, the half-dressed men wouldn't be seen either. And there was no reason why I couldn't take a quick look at the ocean. My promise to Julie had been to stay away from the office. As we drove along, I relaxed and enjoyed the ride. I thought about Zach's mother sitting in the sidecar.

"Did your parents ever take long trips like this?" I asked.

"Maybe a couple of hundred miles or so in a day. There are roads in California unlike anyplace else. The views are incredible."

"Do you miss it?"

"Yes."

We popped over a bump that made me hit my knees against the top of the sidecar.

"Sorry," Zach said. "That one snuck up on me."

We came to Tybee Creek, an indistinct waterway that meandered through the landward side of a large marsh. The tops of the marsh grass rippled slightly in the breeze. A few white egrets stood motionless in the water. The tide was going out, exposing mussel beds at the edges of the watery channels. Expensive-looking homes lined the edge of the marsh on both the island and the mainland. We crossed a bridge onto Tybee Island.

"We'll stop near the main pier," Zach said.

We passed through residential areas with sandy driveways guarded by dune grass and into an aging business district. Several people on the sidewalks pointed in our direction as we passed. It made me feel special. We turned down a narrow street and parked in front of a meter. Zach turned off the engine. I climbed as gracefully as I could from the sidecar and removed my helmet.

My skirt was wrinkled.

"That was fun," I said before Zach asked me. "You're a good driver."

"Thanks, but you drive a car; you ride a motorcycle."

Zach put on a pair of dark sunglasses. He locked the helmets to the motorcycle with a thin steel cable.

"You don't need any money," he said. "Bring your bag or I can lock it in the sidecar."

"Lock it up. All I want is my hat."

There was a cover that slid over the sidecar, turning it into a storage compartment. Without the helmet over my face, I could smell a tinge of salt in the air. The morning breeze was coming in from the ocean. I put on my hat.

"Ocean views, this way," Zach said, retying his hair in a tight ponytail.

Two- and three-story frame houses with rooms to rent crowded against the sidewalk. There weren't many people on the street.

"It will be crowded here by noon," Zach said.

After a couple of blocks the street made a turn to the left, and I could see the blue glint of ocean in the distance. There were seagulls riding the air currents. Sand scattered the sidewalk. The street ended at a modest sand dune. Looking to the right, I could see the pier stretching its thick finger past the surf into deeper water. Tiny figures of fishermen stood at the end of the pier. I took a deep breath, enjoyed the sensation for a few seconds, and exhaled.

The pier was thirty feet above the water and wide enough for two cars to drive side by side. We passed fishermen using long, sturdy poles. Coolers of bait shrimp and fish rested beside the poles. Most of the fishermen were shirtless, tanned, and smoking cigarettes. I kept my eyes directed toward the water.

"What are they fishing for?" I asked Zach.

"Fish."

"What kinds?"

"Saltwater varieties. I'm not an expert about pier fishing."

We passed several black men with poles in the water. "Moses could tell me what kind of fish live in these waters," I said.

"Who?"

"Moses Jones. Our client charged with trespassing."

"Maybe, but as I remember he also sees faces in the water."

We reached the end of the pier. Here were the serious fishermen, each with multiple poles. I watched one man bait four hooks on a single line and fling it into the air. It plopped into the water far below. Nobody seemed to be catching any fish. Gulls cried out as they swooped down, landing on the pier to scoop up bits of discarded baitfish and shrimp.

The pier gave a panoramic view of the beach. When I was eighteen, I'd traveled to the east coast of Florida for a mission outreach sponsored by our church and waded briefly in the Atlantic early one morning before the sunbathers wearing nothing more than brightly colored under-wear made their appearance. Even that brief contact with the sea intrigued me. Like a mountain panorama, the ocean revealed the expanse of creation — a vista so big and unfathomable that only an omnipotent God could have fashioned it. With the tide going out the strand was broad, the waves small. Zach and I found an empty spot along the north side of the pier to watch.

"Are there many shells on this beach?" I asked. I couldn't see anyone stooping over.

"No. It's sand, sun, and water."

"The one other time I was at the ocean, I loved collecting shells," I said. "I have a jar-ful on a shelf in my bedroom at home. Most are broken, but there is still beauty in them."

Zach nodded his head. "People are like

that too."

I turned toward him. "Are you teasing me?"

"No."

More people streamed from the ocean-front motels toward the water. Included were the beginnings of the bathing suit crowd. Seeing the bikini-clad women made me wonder where Julie would spend the day.

"I'll help you with the Jones case this week," Zach said, breaking the silence.

"Okay. Just let me know."

We stood beside each other without speaking for a long time. A crazy thought raced through my mind that Zach wanted to throw me off the pier. I gauged the distance to shallow water. If I survived the fall it would be an easy swim. Zach touched my arm, and I jumped.

"Are you ready to go back to the motorcycle?" he asked.

"Yes."

As we walked off the pier, the fear of harm at Zach's hands didn't leave me. It would be easy for him to ram the sidecar into a tree, endangering my life.

"Why did you invite me on the motorcycle ride?" I asked.

"I'll tell you at our next stop."

"How far is that?"

"It's on the island."

I put on my helmet and stepped into the sidecar. I wanted to return to Mrs. Fairmont's house as soon as possible. Zach backed the motorcycle away from the curb with his feet and started the engine. We retraced our route onto the island. Before crossing the bridge at the marsh, Zach abruptly took a side road.

"Where are we going?" I asked, my anxiety rising.

"You'll see."

After a few hundred yards, the paving gave way to sand. There were a few houses hidden among the trees. Zach turned down a driveway with no house at the end of it and stopped the motorcycle. It was a lonely spot. My heart was pounding in my chest. I sat in the sidecar, not moving.

"Get out here," he said.

"I'm ready to go back to Mrs. Fairmont's house," I said, trying to keep my voice calm.

"And I need to spend several hours at the office. We'll only be here a few minutes."

I licked my lips and climbed out. Zach didn't bother to lock up the helmets.

"It's a short path," he said, heading off into the underbrush.

I didn't know whether to refuse and stay by the motorcycle or run down the road for help. I reluctantly followed. After about twenty yards we came into a clearing. There was the foundation of a destroyed house and a rickety pier with a lot of the boards missing. Zach pointed at the outline of the house.

"The house burned down shortly before I moved to Savannah. Mr. Appleby represented the owners who had to sue the insurance company on the policy."

"Why?"

"The company alleged arson. There was no question it was a set fire, but the evidence connecting our clients was sketchy. They used the insurance money to pay off business debts and avoid bankruptcy instead of rebuilding the house."

The strip of land extended out and provided a nice view up and down Tybee Creek. In the distance I could see cars crossing over the bridge.

"It's a pretty spot," I said. "Can we go now?"

"You can see better from here," Zach said, walking toward the water.

I followed him to a gazebo near the edge of the water. It didn't take many months for wood to weather in the salt air. Only a few flecks of white paint remained. The vines planted at the edge of the structure were in summer green. Zach didn't enter the gazebo but sat on the front steps. I stood beside him. He was right about the view.

"I like to come here and pray," he said. "I've been in every season of the year."

I looked at him in surprise. I'd been thinking about him in such a negative way that his comment caught me off guard.

"Why here?" I managed.

"It reminds me of a place I liked to go in California. It wasn't near the ocean, but it felt the same."

"What sort of place?"

"Up in the mountains near an abandoned cabin that had fallen in on itself. That's where the Lord told me to come to Savannah."

I sat down on the far end of the steps, leaving a healthy distance between us. "How did that happen? You promised to tell me."

"I know." Zach smiled and took off his sunglasses. "And I try to always keep my promises."

It was such a sweet smile that I blushed in embarrassment at my fears of a few moments before.

"Mr. Appleby read an admiralty case note I wrote for the *Pepperdine Law Review* and contacted me. I'd never visited this part of the country and agreed to fly out for a visit.

I already had three offers from law firms on the West Coast but thought it wouldn't hurt to check out Savannah. I met with Mr. Appleby, and he offered me a job before I left town. The money didn't compare with the other firms' offers, but the cost of living is so much lower here that it was worth considering. Of course, like you, the most important consideration for me was God's will."

"Did you ask your parents?"

"We discussed it. They wanted me closer to home but tried not to let their emotions get in the way. In the end, they left it up to me. That's probably easier to do with a son than a daughter."

"My parents allowed me to make my choice this summer."

"Good for them. Anyway, I rode the black motorcycle into the mountains so I could spend time praying about the decision. I took a tent and sleeping bag so I could spend the night."

"Alone?"

"Except for the bears and mountain lions. The old cabin was built on land purchased by the state to include in a park. It was okay to camp there, but I couldn't build a fire. Just before the sunset I was reading in Acts about the fellowship the early Christians enjoyed in Jerusalem."

"When they had all things in common?" I interrupted.

"Yes, only the part that touched my heart was the phrase 'fellowship of believers.' In my family, relationship with other Christians stood at the center of everything. I knew if I took one of the other jobs, I might make more money, but that the fellowship of believers waited for me in Savannah."

"Where are these people?" I asked, feeling excitement rise up inside me. "I could go to church with you tomorrow."

Zach shook his head. "I'm not sure I've met them. I'm part of a church that meets in a house on the north side of the city. It's a great group, but as I've continued to pray about the verse, I think it may be more personal than corporate."

"I don't understand."

"The best fellowship often happens one-on-one with another person, not in a crowd of people."

I swallowed. "Are you talking about male/female fellowship?" I asked.

Zach laughed. "With everything shared in common. You're already good at cross-examination."

"Why are you telling me this? You're not talking to me as you would a summer clerk."

"That's right. You're the type of girl who deserves the truth, the whole truth, and nothing but the truth. I want to be completely up front with you. I'm interested in getting to know you better, but only with your permission. If you say no, I won't bring it up again, and there won't be any hard feelings on my part."

It was the most flattering, pure-hearted invitation I'd ever received from a male.

"I'll need to talk to my parents about it."

"Sure. You can talk to Joe Carpenter if you like. I'm not suggesting we date or agree to anything beyond getting to know each other in a transparent way." Zach gestured with his hand across the expanse of the marsh. "Without the distractions of phony barriers."

I stared at the marsh for a few moments. My heart beat a little faster. "I've never had anyone approach me like this," I said.

Zach pulled on his ponytail. "And I'd bet you've never met a Christian lawyer from California with long hair who owns two motorcycles."

17

During the return trip to Mrs. Fairmont's house, the sun climbed higher in the sky. The artificial breeze created by the speed of the motorcycle kept me outwardly cool, but inside I felt flushed.

I barely knew the young lawyer, but he'd already shown the ability to get behind my defenses. No one, not even the boys at church who'd known me all their lives and shared the same religious convictions, ever came close to relating to me as a person. The novelty of the ride in the sidecar couldn't compete with the new thoughts racing through my head. I spoke into the microphone.

"How long have you been thinking about what you said to me on the island?"

Zach glanced sideways. "Is this a good time to talk about that question?"

"Yes."

"Since the first time we met."

"Was it the homeschool connection?"

"It was everything. Put yourself in my shoes. How hard is it to meet people whose main goal in life is to love and obey God?"

We stopped in front of Mrs. Fairmont's house. I handed him the helmet. "Do you want to come in for a few minutes?" I asked.

"No, I'm going to the office."

"Thanks for the ride."

As I reached the front door, I heard Zach pull away from the curb. I couldn't resist stopping to watch him ride down the street until he was out of sight.

Flip greeted me at the door. Mrs. Fairmont was sitting in the den with a book in her lap. Her eyes were closed. I quietly walked over to her chair. The book in her lap was a biography of Abigail Adams, wife of John Adams. I wondered how many pages she'd read before falling asleep or losing the ability to concentrate. She stirred and opened her eyes.

"It's Tami Taylor," I said quickly.

She rubbed her eyes. "I know who you are, but thanks for reminding me. Did you have a good time?"

"Yes ma'am. We rode out to Tybee Island."

"When I was a little girl one of the highlights of the summer was the train ride to Tybee."

"A motorcycle was exciting for me."

Mrs. Fairmont nodded and pointed a frail finger at the book in her lap. "Life has to be lived while you can. You only have one chance."

It was no use trying to call home. I knew Mama and Daddy would be working all day Saturday. So, I cleaned and scrubbed my apartment for several hours, then offered to take Flip on a walk through the neighborhood. As soon as he saw the red leash, Flip ran to the front door and began jumping up and down. I fastened the lead to his collar and headed out the door. The leash seemed unnecessary. The little dog stayed by my side with his head held high in the air. We walked all the way to Forsyth Park where I let him drink from a special water fountain just for dogs. When we returned to the house, Mrs. Fairmont held him in her lap and made me repeat in detail everything that had happened. The two of them took a long nap in the den.

Late in the afternoon Mrs. Fairmont woke up and started watching TV. I slipped into the kitchen to phone home. One of the twins answered. It sounded like Ellie.

"It's Tami. Is this Ellie?"

"Do I sound like Ellie?"

"Yes, I need to talk to Mama and Daddy."

"Are you in trouble?"

"No."

"Then why are you in such a hurry to talk to them? Don't you want to know what Emma and I have been doing today?"

I realized that I'd sounded curt. "Sure. Did you clean the chicken coop?"

To my surprise, the girls hadn't worked much at all. After they cleaned their room, Mama took them to a basketball scrimmage for girls their age at the high school.

"We each wore one of your old uniforms," she said. "It was funny because we looked alike and had the same number."

I'd purchased my high school uniforms because no one else would want to wear extra-long shorts and baggy shirts.

"Who had the most assists?" I asked.

"They didn't keep up with that, only points and rebounds. I had four more points than Emma."

"What about rebounds?"

"She got some lucky bounces."

"And then threw the ball to you while you were running down the court. If you scored on her pass that would be an assist."

"Yeah, that happened a couple of times. Anyway, the new coach for the middle school team was there watching. She talked to Mama after the scrimmage about us being on the team."

"But you won't be enrolled at the school."

Ellie spoke with excitement in her voice. "The coach says the school board has adopted a new policy for homeschoolers that lets them play sports. I'm not sure how it works, but Mama and Daddy are going to pray about it. Would you pray too? The other girls were nice to us and had fun trying to tell us apart."

It would be much easier for Ellie and Emma to face the world together than it had been for me going it alone.

"Two are better than one," I said, quoting part of a verse from Ecclesiastes.

"Yeah, but I also sank some free throws," Ellie said. "It's only one point, but most of the girls didn't come close. Emma and I only missed two each."

I didn't try to correct her. "Now, will you let Mama and Daddy know that I'm on the phone?"

"I love you," Ellie said.

"I love you too."

I could hear the television in the den. It sounded like Mrs. Fairmont was watching a war movie. Mama came on the line.

"I'm here," she said. "Ellie said it was urgent. Are you all right?"

"Yes ma'am. It couldn't be too urgent. I listened to Ellie talk for ten minutes about the basketball scrimmage. Are they going to play on the middle school team next year?"

"We're praying about it."

"Is Daddy there?"

"He's gone with Kyle to look at a few head of cattle. I think Kyle has them sold for a profit before he buys them. That boy is going to be a success. I just hope it doesn't become too important to him and draw him away from the Lord." Mama paused. "But tell me everything about your week."

I'd already thought out an efficient way to summarize my activities. When I mentioned interviewing Moses Jones, Mama interrupted me. "You met with a criminal alone?"

"Yes ma'am. But it took place in an interview room at the jail with deputies everywhere."

"That part of being a lawyer has always worried me. Be careful."

"Yes ma'am." I took a deep breath. "And I've enjoyed getting to know most of the people I'm working with. One of the associate lawyers is a serious Christian. He's supervising my work in the criminal case."

"Then he should be with you when you meet with this man. Don't be shy in insisting that he come along."

"I won't. He's already told me that he wants to be there at the next meeting with the client."

"Good. How is Mrs. Fairmont's health? Your father and I have been praying for her."

I told Mama about the rough night and how God helped me. When I described the time of singing and prayer, she interrupted. "Amen! The Spirit is all over what you're doing at that house. To me, it's a thousand times more important than any work at a law firm. I'll mention it in our Sunday school class. Once Gladys McFarland hears about the need, you know she'll pray."

"Yes ma'am."

"Are you going to a church in the morning?"

"No. The Christian lawyer mentioned a home group he attends. I may visit, but not tomorrow."

"Be careful, but you've learned how to discern truth and error."

"Yes ma'am. And the lawyer also asked permission to get to know me better."

I stopped. The news was out. I waited.

"Did you say something?" Mama asked. "The phone went dead."

"Yes ma'am. The Christian lawyer wants to get to know me better."

"Isn't that why they offered you a summer job in the first place? That shouldn't be too hard if you're working on a case together."

I spoke rapidly. "Yes ma'am, but he meant on a personal level. He has a homeschool background all the way through high school. We have a lot in common."

There was silence. This time, I knew why.

"How old is he?" Mama asked in a measured tone of voice.

"I'm not sure, but he's only been practicing law for three years. He's probably twenty-seven or twenty-eight."

"So you don't know much about him."

"He's from California and very polite. He's smart and a hard worker. The senior partner he works for has a lot of confidence in him. This week he was working on an important case involving a company in Norway."

Mama ignored the data. "Tell me exactly what he said to you."

"That he would like to get to know me on a personal level. I told him I would need to talk to you and Daddy, and he thought that was a great idea. I've never met anyone like him. He understands my convictions and doesn't criticize me."

"How could he know that much about

your beliefs? You've only been in Savannah a few days."

"It seems longer than that to me. Zach and I have discussed things at work and spent time together." I stopped. Mention of the motorcycle ride to Tybee Island at this point would kill all prospects. "We talked this morning. He came by the house, and we sat on the back porch with Mrs. Fairmont and had a great time."

Slightly breathless, I stopped and waited.

Mama spoke calmly yet firmly. "I'm sure your father and I would want to meet this young man before agreeing to anything. If he's as spiritually mature as you say, he shouldn't have any problem with that approach."

It was a predictable response. But as I'd presented my brief case, I'd realized how badly I wanted Mama to give me the okay. Parental approval of a budding romance was a safeguard against the anguish and heartache caused by aborted attempts to find the right soulmate. Mama said the serial dating practiced by most girls was often nothing more than preparation for multiple divorces.

"Yes ma'am. Talk to Daddy, and I'll keep my interaction with Zach strictly business."

"And remember that our home is open if you want to bring him here for a visit. You're mature enough to get married. It's just a question of letting God find your mate."

I raised my eyebrows. "You really think I'm ready for marriage?"

"Yes, but the timing should be in the Lord's hands. How many times have we prayed for your husband without knowing his name?"

"Hundreds, ever since I was a little girl."

"We want you to have your own home and family. I'm not the perfect wife and mother, but I hope I've given you a good example."

"Yes ma'am."

"I miss you most as a daughter, but also as a worker." Mama chuckled. "You'd think I would get twice the help from Emma and Ellie, but I think, with them, the help is divided rather than multiplied."

Mama's lighthearted comments encouraged me.

"Tell me about your week," I said.

Listening to Mama felt good and bad. It was good to hear about home, bad to face again the ache of separation from my family.

"Tammy Lynn," she said when the conversation was coming to an end, "thanks so much for telling me about your conversation with Zach."

Hearing Mama speak his name startled me.

"We trust you," she continued. "Which is one of the greatest gifts a child can give to a parent."

I felt a stab of guilt because I'd not told the whole truth. I quickly searched my heart for a way to provide additional information.

"We love you," Mama said. "Bye."

The call ended. I stared for a few seconds at the phone receiver in my hand. Even if I didn't tell Mama the whole truth, I could still honor her wishes.

Monday morning, I arrived early at the office and went directly to the library. I already felt more comfortable in my surroundings. A few minutes later, Julie and Vince, their faces reflecting the red of a glorious sunset, came in together.

"I don't have as much Middle Eastern blood in my veins as I thought," Julie said. "And Vinny is a pure Caucasian."

"Did you go to Tybee Island?" I asked.

"No," Vince replied. "Ned Danforth invited Julie to spend the day on his boat, and she brought me along."

"As my bodyguard," Julie added. "I could tell Ned was miffed when we drove up to the marina together, but I pointed out that it was an opportunity to get to know both of us at the same time. Ned and Vinny ended up spending a lot of the time fiddling with the navigation system while I served as a hood ornament."

"I think you were a bow ornament," Vince corrected. "We were on a boat."

Julie looked at Vince in surprise. "Did the sun shining on your head give you a sense of humor? Either way, you ignored me by asking question after question about Tami."

Vince's expression changed, but he was so sunburned that I couldn't tell if Julie's comment embarrassed him or not. She continued. "Summer clerks have to stick together, and you two should go to lunch today and satisfy your mutual curiosity."

Before I could deny curiosity, Vince gave me a hopeful look that stopped my words in their tracks.

"I'd like that," he said. "Are you available?"

"I'm not sure," I answered. "I haven't checked with Mr. Carpenter."

"Be here at noon," Julie said to Vince.

After Vince left, Julie sat across the table from me. "I owe you an apology," she said.

"Why?"

"For giving you such a hard time about not putting on a bathing suit so you could meet men. Friday night I get a predatory call from Ned Danforth. At least, I could tell what he had in mind and convinced Vinny to ruin the party. You might not have been savvy enough to see it coming. Anyway, after we spent four pleasant hours sailing along the coastline, I thought I might have been paranoid. But then while Vinny was below deck with his nose stuck in an on-board software program, Ned came up to the bow and made a comment I couldn't ignore. I had to put him in his place like a ninth grader. It was awkward for both of us. He immediately turned the boat around. The sail back to port seemed twice as long as the ride out. Ned spent the rest of the trip hanging out with Vinny, and I got cooked because I didn't want to join them. Fraternization between associates and summer clerks is so unprofessional." Julie looked down at the paperwork in front of her. "What did you do this weekend besides read the Bible and pray?"

"Fraternized with one of the male associates."

Julie's mouth dropped open. "Get out."

"Yeah, one of the attorneys and I went to Tybee Island."

"Who?"

"Zach Mays, but don't get the wrong

idea," I added. "It was nothing like your boat cruise with Ned. He had me back to Mrs. Fairmont's house before noon so he could come to the office and work."

"I didn't peg you as a pathological liar, but that makes no sense. Tell me straight what happened."

I pointed to the books open on the table in front of me. "Don't you think we should get to work?"

"No!"

Julie sat back in her chair and folded her arms across her chest. It took twice as long as it should have to tell her about the motorcycle ride because she constantly interrupted.

"I'm just trying to make sure you're not holding back. So when did he talk to you about the homeschooling thing?"

"Weeks ago."

"How is that possible if you didn't interview in person for a summer job?"

"Let me finish telling you about Saturday before you drag up another example of fraternization."

Julie shook her head. "Maybe you're not as uptight as I thought."

"No, I'm more uptight than you can imagine, but it feels right to me." I finished as quickly as I could. I left out the entire discussion about asking my parents' permission to get to know Zach on a personal level.

"I had no idea the two of you had something brewing so fast," Julie said thoughtfully. "He doesn't look religious, and the motorcycle deal doesn't fit the stereotype. I just hope he didn't come up with a strategy to seduce you after the first meeting."

It was such a brusque comment that it shocked me.

"He's not a Ned Danforth. I would be able to see through that in a second."

"Maybe." Julie paused. "But where does this leave poor Vinny? I had him all psyched up about what a great girl you are."

"I thought he asked you question after question."

"Maybe one, but I felt so rotten about the way I talked to you on Friday that I tried to make it up by praising you to him. Now, he's going to find out that he's a lap down before the race even starts."

I studied Julie carefully for a moment. "Did you make him think I was interested in him?"

"Uh, no. Except that like a good Christian you love all people equally, no matter their age, race, gender, or hair color."

"That's how you put it? It sounds like a sentence from the federal antidiscrimina-

354

tion laws."

"In so many words or less."

"Maybe I'll get the truth from Vince at lunch."

Julie held up her hands. "Just leave me out of it. I need a social director more than you do."

18

Midmorning, Myra Dean came into the library and summoned Julie to a meeting with a prospective client in the main conference room.

"Bring a blank legal pad and a pen," Myra said. "You won't say anything. Mr. Carpenter wants you to take notes while he conducts the interview. It's a new client who is the money guy behind a huge real-estate deal that is heading toward litigation. He's checking us out, and Mr. Carpenter will be putting on a full-court press to get the business. Rich clients like to know they have a bigger army of lawyers and staff than the people on the other side."

"Will I be the only person taking notes?" Julie asked. "Vince is so quick on the computer. I might miss something important."

"No," Myra replied. "I'll be there too. You're my backup."

After they left the library I stood up to stretch and take a break. Julie's tough exterior was showing cracks. While in college, I'd led several girls to faith in Christ. Some of them came from religious backgrounds. Others were crying out for help from a pit of sinful despair. But I'd never had the chance to pray with a Jewish person. There was a buzz on the phone extension located in the library and a female voice spoke into the room.

"Tami Taylor, please pick up on line 127."

I pushed the three buttons. "Hello," I said.

"It's Zach. Can you take a break?"

"That's what I'm doing right now."

"Good. Come to my office."

The phone clicked off without giving me a chance to reply. Zach was definitely more abrupt in his conversations at the office during the week than on Saturday at the beach.

Upstairs, people were walking back and forth carrying papers, folders, and documents. Everyone was busy and no one paid any attention to me. I walked down the hallway to Zach's door and knocked.

"Come in," he called out.

I opened the door and peeked in. Zach was on the phone with his hand over the mouthpiece. He motioned for me to sit down.

"I understand," he said, removing his hand, "but I haven't had a chance to talk to our client. The judge isn't going to make me go to trial a couple of weeks after he assigned the case to our firm."

Zach listened for a moment. "Just because the jail log shows that Tami was there early last week doesn't constitute effective assistance of counsel. We haven't filed the standard pretrial motions or learned the names and addresses of any of your witnesses."

There was another pause.

"Yes, it will help if you open your file and allow us to review everything you have, but that's just the beginning. We'll need to do our own investigation." Zach turned toward his computer. "Yes, I'm available tomorrow afternoon, but I need to check with Tami to confirm her schedule. The main reason Judge Cannon assigned the case to our office is so she could gain courtroom experience, even if it's limited to preliminary matters."

Zach pushed a button and changed the computer screen from a calendar to his mailbox.

"Right," he said. "I appreciate the pressure you're under. We'll consider the offer and discuss it with Mr. Jones."

Zach hung up the phone. "Good morning," he said.

"I'm not sure," I replied. "That conversation didn't sound like a good way to start the day or the week."

"Don't worry; we'll sort through it in a minute. Did you talk to your parents?"

"Uh, just my mother." I tried to put a hopeful look on my face. "I told her how nice you've been to me and that we had a lot in common. I mentioned your home-school background and that you're well respected in the firm." I stopped. "It's very awkward repeating this to you."

"I'm not trying to embarrass you. I respect you."

"I told her that too." I sighed. "She's going to talk to my father, but she thinks we shouldn't take any steps toward a personal relationship until they have a chance to meet you."

"Did you make it sound more serious than I intended?"

I stared at Zach for a second, not sure whether to cry or run out of the room. My face must have revealed my feelings.

"No, that was wrong," he added. "Can you forget that last sentence and back up to the part about me respecting you?"

"I'll try."

"Thanks. Would it be okay for me to talk to them?"

"I wondered about that," I admitted. "But not until I hear from my father. I don't want to manipulate them."

"Of course, they taught you to appeal to authority, not rebel against it."

"Exactly," I replied in surprise.

"It's good training for becoming a lawyer. Including the case of *State v. Moses Jones,*" Zach replied, tapping a folder on his desk. "That was Ms. Smith, the assistant DA. Her call was routed to me instead of you. The bottom line is that she wants to fast-track *State v. Jones* and bump it up the trial calendar. Several of the complaining home-owners are going to leave town for the summer and don't want to be held hostage as witnesses for a trial. I guess they have homes in the mountains so they can escape the malaria on the coast."

"Malaria? Are you serious?"

"A hundred years ago, it was a big problem."

"Whether a few people are here or not shouldn't matter," I said. "There are twenty-four counts. It would still be a minority."

Zach flipped open the folder on his desk. "How closely did you read the charges?"

"What did I miss?"

Zach ran his finger down the sheets of paper in front of him while I fidgeted.

"There are twenty-four counts but only five different physical locations," he said after a minute. "Think about it. Jones was looking for a convenient hookup for his boat, not a change in scenery. He wouldn't have sought out a different dock every night."

"I missed that."

"And I'm no criminal law expert, but the first rule of an admiralty case is to carefully read the documents. It's the same for any area of the law. Check out the paperwork."

"I'm sorry."

"Just learn the lesson."

"What did Ms. Smith say about a plea bargain?"

"I'm getting to that. A few of the rich folks on the river want Jones removed from polite society. Each count carries a sentence of up to twelve months plus a one-thousand-dollar fine. If you laid those end to end, Moses Jones could be in jail the rest of his life."

My jaw dropped.

"But no judge would lock him up and throw away the key," Zach added. "The DA's initial offer is six months in jail followed by three years on probation with no monetary fine."

I thought about Moses sitting in the interview room breathing through his few remaining teeth. In spite of my mother's fears, he didn't seem to be a huge threat to society.

"That sounds harsh. I mean, he didn't steal or damage anything."

"And that's her first offer. You can make a counterproposal."

"Me?"

"Remember, it's your case. I'll help, just like I promised. However, we need to meet with him as soon as possible. The case is set for Judge Cannon's arraignment calendar tomorrow afternoon. If we work out a deal, it could all be taken care of at that time."

I took a deep breath. "That sounds great."

Zach glanced at a clock on the corner of his desk. "We can run over to the jail, discuss options with the client, and grab a late lunch on the way back. All in the context of business."

"Could we go to the jail later today? I promised Vince that I'd have lunch with him. We tried to get together several times last week, and it kept getting pushed back. I don't want to hurt his feelings."

"Hurt his feelings? What kind of lunch is it?"

"What do you mean?"

"Did you talk to your mother about Vince Colbert?" Zach asked.

I felt my face flush. "No. He didn't ask me to."

Zach looked up at the ceiling for a few seconds before lowering his eyes and meeting my gaze. "For a laid-back California guy, I'm not doing very well," he said. "Have a good lunch with Vince; then check with me. I'll carve out at least two hours for a trip to the jail to meet Mr. Jones."

In the hall outside Zach's office I ran into Gerry Patrick.

"Hope your first week wasn't too dull," she said cheerily. "We have some events planned that will liven things up."

"No ma'am. It's been very stimulating," I replied. "Much more than I'd guessed."

"Good. I'm here if you have any questions."

I returned downstairs to finish a memo for Bob Kettleson. In double-checking my research, I discovered that one of the cases I relied on had been seriously criticized in a recent appellate court opinion. After offering a quick prayer of thanks, I pointed out the potential pitfall in an extra two paragraphs of the memo before sending it to the senior associate. No one came into the library until Vince, the ubiquitous notebook computer in his hand, arrived at precisely 11:50 a.m.

"Are you still available?" he asked.

"Yes."

I noted my time on a log and closed the folders.

"Julie is in a big meeting with several of the partners and associates," Vince said as we checked out at the reception desk.

"I was there when Myra Dean asked her to come."

We walked outside into the hot sun. The slight coolness I enjoyed during my early morning runs didn't last past the point most people in the city were sipping their first cup of coffee.

"How does Savannah compare to Charleston?" I asked.

"Same and different."

We walked in silence. A lunch with Vince might be similar to my morning quiet time. He unlocked the passenger door and held it open for me. Before he reached the driver's side, the car's engine started and the air conditioner started blowing warm air.

"I've never been to Charleston," I said. "Does your family live near the Battery?"

Vince smiled. It was a nice smile without a hint of mockery.

"No. I have a great-aunt that lives south of Broad Street, but I grew up in a newer area. My father is a chemistry professor at the College of Charleston. He also holds several patents in the plastics industry."

I thought about my daddy working at the chicken plant in Powell Station. He was more into biology than chemistry.

"Would you like to go to a café I found before you and Julie arrived?" Vince asked.

"Sure."

Without Julie around to interrupt, I found Vince capable of holding up his end of a conversation. During the drive, I learned that he had two older sisters: the one who was married in Savannah and another who lived in Boston.

"Did you think about going to Harvard?" I asked, expecting him to say that he'd not been accepted for admission at the older institution.

"Yes, it was a tough choice," he replied. "Both Yale and Harvard are good schools."

I stifled a laugh. He glanced over at me.

"What's so funny?"

"Oh, you know, the dilemma of having to pick between two of the finest law schools in the country. At least you didn't have to worry about Virginia, Michigan, and Stanford."

"Virginia and Michigan accepted me, but I didn't apply to Stanford. I didn't want to be on the West Coast."

I looked out the car window. Vince parked on the street.

"The café is a block north," he said. "I hope you'll like it."

The restaurant was in the downstairs of an older home near Greene Square. A hostess wearing a black skirt and white blouse placed us at a table for two where we could look through a window into a garden much more elaborate than the one at Mrs. Fairmont's house. Everything about the place, from wall decorations to furniture, had a French flavor.

"This is really nice," I said after I'd had a chance to look around.

"The food is good too."

I opened the menu and didn't recognize a single entrée by name. Only when I read the ingredients could I partially decipher what was offered.

"It really is a French place, isn't it?" I said.

"The chef is from Marseille."

"How do you know?"

Before he answered, a short waiter wearing rimless glasses came to our table. Vince spoke to him in French, and the man left.

"Is he from Marseille too?" I asked, dumbfounded.

"No, he's from a little town in Provence. He'll send out the chef so we can find out what he recommends."

"You speak French?"

"Enough to get by."

I took a sip of water. The more I learned about Vince, the less confident I felt in his presence. The waiter returned accompanied by a rotund man wearing an apron and a tall white chef's hat. Vince continued to speak exclusively in French. The chef bowed toward me. Vince held out the menu while the three men had a rapid-fire conversation. Most of the other patrons in the restaurant turned to watch. I pressed tightly into my seat, not even trying to pretend I could understand. The chef and waiter left.

"How did it go?" I asked.

"He's going to put together something special that isn't on the menu."

"The menu didn't have any good options?"

"Yes, but he wants to make the lunch memorable."

"It's already that. I've never been in the middle of a French conversation before."

"What foreign language did you take in college?"

"Spanish, but I've only used it in public

367

with a few of the workers at the chicken plant."

As soon as I mentioned the chicken plant, I wanted to cram my napkin in my mouth. This was not the time or place for another discussion about my previous experience as an eviscerator. Vince looked across the room.

"Do you see that painting?" he asked, nodding toward the far wall. "The one above the fireplace."

I turned my head and saw a pastoral scene with vibrant colors. "Yes."

"It's an original. Twentieth-century but in an earlier style. What do you think?"

"I like it."

When I looked back, Vince was staring at me.

"Tell me more about you," he said. "Where you're from, something about your family, your travels."

"Well, I've lived my whole life in rural north Georgia with my parents, two brothers, and twin sisters. I didn't apply to any law schools except Georgia because I can't afford out-of-state tuition. Yesterday, I saw the ocean for the second time in my life. My conversational Spanish doesn't function past basic communication. I can't compete with you in any area of life or experience."

"Life isn't primarily about competition, is it?"

"No, it's about glorifying God," I said.

Vince nodded. "Gerry Patrick told me you were a serious Christian. Your faith made an impression on her, and I wanted to find out why."

"I'm not sure it was a good impression."

"She seemed positive, but the Bible says we shouldn't be surprised by persecution and misunderstanding."

I couldn't believe my ears. "Are you persecuted?"

Vince shrugged. "Imagine how people at the law school react when they find out I believe the Bible is true and Jesus Christ is the only way of salvation. The only acceptable belief is no belief, and the greatest foolishness is commitment to truth."

"How did you come to believe?" I asked.

Vince rubbed the back of his scarred right hand. "In high school I suffered a serious chemical burn to my right hand and arm when a lab partner caused a minor explosion during an experiment. The corrosive activity of the chemicals didn't stop until they took me into surgery."

I winced.

"I spent almost a week in the hospital and have had multiple skin grafts. I usually don't

369

tell people this, but as I suffered, I thought about hell, where the fire never stops and the pain never ceases."

The waiter brought two cups of chilled soup.

"This is an asparagus-based soup," he said. "It sounds weird, but give it a try."

I touched a tiny spoonful to my lips. It was a puree with a much lighter flavor than I expected. I ate a larger spoonful.

"It's good," I said.

Vince ate several bites without speaking. I waited for him to continue. He kept eating, occasionally glancing around the restaurant.

"Are you going to leave me wondering why you decided not to go to hell?" I asked. "That would be stranger than this soup. Which is delicious," I quickly added.

Vince put down his spoon. "Sorry, I have a tendency to focus on one thing at a time. I'm not the best multitasker."

"Then eat your soup before you tell me more."

Vince efficiently reached the bottom of the cup.

"I'm listening," I said when I saw he'd finished. "Why did you think about hell at all? Not many preachers ever mention it."

"In a literature class I'd read Dante's *Inferno* and Jonathan Edwards' 'Sinners in the

Hands of an Angry God.' I had a cultural knowledge of the Bible and was familiar with the concept of eternal punishment. But until the accident, everything was theoretical. Afterward pain dominated my life. In between morphine injections I suffered horribly. The pain would ease, but I knew it would return and my mind couldn't escape the thought of suffering at an even more extreme level — forever."

"That's terrible."

"Do you want to change the subject?"

"No, no. Our church believes in hell, but I don't like to think about it. I'm more interested in learning how to obey the Lord in my day-to-day life."

The waiter brought our meal. The food looked like a picture from one of the magazines at Mrs. Fairmont's house.

"What is it?" I asked.

"*Blanquette de veau.* It's a veal dish."

I took a bite. There were unusual flavors with a hint of onion.

"Can you keep talking?" I asked. "In between bites?"

Vince nodded. "Hell wasn't the only thing I thought about in the hospital. Of course, I thought about my lab partner. He should have been the one suffering, not me. Many times I imagined the chemicals spewing onto his hand and arm instead of mine. Then I read what Paul wrote about forgiving people who have sinned against us. It made logical sense. If I wanted God to forgive me so that I wouldn't go to hell, I needed to forgive the student who sinned against me. I talked to my parents about it. My father listened, but my mother thought I was delusional."

"What did she say?"

"That my mind was too precious a gift to throw away on Judeo-Christian mythology. She's a strict humanist. My father sees the order in science and that makes him doubt random chance as the explanation for the universe."

"Discussions around your supper table must be interesting."

"Anyway, after I got out of the hospital, I started reading the Bible and started attending an Episcopal church not far from our house. The thoughts of hell went away, and the love of God filled my heart."

Vince's description of his conversion left me with doubts. It didn't sound like he'd prayed it through.

"What about your lab partner? Did you forgive him?"

"Yes, and when I told him what happened to me, he prayed to receive Christ too. Now, he's in a postgraduate chemistry program at Rutgers."

We ate in silence for a minute.

"But how do you know God's love is in your heart?" I asked.

Vince smiled. "Oh, when it happens, you'll know."

During the remainder of the meal, he plied me with questions. I had to fight the sense of being interviewed by an anthropologist studying a primitive religious sect. Several times he appeared puzzled, but there was no hint of criticism. I finally decided everything I told him was going into an internal computer file to be processed later.

Dessert, custard topped with fresh blueberries, arrived. The custard was the creamiest substance I'd ever put in my mouth.

The chef returned at the conclusion of the meal. I smiled as sweetly as I could while Vince complimented him on the meal.

"Why did you take a summer job with Braddock, Appleby, and Carpenter?" I asked him during the drive back to the office. "With your academic background, you could have worked anywhere."

"One, it's close to home without being there. I'll spend next weekend in Charleston."

Vince turned onto Montgomery Street. I waited for other reasons. None came.

19

After I thanked Vince for lunch, I grabbed the Jones file from the library and rushed upstairs to Zach's office. His door was open. Fast-food paper wrappers from lunch were strewn across his desk.

"Are you ready to go?" I asked.

Zach looked at his watch. "I worked until one o'clock, then went out for a burger. Mr. Appleby doesn't take a two-hour lunch unless there is going to be a twenty-thousand-dollar fee on the line."

"Vince took me to a French café near Greene Square. The food was good, but the service was on European time."

Zach wadded up the food wrappers and threw them across the room into a round trash can.

"Nice shot," I said.

"When did you go to Europe?" he asked, standing up.

"I haven't. Vince told me the French take

a lot of time with their meals. Eating is more of a social event with them than it is for us."

"Let's socialize with Mr. Jones at the jail," Zach said. "While you were leisurely dining, I stopped by the courthouse and copied the district attorney's file."

"What did you find?"

"I'll let you look it over in the car."

I'd never seen Zach's car. He owned a white Japanese compact. The engine didn't start until he turned the key in the ignition. He handed me the file.

"See what you think," he said.

I opened the folder. There was a one-page arrest record, and the names of the five property owners mentioned in the criminal charges. Beside each name were several dates and the words "video surveillance."

"Do you think the police were watching Moses for several weeks and videotaped him each time he tied up at one of the docks?" I asked.

"No. Video surveillance refers to images from security cameras. That's how they knew which night Moses was at each location. Each count has a specific date. While I was waiting for you, I called three of the five homeowners. They were nice enough to talk to me. That's how I found out about the surveillance cameras. The homeowners association has a contract with a security agency that services everybody."

"What else did you find out?"

"That Moses Jones did not have permission to trespass. One woman said she was terrified that Jones was going to assault her and burglarize her house. She saw his boat floating at the end of her dock early one morning and called the police. He was gone by the time they arrived, but that's when the investigation started."

"Did she talk to Moses?"

"None of them did. The two other owners I reached didn't know he'd been there until the security company checked the recordings for all the houses on the river. Jones was arrested at the dock of a homeowner who didn't answer the phone."

I turned to the next page in the folder and found the statement Moses gave to Detective Branson.

"Moses doesn't talk anything like this," I said after quickly scanning the four-paragraph statement with my client's crude signature at the bottom. "These are the detective's words put into Moses' mouth."

"Stylistic objections aside, what is your opinion of the statement?"

"Moses admits tying his boat up at the

docks. I know he's guilty, but the way the detective crafted the statement bothers me."

Zach glanced sideways at me. "Are you turning into a left-wing criminal defense lawyer before my eyes?"

"No, I don't want to miss anything else. I didn't pay enough attention to the charges."

"Should we file a motion to suppress the confession?"

"I don't know if there are legal grounds."

"Research it before we appear in front of Judge Cannon tomorrow afternoon."

We arrived at the jail complex. I pointed to a parking area.

"That's near the entrance for the cell block where he's kept. Didn't you handle a criminal case when you clerked for the firm?"

"Remember, I didn't clerk in Savannah."

I felt embarrassed. Zach had told me he had clerked in Los Angeles, not Savannah, but I hadn't paid attention to the details. I started to apologize, but that would have only reinforced my blunder. We entered the waiting area. A different female deputy was on duty. I showed her the order from Judge Cannon, and a deputy took us to the interview area.

"I'll have the prisoner brought up," the deputy said.

In a few minutes the door to the cell block opened and Moses came in. He saw me and smiled. I couldn't help feeling some compassion for the old man.

"Mr. Jones, this is Zach Mays," I said. "He's a lawyer who is going to help you."

"Call me Moses," the old man said. "No one calls me Mr. Jones unless they be wanting my money, which I ain't got none."

We entered the interview room.

"What you do about my boat, missy?" Moses asked before we were seated. "It be in the same place as before."

I'd forgotten my promise to check on the status of his boat.

"Uh, that's not been decided. We'll talk to the district attorney about it and include return of the boat as part of the plea bargain in your case. Mr. Mays has been working hard on your case and has some things to tell you."

Zach told Moses about his interviews with the homeowners and Ms. Smith's plea offer. When the subject of jail time came up, Moses looked puzzled.

"She want me in this here jailhouse for six months more? I done been here 'bout two months."

"Which is long enough," Zach said. "I think they should let you out for time already served and put you on probation for less than three years."

"Oh, yeah. Plenty boys get prohibition. But the policemans, they turn that into hard time if they be wanting to. This ought to be over and done with."

"That may not be possible," Zach said. "Some probation, or 'prohibition' as you call it, will be included in your sentence. Do I have your permission to talk to the district attorney about a deal? You would have to be willing to plead guilty to at least some of the trespassing charges and agree not to do it again."

"I told missy here, I be tying up to an old tree from here on." The old man's eyes watered. "I just be needing a place of peace where they can't find me."

"Who?" Zach asked.

Moses looked at me. "The faces. I ain't on the river, but that little girl, she found me last night. I dream 'bout the river an' there she be. How she do that? In my dream, miles from the river edge?"

"What is the girl's name?" Zach asked. "Do you know her?"

"It's not relevant to the case," I said to Zach. "We don't need to ask about this. Please leave it alone."

"What's her name?" Zach persisted, leaning forward in his chair.

Moses licked his lips. "It be Prescott. She a pretty little thing. No more than ten or eleven year old. I don't do nothing bad. So, why she bother me all these years?"

I remembered the photograph in Mrs. Fairmont's room. The blood rushed from my head, and I felt slightly dizzy.

"Did you say Prescott?" I asked in a voice that trembled slightly.

"That be right, missy."

"What color eyes and hair does she have?"

"She be yellow-haired with eyes like the blue sky. Even in the dark, dark water, that hair, it still glows, those eyes, they see right through my soul."

"Is she the girl who was murdered?"

Moses stared at me and blinked.

"What are you talking about?" Zach asked me sharply.

I bolted from the room and let the door slam behind me. I leaned against the wall and took several deep breaths. The deputy on duty in the room started walking toward me. Zach came out of the interview room and joined me.

"Are you okay?" the deputy asked.

I held up my hand. "I just needed to leave the room for a minute. I'm okay."

"Are you sure?"

"Yes sir."

The deputy backed away.

"What's going on?" Zach asked as soon as the deputy was on the other side of the room. "Who is the Prescott girl?"

I didn't answer. Zach put his hands on my shoulders and came close to my face. "Talk to me!"

I pushed away his hands. "That's not necessary," I said. "Give me a second."

He backed away.

In a shaky voice I told him about the old photograph and Mrs. Fairmont's story.

"A terrible crime like that would have been the talk of the town for months," Zach said matter-of-factly. "Everyone else in Savannah would have known all about it. The girl's picture would have been on the front page of the paper every time it ran an article."

"But that doesn't explain why Moses sees her face in the water. You heard him. He wanted to make sure we didn't think he'd done anything wrong."

"Which proves?"

My frustration with Zach flew to the surface. "That you don't understand we may be representing a man who should be charged with murder, not trespassing!"

"Keep your voice down," Zach whispered

382

as he glanced across the room toward the deputy. "We're here to talk to Moses Jones about a misdemeanor trespassing case."

"Then why did you keep going on about the girl in the water after I asked you to stop? This isn't my fault!"

"I'm not blaming you," Zach answered. "But we can't leave Jones alone while we argue. I'm going back in. We need to finish meeting with him about the trespassing case before thinking about anything else."

We returned to the interview room.

"Sorry to leave you like that," Zach said to Moses.

I stared at the old man's hands. They were arthritic now, but when he was younger they could have been lethal weapons.

"How did the Prescott girl die?" I blurted out. "Was she strangled and drowned?"

"No, Tami," Zach said. "Leave it alone."

Moses didn't pay attention to Zach. "People, they know. I not be telling the policemans. How could I?"

Zach spoke. "Mr. Jones, you don't have to talk about this if you don't want to." Moses blinked his eyes and began to cry softly.

"Tami, do you have a tissue?" Zach asked.

I reluctantly took one from my purse and handed it to Moses. The old man wiped his eyes and put his head in his hands. There was nothing to do but watch. Moses' shoulders shook slightly from the sobs. He sniffled several times.

"Mr. Jones, maybe we should come back later," Zach said.

Moses raised his face. His eyes were bloodshot.

"I be tired," he said. "I been rowing this boat way too long. Time to pull it up on the bank and lighten my load."

"What do you mean?" Zach asked.

Moses turned to me. "Do you believe I done hurt that little girl, missy?"

The old man's face didn't look sinister, but how could I trust my eyes?

"I don't know."

"Row my boat," he replied softly. "All I done, is row my boat. That be the whole truth. He give me a shiny silver dollar, but I throwed it in the river."

"Who?" Zach asked.

"He gave me that dollar, and talk about that little girl," Moses said with a faraway look in his eyes. "But it make me scared."

"Who gave it to you?" Zach persisted.

Moses refocused his eyes on Zach. "Ol' Mr Carpenter, the big boss man, he give it to me. He be toting a wicked-looking gun."

I looked at Zach. "Joe Carpenter?"

Moses turned to me and shook his head.

"No, missy. Ol' Mr. Carpenter, he be dead and in the water hisself."

Zach pushed his chair away from the table. "Okay, that's enough. Mr. Jones, I need to apologize to you. I let my curiosity get the best of me and asked you questions that don't have anything to do with your trespassing case. Ms. Taylor and I are here to discuss the hearing in front of Judge Cannon tomorrow. You'll have to plead guilty or not guilty. I need your permission to work out a plea bargain with the district attorney's office. If I can get you out of jail for time served followed by a reasonable period of probation and the return of your boat, does that interest you?"

"I be listening," Moses replied. "You be the lawyers."

Zach looked at me before he answered. "I'll interpret that as your agreement for us to negotiate a better plea bargain; however, you'll make the final decision tomorrow."

Moses stared at me for a few seconds. I waited for him to speak.

"Yes, missy," he said. "You be thinking about all Moses done told you. That other tall girl. She listen, but I think you be knowing more than she do. Taking a green pill, that don't change the past."

Zach rose to his feet. "We'll see you in the

courtroom tomorrow," he said to the old man.

I watched the deputy return Moses to the cell block.

"Who is the 'other tall girl'?" Zach asked when Moses was gone.

"Probably a mental health worker who prescribed medication. Detective Branson knew Moses needed professional help."

A deputy led us back to the main entrance.

"Should we talk to Mr. Carpenter about this?" I asked as we left the building.

"And ask why his family name was linked by an insane old man to the death of the Prescott girl?" Zach replied. "That kind of conversation might shorten your stay as a summer clerk."

"No, I want to ask his opinion of whether it's right to get Moses out of jail on probation when he may be guilty of murder."

We phoned Maggie Smith from Zach's office. The assistant district attorney wouldn't be available until the morning.

"What do we do in the meantime?" I asked.

Zach pulled on his ponytail. "Wait."

"I know what I'm going to do," I said. "Find out more about the Prescott girl's death."

"Are you sure that's smart? Our job is to represent him in a trespassing case. The rest of it is probably a fantasy of random information swirled together in his mind. We don't even know there was a murder investigation."

"Mrs. Fairmont wasn't confused when she mentioned it."

"And could be remembering a rumor. On something like this, it's best to be skeptical. I'm not sure I'm going to let you —"

"Investigate it at all?" I interrupted sharply.

"Calm down," Zach answered.

I imagined steam coming out of my ears. After a few moments, Zach spoke. "We'll get on the phone to the district attorney's office first thing in the morning about a plea bargain on the trespassing case. After that's taken care of, you can decide if you want to talk some more with Moses about the faces in the water or let him slip back into the marsh. If you still want to check it out, I won't stop you."

When I returned to the library, Julie was sitting hunched over one of the research terminals. She turned around when I entered and held up her right hand. It was clenched in the shape of a claw.

"See my misshapen hand?" she asked. "That's what two and a half hours of non-stop note-taking will do to otherwise healthy fingers. While you were laughing it up with Vinny, I barely had time to take a sip of water."

"Is it an interesting case?"

"If you think sorting through fourteen shell companies, some registered overseas, others with dummy boards, is more fun than the Sunday crossword puzzle, this client will be a blast. At one point, I think Mr. Carpenter was having second thoughts about trying to get the business, but when the main guy agreed without argument to the amount of the retainer, all reservations flew out of the room. Now, I'm researching information about the other side. They seem as devious as our client." Julie pushed her chair away from the computer. "So, what about Vinny? Did you tell him you have a crush on Zach Mays?"

"No and no."

"What do you mean? You have to tell me!"

"Why? So you can make fun of me?"

Julie held up her claw hand. "Don't make me use the claw on you. Your arms are longer than mine, but I'm tough in a cat-fight."

"I'm not scared, but there is a lot more to

Vince than either of us realized." I paused. "And I don't have a crush on Zach Mays."

"More," Julie commanded.

I gave her a quick summary of lunch.

"Vinny is a genius," Julie sighed. "If they only make an offer to one clerk, there's no way you or I will land a permanent job with the firm. We may as well goof off the rest of the summer."

"They're paying us to work."

"Oh, don't bring that up." Julie turned back toward the computer screen. I decided not to tell her anything else about Moses Jones. The old man might be delusional, but I wanted to keep his strange comments confidential. I opened one of the Folsom files and began working. Shortly after 5:00 p.m., Julie announced it was time to go home.

"I need to ask Ms. Patrick a question," I replied.

"Don't be long. I have a headache."

I ran upstairs to the administrator's office. Her door was open, and I knocked on the frame.

"Come in," she said. "How are you?"

"Fine. I'm going home now but may want to come back tonight and do some research. Do I need to be concerned about a security system?"

"Not until eleven o'clock. After that, a code has to be entered."

"I won't be that late."

I started to leave.

"Tami, are you respecting the opinions and beliefs of others?" Ms. Patrick asked.

I turned around. "I think so. Have there been any complaints?"

"No, but misplaced zeal can be unprofessional."

"And I hope strong convictions aren't squelched," I responded.

Ms. Patrick had caught me off guard, and the words popped out before I scrutinized them. I inwardly cringed.

"Use restraint," she answered curtly. "I think that is a universal virtue."

"Yes ma'am." I returned more slowly down the stairs. Julie was waiting for me in the reception area. We stepped into the oppressive late-afternoon heat.

"If I'm not offered an associate job at Braddock, Appleby, and Carpenter, I don't think it will be because of Vince," I said.

"Why?"

"It's hard to get a job when you're competing against yourself."

Julie rubbed her left temple. "I'm not feeling well enough to figure that out."

She dropped me off in front of Mrs. Fairmont's house.

"I'll pray that you feel better," I said.

"And I'll take an extra painkiller in case that doesn't work. See you tomorrow."

Mrs. Fairmont was dozing in her chair in the den. Flip barked when I entered and ran across the floor to greet me. Mrs. Fairmont stirred in her chair. I waited, hoping she was lucid. Her eyes opened and focused on me.

"Good afternoon, Tami," she said. "Have you been home long?"

"No ma'am. I just walked in the door. How are you feeling?"

"A little groggy. Gracie fixed supper. It's in the oven and needs to be warmed up."

"Are you ready to eat?"

Flip barked loudly.

"I know you're hungry," I said to the little dog.

Mrs. Fairmont pushed herself up from the chair. Even on days when she didn't leave the house, she wore nice clothes. When I'd asked her about it, she told me that unexpected company could arrive at any moment.

"Let's feed Flip and turn on the oven," she said.

I knew where Mrs. Fairmont kept the dog

food, but taking care of Flip was one of the things she enjoyed most. She carefully measured a scoop of food and poured it into the dog's dish. He immediately began munching the multicolored food with gusto. Gracie had left a note on the oven door with cooking instructions.

"It's a chicken dish," Mrs. Fairmont said. "I think there's garlic in it. I could smell it in the den when she put a clove in the crusher."

"That's fine so long as we both eat it," I replied.

"And the vegetables are in the refrigerator."

The vegetables, succotash and new potatoes in butter, were in pots. I put them on the stove. Without Gracie's help, Mrs. Fairmont wouldn't be able to stay in her house.

Flip finished his dinner and ran out the doggie door. Mrs. Fairmont slowly leaned over, picked up his water dish, and filled it with fresh water. It was time to ask the question that had been in the forefront of my mind since I walked through the front door.

"Do you remember showing me the picture of your friend, Mrs. Prescott, the woman whose daughter died?"

Mrs. Fairmont straightened up. "Yes."

"You and Mrs. Prescott were really good

friends?"

"Yes. That's why I have her picture beside my bed. We were really close all through school and beyond. We had a lot of pleasant times before Lisa's death."

"Lisa Prescott," I said softly.

"It's a pretty name, isn't it?"

"Yes ma'am."

I stirred the succotash and checked the potatoes. "Mrs. Fairmont, I don't want to bring up any painful memories, but how much do you know about Lisa's death? Are they sure it was murder? Was anyone ever arrested and charged with a crime?"

"They never caught whoever killed her. I saved all the newspaper clippings."

"May I read them?"

"I think they're in a box downstairs, but I'm not sure where."

"Could I try to find it?"

Mrs. Fairmont shrugged. "Better let me help. Even as young as you are, you could spend the rest of your life going through the junk I've saved. Christine will probably send it all to the dump, but a lot of it meant something to me."

I checked the clock. The chicken would be ready in ten minutes. The vegetables were on simmer.

"Could we look now?" I asked.

393

"No, child," Mrs. Fairmont said. "I can't go right to it."

"After supper? It's important."

Mrs. Fairmont gave me the same look I'd seen when she first inspected me at the front door.

"Why are you so interested in Lisa Prescott's death?" she asked.

I avoided her eyes. "I can't tell you, except something happened at work today that made me want to find out."

"Christine probably remembers more than I do," Mrs. Fairmont replied. "Let's give her a call."

"No!" I said more strongly than I intended. "Uh, there may not be anything to my curiosity. At this point, I'd rather keep this between us."

"Christine is a blabbermouth," Mrs. Fairmont said, nodding her head. "I don't tell her anything that I don't want spread all over Savannah."

Mrs. Fairmont was quiet during supper. I'd enjoyed the fancy lunch with Vince, but preferred the chicken and nicely seasoned vegetables prepared by Gracie. Mrs. Fairmont yawned several times. I talked, trying to keep her alert enough to lead an expedition into her basement archives after supper.

"Bring the sliced cantaloupe from the refrigerator," Mrs. Fairmont said when we finished eating. "Let's have some for dessert."

I brought the cantaloupe to the table. Mrs. Fairmont ate the fruit with maddeningly slow deliberation.

"This is perfect," she said. "I love it when it's firm and sweet."

"Yes ma'am," I answered as I tried to will her to eat faster. "My family grows very good cantaloupes and watermelons."

She finished the meal with a final large yawn. "Excuse me," she said. "That is so rude, but I can't help it."

She pushed her chair away from the table.

"Have a good evening," she said. "I wish Flip could carry me upstairs to bed. I'll sleep for a while and probably be wide awake in the middle of the night. That's how it is with my condition."

"Yes ma'am," I answered. "Do you think you could put off going to bed for a few minutes so we can locate the newspaper clippings you saved about Lisa Prescott?"

"I forgot," she said with another yawn. "It all happened so long ago, it's hard to imagine it being terribly urgent."

"It is," I said bluntly. "I need to have the information by the morning."

"Very well. But you'd better hold my arm while we go downstairs. I don't want to break my neck."

It was a horrible image — Mrs. Fairmont lying in a twisted heap at the bottom of the stairs. I'd been hired to protect the elderly woman, not to place her in harm's way.

"Maybe we should wait until you wake up in the night," I said. "I can adapt to your schedule."

"No, no. That cantaloupe was sweet enough to give me a few more minutes of energy."

"Are you sure?"

She didn't answer but started walking toward the basement. Flip and I followed. I firmly held her arm, and we made it to the bottom of the stairs without mishap. I turned on the bare lightbulbs that illuminated the open area opposite my apartment. Large cardboard boxes were stacked on top of one another. Furniture not in use was covered by white bedsheets. Shelves affixed to two of the walls contained scores of smaller boxes. I wouldn't have known where to begin. Mrs. Fairmont stood at the bottom of the stairs and stared at a lifetime of accumulation.

"I think I keep the older records over here," she said, moving down a row of the large boxes.

I followed. Most of the boxes were labeled. We passed dishes, extra china, and souvenirs from travel. Mrs. Fairmont stopped and pointed.

"Could you lift that one out?" she asked.

"Yes ma'am." I sprang into action.

It was marked "Of Interest." I placed the lightweight box at Mrs. Fairmont's feet and removed the top. It was filled with yellowed newspapers.

"This is it!" I exclaimed.

"Maybe," she said.

I reached in and grabbed a newspaper that promptly crumbled in my hands. "Oops," I said.

"Don't worry. I'd never have seen it again if you hadn't asked me about Ellen's daughter."

I carefully retrieved what was left and held it up to the light. It was a Savannah paper almost seventy years old. Mrs. Fairmont leaned close to my shoulder.

"That's from my school days," she said. "My mother probably saved it because it contained news about me and my classmates."

I stared at the other papers in the box. "Would everything in this box be that old?"

"At least," she said. "Put it back. I don't

want to read it."

I returned the box to its place. Mrs. Fairmont pointed to another box. This one was labeled "Newsworthy Items." I put it on the floor and removed the top. Inside were stacks of manila folders grown discolored with age.

"That's Christine's handwriting," Mrs. Fairmont said, pointing to the tab on the top folder. "These will be more recent."

One by one I took the folders from the box. They contained everything from Christmas punch recipes to information about horses.

"Christine loved to ride jumpers when she was younger. She wasn't afraid of anything."

I remembered my brief ride in the car with Mrs. Bartlett. I thought she might try to jump the curb in her Mercedes. Toward the bottom of the box, I saw a folder with the name "Lisa" on it and opened it. My eyes fell on the front page of the Savannah paper and a grainy picture of a little girl. I showed it to Mrs. Fairmont. She stared at it for a second.

"It's Lisa," she said in a sad voice. "That picture brings back a lot of memories. Lisa loved dressing up and sitting in a parlor chair with her feet dangling in the air. Ellen brought her over several times for afternoon tea."

While Mrs. Fairmont talked, I quickly scanned the article. On a Tuesday afternoon, the ten-year-old girl vanished following a piano lesson. The piano teacher, a woman named Miss Broadmore, was questioned by police and reported that Lisa left the teacher's house at precisely 4:30 p.m. for the five-minute walk home along familiar streets. Lisa never made it. Within an hour the police were notified. Requests for assistance were broadcast on the local radio stations. Anyone seeing her was urged to come forward.

"It was a sad time," Mrs. Fairmont continued. "The whole city was touched by the Prescotts' loss. I think Christine saved all the articles she could. Most of my news came directly from Ellen."

There were other articles in the folder. All of them featured the same photograph. Even in a black-and-white image, Lisa fit Moses Jones' description.

"Do you remember anything else Ellen told you?"

Mrs. Fairmont shook her head. "There are lots of things jumbled up in my head. Trying to sort them out would be an unhappy way to end the day."

"Yes ma'am. I understand. Thanks for helping me."

I assisted Mrs. Fairmont up the stairs to the main floor and then to her bedroom. I examined the picture of Ellen Prescott on the nightstand more closely. Lisa looked a lot like her mother.

"How old were you and Ellen in that picture?" I asked.

"About seven or eight. Young enough that a trip to the park with a friend was a special treat."

I turned to go downstairs. I was anxious to read the rest of the newspaper articles.

"Tami?" Mrs. Fairmont asked.

"Yes ma'am."

"I like having you in the house. It makes me feel safe."

"Thank you."

I took the box into my apartment and carefully removed the newspapers. They weren't as brittle as the very old ones. Beginning with the first account of Lisa's disappearance, I read the unfolding story more slowly.

There wasn't much to tell.

One day Lisa was a bright, vivacious girl. The next she vanished without a trace. The second article was the longest and featured a map with Lisa's most likely route from

Miss Broadmore's house to the Prescott home on East McDonough Street. Close to the Prescott home was the Colonial Park Cemetery.

Several follow-up articles included quotes from people claiming to have seen Lisa during her walk home. Unfortunately, the claims were inconsistent and would have required Lisa to walk several blocks out of her way instead of following the most direct route. The police chief offered cryptic comments without substance to the newspaper reporters. One fact seemed clear. No one saw the little girl after she neared the cemetery. The police focused their investigation on that area and scoured it for physical evidence. Not a piece of sheet music or bit of clothing was discovered. No ransom note was delivered. The possibility of a kidnapping faded.

After a week of daily articles, there was a two-day gap followed by a brief update without any new information. A week went by before another article repeated familiar facts with the conclusion that the police suspected "foul play" but had no suspects. Two months later there was a notice on page two of "Memorial Service for Girl Presumed Dead." It was a harsh headline. More than eight hundred people attended the service at a local church. I returned the newspapers to the box. I looked over my notes and decided I hadn't uncovered anything that warranted a nighttime walk to the office.

And, even though Lisa Prescott's unexplained disappearance occurred decades earlier, I didn't want to go out after dark.

20

The world appeared less menacing in the morning when I went for my run. I modified my route to include Lisa's likely course home from her music teacher's house. It wasn't far. And in a simpler time, when children played outside without constant supervision, the brief walk would probably have been considered good exercise. I did a slow loop around Colonial Park Cemetery. The graveyard had many old headstones and looked like it had been closed for business for many years. It probably hadn't changed much since Lisa Prescott saw it.

Returning to the house, I was surprised to find Mrs. Fairmont, wearing a green silk robe with flowers embroidered on it, standing in the kitchen. Coffee was filling the pot.

"Good morning," I said, pouring myself a glass of water from a jug in the refrigerator.

"Good morning. Did you read the newspaper articles about Lisa?" she asked.

"Yes ma'am. They never mentioned murder, but there wasn't another explanation."

"We hoped for a while that it was a kidnapping. Money wouldn't have been a problem."

"But no ransom note came."

"Right." Mrs. Fairmont nodded. "You know, the Prescotts had a funeral for Lisa. Ellen didn't want to do it, but her husband and the rest of the family insisted. It was a pathetic affair, no casket, all the unanswered questions. Ellen maintained hope Lisa would return. I grieved when Ellen died, but I also thought at least she was with Lisa again."

It was a poignant thought. I poured Mrs. Fairmont a cup of coffee. The elderly woman seemed particularly lucid.

"What can you tell me about the criminal investigation?" I asked.

"Ellen and her husband met with the police several times, and she told me what was said. The detectives had ideas." Mrs. Fairmont stared across the room.

"Do you remember?" I asked.

"There was the blood on the curb at Colonial Park Cemetery. They didn't have all the fancy tests they do now. At first, the police thought it was from an animal hit by a car because they found a dead dog nearby,

404

but later they figured out it was human blood."

"That wasn't in any of the newspaper articles. Was it Lisa's blood type?"

"They weren't sure. The tests back then weren't very accurate. Ellen and I went to the curb before rain washed away the stain. Even though she wasn't positive the blood came from Lisa, Ellen stared at the spot for a long time and cried. I didn't know what to say." Mrs. Fairmont looked directly at me. "What would you have told her?"

"I don't know. I've never lost a close family member. I hope God would give me a special grace for that time. Just loving her was probably the best thing you could do as her friend."

Mrs. Fairmont placed her coffee cup on the counter. "Do you think God will give me a special grace for the time I'm going through?"

"That you will get better?"

She nodded.

It was a difficult question, and I didn't want to give a casual answer. I believed with my whole heart in divine healing. Some people in our church had been healed of serious diseases; others died.

"I know God loves you," I said slowly. "Asking for his help is up to you."

Mrs. Fairmont smiled. "You sound like Gracie, only she puts a lot more feeling behind it. God brought her into my life to help me years ago, and it looks like he's added you for reinforcement."

"Yes ma'am. I want to help."

"I know. Run along and get ready for work."

I turned to leave.

"And promise you'll tell me as soon as you can why you're interested in Lisa Prescott's disappearance," Mrs. Fairmont said. "That's an old wound, and it's not right to open it up without a reason."

"Yes ma'am."

I returned the newspaper clippings to the folder so I could copy them at work. When I came upstairs, I saw the back of Mrs. Fairmont's head above the top of a chair in the den.

"I'm leaving for work," I said.

"Christine?" she called out without turning around.

"No ma'am. It's Tami." I stepped into the older woman's line of sight. "Do you want to call her?"

Mrs. Fairmont stared intently at me. "No, no. I thought you were Christine. What were we talking about earlier? My brain has gotten fuzzy."

"I asked you about Lisa Prescott."

Mrs. Fairmont shook her head with a sad expression on her face. "You know, they never did find her body."

"Yes ma'am, I know. Don't worry about that today."

All the way to work, I prayed for Mrs. Fairmont.

I went straight to Zach's office. His door was open, and papers were stacked on his desk. His tie was loosened around his neck. He was taking a sip of coffee when I entered.

"I didn't know you drank coffee."

"I'm a backslider," he replied.

"No, I didn't mean it that way."

"I'm not offended. I needed a boost since I came in to work a couple of hours ago. Getting a head start on this project for Mr. Appleby is the only way I can create enough time in my schedule for the Moses Jones case this afternoon."

"Could I go alone?"

"No." Zach smiled. "You'll do all the talking, but Judge Cannon wouldn't appreciate a law student showing up in his courtroom without a supervising attorney."

"I did some research about the little girl, but the most interesting information came from Mrs. Fairmont."

I handed him the initial article and waited for him to read it.

"What did Mrs. Fairmont say?"

Zach listened without taking notes while I talked. He took another sip of coffee before he spoke.

"It's obvious. Moses Jones was hired by a man named Floyd Carpenter to dispose of Lisa Prescott's body and was paid a shiny, silver dollar to do it. He dumped her in the Ogeechee River, and the little girl's face has haunted him ever since."

Hearing Zach succinctly state my fears made me shudder. "That's awful."

"Yes, if there's a shred of truth to it."

"But it makes sense. Why else would Moses say the things he does?"

"Because he may be in a permanent mental fog. Did you research our obligation to suggest half-baked theories implicating our client in a forty-year-old missing child case to the district attorney while trying to convince her to release him on probation on a trespassing charge?"

"No."

"And you don't have to." Zach pushed his chair away from his desk. "Before I began my other work this morning, I spent time praying about the Jones case. Once my head cleared of the misguided curiosity that dominated our interview session with him yesterday, I realized we shouldn't be pretending to be a cold-case investigation team. We're not actors on a TV show. Moses Jones is a real person who trusts us to help him with an immediate problem."

"But what about Lisa Prescott?"

"Her disappearance was a tragedy. But why should we try to solve what police officers and detectives close in time to the events couldn't figure out?"

I took a deep breath to avoid getting angry. "I believe everything happens for a reason," I said deliberately. "It wasn't an accident that I saw the picture of Ellen Prescott on Mrs. Fairmont's nightstand and asked about it. It wasn't a coincidence that Moses mentioned the Prescott girl to me. And this morning, Mrs. Fairmont tells me information known only to the police and Prescott family."

"So God sovereignly brought all this together?"

"Maybe."

"Which still doesn't get you off the hook about making a choice. I've made my choice, and so should you. I think you should focus on what Judge Cannon appointed you to do — represent Moses in the trespassing case."

I scrunched my eyes together but held my tongue.

"Make a face if you like," Zach said, "but I'm trying to teach you to be a professional. It's my job. Come back at nine o'clock, and we'll call Maggie Smith."

He looked down at some papers on his desk. Steaming mad, I left his office and walked down the stairs to the first floor. My shoes clipped against the wooden floor. One choice was easy. My interest in getting to know Zach Mays better on a personal level was gone. Julie was in the library when I arrived.

"Good morning," Julie announced brightly. "My headache is gone. A bad one can hang around for a couple of days, but I'm feeling super."

"That's great," I managed.

"Uh-oh," Julie responded. "It's too early in the day to be depressed. Is the pressure of maintaining two boyfriends getting to you?"

"Shut up," I said.

Julie's jaw dropped.

"I did it," I said softly.

Tears rushed into my eyes, and I stumbled out of the room.

Right into the arms of Mr. Carpenter.

The older lawyer steadied me for a moment, then let go. Julie opened the door, saw Mr. Carpenter, and quickly closed it.

"What's going on here?" Mr. Carpenter asked.

I sniffled. "It's been a rough morning," I said.

"That's obvious. Come to my office."

"Now?"

"Yes."

As I walked down the hall I glanced back and saw the library door close again. My tears receded, but my eyes were still red as we passed the secretary's desk. She didn't pay any attention to me.

"Sit down," Mr. Carpenter said.

I sat in a blue leather chair.

"Answer me directly," the lawyer continued. "Why were you crying in the office hallway at eight thirty in the morning?"

"It's a combination of things."

"Tell me every one. As managing partner, I'm responsible for this office and the people who work here. It's better to address problems as soon as they surface instead of letting them fester."

"I don't want to get Julie in trouble."

"I appreciate your sentiment, but I don't know what took place. You might be the one in trouble."

I hadn't considered that possibility. Confessing sin, even if I wasn't the primary guilty party, happened all the time in my family and wasn't a new concept to me.

"I told her to shut up," I said. "And I'm sorry. I'll apologize as soon as I can."

Mr. Carpenter tilted his head to the side. "Much worse things than that have been said in our partnership meetings. Why did you tell her to shut up?"

I realized Mr. Carpenter was going to ferret out every piece of information hidden in my brain, so, in a methodical manner, I told him about Julie's challenge. He listened without interruption.

"Anything else at the office upset you this morning?" he asked.

"Yes sir, I'm struggling with the best way to represent Mr. Moses Jones, my client in the misdemeanor criminal case. Zach Mays and I don't agree on the best way to proceed."

"What did you say was the client's name?"

"Moses Jones."

"Tell me about the client."

"He's an African-American man in his early seventies. He had a prior criminal conviction many years ago, something to do with moonshine whiskey."

"Been in Savannah a long time?"

"I think his whole life."

Mr. Carpenter touched his fingers together in front of his chin. The phone on his desk buzzed. He picked it up.

"Tell Bob Groves that I'll be there in a couple of minutes. I'm almost finished with Ms. Taylor."

I waited, not sure whether the next few minutes would be my last on the job. If I left, it would be with a clear conscience. Mr. Carpenter hung up the phone.

"I've received good reports from several sources about the way you and Ms. Feldman have been working together," the lawyer said. "The incident this morning is an opportunity for growth. Julie is probably scared that you're telling me a boatload of bad things about her. That may be punishment enough for baiting you. When you go back, I expect you to confront her actions in a gracious yet professional manner."

"Yes sir."

"I'll meet with her later today." Mr. Carpenter paused. "And keep me posted via weekly memos on the Jones case."

"Yes sir."

I left Mr. Carpenter's office. I still had a job. I looked at my watch. It was past time for the phone call to Maggie Smith at the district attorney's office. I turned to go upstairs, then remembered my obligation to

Julie. I walked quickly to the library and opened the door. Julie looked up from a casebook.

"I'm sorry," she said hurriedly. "What's he going to do?"

"Mr. Carpenter thought you'd be worried."

"Worried? I've been frantic! Trying to figure out how I was going to break the news to my parents if I lost this job."

"He wants to talk to you later."

"Am I going to get in trouble? What's he going to do to me?"

"Probably tell you to act more professional," I said. "That's what he said to me. He knows we've been working well together. He realizes this was a temporary blowup."

"Are you sure?"

"Yes."

"Okay. Anything else?"

I looked directly in her eyes. "I'm sorry I told you to shut up. We can joke around but shouldn't be cruel."

Julie looked down at the table. "Sure, like I said, I'm sorry too."

I went upstairs to Zach's office, determined to act professional. The stack of papers on his desk was higher than before.

"Sorry I'm late. Mr. Carpenter called me

into his office," I said.

"You didn't miss anything. I just got off the phone with the DA's office. Smith won't want to commit to any modification of her plea offer without the judge getting involved. It's an extreme position for a misdemeanor case, but she wouldn't budge. We won't know anything else until we go to court this afternoon."

"Okay."

"Why were you talking to Mr. Carpenter?"

"He had some questions for me."

Zach stared at me for a few seconds. I remained silent.

"Fine," he said. "We'll leave for the courthouse thirty minutes before the calendar call. The order of cases isn't released in advance. We could be first; we could be last."

I nodded and left.

Julie wasn't in the library when I returned. On my side of the desk was a memo from Bob Kettleson. He wanted me to research a complicated municipal corporation issue before the end of the day. I read the memo again, thankful that I'd completed the course in law school and received an A.

Shortly before noon, the library door opened. I looked up, expecting to see Julie. It was Vince.

"Lunch plans?" he asked.

I smiled. "Thanks, but I don't have time for a long meal. Bob Kettleson needs an answer to a question, and I have a hearing in my criminal case this afternoon."

"My appointed case is on the calendar too," he said. "The client is going to pay a speeding fine and replace his muffler in return for dismissal of the racing charge."

"I wish my case was so simple," I sighed.

"What's the problem?"

I eyed Vince for a moment. He was smart and less likely than Zach to try to impose his will on me in a condescending way. His input might be helpful.

"I'll tell you if we can grab a quick sandwich."

"I know a place," he replied.

While notifying the receptionist that we were leaving for lunch, I glanced up the staircase and saw Zach looking down at us. He quickly walked away.

It was hot outside, and Vince started his car with his remote as soon as we left the building.

"It won't do much good," he said, opening the car door for me. "But it's a nice thought."

He drove a few blocks to a deli near the river. There was a parking place directly in front on the curb.

"Do you ever pray for parking spots?" he asked.

"No, I don't own a car."

"That will change once you graduate and get a job," Vince said.

"I wonder where I'll be."

"Why not here?"

There was no tactful way to mention what Julie and I knew — Vince would be the summer clerk offered an associate attorney job.

"We'll see," I said.

The deli featured a dizzying selection of meats, cheeses, and breads. Vince waited while I looked at the menu.

"Could I order for you?" he asked.

"Sure. You did fine with lunch yesterday."

"Is there anything you don't like?"

"Chicken livers. My mother has cooked them every way possible, but I always have trouble convincing my mouth to send one down my throat."

Vince placed the order, and I watched a man behind the counter slice two types of meat, three kinds of cheese, and add an assortment of unknown condiments to a piece of dark bread. We took our food and drinks to a booth for two next to a window. I could see the river glinting between two buildings. Vince prayed. I took a bite of the sandwich.

"This isn't dull at all," I said after I'd

chewed and swallowed a bite. "I'm not used to a sandwich like this having much flavor."

"Okay. Do you want to tell me about your case?"

I had the sandwich halfway up to my mouth. I stopped. "Not until I eat."

Vince made a few comments while we ate. He seemed more relaxed than the previous day, and I realized he might have been nervous during our lunch. The thought that a man would be nervous around me suddenly hit me as funny, and I laughed.

"What is it?" Vince asked, quickly touching a napkin to his mouth. "Is there sauce dripping off my chin?"

"No." I sipped my drink. "You're fine. It was a private thought about me."

I ate most of the sandwich and wished I could give what remained to the twins. They would have turned up their noses until coaxed into trying a bite.

"Now, tell me about *State v. Jones*," Vince said.

"You remember the name of my case?"

"Your client is charged with multiple counts of trespassing, and Julie's client, Mr. Ferguson, was allegedly impersonating a water-meter reader."

"Why am I surprised?" I shrugged.

I began with the first interview. As I

talked, I had the impression Vince would remember more about the case than I would.

"Did Jones say anything else about the man named Carpenter?"

"No."

"Have you done any research at the court-house or on the Internet?"

"No."

Vince looked at his watch. "We need to get back to the office. Let me think about it."

With Vince, I knew the statement wasn't a put-off.

I was able to deliver a memo to Kettleson with fifteen minutes to spare before leaving for the courthouse. I opened my *State v. Jones* folder and reviewed my notes. I knew if a plea bargain wasn't reached with the district attorney, Moses would be expected to plead not guilty to the charges. I ran over in my mind Moses' argument that he couldn't be convicted of trespassing because the river belonged to God. If that was true, the posts put there by man were the real trespassers. Even a summer clerk couldn't make that argument to a jury of sane adults. I went upstairs to Zach's office. He was pulling his tie tighter around his neck.

"I'm ready," I said.

"Really? Did you contact the homeowners I hadn't interviewed?"

"No."

"I did. One of them will be in the court-room."

Zach picked up his briefcase. "I'll fill you in on the way over there."

As I followed Zach to the first floor of the office, two thoughts crossed my mind. Both Zach and Vince were smarter than I was; however, Vince didn't go out of his way to remind me.

21

"You're kidding," I said, standing beside Zach's black motorcycle with the sidecar attached.

Zach handed me the helmet I'd worn on Saturday. "Ride or walk. It's not very far. I didn't unhook the sidecar after our ride to Tybee Island."

"But you knew we had the arraignment calendar today. You could have driven your car."

"Maybe I forgot," he said with a grin.

I debated whether to go back inside and request use of the law firm car, but when I looked around the lot it wasn't there. I took the helmet.

"This isn't funny," I said, slipping it over my head.

Zach put on his helmet and spoke into the microphone. "We'll be able to park close to the entrance. There are special spaces reserved for motorcycles."

I didn't answer. Refusing his offer of a hand to steady me, I got into the sidecar as gracefully as I could. Zach turned on the motor and backed up. As he did, a car passed behind us as it entered the lot. I turned my head and saw Julie, her mouth gaping open, staring at me from the passenger seat.

"Do you want to know what the homeowner told me?" Zach asked.

"Tell me after we get there."

The pleasure I'd felt toward the end of the motorcycle ride on Saturday didn't return during the short, bumpy trip to the courthouse. I clutched the Jones file in my lap and looked straight ahead. I didn't have to wonder if every pedestrian or the people in other vehicles were staring at me. Zach turned into the courthouse parking lot and stopped next to a green motorcycle.

"That's a nice bike, made in Italy," he said as we took off the helmets.

I pushed myself up with my hands and got out of the sidecar. "I'm not wearing motorcycle clothes. Did your father take your mother to church in a motorcycle sidecar?"

"Sometimes. But you have to remember, my parents were living near L.A."

Zach locked up the helmets.

"Which courtroom?" he asked as we climbed the steps.

"I'm not sure."

"Follow me."

I held back for a second, but it looked silly for me to walk two steps behind him. We entered the building together.

"What about the homeowner?" I asked.

"After I told Mr. Fussleman about Moses' life on the river, he said it reminded him of Huck and Jim. He's willing to ask the judge for a lenient sentence."

"What about the other dock owners?"

"I hope they won't be here. Moses used Mr. Fussleman's dock more than any of the others, so you can argue he's the party who suffered the most damage." Zach glanced sideways at me as we waited for an elevator. "Have you written out your argument for the judge?"

"No."

"You'll have a few minutes after we talk to Mr. Fussleman, and maybe our case won't be the first one called."

"Vince has a case —" I stopped. I could have ridden with Vince and avoided the sidecar.

We got off the elevator and turned left down a broad hallway. A cluster of people were milling around.

"I hope all these people aren't on our calendar," Zach said.

He opened the door to the courtroom. It was a large room with bench seating. At least a hundred people were already present. The thought of making my unprepared argument to Judge Cannon in front of a big crowd made my hands sweat. Zach walked to the front of the courtroom. I followed. He turned around and spoke in a loud voice.

"Is Mr. Fussleman here?"

All the conversations ceased, and everyone looked around to see if Mr. Fussleman identified himself. No one raised his hand or came forward. There was a row of chairs in front of a railing that separated the crowd from the area in front of the bench and the jury box on the right-hand side of the room. Zach sat down and motioned for me to join him.

"What is Mr. Fussleman going to say?" I asked.

"Fussleman grew up here and knows men like Moses who roam up and down the river. I want him to meet Moses before the calendar call. Once Fussleman sees how harmless he is, he may ask the judge to let Moses go free without any more jailtime and even allow Moses to use his dock as long as he doesn't do anything except tie up for the night. That would take care of two problems at once."

It was a much better plan of action than the nonexistent one I'd come up with.

"That's great," I said.

Zach glanced sideways at me. "I promised to help."

I felt ashamed. I'd been petty and prideful. I pressed my lips together and silently asked God to forgive me. Zach stood up again. An apology to him would have to wait.

"Is Mr. Fussleman here?" he called out again.

An older man with gray hair and wearing a business suit raised his hand in the air.

"Come on," Zach said to me.

We walked to the rear of the courtroom. Zach extended his hand and introduced himself. "Thanks so much for coming," he said. "I know it's inconvenient."

Zach introduced me to Mr. Fussleman, who smiled.

"Mr. Mays told me this was your first case," he said. "One of my daughters is a young lawyer in Washington, D.C. When I thought about her, I had to see what I could do to help you sort this out."

"Thank you," I said gratefully.

"Let's step into the hallway," Zach suggested.

More people were entering the courtroom. We found a quiet spot. Mr. Fussleman looked at me expectantly. I knew my job — to tell him Moses Jones was a harmless old man who wouldn't hurt anything except the fish he caught for supper. I did my best, but I kept thinking about the newspaper photograph of Lisa Prescott and her face that continued to accuse Moses from a watery grave. Mr. Fussleman listened thoughtfully. The few times I glanced at Zach, I couldn't decipher his expression. Vince walked past us and into the courtroom.

"What do you want me to do?" Mr. Fussleman asked when I finished.

"Tell Judge Cannon that as one of the dock owners, you support releasing Mr. Jones for time already served in jail, and in the future would allow him to tie up for the night at your dock so long as he didn't interfere with your use of the facilities or cause any damage to your property."

"I want to meet Mr. Jones before I agree to anything, but I don't think I have any objection to releasing him from jail." He hesitated a moment before continuing, "But I can't agree to let him use my dock."

My face fell.

"Unless he checks with me first," he finished.

"It may be late at night," I replied.

"I'm usually up past eleven. If it's later than that, he will have to pole his boat back down the river."

His proposal was more than fair.

"Can we meet with Moses?" I asked Zach.

"Let's try."

We returned to the courtroom.

"There's Maggie Smith," Zach said.

There were three female members of the district attorney's staff stacking up files at one of the tables used by the lawyers.

"Which one?"

"The shorter one with brown hair."

Zach ushered Mr. Fussleman to a seat directly behind the railing. We approached Ms. Smith. Zach extended his hand.

"We met at a young lawyers section meeting last year," he said. "You may not remember me —"

"It's hard not to notice a male lawyer in Savannah with long hair who rides a motorcycle."

I glanced down. Ms. Smith wasn't wearing a wedding ring.

"One of the dock owners, a Mr. Fussleman, is here," Zach said. "He'd like to meet our client."

"Why?"

Zach turned to me, and I explained our purpose. Smith shrugged.

"Okay. If none of the other dock owners show up, I won't oppose a guilty plea for time served as long as there is a period of probation. I don't want Jones claiming ownership of a dock by adverse possession."

"Will you support the plea?" Zach asked.

Smith looked at Zach and smiled. "No, but I'll be very clear that I don't oppose it."

"Thanks," he said.

We returned to the area where the lawyers were sitting. Vince and Russell Hopkins, his supervising attorney, were at the opposite end of our row. A side door opened, and a long line of prisoners wearing jail uniforms entered. Toward the end of the line I saw Moses. None of the men in his group were shackled. A smaller group in leg irons and handcuffs followed.

"Why are some of them wearing hand-cuffs?" I asked Zach.

"Probably felony cases. Moses and the others are the misdemeanor, nonviolent cases."

Moses saw me and smiled. It made me feel creepy.

"Let's talk to the deputy," Zach said.

Zach went up to one of the deputies I

recognized from my visits to the jail and told him about Mr. Fussleman. The deputy motioned to Moses.

"You can talk to him at the end of the row," the deputy said. "But you'd better make it quick. The judge will be here in a minute, and he'll want everyone in their places."

"Get Fussleman," Zach told me. "I'll tell Moses what we're trying to do."

I brought Mr. Fussleman over. Zach was whispering into Moses' ear.

"What dock be yours?" Moses asked Fussleman.

"The one with the blue and white boat."

Moses nodded. "Yes sir. That's a mighty nice piece of boat."

"Thank you."

"Moses, are you sorry that you used Mr. Fussleman's dock without permission?" Zach asked the old man.

Moses looked at Zach then Mr. Fussleman. "I didn't use nobody's dock except as a place to put a piece of cotton rope. I'm sorry that the policemans put me in jail and lock me and my boat up. That's what makes my heart cry in the night."

"Moses doesn't believe the river belongs to anyone," I said, "but he's agreed not to tie up at private docks without permission in the future, right?"

I held my breath for a second, hoping Moses wouldn't back down on his promise.

"That be right, missy."

"And Mr. Fussleman might be willing to let you tie up if you ask his permission in advance before eleven o'clock at night," I added.

Moses looked at Mr. Fussleman. "That's mighty nice of you, boss man. You let Moses know, and I'll clean that blue and white boat for free and scrub your dock. And you know that yellow line at the edge, the one that be going away fast? I paint it for you."

Mr. Fussleman shook Moses' hand. "Come by when you get out of jail, and we'll talk about it." The dock owner turned to me. "This man doesn't need to be locked up. I'll testify if you need me."

"All rise!" announced one of the bailiffs on duty. "The Superior Court of Chatham County is now in session, the Honorable Clifton Cannon presiding."

The judge, an older, white-haired man, sat down without looking in the direction of the lawyers.

"Be seated!" the bailiff called out.

The judge turned toward the DA's table. "Ms. Smith, are you ready?"

"Yes, Your Honor."

"Let's hear pleas first, reserving the motion to suppress in *State v. Robinson* to the end of the calendar."

"Yes sir, we have twenty-six cases here for arraignment. Based on the discussions with counsel, several of those intend to plead guilty."

I licked my lips. There was less than a five percent chance that Moses' case would be the first one called. I desperately wanted to watch a few experienced lawyers navigate the waters before I was thrown in. I leaned close to Zach.

"What if we're first?"

"Then I'll be back to the office in time to get some work done."

It was an unsympathetic answer. Ms. Smith picked up a file from her stack.

"State v. Jones," she called out.

Zach stood up. I was so shocked that I didn't move.

"Come on," Zach said.

I got to my feet and stepped into the open area in front of the judge. A deputy culled Moses from the rest of the prisoners and brought him to stand beside me.

"Your Honor, I'm Zach Mays, and this is Ms. Tami Taylor, a summer clerk with our firm," Zach said. "You appointed Ms. Taylor to represent Mr. Jones, and the firm asked me to supervise her work on the case."

Judge Cannon had bushy white eyebrows. He brought them together and glared at me. Ms. Smith spoke.

"Mr. Jones is charged with twenty-five counts of trespassing by tying up his boat at private docks on the Little Ogeechee River."

"I believe it's twenty-four counts," I corrected.

"A difference without a distinction," the judge grunted. "How does he plead?"

I looked at Zach.

"Mr. Mays is not your client," the judge barked at me.

"Uh, Your Honor, Mr. Jones has been in jail for over two months, and we would like to enter a guilty plea as long as he is released for time served followed by a one-year period of supervised probation."

Moses' voice startled me. "My boat, missy. Don't be forgetting."

"Yes sir. His boat was seized, and he would like it back."

"Ms. Taylor, you do not enter into plea negotiations with me while I'm sitting on the bench trying to work my way through a crowded calendar."

"Yes sir. We talked to Ms. Smith," I responded quickly. "She has no objection to my proposal."

"Is that right?" the judge asked the assistant DA.

"We will leave the sentence to Your Honor's discretion but do not oppose defense counsel's suggestion."

"Was there any physical damage to property warranting restitution?" the judge asked.

"No sir," I replied. "And one of the dock owners, Mr. William Fussleman, is present and willing to testify in favor of the proposed plea."

I pointed in the direction of Mr. Fussleman, who stood up.

"That won't be necessary," the judge said. "Mr. Jones?"

Moses looked up.

"Are you Moses Jones?" the judge repeated.

"That be me."

"Are you aware of the charges against you?"

"Yes sir."

The judge looked down at the papers before him. "Did you illegally tie up your boat at these docks without permission of the owners?"

"I just be stopping by for a while to get some sleep. I don't hurt no one or nothing."

"Counsel, will you agree your client's statement is the equivalent of an affirmative answer?" the judge asked me.

"Yes sir."

"Mr. Jones, do you realize that I do not have to accept your lawyer's suggestion about releasing you from jail and could sentence you to twenty-four one-year sentences to run consecutively, said sentences to be served in the Georgia State Penitentiary?"

Moses stared at the judge without a hint of understanding in his eyes.

"Your Honor," I began. "I explained —"

"I wish I had more time for you to practice being a lawyer, Ms. Taylor, but I don't. I'm not going to accept your recommendation for sentence. Mr. Jones has demonstrated a repeated and callous disregard for the property of others, and I have no confidence he will modify his conduct in the future. If he wants to plead guilty, I will refer him for a presentence investigation, then sentence him in a way I deem appropriate. If that is acceptable we'll proceed. Otherwise, you may withdraw your offer of a guilty plea."

I turned to Zach in panic and whispered, "What do I do?"

Zach spoke. "Your Honor, we withdraw the plea."

"Very well. Have him enter his not-guilty plea on the accusation."

Ms. Smith pushed a piece of paper in front of me and pointed to a place beneath the words "Not Guilty." Moses scrawled his name in the space provided. It was the same signature I'd seen at the bottom of the confession. The deputy led Moses back to the group of prisoners. When I turned away, Vince, a look of genuine sympathy on his face, caught my eye.

"State v. Brown," Ms. Smith called out.

Vince and Russell stood. Zach and I passed them as we walked down the aisle. Mr. Fussleman joined us. The three of us returned to the hallway.

"Was that a surprise?" Fussleman asked.

"Yes," Zach answered. "There is no guaranteed result in front of a judge, but they often look to the prosecutor for recommendations on sentencing. Otherwise, the system totally bogs down."

"We're bogged down," I said. "What do we do next?"

"Get ready to try the case," Zach said, his jaw firm.

Moses watched the tall girl who wasn't a real lawyer and the young lawyer helping her leave the courtroom. The man sitting next to him nudged his arm.

"They gave you a couple of practice lawyers?" the man asked in a low voice.

Moses grunted.

"Judge Cannon," the man continued. "They named him right. He'll blow you up into a million pieces. I saw what he did to you. One of my cousins pleaded guilty to writing a few bad checks and got sent to a work camp for a year and a half."

"I couldn't handle no work camp," Moses said.

"Oh, they wouldn't do that to you," the man reassured him. "At your age you've got nothing to worry about. They have a special prison over in Telfair County that's like a nursing home. They bring three meals a day on a tray to your room and change your bedsheets three times a week."

Moses glanced sideways at the man to see if he was telling the truth. A faint smile at the corners of the man's mouth betrayed the lie. Another prisoner was called forward. Moses watched and listened. The man was charged with destroying the front of a convenience store by ramming it with his truck when the clerk inside wouldn't sell him any beer. The man's lawyer wore a fancy suit and smiled when he spoke to the judge. The prisoner received probation and was ordered to pay for the damage. He returned to the group with a grin on his face. Moses heard him speak to the deputy.

"General, once I get my civilian clothes, you won't be seeing me anymore."

"You'll be back as soon as you get your hands on a fifth," the deputy replied impassively. "We'll save a spot for you."

Moses rubbed his head. He hadn't put a scratch on anyone's dock. Why couldn't he be set free? The next defendant was represented by a different lawyer. He also received probation. The man sitting next to Moses was called forward. He had a long history of drunk driving. The lawyer with the fancy suit represented him too. Moses expected the judge to give the man probation, but instead he sentenced him to three years in prison. When the man returned to the other prisoners, the smile at the corners of his mouth was gone.

As the afternoon dragged on, a deep ache was churned in Moses' gut. He would be returning to the jail and didn't know how long he'd be there. Locked behind the thick walls with the high, narrow windows was little better than living in a casket. He closed his eyes and found himself in the dark on the river. The pain in his stomach was joined by a black sadness in his mind. *Hope* hadn't been in the vocabulary of his heart for many years, but at least he'd been a survivor. Now, he wasn't sure he wanted to live. The ache in the darkness increased. He saw the little girl's face. Her golden hair, like wispy cords of death, reached out for him.

22

Neither Zach nor I spoke into the helmet microphones during the return trip to the office. I was sorry that he would have to find time in his busy schedule to help me, and I felt bad that I would have to defend a man who was guilty of trespassing — and probably much worse. Zach parked the motorcycle. I climbed out, handed him the helmet, and tucked my folder under my arm.

"The case will have to be placed on a trial calendar this summer," Zach said as we walked up the sidewalk. "Otherwise, you'll be in school."

"How soon?"

"That's up to the DA's office. I don't know much about the criminal court schedule. Call the court administrator and find out possible dates, then let me know so I can enter them on my calendar. You'll need to get ready."

Zach held the door open for me. Usually, the cool interior of the office refreshed me. This afternoon, I didn't notice. We stood in the reception area at the base of the staircase. I faced Zach.

"How do I prepare to try a case for a man who signed a confession and whose only defense is based on an argument that God, who created the rivers and oceans, is the only one who can complain about trespassing on waterways in the state of Georgia?"

"You said the confession doesn't sound like Jones."

"I know, but would that be grounds to suppress it?"

"No, but it can be argued to a jury." Zach stopped at the bottom of the stairs. "Look, I'm not a criminal law expert. I'm doing the best I can."

"I'm not criticizing you," I responded quickly. "It was a great idea to ask Mr. Fussleman to come to the hearing. I wouldn't have had the courage to ask him for help."

"You saw how that worked out."

"Yes, but I owe you an apology. You took care of me when I wasn't looking out for myself or the client. I'm learning as fast as I can."

Zach put his hand on the stair railing.

"And you're about to learn a lot more."

Julie was in the library when I opened the door. I placed the Moses Jones folder on the worktable and sighed. Julie put down her pen.

"You look upset, but I'm not going to say anything stupid about Zach or Vinny," she said. "Mr. Carpenter assured me that you didn't try to get me in trouble, which I really, really appreciate. He told me to apologize, put the incident behind me, and be more professional."

I waited.

"What?" she asked.

"Is that your idea of an apology?"

"Oh, I'm sorry."

It was such a lame effort that I had to smile.

"Hey, great," she said. "I heard you and Vinny got rid of your criminal cases today."

"Vince's case may be over, but mine is getting more serious."

"What happened?"

In telling Julie, the magnitude of the disaster grew.

"Wow," she said. "That stinks."

I touched one of the Folsom divorce files with my right hand.

"Divorces and criminal law," I said. "I

think my mother knew this was going to happen and tried to warn me before I came here."

"How did she want you to spend your summer?"

I thought about endless rows of dead chickens. Surely, that wasn't Mama's desire for my future.

"She left it up to me," I replied. "Now, as my father would say, I have a chance to grow in the midst of difficulty."

The family platitude sounded hollow in the moment. I sat down at one of the computer workstations and began typing a memo to Mr. Carpenter about the status of *State v. Jones.*

By the end of the day, Julie had returned to her chipper self. We worked together on the Folsom case, but Moses and Lisa Prescott stayed at the edge of my mind. I expected Vince to stop by and offer his condolences on my courtroom fiasco, but he didn't appear. Julie dropped me off at Mrs. Fairmont's house.

"Are you sure you don't want a ride in the morning?" she asked.

"No thanks. I enjoy the walk when it's still cool."

"Okay, but remember to call me if it ever rains."

Mrs. Bartlett's car was parked at the curb in front of her mother's house. I could hear her voice as soon as I entered the foyer.

"It's Tami," I called out.

"We're in the den," Mrs. Bartlett responded.

Mrs. Fairmont was in her favorite chair facing the television. Mrs. Bartlett was on a leather sofa to her right with a cup of coffee beside her. I sat in the remaining chair.

"How are you feeling?" I asked Mrs. Fairmont.

"Well enough to listen to Christine talk nonstop for an hour."

"Don't be ridiculous," Mrs. Bartlett replied. "You've held up your end of the conversation very well."

"Did you have a good day at work?" Mrs. Fairmont asked me.

"It was difficult," I replied.

"Mother tells me you're snooping around looking for information about the Lisa Prescott case."

"Yes ma'am." I couldn't blame Mrs. Fairmont for forgetting to keep our conversation secret.

"If you solve the mystery, it would be a great story to tell on one of those television shows where they go back in time and figure out what really happened. Only, I'd prefer not to have a TV crew filming inside Mother's house. With all the antiques and valuables around here, it makes no sense giving a thief an inventory of what he might find."

"I'll remember that when the producer calls."

"Ellen Prescott was one of Mother's dearest friends," Mrs. Bartlett continued. "Lisa was a bit of a brat. I know it sounds harsh to say, but it's true. I took care of her a few times when our parents went out for the evening. Lisa was sharp as a tack and had a mind of her own." She turned to Mrs. Fairmont. "Do you remember the time she unlocked the front door of their house and ran out to the sidewalk to hitchhike a ride to the ice-cream shop? I don't know where she got the idea that a young girl could ask a stranger for a ride. I ran out and grabbed her, of course. Later, when I heard that she didn't come home one afternoon, the first thought in my mind was about her running to the sidewalk and sticking out her thumb like a homeless person."

"How long before she vanished did that happen?" I asked.

"Oh, I don't know. It couldn't have been more than a year or so."

"Do you remember anything else?"

"There were all kinds of wild rumors."

444

"What kind of rumors?" I asked.

"Some I wouldn't want to repeat, but we almost had a race riot when some vigilantes marched into the black district and started searching houses."

"Why did they do that?"

"It was a sign of the times. Anytime a white girl disappeared, there were people who immediately blamed the black population. When the police didn't come up with a suspect, low-class troublemakers would take to the streets and try to find a scapegoat."

"The Ku Klux Klan?"

"No, they didn't try to cover their faces. The KKK wasn't around much when I was a child."

"Did they have a particular person in mind?"

Mrs. Bartlett rolled her eyes. "Don't expect me to remember details like that. It was a mob. My father locked the doors and turned out the lights when they came by our house. My bedroom was upstairs. I peeked outside and saw that some of the men were carrying guns. I'm surprised you didn't see an article about it in the newspaper. Do you remember that night, Mother?"

"Yes. It was scary."

"And there wasn't a particular black man who was a suspect?" I asked.

Mrs. Bartlett studied me for a moment. "Do you have a name? Mother and I have lived here all our lives. Between us, we've known a lot of people of every color under the sun."

"I can't say."

"Attorney/client privilege?"

"I can't answer that either."

"Do you hear this, Mother?" Mrs. Bartlett said. "Tami has found out something about Lisa Prescott after all these years. Does the newspaper know you're conducting an investigation?"

"No!" I said. "And please don't mention this to anyone."

"I'm not subject to any rules of confidentiality." Mrs. Bartlett sniffed. "This is hot news for anyone who has been in Savannah for a long time."

I gave Mrs. Fairmont an imploring look.

"Don't give the girl a heart attack," Mrs. Fairmont said. "If you spread this around town, she could get in trouble."

"That's right," I added. "I could lose my job."

Mrs. Bartlett appeared skeptical. "Okay, but I have to mention it to Ken. I'm sure he remembers the Lisa Prescott mystery."

"Will you ask him not to say anything?" I asked.

"Of course. Don't panic. Anyway, hasn't the statute of limitations run out on that case?"

I didn't respond.

"Well?" she repeated.

I looked directly in her eyes. "There is no statute of limitations for murder."

Mrs. Bartlett didn't stay for supper. After she left, Mrs. Fairmont joined me in the kitchen while I warmed up leftovers from Gracie's Sunday dinner.

"Do you think Mrs. Bartlett will keep quiet about my interest in the Prescott case?" I asked as I stirred the black-eyed peas.

"I never could bridle Christine's tongue," the older woman said. "I'd be surprised if you have any success either."

After we ate, Mrs. Fairmont returned to the den to read magazines. She would read the same ones over and over. She'd tell about articles that piqued her interest, not realizing that she'd mentioned the same piece a few days before. After listening for the third time in a week to new ideas for Savannah-area flower gardens, I excused myself to call home. Mama answered the phone.

"It's me," I began.

"What's wrong?" she asked immediately.

"How do you know something is wrong?" I asked.

"I'm your mother. I could tell what was the matter by the way you cried as a baby."

The thought of cuddling up in Mama's arms held a lot of appeal to me.

"Mostly work matters that I can't discuss. Is Daddy there?"

"No, he and Kyle are out again checking on some cows. I think Kyle is going to make enough money to get a new truck by the end of the summer."

"Maybe his cattle business will get big enough that he'll need a corporate attorney."

"I told Daddy about the young lawyer who wants to get to know you better."

"That's not an —"

Mama kept talking. "He agrees with me that you should keep your distance until we can meet him. However, we talked it over, and you can bring him home for the July Fourth holiday if he can give you a ride home."

The thought of a five-hour ride in the sidecar followed by the shock on my parents' faces when Zach parked the motorcycle beneath the poplar tree in our front yard made me smile. Of course, Zach owned a car, but in my mind he was inextricably linked to the motorcycle.

"That's sweet of you, Mama, but I'm not sure I want to invite him." I paused. "However, there is someone else, one of the summer clerks who's a Christian and very nice. He lives in Charleston, so I don't know what he's doing for the holiday, and I may have to stay here to prepare a court case. If I can get away, and Vince wants to drive me home for a visit, would that be okay?"

"Who is Vince?" Mama sounded slightly bewildered.

I told her a little more about him. As I talked I realized that compared to Zach Mays, I had little to hide about the brilliant law student.

"And he maintains his Christian witness at Yale?" Mama asked.

"Yes ma'am. He's had to face challenges and overcome them, just like me."

"I'll mention it to your daddy."

"Thanks. Now, tell me about the twins, the garden, Bobby, church, the chickens, the dogs, anything about home."

Later that night in my apartment, I read the

449

old newspapers, seeking more information about the mob described by Mrs. Bartlett. Two-thirds of the way through the stack, I found a second-page article. Scant on details, it was obviously a major event that should have received front-page coverage. A group of fifty men invaded the black district in response to "unfounded rumors" related to Lisa Prescott's disappearance. Rocks were thrown, windows broken, and a fire started in the front yard of one residence. The mob was confronted by a squad of police officers that included several on horseback. Five men were arrested for disorderly conduct, and the rest dispersed. The incident wasn't mentioned again.

The following morning, the receptionist stopped me when I arrived at the office.

"Vince Colbert wants to see you," she said. "He's in the small conference room near Mr. Braddock's office."

Puzzled, I went to the opposite end of the building from the library. The conference room door was shut. I knocked.

"Come in," Vince called out.

Vince, his laptop open before him, was sitting at one end of the shiny table. He always wore a suit, tie, and starched shirt. This morning he'd taken off his jacket and hung it on the back of a chair.

"What's going on?" I asked.

"Sorry about court yesterday."

"It was a blow. What happened in your case?"

"No problems. My client will be on the road in his quieter car by the weekend. But I spent time last night doing some research that I wanted to tell you about."

"You came back to the office last night?"

"Yes, there is a code needed after eleven o'clock. I can give it to you —"

"I know," I interrupted. "What were you looking into?"

"Please shut the door and sit down."

I closed the conference room door and sat in a chair beside him.

"Careful with the jacket," he said. "I have a meeting in an hour with Mr. Braddock and one of his clients."

"Sorry." I moved the jacket to the back of another chair.

"I've been doing some research to update the firm website. This firm has been in existence since 1888," Vince began. "The founding partners were Mr. Braddock's great-grandfather and an attorney named Vernon Fletchall. After Mr. Fletchall died, the firm was simply known as the Braddock firm until Mr. Braddock brought in another partner in the early 1900s. Mr. Braddock's son joined the firm, and about thirty years later his grandson, the current Mr. Braddock's father, a man named Lawrence, who graduated from Vanderbilt after World War II, started practicing in Savannah. In the meantime, the founding Mr. Braddock died and not long after that, his son also died."

"I'm not taking notes. Is there going to be a test?"

"No, but learning more about the history of the firm gave me an idea."

"Okay," I answered, mystified.

"Mr. Samuel Braddock and his father practiced law together for a long time. Lawrence died about ten years ago, although he'd been retired for many years. Mr. Appleby is originally from Norfolk and joined the firm when the father was still practicing." Vince paused. "Mr. Carpenter did too. Mr. Carpenter's family —"

Realizing another long genealogical recitation was coming, I couldn't stifle the giggle that bubbled up within me.

"What did I say?" Vince asked.

"I'm sorry. I don't know where you're going with this, but your attention to detail is incredible. Are you the same way with your Bible study?"

"I try to be."

"How many books of the Bible have you memorized?"

Vince shook his head. "I'm not answering that. Are you going to let me finish? It's going to be hard to find time later today."

"All right. You were starting Mr. Carpenter's genealogy."

"Mr. Carpenter's family is from Savannah too, but his family history isn't documented except for the names of his parents. When I saw his father's name, I remembered our conversation the other day at the deli."

"Floyd Carpenter?" I asked in shock, putting my hand to my mouth.

Vince nodded. "Yes."

"I never really thought —" I stopped.

"Did you mention that to Mr. Carpenter?" Vince asked.

"No. I thought it would sound foolish."

"That was probably very wise." Vince moved the cursor on his laptop. "At that point, I stopped working on the website and started searching the closed file records."

"Looking for what?"

"References to the significant names: Prescott and Carpenter as clients of the firm."

"What did you find?" I asked.

"Not much. Floyd Carpenter died not

long after Mr. Braddock's father passed away."

My heart sank.

"However, the old files haven't been destroyed," Vince continued. "The State Bar Rules would allow it, but the firm is proud of its history and put its records on microfilm in the 1980s. They're stored off-site. I'm just not sure how to get access."

"Mr. Carpenter obviously isn't an option."

"Why don't you ask Zach?"

I shrugged. "I'm not sure he'll help. He thinks I need to concentrate totally on helping Moses with the trespassing case and forget about Lisa Prescott."

"You can do both." Vince closed his laptop. "There may be nothing to it, but access to privileged information is a unique opportunity, something the police didn't have when they were investigating Lisa's disappearance."

Everything Vince said made sense.

"How long did it take you to do this?"

Vince smiled. "Less time than it took to memorize the first two chapters of Ephesians. I'll check with you this afternoon."

I left the conference room. When I passed Mr. Carpenter's office suite, his secretary stopped me.

"Tami, hold on. I was about to come looking for you. I'll let Mr. Carpenter know you're here."

"Could it wait?" I asked, trying to think of a good reason to postpone a meeting.

The secretary already had the phone receiver in her hand. She shook her head. I had no choice but to wait. I offered up a rapid prayer for help. Mr. Carpenter opened the door to his office.

"Good morning, Tami," he said. "Come in."

I entered the office and sat down. He didn't go behind his desk but sat across from me in a leather side chair. Sitting so close to him increased my anxiety.

"I hope I'm not in trouble," I said lamely.

"Of course not," Mr. Carpenter answered lightly. "I read your memo about the Jones case with great interest. Clifton Cannon can be hard to deal with, especially if his sciatica is acting up."

"I don't know, but it must have been bad yesterday. It's disturbing that the judge's back condition might affect how many years a man or woman spends in prison."

"The practice of law is filled with intangibles that law school doesn't prepare you for."

"Yes sir."

"What are you going to do next on the case?"

"Uh, get ready to try it. I have to phone the courthouse and find out the dates for criminal trial calendars this summer."

"Zach will guide you. He's a bright young man. If both of you get in over your heads, call on me."

"Yes sir."

Mr. Carpenter stood. "Keep those memos coming. You're a good writer. Written and verbal communication skills are the main keys to success for an attorney."

23

I went to the library and picked up my folder containing the old newspaper clippings. Julie wasn't there, but I needed a place to think without interruption. I'd not told Julie anything about Lisa Prescott and didn't want to start now.

I went upstairs to Gerry Patrick's office. The firm administrator's door was open. She was on the phone but motioned me to come inside. I stood in front of her desk and waited until she finished the call.

"How can I help you?" she asked.

"You'd mentioned the possibility of a cubicle where I could work. Is that still available?"

"Did you and Julie have another problem?" Ms. Patrick asked with an edge to her voice.

The fact that the previous day's incident was common knowledge in the hierarchy of the firm worried me, but I knew interoffice communication only required a few computer keystrokes and the click of a mouse.

"No ma'am. Each of us met with Mr. Carpenter, and our relationship is better than ever. But I need to do some research without any distractions. Julie and I work well together, but we still take a few minutes here and there to talk."

"What are you working on that requires that level of privacy? Julie is also an employee of the law firm."

It was an insightful question that rendered me temporarily speechless.

"You're right," I said after an awkward pause. "There's no good reason for me to set up in a second workstation."

Ms. Patrick looked down at her desk. "Good. Have a nice day."

I made copies of all the newspaper articles and put them in a separate folder. I had no option but to talk to Zach. His door was closed. I knocked lightly and opened it a crack before he answered. He was staring at his computer screen and tugging on his ponytail.

"Hey," he said. "Did you get the dates for the trial calendars?"

"Not yet, but I will. Do you have a few minutes?"

"Yeah."

I sat down next to the now familiar picture of Zach's sister. "Do you promise not to get upset at me if I ask for some advice?"

Zach gave me a puzzled look. "Have I been that hard to work with? My only goal is to help you mature as a lawyer as quickly as possible. The best way for that to happen isn't to coddle you, but to challenge you and keep you focused."

"You're not mad at me?"

"No. I've told my parents all about you."

"What did you say?" I asked in surprise.

"The truth as best I know it." Zach smiled. "They know how unusual it is to meet a woman with your faith and convictions. I'd like to meet your family."

"Really?"

"Of course. How can we make that happen?"

"I'm still working on it," I answered, perplexed. "But this case is all I can think about right now. I need your help. How can someone access the firm microfilm records?"

"Through Gerry Patrick. She has a key to the storage facility. It's on Abercorn Road near the mall."

"Would you mind asking her? Ms. Patrick doesn't like me."

"Why?"

"For some of the same reasons you think I'm a woman of faith and conviction. We've had misunderstandings that make her suspicious of anything I say."

It was Zach's turn to give me a puzzled look. "That makes no sense. Just tell her the name of the case, and the supervising attorney. She shouldn't give you any problem."

I grimaced. "You're the supervising attorney. It has to do with *State v. Jones*."

Zach sat up straighter in his chair. "Start talking."

Thirty minutes later, I finished. Zach read a couple of the articles while I nervously fidgeted in my chair.

"Is that all?" he asked, looking up from the newspaper clippings.

"Pretty much. I don't think I left out any important details."

"And Mr. Carpenter isn't aware of your suspicions?"

"I don't think so."

"He's a smart man."

"I know."

"Do the partners know Vince is helping you?"

"No. I think he worked after hours."

Zach frowned. "Have you thought this

through to its logical conclusion?"

"What do you mean?"

"We've had this discussion before — Moses, a man named Floyd Carpenter, the shiny dollar, and Lisa Prescott's body in the Ogeechee River. What changed?"

"Additional information makes it seem more plausible."

"Which still doesn't address the ultimate issue. What is the significance of solving a missing person case after everyone except our client is dead? Lisa was an only child, and her parents are deceased, right?"

"Yes."

"And Floyd Carpenter is dead?"

"Yes."

"Which leaves Moses, an old man, alive." Zach spoke with emphasis, "And our client."

"But the truth needs to be known."

Zach picked up a pen and twirled it around with his fingers. I steeled myself, determined not to back down.

"What are you going to do if you search the firm archives and find out that Floyd Carpenter consulted with Mr. Braddock or his father about the disappearance of the Prescott girl? What if there are incriminating notes, even a written confession? What if Moses Jones is mentioned by name as an accessory or principal in the commission of a crime? Are you going to violate your ethical duty and turn the information over to Maggie Smith? Would you run to the newspaper and humiliate the Carpenter family in a massive exposé? What would be helped by that except a reporter's career? If you contact the newspaper, make sure you suggest a headline that includes the verse about the sins of the fathers being visited on their children to the fourth generation."

With each question, my resolve weakened. "But don't you want to know what happened to Lisa?"

"Of course I'm curious. But a lawyer has to consider the consequences. It's a boring analogy, but I leave out favorable contract provisions if I think they might trigger a response from the other side that could cause greater harm to my client's primary interests. Your decision is much more important because of the impact on Moses' freedom."

Zach's last comment gave me an idea. "If Moses isn't guilty and can shed light on what really happened to Lisa Prescott, it could help his trespassing case."

I could tell from the look on Zach's face that for once, I'd brought out a point he hadn't considered.

"That's far-fetched," he said.

"It would enable the police and district attorney's office to solve a crime and close a file even if it's decades too late to bring someone to justice."

Zach still looked skeptical.

"And I'm not ignoring all the good points you made about not humiliating Mr. Carpenter and his family, but I can't get away from the belief that I'm supposed to dig as far to the bottom of this as I can. I need to get over pretending to be a crusader and go forward only to the extent I should as a lawyer —"

"Law student."

"Who is acting in a professional, ethical manner. I'm working at the firm with at least a small hope of landing a job after graduation. Throwing that away for no reason would be stupid. I don't want newspaper publicity for myself and don't want to hurt someone else's reputation. I've been persecuted enough to know how it feels."

"But once you release information, you can't control where it goes. We should try to lessen interest in Moses so he can slip back into the river marsh and live out his life in peace, not make him an unwilling celebrity."

"That sounds nice," I said, "but you're wrong. Moses Jones is not at peace."

"And you're not his pastor." Zach glanced at his watch. "Look, I have a meeting with Mr. Appleby and a client in five minutes. Do you still want the key to the storage facility?"

"Yes."

"I'll okay it, but tell me what you find out. I can't escape the responsibility that will fall on me if you get out of line."

I'd not considered the possible risk to Zach's job.

"Yes. And I've listened to what you said."

Zach leaned forward and spoke with intensity. "But have you heard?"

I bit my lower lip and nodded.

Zach left to get the key from Gerry Patrick. In at least one way, this morning's conversation had been a success. I'd avoided an emotional meltdown when Zach Mays challenged me. Returning, he handed me the key.

"It's checked out in my name, so let me return it to her. Are you going to use the firm car?"

"Unless you give me the keys to your motorcycle."

Zach managed a slight smile. "This is a more explosive situation than you realize. A getaway on a motorcycle might be your best means of escape."

"And I'm not going to be reckless, on or off a motorcycle." I stepped toward the door. "I'll talk to you before doing anything else. I promise."

The firm car had been checked out by the runner going to the federal courthouse. She wouldn't be returning for an hour and a half.

Bob Kettleson's paralegal had left me a note on the library door. I went to her cubicle where she handed me a memo instructing me to research the relative priorities of eminent domain for a parcel of riverfront property claimed by a private utility and the city, state, and federal governments. When I returned to the library, Julie was there.

"Oversleep?" she asked.

"No, I've already talked to Vince, Mr. Carpenter, and Zach this morning."

"Not all at once, I hope."

"No, although that could happen."

"Yeah, if Mr. Carpenter served as mediator. Vinny has come by twice looking for you. I think he used a bathroom excuse to get out of a big important meeting with Mr. Braddock and a rich client."

"What did he want?"

"I don't know. I asked him if it had to do

with lunch, and he shook his head. Have you hurt his feelings?"

"No."

"You know how confident he always looks with that laptop under his arm, but he seemed worried about something. I offered to be a sounding board for him if he gets lovesick and needs a friendly ear."

"No, you didn't."

"But I thought about it. I've helped more couples work through issues than a marriage counselor. My mother still wishes I'd become a psychologist."

"Vince doesn't need psychotherapy. He's more stable than the hard drive of his computer."

"That's not bad," Julie said approvingly. "I'm rubbing off on you."

I began working on the eminent domain project but kept a careful eye on the clock. Vince didn't return, and Julie was engrossed in her own research. As soon as an hour and a half passed, I went to the receptionist desk. The car was available until noon, and directions to the storage facility in hand, I drove across town to a modern, three-story building with a reflective glass exterior. Microfilm can't be kept in a miniwarehouse without climate control, and the storage company shared the space with two insurance companies, an investment adviser group, and a CPA firm. I took the elevator to a top-floor office. A nice-looking man about my age with dark hair and dressed in blue jeans and a casual shirt sat behind a tall desk. He wore a name tag with "Eddie" on it. The area was filled with rows of lockable file cabinets in the middle and small rooms around the edges.

"I'm from Braddock, Appleby, and Carpenter. I need access to their microfilm records."

"Sign in," Eddie said, sliding a logbook in front of me. "Have you been here before?"

"No. I'm a summer clerk."

"Where are you in law school?"

"University of Georgia."

While I wrote my name, Eddie typed on his computer. "There is a reader set up in their site," he said. "If you want hard copies, it also serves as a printer. It's a lot like the machines you find in a modern deed room."

I'd not been in enough modern or old-fashioned deed rooms to know what he meant. I followed him to one of the enclosed rooms.

"This is it."

I put the key in the door and opened it.

"Make sure you sign out at the front when you leave," he said.

I hesitated.

"Do you know how to use the reader?" he asked.

"No."

We stepped inside. The walls were lined with lateral filing cabinets that had numbers on the front. The reader looked a lot like a computer.

"Slip the film in here," he said, "then turn this knob until you reach the file you want. If you want to make a copy, press the Print button."

The button was clearly marked.

"How do I find a particular file in the cabinets?"

He pointed to two cassettes lying beside the reader. "You can scroll through the index of files alphabetically and locate the numbers for the cassettes in the cabinets."

It seemed easy enough. I sat down in a chair in front of the reader. "Thanks," I said.

Eddie didn't leave. "If you need specific help, I'll be here," he said. "I'm going to start applying to law schools after the first of the year. How do you like it?"

"It's hard but a great education."

"Do you have a business card?" he asked.

The fact that I was alone in the facility

468

with a man I didn't know made me feel suddenly uneasy. I turned in my chair and cleared my throat so I wouldn't sound nervous.

"No, they don't give those to summer clerks."

"How about your home number or e-mail address?" he asked. "I'd like to chat sometime. You know, get your opinion about schools."

"I don't give out personal information to people I don't know," I said, trying to sound professional.

He pointed to his name tag. "My name is Eddie Anderson."

"Eddie, if you'll excuse me, I have work to do."

He left. I took a few deep breaths and made sure the door to the tiny room locked behind him. However, I suspected the custodian of the records probably had a master key for the whole facility. I offered up a prayer for protection. The thought of looking through old files that might hold clues to Lisa Prescott's disappearance was creepy enough without adding the young man to the mix.

I checked the index for files with Carpenter in the heading and wrote down the locations. Before I had a chance to pull any of the cassettes, a knock at the door made me jump. I didn't want to open it, but couldn't think of a way to avoid it. I stood and planted my right foot firmly in place to prevent him from easily forcing his way into the room. I cracked open the door.

"Yes?" I asked tensely.

"Someone from your office called when he couldn't get you on your cell."

I quickly decided not to inform him that I didn't own a cell phone.

"Is there a message?"

"Call Vince Colbert."

"Do you have a phone I can use?"

"Sorry, but it's not allowed. And you took my request a few minutes ago the wrong way. It wasn't a lame pickup line. I'm trying to find out information about law schools from people who actually go there. I took a tour through the admissions office at Georgia, but I'm sure part of it was propaganda —"

"I'm not the best person to give you a broad view," I interrupted. "I live off campus and keep to myself, but I'll take a minute to talk before I leave. Where is the nearest phone?"

Eddie glanced past me.

"In your purse?" he asked, gesturing toward the place where I'd put it on the table beside the reader.

"No."

"Then you can use my cell. It's at the sign-in desk."

"Thanks."

As we returned to the entrance area, I felt slightly ashamed at my harsh reaction. Eddie reached under the desk and handed me a phone.

"Reception is best in that part of the room," he said, pointing to a place near a window.

"Thanks."

I went to the window, called the office, and asked for Vince. While I waited on hold, I tried to imagine why he'd made the effort to track me down at the storage facility. He picked up the phone.

"What are you doing?" he asked.

"Trying to solve the mystery of Lisa Prescott's disappearance. Is there a problem?"

"Interest in what you're doing has gone up the ladder at the firm. I went into Mr. Braddock's office to get a file for a meeting and saw a memo on his desk from Mr. Carpenter. The subject line included your name."

"What did it say?"

"Both Mr. Carpenter and Mr. Braddock

are very familiar with the Prescott case. Mr. Carpenter attached copies of your memos about Moses Jones and mentioned that it was time 'for us to find a way to finish what our fathers started.' "

"What does that mean?"

"I'm not sure, and I don't know how or why, but Mr. Braddock is also involved. Both of them are very interested in Moses."

"Why?"

"Think about it. For some reason, Moses is a threat that could damage the reputation of their families in Savannah. Can you imagine the impact on the law firm and its business? A lot of money flows through this office. If they think the threat is real, their goal may be to silence him. You could be hurt too."

My stomach turned over. "I can't believe that."

"I don't think they would physically harm you, but there are ways to destroy your future or credibility. I hope I'm wrong, but there's no need to take any chances. Maybe you should put a halt to this."

"How? I don't have enough information to go to Maggie Smith at the DA's office and implicate Floyd Carpenter and Mr. Braddock's father in an unsolved murder."

"That's not what I meant. Maybe you

should ask to be taken off the case. You could claim your religious beliefs prohibit representation of someone who is factually guilty."

It was a plausible argument — one that my mother would agree with. But at that moment, a different kind of religious conviction rose up within me. My faith was a foundation, not a crutch. I'd spent my whole life fighting pressure to compromise my convictions, and in every serious situation I'd passed the test. This was a different type of challenge, but I felt the same resolve and didn't want to yield to what my conscience told me was evil pressure.

"I don't know," I answered slowly. "That's not necessarily true. I'll have to think about it." I paused. "And hear what God says."

24

I closed the cover on the cell phone and waited for a still, small voice to tell me what to do, but nothing came. I stared out the window. No angel with a drawn sword appeared in the sky over Savannah and called me to battle.

I returned the phone to the young man.

"Thanks," I said.

"Are you finished?"

"No," I answered slowly. "I'm just getting started."

I returned to the archive room and began checking the actual records. There were many files involving Floyd Carpenter and the Braddock law firm. The professional relationship between Lawrence Braddock and Floyd Carpenter spanned many years. As I worked my way through the files, a familiarity appeared in the correspondence that revealed a growing friendship.

One thing became quickly apparent. Floyd

Carpenter had considerable problems with the Internal Revenue Service. His written comments to Lawrence Braddock about the federal revenue agents sounded like field reports of a Confederate officer. At one point, massive tax liens were filed against Floyd.

My heart beat faster and my mouth got dry as I scrolled to the next file. The title of the file grabbed my attention: "Floyd Carpenter re Lisa Prescott." I clicked to the next screen that contained a single typed entry: "The contents of this file were not archived."

I stared at the screen for several seconds. I pushed the button to advance the page, which revealed an intake sheet for a divorce case between a couple named William and Lynn Mitchell. I checked the index and found the next folder listing Floyd Carpenter in the subject matter.

It was dated a year after Lisa Prescott's disappearance and confirmed payment of several hundred thousand dollars to satisfy the federal tax liens filed against Floyd Carpenter and several businesses apparently controlled by him. The Braddock firm was paid over fifty thousand dollars for legal services. The next file involved formation of a real estate investment trust four years after

Lisa's disappearance. As I moved through the years, my hope of finding anything relevant faded. One routine business transaction followed another. The last file was the probate of Floyd's will. Joe Carpenter served as executor.

With a sigh, I leaned back in the chair. I'd stared at the screen so intently that I'd gotten a headache. I looked at my watch. It was midafternoon. I suddenly realized that I'd gone way over the time period allotted for my use of the firm car. I turned off the reader and hurriedly returned all the cassettes to their proper places. Locking the door, I walked rapidly toward the exit. The young man was sitting at the entrance.

"I skipped my lunch break so we could talk," he said.

"Sorry, but I'm late getting back to the office," I replied. "Call me at Braddock, Appleby, and Carpenter."

"And your name?"

"Tami Taylor. It's on the sheet I signed when I checked in."

"Right."

I almost never exceeded the speed limit, but during the drive to the office I kept pace with the fastest traffic on the road without looking at the car's speedometer. I parked next to Zach's red motorcycle.

"Did I mess up someone's schedule?" I asked when I returned the keys to the afternoon receptionist.

"Mr. Kettleson's car is in for service. I think he ended up borrowing a car from one of the other lawyers."

"Was he upset?"

The woman leaned forward. "I've been working here for five years, and I'm not sure I've ever seen him smile."

I laid the keys on the counter. It was another nail in the coffin of my legal career. However, if I didn't get a job offer or even a good recommendation from Braddock, Appleby, and Carpenter, it wouldn't be the end of the world. A legal career in Savannah wasn't the dream job of a lifetime. I could always return to Powell Station and beg Oscar Callahan to hire me.

Julie wasn't in the library. Trying to ignore my headache, I began working on the eminent domain memo. Delivering an opinion as soon as possible might soften Bob Kettleson's reaction to my tardiness in returning the car. The library door opened. It was Zach. He quickly glanced around the room.

"I'm alone," I said.

"Did you check out the old files?"

I handed him the key. "Would you return

this to Ms. Patrick? I have a headache and a complicated memo to research for Bob Kettleson."

Zach ignored my problems. "Any smoking guns?"

"Smoke but no gun."

He sat down across the table from me, and I told him about the empty folder, leaving out what I'd learned from Vince about the memo from Mr. Carpenter to Mr. Braddock and his advice that I consider quitting the case. Zach seemed to relax as I talked.

"Do you feel you've reached the end?" he asked.

"Not really."

"What else can you do except show Moses the newspaper articles and ask him if they help him remember anything? If he says something about Floyd Carpenter, what does that prove? Without corroboration, any information from Moses is unreliable because of his mental status."

"What about your mental status?"

Zach's eyes narrowed.

"I'm sorry," I continued. "It's just that all you seem to care about is getting me to drop the whole thing. It's frustrating knowing that something is there but not being able to figure it out."

"Welcome to the practice of law. I had no

idea Floyd Carpenter was a shady character, but that shouldn't cast a shadow on his son. My big concern is that you're going to hurt people who don't deserve it and put a client at risk in violation of your ethical duty to him. You're a disciplined person; transfer that to your professional life and focus on what you're supposed to be doing."

"Don't you get tired of preaching the same message?"

Zach stood up. "Not if I believe it's the truth. You'd do the same thing."

After Zach left, I pressed my fingers against my temples. The pressure felt good as long as I didn't move my hands. After a minute, I released them and continued working on the eminent domain project. I made slow progress but hadn't started to type anything when Julie returned at 5:00 p.m.

"I have a headache," she said. "Are you ready to leave?"

"I have the same problem. What caused yours?"

"Ned and I met with the client in my criminal case and then went round and round about the best way to handle it. Ned is pressuring me to take it to trial in front of a six-person jury for the experience. I think the best thing is to work out a plea agreement that will get my client out of jail and on with his life. Don't you think I should put the client's interests first, not what might be more beneficial or interesting to me?"

"I'm ready to leave," I answered.

That evening, Mrs. Fairmont was in a mild fog. She didn't speak much during supper except to ask me three times if I'd turned off the television before we sat down to eat. My headache eased as we ate, and I realized it was probably caused by lack of food combined with eyestrain.

"Is there anything you would like to do this evening?" I asked as we finished supper.

Mrs. Fairmont blinked her eyes a few times and stared past my left shoulder. "I miss my friends," she said sadly. "So many of them are gone."

I reached across the edge of the table and put my hand on hers. "I'm sure you had many good friends."

Mrs. Fairmont's eyes brightened. "Would you like to look at my picture albums?"

"You have albums?"

"Yes. They're in the small dresser in my show closet. Would you bring one or two to the green parlor?"

I remembered seeing the small white piece of furniture. "Yes ma'am. Are there any particular ones you want to see?"

"No, surprise me."

I cleaned up the supper dishes while Mrs. Fairmont went into the parlor. Upstairs, I discovered that every drawer in the dresser contained photo albums. I grabbed one from each drawer and returned downstairs. We sat beside each other on a firm sofa. I placed an album in her lap, and she opened it.

It was from Christine's early years.

"What was Mrs. Bartlett like at this age?" I asked, pointing at a photo of the family and several other young girls at the beach in front of a huge sand castle.

"Christine has always been social. She recruited those other girls and got them to haul buckets and buckets of sand to build that castle while she bossed them around." Mrs. Fairmont stared at the picture. "I knew she would have to marry someone with plenty of money because she wouldn't lift a finger to do any work herself. What do you think made her that way?"

I didn't try to answer. Mrs. Fairmont turned the page. The faded images seemed to bring a spark of life back to her. We finished one album. I handed her another.

481

"Aren't you bored?" she asked.

"No ma'am."

I'd picked an album of pictures from before Christine was born. It was filled with black-and-white photos of Mr. and Mrs. Fairmont. Mrs. Fairmont spent time inspecting each picture, especially the ones with her friends. She couldn't remember every name, but when she identified one, it was like discovering the missing piece of a jigsaw puzzle. One picture was a group scene from a fancy outdoor party in the spring. I could see the flowers but not the colors in the black-and-white photo. Mrs. Fairmont touched it with her slightly gnarled index finger.

"That was a big soiree. A lot of our social set was there."

The women were wearing fancy dresses and the men stood around in suits and ties. Several servants could be seen in the photo.

"There's Ellen Prescott," Mrs. Fairmont said, pointing to a statuesque woman beside a tall man. "Of course, this was a long time before Lisa was born."

"Is that her husband?" I asked.

"No, it's her older brother Floyd. The party was at his home."

"Her brother was named Floyd?"

"Yes, Ellen was a Carpenter before she

married. Their father worked as a clerk in a shoe store. Ellen was so sweet and married Webster Prescott, who had inherited a lot of railroad stock. Floyd was the black sheep of the family, but he made a lot of money and that has a way of making people forget the past."

My eyes opened wider as I stared at the photo. "Why was he a black sheep?"

"Oh, I never heard anything but rumors."

Mrs. Fairmont reached out to turn the page, but I held it firm.

"What's wrong?" she asked.

"I'm still looking at that picture. What did Floyd Carpenter think about Lisa?"

Mrs. Fairmont gave me a strange look. "I don't know, but I'm sure everyone considered Lisa the little princess. Her blonde curls stood out in any crowd. Christine claims Lisa misbehaved, but I think Christine was probably looking at herself in the mirror."

While Mrs. Fairmont talked, I tried to come up with an innocent way to frame my next question. "Did Floyd's name come up in conversations after Lisa disappeared?" I asked nonchalantly.

Mrs. Fairmont's eyebrows arched downward. "What an odd question. I'm not sure what you mean."

"I'm just curious about Floyd and Lisa and their families."

"Floyd had a son named Joe, who is a lawyer."

"He's my boss."

"Of course, he works with Sam Braddock. Joe and Lisa were the only children in the two families. After Lisa was murdered, the Prescott line ended when Webster and Ellen died."

"But no one is sure Lisa was murdered."

Mrs. Fairmont pushed my hand away from its grip on the page. "If Lisa had gotten lost, someone would have found her. She was either kidnapped or killed. I'm sure there are other interesting photographs in this album."

Mrs. Fairmont turned the page and continued reminiscing about old friends. I barely paid attention and hoped a polite "Yes ma'am" and "No ma'am" would give the impression of interest. There weren't any other pictures of Floyd, and the album ended before Lisa's birth. Mrs. Fairmont's enjoyment returned. I took the book from her hands.

"There's nothing like family and close friends," I said.

"This has been like therapy for me. Would you like to do it again?"

"Yes ma'am."

Flip opened his tiny jaws in an amazingly expansive yawn.

"My baby is ready for a nap and so am I," Mrs. Fairmont said.

"I'll carry the albums upstairs," I said.

I led the way and returned the books to their respective drawers across from the shoe racks. I wanted to take out the other albums and discover if one of them held clues, but without Mrs. Fairmont as a guide, the photos wouldn't have any more significance than a magazine spread.

"I'd like to call my parents before it gets too late," I said as I leaned over to give Flip one last scratch in his favorite place.

"Of course," Mrs. Fairmont replied. "Seeing those pictures probably made you homesick."

I returned to the kitchen. I didn't feel homesick. I was frustrated at my inability to penetrate the deepening mist surrounding Floyd Carpenter and Lisa Prescott.

Daddy answered the phone. I could almost hear his smile when he realized it was me. I touched the top of my head where he liked to kiss me. We talked for a few minutes about the weather and the garden.

"Are you changing, Tammy Lynn?" he asked.

I pondered his words a moment. "That's a good question. I've been too busy to take inventory."

"Being too busy can happen to anyone. It doesn't matter whether you're working in a chicken plant or a law firm. Ask the Lord to search your heart and give you a readout."

"Yes sir."

"That's what Oscar Callahan has been doing," Daddy continued. "Did your mama tell you about his heart attack?"

"No sir."

"It happened a few days after you left for Savannah. We didn't get much information about it at first because they transported him to the intensive-care unit at a hospital in Atlanta. Pastor Vick and one of the elders drove down to pray for him. He let them anoint him with oil and pray the prayer of faith."

"Is he going to be okay?"

"We're praying. The whole church came together at the end of the service last week and spent time at the altar."

"That's good."

"He's been home for a week or so. I spent some time with him yesterday because Kyle is taking care of his cattle. I think he's going to give Kyle a fine-looking calf as payment."

"Good."

"And he felt well enough to tell me a few stories from the old days and asked me to pray for him. He's tender toward the Lord. Talking to him gave me a lot of hope that he'll get right before his time comes."

"What about his clients?"

"He's already brought in an experienced lawyer from Dalton who does the same kind of work. I can't place his name, but he's going to take over the practice. I think he brought along an associate too."

In a split second my safety net had evaporated.

"And he asked about you, of course," Daddy continued. "I told him you were getting along fine."

"Yes sir," I managed. "I guess he had to find someone to help his clients immediately."

Daddy didn't notice the strained tone in my voice.

"I suppose you mainly called to talk about the young man you want to bring home for a visit."

"Which one?" I blurted out, then coughed into the receiver as a diversion. "Excuse me," I said after clearing my throat. "I'd like to put that topic on hold for a while. I need to concentrate on my work without being distracted."

"Good girl," Daddy replied. "That sounds like a wise decision."

"I hope so."

"Continue to seek his will, and he'll take care of helping you find your life partner. Do you want to talk to Mama? She's upstairs with the twins. They had a spat this afternoon and need to do some repenting."

"No sir. Tell her I love her."

That night I lay in bed and tried to come to terms with what had happened to Oscar Callahan. I felt guilty about dwelling on the effect his heart attack had on my future and tried to force myself to pray for the lawyer's recovery. I could concentrate for several minutes before my thoughts drifted back to the air-conditioned white office on the corner now occupied by lawyers who wouldn't need an inexperienced female associate to drive up overhead costs. After tossing and turning for an hour, I turned on the light and wrote a long prayer for Mr. Callahan in my journal. The discipline of writing helped me focus. I wrote "Amen," then started another prayer for the Moses Jones case. It was good seeing the names of the people involved in the sentences requesting God's help. It put them, and the situation, in a better perspective. When I turned out the lights the second time, I quickly fell asleep.

25

After the monotony of days, weeks, and months of unchanging jailhouse routine, the smells and sounds of waking up in his shack by the river began to fade from Moses' memory. The air-conditioned environment of the jail didn't vary more than a couple of degrees, but Moses would have traded confined comfort for the hottest heat of the summer or the coldest rain of the winter along the Little Ogeechee.

Each day, he wondered if the tall girl who wasn't a real lawyer would visit and reveal his future. Twice a day, he pushed his gray buggy down the halls and collected trash. At the dump bin, he always spent a few seconds peering through the fence at his boat, which remained chained to a pole in the stolen-car impound. But as time passed, the boat looked more like a piece of dented aluminum waiting for the scrap heap than a river vessel that became a graceful extension of himself when floating on the water.

He passed from depression to despair. He'd rarely talked to the other prisoners before, but now he was sure some of the newcomers wondered if he could speak at all. The old man had become a familiar part of the jailhouse scene. Years, he'd waited for death. He'd always thought it would come suddenly when the pain that occasionally moved from his chest down his left arm would double back and explode his heart while he was leaning over the edge of his boat, trying to haul in a big fish. The thrill of the moment would trigger the end, and he would tumble easily into the water to join the mystery of the dark beyond.

He now feared that he would pick up a heavy bag of trash one afternoon, collapse in a heap on the concrete floor, and be hauled out by his replacement, in the gray buggy, to the dump bin.

When I arrived at the office in the morning, there was a note on the table in the library asking me to come to Mr. Carpenter's office as soon as I arrived. I read the note twice, hoping it said something different the second time. I'd never been a quitter, but my resolve of the previous day had faded, and for a few seconds I entertained the notion of leaving the building, never to return. I had no idea what Mr. Carpenter had discovered about my activities, but it was naive to think he didn't know what I was doing. I marched as resolutely as my legs allowed down the hallway.

"Mr. Carpenter is expecting you," his secretary said. "Go on in."

I tentatively opened the door. The managing partner was sitting at his desk with a stack of papers near his right hand. He looked up. "What have you been doing?" he asked.

"Mr. Carpenter," I began in the most respectful voice I could muster.

"I thought you were going to have a memo about the status of the Gallagher Corporation holdings in the Folsom case ready for me before you left the office yesterday. I have a deposition scheduled in an hour and a half and want to be able to sort out how Mrs. Folsom finagled her way into a majority position."

My mouth dropped open. "Uh, I left the memo on your secretary's desk two days ago."

Mr. Carpenter picked up the phone. "Sharon! Do you have a memo about Gallagher Corporation from Tami Taylor on your desk?"

The lawyer glared past me at the door, which opened in a few seconds. The secretary entered and walked gingerly past me. She handed Mr. Carpenter the memo without looking at me.

"Here it is. It was placed in another file by mistake."

Mr. Carpenter didn't say anything but grabbed it and began reading it. He grunted several times. I sat still.

"Where is the documentation supporting your opinion?" he asked.

"In the file in the library."

"Get it," he said.

I fled from the office and returned to the library. Julie was there.

"What's going on?" she asked when she saw my face. "Is it Vinny or Zach?"

"Neither. Mr. Carpenter's secretary misplaced that memo I wrote about Gallagher Corporation. She found it, but he wants the documents and research." I riffled through the folders looking for the correct one. "Is being a lawyer worth the stress?"

"Oh, yes. Of course, I don't have a clue myself, but if I believed differently, I would be on my way to the beach this morning."

I grabbed the folder and returned to Mr. Carpenter's office. Sharon didn't look up as I passed her desk.

"Here it is," I said, handing it to him. "I'm sorry for the mix-up."

"It's not your fault," he said with a wave of his hand. "How are the documents organized in the file?"

"Reverse chronological. I flagged the ones that are particularly helpful with red tabs."

Mr. Carpenter flipped through the file and grunted again. "Good work," he said. "Next week I'll have another case for you to work on. It has similar issues."

"Yes sir."

I left his office. It wasn't even 8:30 a.m., yet I felt drained. When I returned to the library, Julie was talking to Vince.

"He wants to see you," she said when I entered the room. "I'm doing the best I can to entertain him, but I can tell he's getting bored."

Vince looked at me. "Are you available for lunch today?"

"I'm not sure. I've been putting out a fire with Mr. Carpenter."

"What kind of fire?" Vince asked a bit too loudly.

"It's not that," I responded quickly. "It has to do with a divorce case."

"What?" Julie interjected. "Are you working on something together?"

I looked at Vince and shook my head.

"Out with it," Julie said, sitting up straighter in her chair. "We're all equal here, except that you're ten times smarter than the rabbi and me put together."

"It's controversial," Vince replied.

I wanted to reach out and put my hand over Vince's mouth.

"And unverified," he added.

"Julie," I said, "I'm not going to discuss this with you." I looked at Vince. "And neither is he. End of the discussion."

"Is it about Moses Jones and the Prescott girl who was murdered?" Julie asked.

I stared at her in shock.

"You left the folder in here a few days ago." She shrugged. "I couldn't help glancing through it, reading the newspaper articles, deciphering your notes."

"That's wrong! You had no business —"

"We're in the same firm," Julie said, shrugging again. "Secrets don't exist."

Before I could respond, the library door opened. It was Zach. Everyone turned and stared at him. He stopped in his tracks.

"What's going on in here?" he asked.

"Tami and her investigation into Moses Jones' involvement in the Prescott murder," Julie said. "I busted her, and she's acting immature about it. Did she try to hide it from you as her supervising attorney?"

Zach surveyed the room. "Tami and Vince, let me talk to Julie for a few minutes," he said.

Vince and I stepped into the hallway.

"What's he going to do?" I asked.

"Not much. She's right."

"What?" I blurted out. "How can you say that? I thought you were on my side."

"I am, but client confidentiality doesn't restrict the flow of communication among employees of the firm. There is no basis for hiding information from one another."

I couldn't believe Vince's position.

"So, you think I should summon Mr. Carpenter and Mr. Braddock to the conference room and confront them with the facts I've uncovered?"

"No, but there's no legal reason why they couldn't order you to disclose your research. Everything you've done originated as work product for a client of the firm. When I came into work this morning, the sign in front of the building read 'Braddock, Appleby, and Carpenter.' This is their law firm, and in our employment contract we agreed that the work we performed this summer belonged to them. That's one reason I urged you to reconsider the scope of your investigation."

I stepped back against the wall. "I might

as well quit and go back to north Georgia for the rest of the summer. There's no way I'm going to ever think like a lawyer."

"I disagree," Vince responded in a matter-of-fact voice. "You know how to focus on the most important aspect of any legal matter."

"Which is?"

"The determination of the truth. If you try the Jones case in front of Judge Cannon, that's one of the first instructions he'll give the jury. It's the practical effects of what you're doing outside the scope of the case that are spinning out of control."

"Thanks a lot . . ." I began.

Before I could continue, the library door opened, and Zach motioned for us to come inside. "I think we're on the same page," he said as soon as we returned.

I waited for a more complete explanation.

"You should have asked for my help," Julie said. "We've worked well together on our other projects."

Vince didn't say anything. I looked at the other three people in the room. "Is that a solution?" I asked.

"Yes," Zach replied. "You don't have to ask Julie to help, but she's available. As your supervising attorney, I'll leave that decision up to you. Did you check the criminal court

497

schedule for the rest of the summer?"

"No, but I'll do it right now."

"Let me know."

Zach left with Vince right behind him. I sat down across from Julie.

"What did Zach say to you?" I asked.

"That it was unprofessional to snoop in your file. Why didn't you tell me the connection between Moses Jones and the disappearance of the Prescott girl?"

"I didn't want you to get all worked up about it."

"And start running my mouth?"

"Yes."

"I wouldn't do anything to prejudice our client. The rules of ethics —"

"I know. Zach has given me more than one refresher course."

"Okay, I won't repeat it. What are you going to do now?"

"Call the courthouse."

After several transfers from one clerk to another, I found out that there were three weeks of criminal court scheduled during the rest of the summer. Two of those weeks were assigned to Judge Cannon, and the judge for the third week was a woman named Linda Howell. I called Maggie Smith, and her assistant informed me the Jones case had not yet been placed on a specific calendar. I sent Zach an e-mail with the dates. He immediately responded with a request that I come to his office. I trudged up the winding staircase that no longer reminded me of a plantation mansion.

"Is there a problem with the dates?" I asked.

"One week in front of Judge Cannon is out because I'll be on vacation in California. I'll let the DA's office know. The other two weeks will depend on my schedule, but I've already let Mr. Appleby know what's going on."

"Okay." I moved away from the door.

"No, come in and sit down," Zach said.

"I don't need another lecture this morning," I replied wearily. "The fruit of patience in my life may not be as mature as I'd hoped, and I don't want to get upset."

"We need to set a day and time to talk to Moses Jones and discuss trial strategy. It will also be a chance for you to show him the newspaper articles if you want to."

"Okay."

Zach studied me for a few seconds. "What else have you found out?"

"Do you care?"

"You can tell me now or later."

I took a deep breath. "I'm not finished in the microfilm records. I want to uncover the connections between Floyd Carpenter and this firm." I paused. "Especially regarding Floyd and his relationship with his sister and niece."

"Who?"

"Ellen and Lisa Prescott. Mrs. Fairmont told me about the Prescott-Carpenter connection while we were looking at old photos last night."

I could tell Zach was surprised by my latest information. He pulled twice on his ponytail. If the lawyer ever cut his hair, he would have to find something else to do with his hands during moments of intense mental activity.

"How does this fit?" he asked.

"I don't know until I do more research. Should I ask Julie to do it?" I asked sarcastically then immediately felt guilty.

Zach ignored my dig. "No, you're so far ahead of her that it would be inefficient. Wait here while I get the key from Gerry so you can finish your research. We can meet with Moses later today."

While Zach talked to Ms. Patrick, I checked on the firm car. It was scheduled to return in a few minutes and I reserved it for a couple of hours. I went to Zach's office where he handed me the key.

"Gerry started asking questions," he said.

"I simply thanked her and left."

"But she's an employee of the firm. According to your logic . . ." I began then stopped. "Will you pray that God will put a rein on my tongue? It's been out of control since I got to the office this morning."

"No man can tame the tongue," Zach said. "Does that include women?"

"Yes." I turned the key over in my hand. "And thanks for confronting me when you think I'm out of line. My mother does a good job of correcting me, but I thought I'd be without that kind of help this summer."

"Sure, but I don't want to be a surrogate mother or father. Did you find out a date and time when I can meet them?"

"Not yet. When will you be in California?"

Zach gave me the dates and eyed me closely. "Is there a reason why you wouldn't want me to meet your parents?"

"Let's not talk about it now. I have too much to think about."

"If there is something —"

"We'll talk soon," I said. "I promise."

I got off the elevator and opened the door to the archive facility. Eddie, the young man who wanted to go to law school, looked up and smiled.

"Welcome back," he said.

I signed in. Only two people had visited the facility since I'd been in the day before. Apparently, business was slow for dead records. I put down the pen, and Eddie started to walk toward the storage room.

"I know the way," I said.

Eddie stopped. "Okay. Let me know if you need to use my phone."

I turned on the microfilm reader and used the index to locate the earliest Prescott file. I found the proper cassette and inserted it into the reader. It was toward the end of the roll, and I scrolled through pages of documents typed with the font of an old typewriter. The letterhead for the Braddock Law Firm still listed the date of birth and death for Vernon Fletchall. When I reached the beginning page it contained records for the purchase of a house near Colonial Cemetery. Nothing relevant.

The next file was on a different cassette and related to a business deal. It contained several pages of handwritten notes by Lawrence Braddock. The lawyer wrote in a tall, yet tightly compacted script and fully utilized a sheet of paper. Once I got used to his style, it wasn't hard to read. On a third cassette, I found a copy of a Last Will and Testament prepared for the Prescotts when Lisa was about three years old. It was a lengthy document. My hand stopped advancing the pages when I reached Item XXI, a catchall provision that designated the beneficiary of the will upon the deaths of Webster and Ellen if Lisa predeceased her parents and there were no other surviving children.

If that event occurred, the sole beneficiary of the will was Ellen's "beloved brother," Floyd Carpenter. I bit my lower lip in disbelief. I pressed the Print button.

I'd found the smoking gun. And it contained three bullets, not one.

The page inched out of the printer. I held it in my hand and read it again. In crafting a plan for wealthy individuals, estate lawyers have to consider remote possibilities that no one expects to happen. Unless, of course, human intervention makes the unlikely certain. Lisa's disappearance and death, followed by the deaths of her parents, was a simple matter of economics and federal tax liens.

It was hard to imagine the evil that could murder an entire family for money. I thought about the grainy picture of Lisa in the newspaper and the picture of Margaret Fairmont and Ellen Prescott as little girls standing on tiptoe to get a drink of water. Tears came to my eyes. I took a tissue from my purse.

After the tears passed, I returned without enthusiasm to the index. I found several more Prescott files. Righteous indignation rose up in me when I found notes from a consultation Webster and Ellen had with Lawrence Braddock a few days after Lisa's disappearance. The Prescotts, upset over the lack of progress with the police investigation, met with the lawyer to discuss the case. In his notes, the lawyer promised to make "appropriate contacts" with state law enforcement officers in Atlanta who could assist in the investigation. However, the last line of Mr. Braddock's notes was the most incriminating. "Call F.C."

I printed the notes. The next file was the probate of the Prescotts' will after the car wreck. Mrs. Fairmont was wrong. The couple lived only slightly over a year after Lisa's death, just long enough to provide a buffer against any suspicion. The circumstances surrounding their car plunging into a tidewater canal weren't mentioned — they were simply listed as the "decedents."

The file contained pages of inventory about stocks, bonds, bank accounts, antiques, art objects, and real estate. I slowed when I came to a petition asking the court to judicially declare Lisa deceased even though no body had been found. Several law enforcement officials were listed as witnesses, and three weeks after the petition was filed, the probate judge signed an order granting Lawrence Braddock's request.

The provisions of the will didn't require an accounting to the probate court identifying the total value of the estate, but I found a handwritten memo from Mr. Braddock to Floyd Carpenter listing a summary of all tangible and intangible assets — the Prescotts left their child's killer slightly under two million dollars, a huge sum at the time, and more than enough to satisfy Floyd Carpenter's tax liens.

I printed out the entire probate file. While I waited for the pages to inch from the printer, I prayed for God's guidance. But I was numb with shock. I returned all the film cassettes to their proper places and put the documents in a file folder. This time, I wouldn't leave the information lying around where Julie could find it. Zach and Vince's claim that no secrets existed among employees of Braddock, Appleby, and Carpenter didn't apply to what I'd uncovered. After forty years, it still bore the stink of death.

"Find everything okay?" Eddie Anderson asked as I wrote down the time on the entry and exit log.

I looked up at him, not sure how to answer. He quickly glanced away.

I drove back to the office and pulled into the parking lot but didn't get out. I didn't know what to do next. I couldn't talk to my parents. Oscar Callahan was at home recovering from a heart attack and, although a lawyer, had no more right to privileged information than the courier I watched walk up the sidewalk to the front door of the office. My confidence in Zach and Vince as reliable counselors had been seriously weakened. And if Mr. Carpenter summoned me into his office again, I wouldn't be able to look him in the eyes and find a way to dodge his probing questions. For the second time, I considered fleeing Savannah like the Confederate army that faced Sherman. I closed my eyes and let the coolness from the air-conditioning vent blow over my face. A knock on the car window made me jump. It was Zach. I pushed the button to lower the window.

"This isn't the place to take a nap," he said.

"I'm not in a joking mood."

"What did you find in the microfilm records?"

"I'm not ready to talk about it."

"Why not?"

I shook my head. "Don't pressure me."

Zach leaned closer to the open widow. "Tami, when a lawyer isolates herself on a case, there's a much greater chance of a mistake."

"I'm not a lawyer yet, as you so gently reminded me the other day. And I'm debating whether I ever want to be!"

I opened the door and pushed Zach out of the way. He backed up as I marched past him and met the courier leaving the firm. I returned the car keys to the receptionist.

"Did you see Mr. Mays?" she asked. "He was looking for you."

"Yes."

It was close to lunchtime, and I desperately hoped Julie wouldn't be in the library. I opened the door and peeked inside. The table where we usually sat was empty. On one of the bookshelves I found a set of out-of-date tax treatises no one would likely use and hid the folder behind them. As I repositioned the books, the library door opened. It was Vince. He looked around the room.

"Are you alone?" he asked.

"Yes."

"I owe you an apology," he said. "Can we talk?"

Given how vulnerable I felt, I didn't want to be around anyone.

"I accept your apology, but let's not talk," I answered.

"I'm sorry, but it can't wait."

Vince shifted on his feet. He was unbelievably persistent about spending time with me.

"All right," I sighed. "But I'm only going to listen. Don't expect me to respond."

26

"Is the sandwich shop near the river okay?" Vince asked as we passed through the reception area.

"I don't care. I'm not hungry."

We rode in silence. Vince had to park a block away from the deli. As we walked on the uneven cobblestones, the sights and sounds of the people along the waterfront seemed out of touch with reality. The deli was crowded. Vince ordered a ham sandwich. I picked up a bottle of water.

"Thanks for coming," Vince said as we sat down. "Where did you go after we talked this morning?"

"That's a question, not an apology."

"I'll get right to it. You were right that your investigation into Lisa Prescott's disappearance shouldn't be common knowledge at the firm."

Vince paused as a waitress brought his sandwich. I took a sip of water.

"At ten thirty I was supposed to go over a research memo with Mr. Braddock in the conference room. He wasn't there so I went to his office but had to wait because he was in a meeting with Mr. Carpenter. The office door was cracked open. I couldn't hear Mr. Braddock's voice because he's so soft-spoken, but I caught some of Mr. Carpenter's side of the conversation. He told Mr. Braddock that you had sent him a memo on Tuesday to update him on the Jones matter and he should be hearing from you again soon. Then he said 'stronger pressure should have been applied to Moses Jones a long time ago.' "

"What does that mean?" I asked.

"I don't know exactly, but it doesn't sound good. Mr. Braddock must have talked for a while; then Mr. Carpenter said, 'As soon as Ms. Taylor is out of the picture, we'll get to him before it's too late.' It was quiet while Mr. Braddock talked, and then Mr. Carpenter came barreling out of the office. I almost fell out of the chair."

"Did he realize you were eavesdropping?"

"I hope not. He was in such a hurry to leave the office that I don't think he paid any attention to me."

Vince took a bite from his sandwich. I glanced past his shoulder at the people lined

510

up at the counter. Two women were pointing at items in the display case as they discussed what to eat. My decision was much more serious — how much to tell Vince about my morning discovery.

"Your intuition or discernment or whatever you want to call it was correct," Vince said between bites. "I thought about going back to Julie and warning her to keep her mouth shut, but that would probably make her more likely to talk."

"Yes."

Vince pushed his plate away from him and covered his sandwich with a paper napkin.

"I'm not hungry either," he said. "It was so bizarre hearing two respected attorneys talk like gangsters that I didn't know what to think."

Vince's dilemma mirrored my own. "I completely understand," I said slowly. "Only this morning I was reading about a forty-year-old conversation between two different men named Carpenter and Braddock."

Vince listened to my story, then spoke. "If I hadn't read the memo and overheard today's conversation, I wouldn't think that the current Mr. Carpenter and Mr. Braddock had done anything wrong," he said. "Now, I don't know. Mr. Braddock was just beginning to practice law with his father when all this happened, and Joe Carpenter was in high school or about to enter college. Maybe they were pulled in somehow."

"I'm not sure I want to know. The immediate crisis is what to do about Moses Jones. Even if he did something wrong a long time ago, he should only be punished by the proper authorities. Do I have a greater obligation to protect him from 'stronger pressure,' or should I just keep quiet and represent him in the trespassing case? Would it be unethical to tell the assistant district attorney that he needs to be kept in jail for his own safety?" My voice trembled slightly. "What if he gets out of jail and something bad happens to him?"

"What does Zach think? Have you talked to him?"

"No! From the beginning, he's been reluctant to help and argues with me about everything. I think it's time to draw a circle around us and agree that we're the only ones who need to know what's going on."

Vince leaned back in his chair. "Okay. But while you're thinking about Zach and Mr. Jones, you need to decide what you're going to tell Mr. Carpenter. He's expecting to hear from you."

"I know, but I think it all leads to the same place. First, I have to talk to Moses. This is his case, his life."

We returned to the office. The firm car was checked out and would be gone for the rest of the afternoon. I was stranded.

"You can borrow mine," Vince offered.

"Are you sure?"

He handed me the keys. "Of course. You're only driving across town."

"Thanks." I walked rapidly to the library. I didn't want to run into Zach or Mr. Carpenter. All I needed was the folder containing copies of the newspaper clippings. It was time to find out whether Moses' memory, like Mrs. Fairmont's, could be unlocked by a picture. I opened the library door. Julie was sitting at the table.

"Any success?" she asked.

"Not yet," I answered quickly. "I'm going to the jail to talk to Moses Jones. The date of trial hasn't been set, but I've got to start getting ready."

"Are you going to ask more questions about the Prescott girl?"

"Maybe."

Julie placed a book on top of the papers stacked in front of her.

"I'm going with you. You'll need a witness of what he tells you."

"That's unnecessary," I answered, trying

to stay calm. "You should be working on your own cases."

"Not if I need to help you. Besides, we can take my car."

"Vince is loaning me his car."

Julie's eyes widened. "When are you going to move into his apartment?"

I felt a flash of heat across my entire body and an overwhelming urge to yell at her. I closed my eyes to fight it off.

"Okay, I'm sorry," Julie said. "I keep forgetting that you don't share my sense of humor."

"And I don't need your help."

Julie held up her hands. "Don't be so touchy. But you can't trust your judgment when you're so upset about everything."

"I'm not upset about everything. Just your crude comment."

"You're wrong about that." Julie held up her right hand and pointed at her fingers. "You're upset with Mr. Carpenter because his questions scare you, mad at Zach because he doesn't agree with you all the time, and tired of me teasing you. I don't know for sure, but I also suspect Gerry Patrick and Bob Kettleson have gotten under your skin. To top it all off, you're frustrated by everything that's been happening in the Jones case. Judge Cannon and the assistant

514

DA are blocking you at every turn, and you don't see a way out. If it weren't for your iron will, you'd be close to cracking."

Julie sat back in her chair with a self-satisfied look on her face. My mother couldn't have done a better job of dissecting my struggles.

"Maybe you should have gotten a PhD in psychology," I replied as evenly as I could, "but I still don't want you to go to the jail with me."

"Suit yourself. But I'm here if you need me."

I picked up my folder and left. The midday heat had driven out the effects of the air-conditioning left from our drive to lunch. I turned the fan motor on high. Backing out of the parking space, I heard the sound of a horn and slammed on the brakes. Turning my head, I saw Mr. Braddock behind me in his silver Mercedes. He shook his head and smiled. I said a quick prayer of thanks that I'd not hit his car, but all the way to the jail couldn't get the look on his face out of my mind. How could a man with such deep-seated evil living within his soul smile and wave? The Old Testament prophet was right when he wrote that the heart of man was deceitfully wicked above all else, who can fathom it?

Arriving at the jail, I identified myself to the female deputy on duty and asked to see Moses. I waited in the open area outside the interview rooms until he appeared, escorted by a corrections officer who looked as young as my brother Kyle. We went into an interview room.

"Hello, Mr. Jones," I said as the door closed with a low thud.

"Yes, missy," he replied as we sat down across from each other. "I be worrying that you forgot about Moses and going to leave him in this place to die."

"No sir, I've been working hard. Your case will be coming up for trial sometime in the next few weeks. I don't know the exact date, but as soon as I do, I'll be here to let you know. There's a chance we will have a different judge."

"That may be help." The old black man nodded. "But I not know what I'm going to say."

"We'll practice going over your testimony until you know everything I'm going to ask you," I replied with more confidence than I felt. "You can't deny tying up your boat at private docks for the night, but we'll let the jury know that you didn't realize it was private property."

"That river, it belong to God who made it."

"Yes, I understand and agree, but that's not our best argument. An innocent mistake on your part will be easier to explain, and we'll also be sure to produce evidence that you didn't damage anyone's property or scare the landowners. Ignorance of the law isn't usually a legal excuse, but the jury can find you not guilty if they think you had an honest misunderstanding. Does that make sense?"

Moses shook his head. "No, missy. You be talking and talking."

"That's okay for now. We'll go over everything and break it down so you can follow."

I laid the folder with the newspaper clippings on the table. When I did, I felt my heart beat a little faster. I cleared my throat. Moses ran his tongue across the most prominent tooth in the front of his mouth.

"Moses, I have something else to show you." I opened the folder and took out the initial article about Lisa Prescott's disappearance. It contained the largest version of the photograph that ran in all the subsequent articles. I slid the sheet across the table and turned it so Moses could see it.

"Do you recognize this girl?" I asked.

He lowered his head closer to the table

and tilted it to the side. "She be dead," he said in a soft voice after a few moments. "Where you get this?"

"It's a copy of an old newspaper article. Is this the girl whose face you see in the water?"

Still staring down, he nodded. I leaned forward. "Why do you see her face in the water?" I asked.

Moses let out a long sigh that slightly whistled as it passed through his teeth. " 'Cause that's where she be," he said softly.

"How did she get there?" I asked, trying to stay calm.

"There weren't nothing else I could do."

I sat back in my chair. Moses looked at me and blinked his eyes. The old man was about to cry. I'd seen many confessions with tears at the altar of the church in Powell Station, but none that involved a murder.

"Do you want to tell me?"

He put his weathered hands on the table and closed his eyes. "I go fishing. Not in that boat chained to the pole out back, but in an old wooden thing that leaked termite-bad. I be minding my own self when I heared the sound on the bank. I thought it must be a hurt critter and rowed over to see for myself. It be getting dark, but I seen a piece of yellow scrap that caught my eye. I touched the bank and hopped onto the ground. I heard another sound. The bushes were thick, and I got cut bad getting to her."

He opened his eyes and pointed to a two-inch scar on his forehead. "I be bleeding bad my own self by the time I got to her. She was a-hurtin' and bleeding here and here."

The old man pointed to his mouth and ears. "Her eyes be open, but not seeing nothing."

He stopped and bowed his head. I could tell he was slipping completely into silent memory and pulled him back.

"Was she alive?" I asked.

He looked up. "She be breathing. I run up the bank to an old dirty road, but no one there 'cause it way out in the country. I yell and holler. No help be coming. I go back and pick up that girl. She not much heavier than an old blanket. I put her in my boat. We both bleeding together. I row down the river as fast as I could go. It be getting darker and darker. I get to the big water so I can get her to the bridge for the hardscape road to town. Cars be there for sure. I put down my ear to listen." He shook his head. "And she be gone."

"She fell into the water?"

"No, missy. She be dead."

"Did you take the body to town?"

Moses shook his head. "I be black; she be white. We both be bleeding. What happen to me if'n I carry her to town? That night I be hanging by my neck from a tree with nobody asking no more questions."

It made perfect sense.

"What did you do with the body?"

"I take her to the place on the river where I be staying. I don't know what to do. I stay up all night a-crying and walking round in circles. Before the sun comes arising, I tie a rope about her little feet and then onto a big rock. I push off into a deep spot, say a prayer, and that's it. She be there today."

"Did you ever tell anyone what happened?"

"My brother, he knew. And my auntie that helped raise me."

"Are they alive?"

"They be long dead."

"What about Mr. Floyd Carpenter? Did he know you found Lisa Prescott?"

"People talk, maybe my brother, and Mr. Tommy Lee bring me into his office and make me see Mr. Floyd."

"Who is Mr. Tommy Lee?"

"My boss man when I run bolita. Mr. Floyd, he be the big boss man."

"What is bolita?"

"The numbers."

I gave Moses a puzzled look. He held out his hand and rubbed it. "You tell me two numbers and give me a dime. If they be right, I give you five dollars the next day."

"Gambling?"

"Yes, missy. But I never did sell bootleg. I drink it way back then, but I don't haul it. That be my brother. Only ways I go to jail for half a year instead of him."

Moses' connection with the sale of untaxed alcohol wouldn't help me find out what I wanted to know.

"Why did Floyd Carpenter want to talk to you about Lisa Prescott?"

"I be thinking they call me a thief, but I turn in all my money. But all the talk is about the little girl, asking me what I saw, where I been. I be scared and say nothing. Mr. Tommy Lee, he holler at me and lift up his fist, but he don't mean it. Next day, I on the street running numbers, just like before."

"Did Floyd Carpenter suspect you found her on the riverbank?"

Moses shook his head. "I don't be knowing, only I see his face to this day."

"Where?"

"In the water. Why do you think that be so?"

It was an unanswerable question.

"Didn't you tell me Floyd Carpenter gave you a dollar that you threw in the river?"

"Later, he come all the way down on the river where I be staying. I was eating my breakfast when he walk out of the woods with a long rifle on his shoulder. 'Bout scared me half to death. But he talk soft. Give me a shiny silver dollar."

"Why did he give you the money?"

"He say if I be telling the truth, that dollar will make me a rich man. If I be lying, then I won't never have nothing. I be poor my whole life except I got my boat."

"Telling the truth about what?"

Moses pointed to the picture in the paper. "That girl with the yellow hair and blue eyes."

"Did you tell him then that you found her on the bank and tried to save her?"

"No, the voice in my head tells me something ain't right. I just shake my head and act dumb, but I be scared if'n he don't believe me. So I start sleeping more on the river, but he find me there."

"He came to see you in a boat?"

"No, missy. Ain't you listening? His face. It don't need no boat." He pointed again at the newspaper article. "He be like her."

I sat back in my chair and studied Moses

Jones in a different way. The old man had lived most of his life haunted by people he'd never harmed.

"I'm sorry this happened to you," I said after a few moments passed. "All of it."

He looked at me and bowed his head slightly. I started to offer another consoling word, but the horrid, unjustified malice directed against Moses by Mr. Carpenter and Mr. Braddock hit me.

"Moses, did you know Mr. Floyd Carpenter had a son?"

"Yeah. He be a big-shot lawyer."

"He's my boss. And he wants to know everything you've been telling me."

Moses gave me a puzzled look. "Why he care about me after all these years done flowed by?"

"Because of Lisa Prescott. He and another lawyer named Samuel Braddock believe there is a connection between you and the little girl. They see you as a threat."

"What you mean?"

"You were scared of Mr. Floyd and his gun. They're scared of you and what you know."

"Why? I be sitting in this jail and can't hurt nobody."

"That's true. But they think you can harm them by changing the way people in Savannah think about them. The guilt of past generations is chasing them. And that guilt doesn't ever get tired." I paused. "Floyd Carpenter was the person responsible for Lisa Prescott's death."

Moses' face revealed his shock. "Why he do that? She not be more than a little thing."

I rubbed my hand as he had earlier. "For a lot more than a chance at five dollars."

27

Moses shook his head after I spent almost an hour explaining as best I could what I'd uncovered.

"That be too much old thoughts for my brain to hold."

"I know it's complicated, but what I really need is your permission to talk to the district attorney's office about the possible danger to you. The DA's office could call in the police to investigate, and you could tell Detective Branson what happened that evening on the river. He seems like a good man."

"You be a nice'un, but out there" — Moses gestured with his arm — "ain't nobody gonna believe me. Nowadays I may not be strung up on a tree limb, but I never get out of this jail. No, missy, you best keep this to me and you."

"Don't you understand? You could be in real danger."

"For sure, every way be a rocky path. But the less folks that knows the way I go, the better off I be."

I searched for another approach to convince him. "Please, think about it. It would be awful if something bad happened to you."

Moses gave me a slightly crooked smile. "That be a kind word. I not hear talk like that since I was a small boy at my auntie's house."

"I misjudged you, and I'm sorry."

Moses didn't answer. I looked down at my legal pad. It was blank. I'd been so engrossed in what Moses had told me that I hadn't taken a note. Perhaps no notes about our conversation would be better.

"I'll be back to see you soon," I promised.

"And don't be forgetting about my boat. If'n I get out of here on prohibition, I want that boat going with me. It ain't done nothing wrong."

The drive back to the office didn't give me enough time to figure out what to do next. Investigating Lisa Prescott's disappearance had been theoretical. The danger to Moses was immediate and certain.

Vince was working in the conference room adjacent to Mr. Braddock's office. Two paralegals were at the other end of the table organizing documents. I placed the keys on the table and leaned close to his ear.

"Thanks," I said. "Do you have time to talk?"

Vince motioned toward the other end of the table.

"They're up against a deadline, and I need to pull off some data from the Internet for Mr. Appleby."

"You're working for Mr. Appleby?"

"Yes. The information is in French and no one else can translate it. I should be finished within an hour. Where will you be?"

"In the library."

To my relief, Julie wasn't in the library. I logged on to one of the terminals and checked my office e-mail. There was a message from Mr. Carpenter asking for an update on the Moses Jones case. I skipped to the next item. It was from Zach.

Tami,

I talked with Maggie Smith. She agreed to place Moses Jones' case on Judge Howell's trial calendar. She also brought up the possibility of running the plea bargain past Judge Howell. If the judge goes along with the deal, Jones could be released in a few days. Thought you might want this good news as soon as possible.

Follow up with me upon your return to the office.

Zach

A few hours before, this would have been welcome news. Now, it doubled the pressure I felt. I noticed that Zach had also sent it to Mr. Carpenter. My mouth went dry, and the pressure doubled again. I glanced at the ceiling and offered up a prayer for help.

I tried to work on the Folsom divorce case while I waited for Vince to finish, but it was trivial compared to the threats facing Moses. I checked my watch every five minutes. Shortly, before the hour was up, the library door opened. I looked up in relief.

It was Zach.

"Did you read my e-mail?" he asked.

"Yes."

"And?" he asked, raising his eyebrows.

"It sounds hopeful, but I'm not sure Moses is ready to get out of jail. You heard what he said when we explained the terms of probation to him. He'll violate the terms of release and go back to jail without any chance of getting out for a long time."

"He's a grown man. As long as he understands what's expected of him, compliance is his responsibility. Do you think he wants to stay locked up? We don't have the right to keep him in jail if there is a reasonable chance to get him out."

"We might get a not-guilty verdict at trial," I responded. "Then he wouldn't have to worry about probation. I met with him this afternoon and explained our trial strategy. As we talked it made more and more sense. I mean, jurors are regular people who can appreciate an honest mistake, especially when no property damage has occurred."

"I don't want to hurt your feelings, but I can't believe what I'm hearing. The case is exactly where we want it to be, and you think the best course of action is for our client to go to trial? What's really going on? This has to do with Lisa Prescott, doesn't it?"

I pressed my lips tightly together.

"What did you find in the microfilm records?" Zach continued. "Even if you uncovered incriminating information about Moses Jones, it doesn't give you the right to be judge and jury, sentencing him to jail."

The door opened, and Vince stepped in. He saw Zach and started backing out of the room. "Sorry to interrupt," he said. "I'll check with you later."

"Hold it," Zach said.

"What?" Vince asked.

Zach stared at Vince, then turned toward me. "Because you two are working on the Jones case together doesn't mean you can withhold information from me. Tami was supposed to take me with her and conveniently forgot to let me know."

"Oh," I said, stung, "I got caught up and —"

Zach interrupted. "I want to hear what's happened since we met this morning."

The three of us sat around the table, with Zach at one end and Vince and I across from each other.

"Out with it," Zach said.

I looked at Vince, who seemed nervous. Zach hesitated for a moment, then spoke. "I'm only an associate. Do you want me to bring in one of the partners to help sort this out? I don't know who's here this afternoon, but Mr. Carpenter is the most familiar —"

"No!" I blurted out. "That would be cruel."

"No more than the accusations you've made against him," Zach shot back.

"Not cruel to me," I replied testily. "Leave me out of this. I've never had a realistic chance of working here, and based on what I know now, I wouldn't accept a permanent job if Mr. Carpenter offered me one. This is all about Moses Jones. You have no idea what you're about to do to him."

Zach's neck was slightly red. "Then tell me. I'm listening."

I looked at Vince.

"Go ahead," he said.

I faced Zach. "First, I need to ask you a question. Is your primary loyalty to Moses Jones as a client or to this law firm?"

"Is there a conflict between them?"

"Yes. And if I don't tell you the details, then you won't have to make a choice."

I saw Zach hesitate. I knew he liked his job working for Mr. Appleby. I turned to Vince.

"And everyone knows you're a lock as the next associate of the firm. You warned me the other day, but have you thought about the negative impact this could have on your future? Are you helping me because God has called you or because it gives us a chance to be together?"

The slightly embarrassed look on Vince's face told me what I needed to know.

"I'm trying not to be cruel to either one of you or anybody else," I continued in a calmer tone of voice. "I came to the conclusion this afternoon that what happens to me doesn't matter as much as taking care of my client." I stood up. "From now on,

I'm not going to discuss this with either one of you. I'm exhausted and ready to go home."

I left Zach and Vince together in the library. I didn't know where Julie might be, but I wasn't going to stick around. I found her coming out of Ned's office.

"Are you ready to leave for the day?" I asked.

She looked at her watch. "Yeah, it's later than I thought. I have a few things to grab from the library."

"I'll wait for you at the car."

"It's blazing hot outside."

"Then you'll hurry, okay?"

Julie glanced questioningly over her shoulder. I hoped the thought of me roasting in the late-afternoon heat would keep her from having a long conversation with Zach and Vince. I walked slowly along the sidewalk in the shade cast by the building. I reached the car and watched the front door. In less than a minute Julie joined me.

"Was anyone in the library?" I asked.

"No, why?"

"Just curious. I'd finished a meeting with Zach and Vince, and they stayed after I left."

"About the Jones case?"

I knew I had to answer, and partial information was much more likely to satisfy

Julie's curiosity so we could change subjects.

"Yeah, I met with him this afternoon at the jail," I said casually. "One of the things we discussed was trial strategy. I think my chances of getting a not-guilty verdict are greater than you might think, but Zach and Vince are unconvinced."

"Your client admits the crime. I can't imagine a credible defense."

I stretched out my explanation until Julie stopped in front of Mrs. Fairmont's house.

"You're dreaming," Julie said. "The best you could hope for would be a hung jury if you convince a couple of people to feel sorry for him."

"And a hung jury might be as good as an acquittal. How many times do you think the district attorney's office wants to take up the court's time trying a misdemeanor trespassing case?"

"You have a point," Julie admitted with a nod of her head. "Once again, I underestimated you. I didn't think you had the guts to force a trial."

As Julie drove away, I wasn't sure I had more guts than an eight-pound chicken.

Inside the house, I greeted Flip, whose excitement at my arrival seemed to increase each afternoon. Mrs. Fairmont was asleep in her chair with the television blaring. I gently touched her on the shoulder. She didn't respond. I shook her harder. To my relief she stirred and opened her eyes.

"How do you feel?" I asked.

"Who are you?" she asked as she glanced up at me with bleary eyes.

"Tami Taylor. I'm staying at your house this summer while I work for Samuel Braddock's law firm."

"Samuel Braddock?"

"Yes ma'am."

It was the first time Mrs. Fairmont's memory for people she'd known for years was fuzzy.

"Are you hungry?" I asked. "I'd be happy to fix your supper."

Mrs. Fairmont closed her eyes for a few seconds, then opened them. "Yes, that would be nice."

Gracie hadn't come that day, but there were leftovers in the refrigerator. I quickly prepared two plates of food and began warming one up in the microwave. After the stress that threatened to crush me at the office, the normalcy of fixing supper was therapeutic.

I returned to the den and found Mrs. Fairmont sitting in the chair with her eyes closed. It was a sad sight that made me ache over the ravages of aging. I heated up the other plate of food and placed them on the dining room table. Flip, smelling the meal, took up his position beside Mrs. Fairmont's chair. I returned to the den and roused her again. At first I thought I might have to assist her to the table, but once on her feet, she walked without any problems to the dining room.

Mrs. Fairmont seemed to enjoy her supper but didn't respond to my attempts at conversation beyond a single word or two. I was just getting to know her and didn't want to see her slip away permanently into a pit of mental confusion.

"Lord, please don't let this be the time," I prayed softly.

Mrs. Fairmont glanced over and gave me a sweet smile. "You're a nice young woman," she said. "Would you like to stay for a cup of after-dinner coffee?"

"Yes ma'am. I'll fix it for you."

I brought coffee to the table along with a cup of tea for myself. We drank in silence. Mrs. Fairmont touched a napkin to her lips.

"I should invite Samuel and Eloise Braddock over for dinner," she said. "They are such a gracious couple, and we have many good memories together."

"It would be best if I'm not here that

evening," I said.

"Why?"

"So you can discuss good memories."

I lay awake that night. Most of the challenges I'd faced in my life seemed theoretical compared to the sober reality facing Moses Jones. My responsibility to the old man rested on my chest like a great weight and reduced me to one of the simplest prayers.

"Help me," I prayed over and over and over.

I finally drifted off to sleep with the words lingering on my lips.

I awoke in the morning and enjoyed a five-second stretch before reality returned. I sighed and reluctantly resumed my burden. During my morning run, I took a new route away from the historic district into the modern part of the city. I needed new scenery.

Mrs. Fairmont wasn't downstairs when I returned, but she responded when I pressed the Call button on the intercom.

"How are you feeling this morning?" I asked.

"Fine. I'm going to call Christine and tell her to take me to lunch. Have a nice day."

I walked as resolutely as I could to the office and went directly to the library. Julie hadn't arrived, and there weren't any notes from Zach or Vince. One of my main goals for the day was to avoid contact with either one of them. I checked my law firm e-mail account. I'd received another project from Bob Kettleson. I grimaced. One consequence of my leaving the firm would be increased work for the senior associate. Julie burst through the door.

"Wow, what a night," she said. "I met the most awesome guy. He lives on my street, and we met while he was walking his dog, a cute little thing with pointy white ears. Joel graduated a few years ago from the design school here and opened his own studio. He's a photographer, and some of his shots were the most amazing things I've ever seen. He asked me out to dinner on the spot and took me to the neatest French restaurant in a house on West Oglethorpe Street."

"I know the place," I said.

"He lived in Paris for a year after graduation. And get this, he's Jewish without being over the top about it. Just like me. We had so much fun. I haven't laughed so hard in months. His work is so good that I've got to get my father to buy a few prints for my mother. He invited me to synagogue Friday night, then to the beach on Saturday. My mother will flip when she finds out. Maybe we can do something clean and wholesome one evening with you and either Vinny or Zach."

Julie stopped and laughed. "That sounds strange, doesn't it?"

"Yes."

The library phone buzzed, and I picked it up. It was the front desk receptionist.

"This is Tami."

"You have a call from Ms. Smith at the district attorney's office. She asked for Zach, but he's not here."

"I'll take it," I said after a moment's hesitation.

Maggie Smith wasted no time on pleasantries once I took the call. "I spoke with Zach yesterday, and I was able to reassign the Jones case to Judge Howell's docket. I ran the plea bargain past the judge, and she's fine with it — release Jones for time served and a year on probation with no monetary fine. It's specially set on her calendar this afternoon at two o'clock. I sent Zach an e-mail confirmation."

"I'm not sure my client —" I began, and then stopped.

Moses had not withdrawn his agreement to the plea, and I couldn't tell her otherwise.

"What about your client?" Smith asked.

"I need to let him know about the hearing."

"Fine, but the prisoner request list went over to the jail first thing this morning. He'll be there and released in time for a cornbread supper. See you this afternoon."

I hung up the phone.

"Good or bad news?" Julie asked.

"It depends. We're going in front of another judge with the plea bargain in the Jones case. The assistant DA thinks it will go through."

There was no avoiding Zach now. No matter how cooperative Judge Howell might be, she wouldn't allow me to appear in court without a supervising attorney. I buzzed back to the receptionist.

"Please let me know when Zach Mays arrives."

"He walked in the door right after I transferred the phone call."

There was no use putting off the inevitable. I slowly set the phone receiver back in the cradle.

"Does Joel have any photos of the river marshes?" I asked Julie.

"Yeah, at all times of the day. They're gorgeous."

"If you want to buy me a going-away

present, that would be a good choice."

I left Julie with a puzzled expression on her face and went upstairs to Zach's office. He turned around when I entered.

"Maggie Smith called," I said. "The case —"

"Is on for two o'clock this afternoon. I read her e-mail."

I turned to leave.

"One other thing," Zach said. "Mr. Carpenter is going to be there."

I spun around. "Who invited him?"

"Nobody. He's been keeping up with the case independently of your information."

"What does that tell you?"

"That he's more interested than I knew. But you're not sharing information with anyone, and I don't want to speculate about his motives."

"*Motive* is a good word." I stopped and took a deep breath. "And I know I'm doing the right thing keeping you and Vince out of this."

28

Somehow, I needed to convince Moses to reject the plea bargain and remain in the relative safety of the jail. All paths might be rocky, but not all held the danger of a fatal rock slide. I needed time to figure out the best way to safety.

I checked on the availability of the law firm car. It was checked out for the entire day. I wouldn't suffer the indignity of riding in the motorcycle sidecar or in the same vehicle with Mr. Carpenter and didn't want to ask Vince to let me borrow his car. That left Julie. I returned to the library.

And came face-to-face with Bob Kettleson.

"Let's go," he said. "We have a meeting with the developer on the eminent domain issue you researched."

"Why do you need me? Everything I know is in the memo, and there is a hearing on my appointed criminal case this afternoon.

I have to get ready."

"It's a plea bargain," Julie said. "And you told me the assistant DA is recommending it to the judge."

"What time is the hearing?" Kettleson asked.

"Two o'clock."

"We'll be back in plenty of time. The main reason for the invitation is that I've been pleased with your work and wanted to get to know you better. It's a forty-five-minute drive to the client's business, and I hate wasting the time."

I'd long since abandoned Zach Mays' rules for summer associates. I silently appealed to Julie. All she gave me was a smirk.

I picked up the folder that contained my memo and followed Kettleson out of the office. Because the client developed real estate up and down the coast, its main office was located between Savannah and Brunswick. We left the city and drove south. Kettleson spent the first thirty minutes of the trip talking about himself and didn't direct a single question toward me. Finally, he asked me to list every course I'd taken during my second year of law school, the professor who taught the class, and the grade received.

"Your municipal corporations background shows in your analysis. I wish you could have had Professor Sentell. He was the best."

"He gave a few guest lectures."

I spent the rest of the trip listening to Kettleson tell me about his experiences in law school where he'd been selected for the law review. I was tempted to ask him to list all his second-year classes and the grades he'd received, but I kept my mouth shut and tried to organize my thoughts about the Jones case. Kettleson's nasally voice didn't help me concentrate.

The meeting with the client included an architectural presentation of the plans for the disputed property and legal analysis by Kettleson in which he read my memo without giving me credit for the research.

"Joe Carpenter, our top litigator, will be the lead lawyer if a lawsuit has to be filed," Kettleson said in conclusion. "But I hope litigation won't be necessary after our senior partner, Mr. Braddock, makes his calls to the politicians. No one is better connected in Chatham County, and he has well-placed friends in Atlanta and Washington."

The client catered lunch. I anxiously looked at my watch.

"Mr. Kettleson, don't forget I have to be back for my hearing," I said.

"Don't worry. We won't stay long."

He was wrong. We stayed until the company's managers began to drift back to work. On the ride back to Savannah, I kept looking at my watch and taking a peek at the speedometer. Kettleson stayed quiet, and I didn't try to interrupt his thoughts. We pulled into the law firm parking lot at 1:50 p.m. If I'd brought the Jones file with me, Kettleson could have dropped me off at the courthouse.

"It's only a couple of minutes to the courthouse," the senior associate said as he turned off the car.

"Except I don't know how I'm going to get there." I rushed into the building. Vince was sitting in the reception area.

"Here's your file," he said. "I'll drive you to the courthouse."

We passed Kettleson on the way out of the building.

"That worked out great," the senior associate said. "Look for another project from me when you get back."

We reached Vince's car.

"How did you know about the hearing?" I asked.

"Julie told me."

"For once, I'm glad she has a big mouth."

It was only a few blocks to the courthouse.

"Did you see Zach or Mr. Carpenter

leave?" I asked.

"No. Why is Mr. Carpenter going to be there?"

"You know he's probably been shadowing everything I've done. I wouldn't be surprised if he knows I've been snooping around the microfilm records."

"Are you going to tell me more?"

"No."

We stopped and waited for a light to turn green.

"I want to help," Vince said, moving forward.

"You're helping right now. Trust me, this is for the best."

"I'll let you out and find a place to park."

Opening the car door, I climbed the steps two at a time. Fortunately, there wasn't a line at the security check, and an elevator was waiting with the door open. It was 1:58 p.m. when I opened the back door to the courtroom. It was much smaller than the one used by Judge Cannon. Zach and Mr. Carpenter were sitting in the area reserved for the lawyers. Moses and a single deputy were in the prisoner dock. There was no sign of Maggie Smith or the judge. I walked breathlessly down the aisle. The two lawyers turned toward me as I approached.

And I had a sinking feeling in the pit of

my stomach that Zach and Mr. Carpenter had been working together all along.

"Glad you could make it," Mr. Carpenter said.

"Bob Kettleson —" I began.

"We know," Zach said. "I checked on you a couple of hours ago."

I couldn't bear to look Zach in the face. "I need to talk to Mr. Jones," I said.

Zach stood up.

"No!" I said so loudly that it filled the courtroom. "Alone."

Zach looked at Mr. Carpenter, who shrugged.

"Okay," Zach said.

I went to Moses. The deputy moved several feet away. I positioned my body so Zach and Mr. Carpenter couldn't see. Up close, the old man's face was as wrinkled as a crumpled-up newspaper. His eyes were slightly yellow around the edges.

"That's Floyd Carpenter's son," I whispered.

"I see that, missy. They favor each other."

"I don't know exactly why he's here, but it can't be anything good. Until I can figure out a way to protect you, I think you should stay in jail. It's the safest place you can be."

"I done told you I ain't gonna die in no jailhouse." Moses spoke louder and gestured toward the deputy. "He brung all my stuff in those two pokes. I be thinking about going home. Is that right?"

"If the judge accepts the plea bargain. But what I'm trying to tell you is that it won't be safe for you on the street."

"I be going straight to the river. Only who gonna tote my boat for me?"

The old man's concern about his boat gave me an idea.

"We'll ask the judge to let you stay in the jail until arrangements can be made to transport you and your boat at the same time. It would be a shame for you to get out and then have the boat sent for scrap."

"It ain't no big beer can —"

Before Moses could finish, a side door to the courtroom opened. Ms. Smith and a slender, dark-haired woman wearing a judicial robe entered the courtroom.

"All rise!" the deputy called out.

"Be seated," the judge said. "Ms. Smith, call your case."

"State v. Jones."

Moses and I stepped into the open area in front of the bench. Zach joined us. I stood between him and Moses. Mr. Carpenter remained in his seat. Vince sat behind him.

"This is Ms. Tami Taylor, a rising third-year law student at the University of Georgia," Zach said in a syrupy voice that made me want to slap him. "She's a summer clerk with our firm. Judge Cannon appointed her to represent Mr. Jones in this matter."

"Welcome to Savannah, Ms. Taylor," the judge said. "I hope you're having a pleasant summer."

I was barely able to muster a crooked smile. The judge nodded toward Ms. Smith.

"Proceed."

Maggie Smith handed a file to the judge. "As you know, opposing counsel gave me permission to discuss a potential plea bargain in this case ex parte with you —"

"I didn't agree to any ex parte —" I interrupted.

"I did, Your Honor," Zach cut me off. "I'm the supervising attorney. Under the circumstances, it was the most efficient way to dispose of the case."

"What circumstances?" I asked.

"Ms. Taylor," the judge said, "we're not in a rush here, but you and Mr. Mays can discuss a better method of interoffice communication at a later time. If you'll be patient, I'd like to hear from Ms. Smith."

"Yes ma'am."

Smith spoke. "The defendant is charged with twenty-four counts of trespassing by tying up his boat at private docks. No property damage occurred, and one of the complainants, Mr. Bill Fussleman, sent a letter to my office offering to accommodate the defendant's boat at his dock upon reasonable notice in the future. We are recommending that the defendant be sentenced to time served of eighty-two days, plus one year probation."

"What 'bout my boat?" Moses spoke up.

Smith continued. "The defendant's boat was confiscated when he was arrested. It's in the impoundment lot at the jail and can be released simultaneously with the defendant."

"So, he should remain in jail until arrangements can be made for the transport of his boat," I said.

The judge gave me a puzzled look. "Is that what your client wants to do?"

I swallowed. "We were discussing that when you called the case."

Moses, Maggie Smith, Zach, and I all stared at one another.

"Our firm will make arrangements for the boat to be removed and delivered to Mr. Jones," Zach said, breaking the stalemate.

"Very well," the judge said. "Are we ready to proceed with the plea?"

"Yes ma'am," Zach responded.

I frantically searched for another delay

tactic but came up empty. Zach's duplicity was infuriating.

I listened numbly as Judge Howell went through the constitutional litany required when a defendant enters a guilty plea. Most of the phrases had been the subject of intense scrutiny in cases that made their way to the Supreme Court. Today, it sounded like meaningless gibberish.

"Is your client prepared to enter a plea of guilty to the charges?" the judge asked.

"If that's what he wants to do," I answered resignedly.

The judge looked from me to Moses. "Do you want to plead guilty, Mr. Jones?"

"Yes'm, so long as I get to go home."

"All right, I'll accept your plea and sentence you to time served of eighty-two days, plus one year supervised probation. The defendant is released on his own recognizance. Mr. Jones, your attorneys can assist you in setting up the initial schedule with your probation officer. After that, make sure the officer knows how to get in touch with you and keep all scheduled appointments. I don't want to see you in court again. Anything else?"

"Yes'm. My boat."

Judge Howell smiled. "Of course. Your boat is released from impoundment without payment of any storage fees. Remove it from the lot within seven days."

Judge Howell rose and left the room. Ms. Smith turned to Zach and me. "I'm glad we could work this out. Trying cases like this gives the public the impression we don't have anything important to do."

"Thanks for your cooperation," Zach said.

Smith shook Zach's hand and smiled sweetly. "I know you don't do criminal work, but I hope to see you around."

The assistant DA left the room. The deputy handed Moses two plastic bags.

"Keep catching those big croakers," he said. "You've been the best worker we've had on trash detail for a long time, but I hope we don't see you again."

"Thank you, boss man," Moses answered.

I took Moses by the arm to guide him out of the courtroom behind the deputy.

"Tami!" Mr. Carpenter called out. "Just a minute."

Moses and I kept moving toward the side door of the courtroom. The senior partner walked over and blocked our way. He faced Moses.

"My name is Joe Carpenter."

"I know who you be," Moses said, staring at the floor.

"And Mr. Jones is leaving now," I said,

trying to keep my voice steady. "I'll see you when I get back to the office."

Mr. Carpenter didn't budge. "It's not you I want to talk to," he answered. "I have business with Mr. Jones."

I knew there was no use appealing to Zach. I frantically looked to Vince for help. He stepped back and didn't say anything.

"Sit down on that bench," Mr. Carpenter commanded Moses.

The old man complied. Mr. Carpenter turned to me. "Ms. Taylor, your business here is finished. Go back to the office. I'll meet with you later this afternoon before you leave."

"I'm not going anywhere," I responded, planting my feet as if guarding a basketball goal.

Mr. Carpenter's head jerked back. "What did you say?"

"I'm staying here with my client," I said more bravely than I felt.

Mr. Carpenter's eyes narrowed. "What I have to discuss with Mr. Jones has nothing to do with you."

I nodded my head toward Moses. "That's for him to decide. Moses, do you want me to stay with you?"

"Yes, missy."

I looked Mr. Carpenter in the eyes. "And

that's what I'm going to do."

"I'm going to ask this man some —"

"Mr. Jones doesn't have to talk to you or answer any questions," I interrupted.

Mr. Carpenter turned toward Zach and Vince. "Go!"

The two young men stared at each other for a second.

"I want them to stay," I said.

"Why?" Mr. Carpenter asked, his face getting red. "They have no more business here."

"So they can witness what you're about to do."

"What I'm about to do is fire you and tell you to get out of my sight," Mr. Carpenter exploded. "Now move aside!"

Zach and Vince stepped back at the sound of Mr. Carpenter's voice. I held my ground. The river had been crossed. All that mattered was protecting Moses.

"Do whatever you want to do about my job, but I'm not going to abandon my client."

Mr. Carpenter turned to Moses. "Mr. Jones, has Ms. Taylor told you she's a lawyer?"

"No sir, she always be saying she's not a real lawyer, but she sure enough got the grit to be one."

"I'd say she has grit where she should have brains," Mr. Carpenter replied sarcastically.

"You can insult me, Mr. Carpenter," I replied, my own eyes flashing. "And you can fire me. But Judge Cannon signed an order authorizing me to represent Mr. Jones, and that's what I intend to do."

Mr. Carpenter glared hard at me for several seconds until a sneer turned up the corners of his mouth. "Ms. Taylor, I want to be totally clear about this situation. Are you refusing to let Mr. Jones talk to me unless you are present?"

"Yes sir. And I'm telling him that he doesn't have to talk to you at all if he doesn't want to." I looked down at Moses. "In fact, I'm advising him not to answer any questions or provide information about recent or past events now or at any time in the future."

"That's quite comprehensive," Mr. Carpenter replied.

"Yes sir. That's what I intend."

Mr. Carpenter nodded his head. "Very well, I have a few things to say to you."

I stood up straight. I had no intention of slouching in the face of the firing squad.

"First, Oscar Callahan told me you were a young woman of exceptional conviction and personal courage. Nice sentiments, but I had no idea how firmly rooted those qualities are in your character. Fearlessness in the face of intense pressure can't be taught; it is forged in the trials of life. Second, I never dreamed that a summer clerk would take representation of a client so seriously that she would risk losing a job and damaging her entire career to maintain zealous though misplaced advocacy. I have no doubt that you will someday be an outstanding lawyer. Third, you have earned the right to know why I want to talk to Mr. Jones."

"It doesn't matter what you say —" I began, aware I was being manipulated.

"Tami! Let him finish," Zach interrupted.

"And I don't mind Zach and Vince staying if those are the terms you set for me. Why don't we all sit down?"

Without waiting for an answer, Mr. Carpenter pulled up a chair and sat across from Moses. My mind reeling, I sat on the bench beside Moses. Mr. Carpenter gestured with his hand, and Zach and Vince sat down. The older lawyer looked at Moses.

"Mr. Jones, I'm going to tell you some things, but I don't want you to say anything to me without Ms. Taylor's permission." He looked at me. "Is that agreeable?"

Mr. Carpenter was a cagey man seeking a way to gain control of the situation through flattery and deceit.

"No sir. Talk to me first."

Mr. Carpenter's jaw tightened, but he kept his composure. "Very well. My father was a businessman here in Savannah. People described him as 'colorful,' which is a euphemism for a criminal who has enough money to buy his way into respectability."

The senior partner's candor shocked me.

"Many years ago while I was in college, his niece, a little girl named Lisa Prescott, disappeared and was never found. Our family always suspected foul play, but the police never found her body or identified a suspect. Through some of his criminal connections, my father heard a rumor that Mr. Jones knew something about Lisa's disappearance. According to information in a file kept by my father, Mr. Jones was questioned at least once but denied knowing anything. Now you know why I took such an interest in this case. Moses Jones isn't a name easily forgotten, and when Sam Braddock and I pulled out the old records, we realized the connection. We didn't even know if Mr. Jones was still alive." He looked directly at Moses. "We're all getting older, and once and for all, I want to know the truth."

Moses turned to me. "What you be thinking, missy?"

Mr. Carpenter's matter-of-fact recitation of the facts threw me completely off guard. His approach bore none of the threatened pressure.

"What are you going to do if Moses doesn't want to talk to you?" I asked, stalling for time.

"Keep working on what my father started. That's more important than anything he could tell me."

"What do you mean?"

"Not only did we lose Lisa; her parents died a year later in an automobile accident. The double tragedy was the catalyst for change in my father's life. He stopped being 'colorful' and moved into legitimate business activities in which he made a lot more money than he ever did on the shady side of the law. Lawrence Braddock helped him go straight. Together, they set up the Lisa Prescott Foundation."

"Foundation?" I asked in a subdued voice.

"Yes. Lisa's mother, Ellen, was my father's baby sister. Her husband didn't have any surviving family, and everything passed to my father under their wills. He didn't touch a penny of the money, but established a charitable foundation that has given away millions to children's causes in Georgia and South Carolina. Sam Braddock and I have served on the board of the foundation for more than thirty years."

"Why didn't you tell me anything about this?"

Mr. Carpenter raised his eyebrows. "Why should I? You were representing Mr. Jones in a trespassing case."

"But why did you want to talk to Mr. Jones alone?"

"I wanted to push him hard for the truth." Mr. Carpenter rubbed his hands together. "However, that won't happen since his attorney has demonstrated a tenacious ability to frustrate my efforts at communication."

"Do you believe Mr. Jones was responsible for Lisa's disappearance?"

"I don't know; the notes in the file mention a rumor that Mr. Jones found her body. The rest is a mystery I'd like to solve. Will you allow me to question him?"

I looked at Zach and Vince. Neither one spoke. I turned to Mr. Carpenter. "Only if it is considered an ongoing part of the attorney/client relationship between Mr. Jones and Braddock, Appleby, and Carpenter."

Mr. Carpenter hesitated. "So that I will be bound by the attorney/client privilege and couldn't disclose the information obtained to the police. That's finesse."

"Agreed?" I asked, ignoring the compliment.

Mr. Carpenter nodded. "Yes."

"And I'll ask the questions first," I continued. "It will go a lot smoother that way; then you can follow up."

"But you don't know what to ask," the older lawyer protested.

"Just listen. You can evaluate my effort."

For the next thirty minutes, I guided Moses through his story. When he described Lisa's injuries after he discovered her on the riverbank, I glanced at Mr. Carpenter, whose eyes were red and moist. The lawyer wiped away tears when Moses told about the simple burial in a watery grave. For the first time since Mr. Carpenter blocked our exit from the courtroom, I allowed myself to relax. The tension flowed out of my shoulders.

Moses concluded with the two times Floyd Carpenter tried to talk to him, and the reason he kept his mouth shut. Mr. Carpenter pulled out his handkerchief and wiped his eyes for at least the third time.

"I'm sorry," Moses said. "But I be too scared to say nothing to your daddy."

"I understand," Mr. Carpenter replied.

I spoke. "Is there anything else you remember about what happened to Lisa?"

"No, missy. That be it."

"Mr. Carpenter, do you have any questions?"

The lawyer bowed his head for a moment. "Do you know the place where you laid her in the water?"

"Yes sir."

"I know she's not there, but could you show it to me sometime?"

"Yes, boss man."

"And did you ever hear any rumors or stories of why she was left on the riverbank or how she got there that evening?"

Moses pressed his lips together. I held my breath.

"I be thinking something myself. That little girl been hit in the head a lot worse than if she'd been in a bare-knuckle fight. Something hard done that. And there be small pieces of glass caught up in her dress. I saved a few of them in a tin can for a long time, but they be lost now."

"A hit-and-run driver," Mr. Carpenter said, turning to me. "Who didn't leave her lying in the road or call an ambulance, but thought she was dead and dumped her off in a secluded place. The police found blood on a curb along the route Lisa would have taken home from a music lesson on the day she disappeared. The first test was inconclusive, but the second came back as a blood-type match. Of course, there wasn't DNA testing back then, and the blood type was one of the more common ones."

"Why wouldn't someone who hit her call for help?" I asked.

"The driver could have been drinking, on drugs, driving a stolen vehicle, or simply panicked. We'll probably never know. People don't always think things through in the heat of the moment."

I could certainly identify with that type of mistake.

Mr. Carpenter continued. "Every car taken in for repair to the front grille or bumper during the next few months after Lisa disappeared was inspected by police, but nothing turned up. If it was a hit-and-run driver, he laid low long enough to avoid being identified. My father hired a private detective firm that continued seeking clues after the police shut down the active file. Nothing turned up."

Mr. Carpenter stood and extended his hand to Moses. They shook hands. I watched in disbelief.

"Mr. Jones, thank you for trying to help Lisa," Mr. Carpenter said. "Knowing someone tried to save her means so much to me."

He choked up again. "And hearing your story gives me hope that she may not have suffered as much as, or in ways, we'd always feared."

"No sir, she never woke up until she passed."

Mr. Carpenter nodded. "How can I get in touch with you about going to her burial place on the river?"

"Through Bill Fussleman," Zach offered. "He's the homeowner who is going to let Mr. Jones tie up his boat for the night at his dock. Fussleman's address and phone number are in the file."

"That be fine, boss man," Moses said. "I be looking out for you."

"Can I take you someplace?" Mr. Carpenter asked Moses. "I'll drop you off anywhere you like."

"No sir. I be walking. It gonna feel good breathing free air and stretching out my own two legs."

"And you?" Mr. Carpenter asked me. "Are you going back to the office? You still have a job."

"Yes, and thanks, but I think I'll walk. Free air sounds good to me too."

29

The three men left the courtroom. I stayed behind with Moses and watched the door close behind them. The courtroom became totally quiet. *State v. Jones* was over. I collapsed on the bench, put my head in my hands, and began to weep.

"What be bothering you, missy?"

The crushing pressure of the past weeks demanded an emotional release. My weeping turned to sobs. I felt the old man lightly place his hand on my back. Several minutes passed before I regained my composure. Thankfully, no one disturbed us. I lifted my head and sniffled loudly. Moses was sitting beside me. I cleared my throat.

"I've been sharing your burden for a few weeks. You've been carrying it for forty years. I don't know how you've done it."

Moses nodded. "That be right, missy. I be toting a very heavy load. Just like the big rock that dragged that poor little girl's body to the muddy bottom."

I took a tissue from my purse and blew my nose. I looked at the old man's weathered face. Pure love for him rose up in my heart. I touched him lightly on the arm.

"And it's time you stopped carrying that load, along with the other loads dragging you down all your life."

"What you mean?"

I turned sideways so I could look directly into his face. "Jesus gave his life so you wouldn't have to carry the burdens of the past, no matter where they came from. His burden is easy and light. Give what's left of your life to him."

The old man blinked his eyes. "You sound like my ol' auntie. I know that be true for young folk, but not for an old broke-down fellow like me. Too much done gone by for me to catch up." Moses looked across the room. "The faces in the water, they be talking to me. They tell me the end of my days."

"No," I answered with feeling. "Listen to Jesus. God wants you to look up, not down."

Moses slowly tilted back his head. After a few moments, there was a puzzled expression on his face. "That be a sweet sound," he said.

I didn't hear anything, but my heart understood. "That's what happens in a court of praise."

And in a gentle, natural way, the Lord used me to guide Moses Jones to a place of freedom and peace. Our tears, young and old, flowed together as he received the love of Jesus with childlike wonder. The spillover blessed me from the top of my head to the tips of my toes. Mama would have shouted in victory. Our celebration, though quieter, was no less triumphant.

"Are you ready to go?" I asked after the last prayer ended.

"I never be more ready." Moses paused. "And you know what, missy?"

"What?"

"I think you be a lot more than a real lawyer."

We left the courtroom and went in opposite directions. It was hot outside, but the heat had lost its power to oppress me. I walked at a leisurely pace. Wisdom adapts to things that cannot be changed, so I took my time returning to the office. The thanksgiving that had bubbled up in my heart while the Lord touched Moses returned. God was good. My mistakes and foolishness hadn't stymied his purposes.

I arrived back at the office ready to confess my sins to Zach. But he wasn't in his office, and the attractive secretary who worked for him informed me that he and Mr. Appleby had left for an emergency weekend meeting in Mobile with representatives of a Chinese shipping company. The Chinese company was going to increase its business on the East Coast and the Gulf of Mexico and wanted a single law firm to coordinate their activities in the United States.

I was a bit ashamed as I admitted to myself that I was relieved he was not in. I dreaded rehashing my embarrassing miscalculation of Mr. Carpenter's interest in Moses Jones and Lisa Prescott.

"Zach will be making trips to Shanghai if this deal goes through," the young woman said. "I told him I'd like to stow away, carry his suitcase, do anything to see that part of the world."

"What did he say to that?"

"Oh, you know how he is," she gushed. "He pulled on that cute ponytail and smiled."

"Did you get the case taken care of?" Julie asked lightly when I entered the library a few minutes later. "Joel is going to the cocktail reception at Mr. Carpenter's house tonight. I want you to meet him, but promise you won't say anything goofy. I told him you were super-religious — kind of like my cousins in New York — so he won't be totally shocked."

"Has he told you to shut up yet?" I asked.

"No, don't be silly. He's a great conversationalist, especially for a guy. He said more in thirty minutes than Vinny has all summer. Not that I'm trying to dump on Vinny, but you know what I mean. What happened in your case?"

"Judge Howell accepted the plea agreement. Moses is free."

"Awesome. I know that's a relief. What about the little girl? What did you find out?"

"That he didn't do anything criminal. He tried to help her."

"How sweet. Oh, I almost forgot." Julie pointed to a fresh folder on my side of the table. "Bob Kettleson's secretary left that for you. She says he wants an answer Monday morning."

I sat down and flipped open the folder. Fortunately, the problem was in an area of civil procedure familiar to me. I spent the next forty-five minutes documenting what I knew to be true. The memo could be typed first thing Monday morning.

Julie looked at her watch. "Listen, do you think we could sneak away early? I'd like some extra time to get ready for the party."

"Why don't you go ahead. I'd like to get a head start on this memo. I can just walk to Mrs. Fairmont's." I didn't want to get into a big discussion with Julie about it, but I really didn't plan on attending the party.

The door opened, and I looked up to see Vince entering the library. Julie greeted him first.

"Tell me everything that happened in court today. Tami made it sound so vanilla that I know she's holding out on me. She is absolutely the worst liar on the planet."

Vince looked at me.

"I didn't lie," I answered.

"But I didn't get the truth, the whole truth, and nothing but the truth," Julie responded.

"I don't have time now," Vince replied. "I broke away from a meeting for a couple of minutes. Maybe we can talk tonight at Mr. Carpenter's house."

"That won't work. I'll be with Joel at the party, and he's not within the attorney/client relationship."

"We'll get alone for a few minutes and make him jealous," Vince answered.

"Where did that come from?" Julie asked. "But it's a great idea."

Vince looked at me. "Would you like me to pick you up?"

"I'm not sure that I'm going to make —"

"You'll be there," Julie interrupted. "I'm sure there will be fancy flavors of water for the nondrinkers in the crowd. You might even have time to witness to Ned before he tosses down too many martinis. If anyone needs to repent, he's it."

"I wish you would go, Tami," Vince added. "I'd really like to talk to you about something."

"If I go, it's only a few blocks from Mrs. Fairmont's house. I can walk."

"Pick her up at seven thirty," Julie cut in. "Cinderella never walks to the ball; she always arrives in a coach."

Vince held out his hands, palms up.

"Okay," I replied with a smile. "I'll see you at seven thirty. Do you know where I'm staying?"

"Of course he does," Julie answered. "He's been stalking you since day one."

"I know the house," Vince said.

After Vince left, Julie turned to me. "What are you going to wear? This is a dressy occasion."

"Maybe the blue suit I wore the first day of work."

Julie rolled her eyes. "I'm not saying you need to buy a strapless cocktail dress, but please don't wear something frumpy. I'd of-

569

fer to go shopping with you, but that would destroy our friendship."

After a moment of rare silence, Julie asked, "So, is Vince the front-runner?"

"I'm not sure if either he or Zach is a runner."

Shaking her head, Julie expelled an exaggerated sigh.

I went upstairs to see Gerry Patrick and knocked on the door frame.

"Come in," she said, looking up from her desk.

"I need to buy a dress for the party tonight at Mr. Carpenter's house. Any suggestions?"

"Waiting till the last minute, aren't you?"

"Yes ma'am."

The office manager tapped her pen against a legal pad, then began writing. She tore out the sheet and handed it to me.

"Use the firm car. You can just bring it back on Monday. Tell Marie I sent you. She knows how to make modest Jewish girls look classy; she can do the same for you."

An hour later, I left the shop with a beautiful pale green dress that, while not hugging my figure too closely, didn't deny the fact that I was a woman. Mama wasn't there to judge it. I was on my own.

■ ■ ■ ■

Christine Bartlett's car was parked along the curb when I arrived at Mrs. Fairmont's house.

Flip didn't greet me in the foyer. With Mrs. Bartlett present, I suspected the little dog had been banished to the basement. I found the two women in the kitchen. Mrs. Bartlett had fixed a late-afternoon pot of coffee. Mrs. Fairmont was sipping from a cup as I entered.

"It's decaf," Mrs. Fairmont said. "Guaranteed not to give me a brain freeze."

"Mother and I have had a great afternoon," Mrs. Bartlett chimed in. "It's been like old times. We went to a cute place for a mid-afternoon snack but wanted home-brewed coffee. Did you have a nice day at work?"

I smiled. "That wouldn't be the word I'd use to sum it up, but all's well that ends well."

"That's somewhere in the Bible, isn't it?" Mrs. Bartlett asked.

"No ma'am. It's John Heywood. He lived in England a generation before Shakespeare."

"Did your mother teach you that at

571

home?" Mrs. Bartlett asked, her eyes slightly buggy.

"Yes ma'am, and a lot more."

"Amazing."

I poured a drink of water and leaned against the counter. "Have either of you heard of the Lisa Prescott Foundation?" I asked.

"Of course," Mrs. Bartlett replied. "It made a big gift toward the new pediatric wing of the hospital a few years ago. I think it only supports projects that will benefit children. Mother, who runs that foundation?"

"Sam Braddock and Floyd Carpenter's son are involved," Mrs. Fairmont answered. "Which makes sense given the family connections. Was it mentioned in the newspaper articles you found in the box downstairs?"

"No ma'am, but I wish it had been."

Mrs. Bartlett stepped closer and lowered her voice. "What else have you found out about Lisa? Mother says you promised to fill her in on the details of a new investigation into her death as soon as possible."

"I'm not the person who can answer that question. My role in the case is over without anything to report."

"Drat," Mrs. Bartlett said. "It's not often I have a chance for a scoop guaranteed to be ahead of everyone else in the city. The whole mystery came up Monday at my bridge club, and I promised to get back to everyone."

"Tell them about the foundation," I suggested.

"That's old news, but I'll come up with something." Mrs. Bartlett placed her coffee cup on the kitchen counter. "Mother is going to eat dinner with Ken and me tomorrow evening. Will you join us?"

It was a nice gesture and made me feel less like the hired help. "Thank you, but this has been a long week, and I'm going to rest up this weekend. I'll stay here and take care of Flip. Is he downstairs now?"

"Yes," Mrs. Fairmont answered, giving her daughter a resentful look. "We'll set him free when Christine leaves."

A few minutes later as Mrs. Fairmont walked out on the front porch to bid her daughter good-bye, I liberated Flip. He rewarded me with a backward somersault that I rated ten out of a possible ten.

I didn't say anything to Mrs. Fairmont about the party at supper, but when she saw me come upstairs wearing the dress, she immediately insisted I wear a necklace.

"And it will look better if you put your

hair up," she added. "How long will it take you to do that?"

"Five minutes."

I returned with my hair caught up behind my head.

"No," she said after making me turn around several times. "I was wrong. Leave it down until your wedding."

I brushed out my hair. At seven thirty the doorbell chimed, and Flip raced into the foyer. I picked up the dog and opened the door.

"This is Flip," I said. "Can he join us?"

Vince stared at me.

"Come in and meet Mrs. Fairmont," I said after an awkward pause.

Mrs. Fairmont and Vince chatted about Charleston for a few minutes. Vince held the door open for me as I got into the car.

"We'll be there in a couple of minutes, so I have to talk fast," Vince said as he pulled away from the curb. "I totally messed up the Moses Jones case and led you astray. I meant well, but that's no excuse. Will you forgive me?"

"What?"

"You trusted me, and I let you down. It's as simple as that. When I saw that Mr. Carpenter was about to fire you, I should have jumped in and taken the blame, but I froze. It was a cowardly thing to do."

"But what did you do wrong?" I asked, mystified.

Vince glanced sideways at me. "You're nice to say that. And you look great too. If I hadn't fed you wrong ideas about the reason behind the memo from Mr. Carpenter to Mr. Braddock and sent you off to the microfilm records operating under a false assumption as to their motivations, none of this confusion would have gotten past first base. When you toss in the spin put on the conversation I overheard outside Mr. Braddock's office, there's no wonder you were confused."

Vince turned onto Congress Street. "Here we are," he said, turning sideways in the seat. "Before I let you out near the front door, I need to know you forgive me."

"Of course."

"Thanks. That takes a tremendous load off my mind."

"And park the car. We'll walk together."

He found an empty space around the corner from the large home. I'd bought new shoes at the dress shop, and the narrow heels made me wobble on the cobblestones. Vince put his hand on my elbow to steady me. I instinctively pulled away.

"I need to ask your forgiveness too," I

said. "I dragged you into the Jones case in the first place. You were only trying to help me."

"I knew you would say that, but most of the blame flows my way."

We reached the house simultaneously with Bob Kettleson and a very thin woman whom he introduced as his wife, Lynn.

"Bob has enjoyed mentoring you," Lynn said. "He says you're a quick learner."

"Thanks. He's quite a teacher."

We entered the house, which was as lavishly furnished as I'd expected. Mr. and Mrs. Carpenter were standing on a silk rug in the foyer greeting their guests. Vince was immediately ushered into the living room by one of the younger partners.

"Welcome, tiger," Mr. Carpenter said, shaking my hand.

"Actually, I already have a nickname."

"What is it?"

"Jaguar."

Mr. Carpenter nodded. "Did you know they are the most unpredictable of the big cats?"

"No sir."

Mr. Carpenter turned to his wife, a tall, stately woman with silver hair. "Maryanne, this is the summer clerk I told you about. I've never seen anyone take the duty to zealously represent a client so seriously." He lowered his voice and leaned closer to me. "And coax open a rusty old memory that might have remained closed to a heavy hand. Come, I want to show you something."

"But your guests —"

"Won't miss me for a few minutes. Besides, I'm the boss."

I followed the senior partner down a hallway and into a paneled study. He pointed to a bookshelf that held a row of pictures — all of Lisa Prescott.

Placed in chronological order, they began with a baby photograph in a lacy bassinet and continued, one per year, to a pose similar to the picture in the newspaper. I spent a few moments with each one, imagining what the little girl was like, comparing her to Ellie and Emma. I reached the end and sighed.

"Thank you," I said. "It's sad, but it helps me to see more of her life."

"None of us knows the number of our days," Mr. Carpenter replied.

I glanced sideways, wondering if the lawyer knew his words were lifted from a Bible verse.

"And over here is a picture of the first board of the foundation," Mr. Carpenter continued.

On the wall was a picture of five men in dark suits. It was easy to spot Floyd Carpenter. None of the others looked familiar.

"Which one is Lawrence Braddock?"

"There he is," he said, pointing to a slender, balding man. "Sam Braddock favors his mother's family and their much higher cholesterol count."

When we returned to the foyer, Julie and a dark-haired young man were talking to Maryanne Carpenter. Julie was wearing a revealing black dress that made me blush. She saw me and waved.

"This is Joel," she announced proudly.

The young man was wearing clothes that hinted at his artistic bent.

"Julie has told me a lot about you," he said.

"All positive," Julie cut in. "Let's get something to eat. I'm starving."

There was a rich selection of hors d'oeuvres laid out in the dining room. I could have skipped supper with Mrs. Fairmont. I collected a small sample of cheeses, fruit, and a pair of chicken wings that might have come from the processing line in Powell Station. Thankfully, Mr. and Mrs. Carpenter included a nonalcoholic punch option. Taking my plate into the living room, I encountered Mr. Braddock.

"You've been at the firm for weeks, and we haven't had a chance to talk," the portly lawyer said. "Although we did have a close call the other day in the parking lot."

"Yes sir. I'm thankful I didn't hit you. I was driving Vince's car. He was kind enough to loan it to me."

"Vince is quite remarkable, isn't he?"

"Yes sir."

"He's so much smarter than I am that it's intimidating," the lawyer added.

"I've felt that way too," I answered in surprise.

Mr. Braddock smiled. "But practicing law isn't just brainpower. Learning how to read people and discern their real motives and interests is often more important than the black-letter rules of statutes and analyzing judicial precedent."

"I have a long way to go in that department too."

"Really? That's not what Joe Carpenter tells me. I can't remember when he was as impressed with the way a summer clerk or associate handled a pressure situation. He says you pushed him so hard he cracked." Mr. Braddock laughed. "There is a boatload of lawyers in this city who would love to make that boast."

"The truth is —"

"That you're also very humble," Mr. Brad-dock interrupted. He pointed toward Bob Kettleson. "And don't think I'm unaware what you're contributing without getting credit for it. Keep up the good work, and we may be talking about a longer-term relationship."

The senior partner moved away. Vince came over to me.

"Did you impress Mr. Braddock without even trying?" he asked.

"Who knows? I feel more out of my league than I did as a ninth grader on the basketball court."

"That's not what everyone else thinks, especially me."

30

I woke up Saturday morning, stretched, and relaxed for a few extra minutes as I enjoyed again the release of Moses' burden. My burden, too, was lighter. As I lay in bed, I also reflected on the validation I'd received the previous evening at the cocktail party. It felt good, but I knew the praise of men was a hollow substitute for the approval of God.

After my morning run, I showered and brewed a pot of coffee. I tiptoed up the stairs and peeked into Mrs. Fairmont's bedroom. Flip, who was curled up near her feet, barked in greeting. Mrs. Fairmont opened her eyes.

"Can I bring you a fresh cup of coffee?" I asked.

The old woman scooted up in bed and repositioned her pillows. "That would be nice, and you can tell me all about the party while I drink it."

I'd just about finished my account of the

previous evening when the doorbell chimed.

"Who could that be so early?" Mrs. Fairmont asked.

I bounded down the stairs and glanced through the sidelight. Standing outside with his black motorcycle helmet under his arm was Zach. I opened the door with a puzzled look on my face. "What are you doing here? I thought you and Mr. Appleby had a meeting in Mobile today."

"We were supposed to, but the representatives of the shipping company had to reschedule the meeting, and we ended up returning just late enough last night to miss the party." Zach looked at me and smiled. "Am I too late this morning to invite you for a ride?" he asked. "I know you like to get an early start on the day."

Parked at the curb in front of the house was the motorcycle with sidecar attached.

"I don't know," I answered. "Riding in the sidecar was a once-in-a-lifetime event, and I've already done it twice. Why don't you ask your secretary or Maggie Smith?"

Zach pointed to his watch. "What female besides you is up at this time on a Saturday morning having already run ten miles?"

"It was four miles."

"At least you're wide-awake." Zach stepped toward the door. "Do I have to enlist Mrs. Fairmont's help to convince you to come out and play?"

"She's still in bed, sipping her first cup of coffee."

"Then you've finished your morning chores. I promise to have you back before the sun gets hot."

"Can it wait until Monday?"

Zach pointed up at the blue sky peeking through the trees. "This is the day which the Lord has made; we will rejoice and be glad in it. Let's go or we'll miss a great opportunity."

"I know we need to talk —"

"And we will." Zach tapped the helmet. "Microphones."

Zach's charm, when he turned it on high, was a worthy opponent for my willpower.

"Okay, I'll tell Mrs. Fairmont. Where are we going?"

"To familiar places."

I returned with my bag packed, and Mrs. Fairmont's words to have fun chasing after me. I slipped into the sidecar and positioned the helmet without assistance. Zach drove slowly through the historic district, providing tour-guide commentary.

"How did you learn all these facts?" I asked into the microphone.

"Until you started working at the firm,

Tammy Lynn, I had nothing to do in my free time except study local history."

"Why did you call me Tammy Lynn?" I asked in surprise.

Zach turned his head sideways. I could see him smiling. "I'm not the only one who can research old records," he said.

We turned onto the highway to Tybee Island. As we increased speed, I let myself enjoy the ride. We reached the marsh, crossed the bridge, and turned down the sandy road where I'd been so afraid. Zach pulled into the driveway of the burned-out house and stopped the motorcycle. We took off our helmets.

"The marsh looks different early in the morning," I said.

"The tide is in; it's deeper water."

I smiled. We walked down the path to the gazebo. Zach sat on the steps; I stood between him and the marsh.

Zach reached down and pulled up a few straggly strands of grass. "I thought a lot about the Moses Jones case while we were traveling yesterday," he said. "Did you talk to Vince and Mr. Carpenter?"

I nodded. "Vince apologized to me, which was crazy but sweet. He barely let me get in a word of remorse. Mr. Carpenter showed me pictures of Lisa in his study at home last night and has no idea what I thought he was doing. He thinks I'm a tiger or a jaguar."

"Jaguar?"

"They're the most unpredictable of the big cats."

"And Moses? How did you leave it with him? I know you stayed behind after we left the courthouse."

I looked out over the marsh. Somewhere in the backwaters of the coastal rivers, I prayed, an old, almost toothless man was having a pleasant morning. Tears came to my eyes.

"It was wonderful," I said simply.

"Can you tell me?"

I sat down on the steps, and in a soft voice I told Zach what had happened in Moses' heart and soul, the unforeseen fulfillment of a promise birthed in my heart in Powell Station. He listened quietly. When I finished, we left the gazebo and walked to the edge of the water. The marsh grass looked more vibrant than I'd remembered.

"It's your turn," I said. "What is your evaluation of *State v. Jones?*"

Zach leaned back against a post. "There's so much you did wrong I don't know where to begin. But you hung in there with Moses past the point anyone else would have bailed

585

out, and in the end earned Mr. Carpenter's respect."

I waited. Zach's eyes revealed more thoughts.

"What else?" I asked.

He leaned closer to me. "My opinion doesn't matter. Heaven only sees what you did right."

Later that evening I called home. Mama answered.

"I finished the criminal case I mentioned," I said. "My client pled guilty and received probation."

"Thank goodness for that. It worried me that you would help someone who is guilty try to escape justice."

"He got justice and mercy."

I expected Mama to ask for details, but she wanted to move on. "Now that the case is over, are you going to be coming home for a long weekend?" she asked. "We really miss you."

"Yes ma'am. And I'd like to bring some-one. Is that still okay with you and Daddy?"

After a brief moment of silence, she said, "Yes. Who is it?"

I'd known this important question was coming and had given it prayerful consider-ation. I'd imagined Zach Mays and his ponytail sitting at the kitchen table explaining to my parents why his family, like the early Christians, spent years in a commune sharing everything; and I'd wondered what would happen if Vince Colbert, his BMW coated with red clay, sat on the edge of the sofa in the front room and told my daddy and mama how he'd become a Christian in the Episcopal church.

I took a deep breath.

It was pitch dark when Moses woke from his nap and untied his boat from Mr. Fussleman's dock. A neatly lettered sign on the gray post read "Reserved for Mr. Moses Jones — Trespassers Will Be Prosecuted." He quietly slipped the long pole into the murky water and pushed the boat downstream. Twenty minutes later, he let it drift closer to the bank. When he reached the right spot, he lowered the cement-block anchor and waited for the ripples to fade. Dawn was still a hope away, and he wanted to catch something fresh for breakfast. He hummed a note or two — with a smile on his face.

Moses wasn't far from the spot where he'd taken Mr. Carpenter. One Sunday morning the lawyer met him near the base of the new highway bridge and sat in the front of the boat while Moses took him to the burial place. Neither man spoke as the boat, like a funeral barge, passed noiselessly through the water. Trees along the shore had grown tall, died, and fallen into the water since Moses laid the little blonde-haired girl to rest, but he knew when he reached the right spot.

"This be it," he said, halting the forward progress of the boat.

Mr. Carpenter bowed his head for a moment, then placed a bouquet of fresh-cut flowers on the water. An invisible eddy caused the flowers to swirl slowly in a circle before the main current captured them and carried the memorial toward the ocean. The two men watched until the bouquet disappeared from view.

"She be gone for good," Moses said.

"Yes, Mr. Jones. And it's good that I finally know where she's gone."

"You ready to get home?"

Mr. Carpenter nodded. Moses pushed against the slow current toward the bridge. After a few minutes, he spoke. "That tall girl who isn't a real lawyer. She help me more than you be knowing."

"How is that?"

"She show me where to lay my burdens down and not be picking them back up again. That day at the big court, it change me forever and forever."

"Tell me what you mean."

And for the next few minutes a man with little formal education taught a man with multiple advanced degrees.

When they reached the bridge, Moses skillfully held the boat steady while Mr. Carpenter stepped onto the bank.

"Thank you, Mr. Jones," he said. "For everything."

"You be more than welcome. And if'n you need my help, I be here for you."

Moses deposited two fat fish into the white five-gallon bucket. Breakfast was secure. Dinner still swam beneath him. He baited a hook and lowered it into the water. There was a slight effervescence to the fishing line that caused it to shimmer in his fingers as he played it out. He waited. A fish broke the surface. It was a top feeder. Moses leaned over the edge of the boat and peered into the dark water.

No images rose to terrify him. The faces had fled. Fear no longer held his future.

The water stilled and became a mirror to the few remaining stars. Moses looked up and tilted his head to the side. Sometimes, if he listened closely, he could hear a whisper of an invitation.

One day, he would rise to accept it.

ACKNOWLEDGMENTS

Writing a novel is both a solitary and collaborative process. I greatly appreciate my wife, Kathy, who safeguards my creative solitude. During the collaborative stage, Allen Arnold and Natalie Hanemann at Thomas Nelson Publishing, along with Traci DePree (tracidepree.com) and Deborah Wiseman, provided invaluable input.

READING GROUP GUIDE

1. In the Bible, a name change bears notable relationship to a life transformation (e.g., Saul to Paul, Abram to Abraham). What significance does Tammy Lynn's name change to "Tami" bear?

2. Compare and contrast life in Powell Station for Tammy Lynn with life in Savannah for Tami. What are her support systems in each? How are those lives different from her life at school at the University of Georgia in Athens. Where is she most alone?

3. Are all the standards of Tami's family faith as hard and fast as she believes? Discuss times when her parents were more flexible than she had thought they'd be. Discuss instances in which Tami makes allowances in her beliefs. Is this hypocritical

or part of maturing as a believer?

4. Is Tami judgmental? Does her character evolve?

5. In what ways does Zach's shared background and beliefs comfort Tami? Likewise, how do their dissimilarities challenge or frighten Tami?

6. How do Vince's and Zach's differences with one another affect Tami? Which character holds the stronger possibility of courtship with Tami?

7. What accounts for Tami's relaxing the rules where Vince is concerned while she passes all considerations regarding Zach through her parents?

8. There are several biblical references in this book ("Joseph and Maryanne Carpenter," "Moses" in the river, etc.). Is there a "Christ figure" (traditional redemptive character)? If so, who is it?

9. How has Tammy Lynn's upbringing, background, and birth order prepared her to be a caretaker for Mrs. Fairmont?

10. Shakespeare frequently raises the theme of mental instability in characters vital to the storytelling process. This creates issues of doubt and trust with the reader. How does the question of Moses' and Mrs. Fairmont's states of mind affect this narrative? Are the most factually reliable characters necessarily the most trustworthy?

11. For all of her endeavors to do the right thing, how does Tami misstep? Recall instances of her not revealing the whole truth. How does her selective editing strike you? Is this an oversight or a calculation?

12. Who do you believe Tami brings home to visit her parents?

13. Deeper water can be more challenging to ford or more buoyant. It can reveal spots teeming with fish to delight fishermen or conceal corpses and frustrate lawmen. In what ways did this book lead you to deeper waters?